My Name is War

Evan DeShais

Evan DeShais Books

Copyright © Oct 2023 by Evan DeShais Books

ISBN Print: 978-1-962732-01-7
ISBN eBook: 978-1-962732-00-0

First Edition, October 2023

Cover art by Brad Fraunfelter

Published in the United States Of America

Intro

L ightning has not only boiled my flesh, it also charred my bones.

A colony world is lost; twenty-seven thousand colonists are severed from humanity, and my former employer blames me.

The incident has killed two people. I am broken, alone, and recuperating when my old life knocks on my door with an explanation and an offer.

I learn that the attack on the colony is not my foe's first attempt, nor do I believe it will be the last.

Dedication

Where to start, possibly with my great-grandmother Mable for reading to me? Yes, I think that is a perfect place. It took a number of years for it to sink in, but the love for reading took. As for this book, I must thank a few people. The thanks go to my wife first and foremost, followed by my parents, who've been along since its rough outline. They've read the drafts of all five books, eleven short stories, and spent countless hours in over-the-phone chats. To my cover illustrator, Brad Fraunfelter, thank you for taking on my project. To my Editor, Sarah Clithero, thank you for the encouragement; I've got such a fun tale for you to read. To Mark and Joy, who would have known that lunch five years ago would encourage me to put my story out there for all to read? Thank you. Finally, and most importantly, I'd like to thank you, the readers who've read my intro, looked at the cover and decided to entrust your precious time to me. That, in my opinion, is worthy of note and dedication. To all of you, thank you for your support. ~Evan

Contents

Chapter 1
Walking the Gate

C1 S1

My name is Raylan. I have a first name; I do not know my last. It was never given to me by my elders, by my family, or my parents. I am doing what I can, living how I can, and I remain indenture-free. I have a job, not a good job, but a steady job. I have someone who cares for me in my life. Why is it then that not knowing my last name bothers me?

Jacki rounds the small, beige hallway from the bathroom into the main sitting area of our 1.5 living room, dining room, kitchen, (1.5 LDK), blockhouse. While managing to toss her hair forward and put it back into a sort of tail, she asks in a pique of frustration, "Hun, you are going to do it, right, Ray?" There is a pause as she tries to pull her hair back a second time. "You are going to talk to MacCallister about getting on day shift?" She asks for a second time without giving me a chance to answer.

I know that emphasis on the word "right." Looking briefly at Jacki while she tries for a third time to get her hair into a semblance of order, I grumble, "Yeah,

I plan on it. I am not sure how much good it is going to do. Dave has it nice and comfortable and does not want to go anywhere."

In her sweetest Southern twang, she needles as she walks over and sits on my lap. "You know it is so that we can spend more time together. We've been on separate shifts for two years. You were on call every weekend before that."

I start to reply. "Yeah..."

Jacki continues, pushing my chin down with a finger and placing a kiss on my forehead. "If we are going to start that family, find a larger space, and move up when my nursing indenture ends in five months, we need you off the night shift." She pops up like a jack-in-the-box as I am about to respond. "Oh, sugar sticks, I am late for the ride share."

Letting out a small sigh, I lean in to kiss her, and receive an exasperated, "Ugh, tell Dave to wash the damn suits" for my trouble.

I head down the narrow hall to the bathroom. After a long night, the handrails along the hallway give my left lower leg a rest. It is not much, but for a kid who grew up in the wilderness, accessible by bush tram only, the magic of a hot shower is mind-blowing. I prop open the door to keep the room from being layered in steam, and I take a long shower. I relax from my night walking the SkipJack back and forth at the demarcation zone.

Unlike Dave, who simply sweats because of his bulk, I sweat in my haptic suit because of exertion. Dave, I am told, runs his haptic suit at fifteen percent load. My old drill instructor would shout me up the mountain and down again if I had the haptic suit any lower than ninety percent. Even with my bum left leg, the pod I use for piloting allows me to function well when piloting a SkipJack. I am not as fast as I was pre-injury, but I am still better than most.

I pull the shower's retractable head off the stand and turn the water to scalding. Well, as hot as the community block housing can manage. With care, I begin to heat the muscles around my replaced lower left leg. As the heat soaks in, and the artificial muscle bundles relax, I lean against the ubiquitous subway tile of our blockhouse bathroom. First, I use the heat of the shower to reset the myomere muscle group. When fully pliable, I knead out the balls of myomere into smooth bundles again. After my shower, I will grab food, head to bed, and tonight I will be back at work. I have worked this monotonous cycle for too

2

long.

With the shower done, I head to the kitchen for food and find a heaping plate of Pad Thai tofu made up for me. With an inhalation of the scent, I look at the plate Jacki left for me. I am thankful I do not have to cook, and I appreciate the effort Jackie went to, but I yearn for a moose steak, moose roast, caribou roast, dried caribou, and bear steak. Meat. I want meat, but meat is well out of our budget.

I settle in for this meal, such that it is. My mind wanders about the potential conversations around moving to the day shift. Before I know it, I find myself nodding off at the table. I head to bed.

When I wake, I realize that I did not wash the haptic suit. I groan: it is too late to change that now. After a quick shower, I use my Forward Elliptical Enhanced Email and Educational Display (FEED) system to check the time and review my FEED messages. Jacki is covering for another nurse whose kid has a recital. She will not be home until after I leave. With a military prep for the day, I get my morning ablutions done. While it is morning for me, it is near dusk for everyone else. I have a slight limp to my step when I head out the door to meet my community ride share.

***

C1 S2

With a limping walk down the steps to the roadway, I step into the eight-passenger Mag-lev-roller (MLR). Not one person says anything. No one ever does. I hear a couple of sniffs at my rancid haptic suit in my bag. I ignore it. I tried to be cordial when I first joined this community ride share.

I opened with my name, where I worked, and what I do. I found out the driver, well, drove. His name was "grunt," or at least that seems to be his only answer to questions and comments. The two ladies in the back are always thumbing through their live FEED systems. The other passenger upfront, a lanky balding man with oily hair, seems just to sleep. When he is not there, no one ever tries to take his seat. The two behind me in the middle row always type into the air using their FEED systems to complete their work. One is older, nearing his retirement age. The other is a younger man, a couple of seasons into repaying his indenture.

I share the seat with a lady I like to call Joan. Joan seems nice, and happy. She is always knitting these little sweaters. Small things. The type of shirt you would put on a large doll. I used to think the bits of clothing were for dolls. One day I noticed she had little bits of fur on her jacket, and I realized they are cat sweaters.

That describes my ride for the last two years. Grunt the driver, the narcoleptic co-pilot, the live FEED ladies in the back, the beaten man, the soon-to-be beaten man, the lonely cat lady, and the SkipJack pilot with whom no one wants to converse. I sometimes wonder if there are conversations in the ride share before I load in and after I step out. Since I am the last on and first off, I will never find out.

The ten-minute ride to the outer perimeter of Dillon Gate Montana West (DGMW), North American Compact (NAC) is in silence. I am nervous, as my boss, Mark MacCallister, is a slippery guy. He is always putting your concerns and questions into a holding pattern while changing to a nonsensical topic—usually, how he needs you to do the extra work that is not required.

With a small staccato of quad thuds, then three more sets of thuds, I know we have passed over the Mag-Lev train tracks and arrived at my stop.

Picture every movie, FEED video, documentary, and government office space where top-secret clearance is needed. Picture all those grandiose public buildings with their high-tech displays and fashionable employees, buildings where all those super-important people work. Yeah, DGMW is not any of those places in the FEED vids. It is an old prefab construction trailer, not even a double-wide. The shade is dull yellow, almost a tan. It stands on blocks about forty-five centimeters off the ground, maybe seventeen meters long, large enough to be trailered, small enough to be shipped.

There is a patchwork of skirting to hide the plumbing from view. The roof is a baby-poop brown. It has one single door on this side and one massive door at the other end. One large window is on the far righthand side where Mark's office is. Finally, there is a tiny ventilation window where the bathroom is on the far left. These were purchased by contract lot as emergency accommodations, housing, or offices. Ours is old, beaten down by the winds rolling south from the northern portion of the Compact as they bounce off the Rockies. It always looks even more depressing at night. It becomes downright dreadful when it is raining.

With a quick ID check, temperature scan, then handprint scan, access is granted to the main building. For all the security to get into the building, it always surprises me that the dimensional Gates don't have any more protection than us demilitarized (demilled) SkipJack pilots.

Take the venerable MKII Compact Military (CM) trainer, strip its weapons off, cut the power systems for those weapons, and you have the ubiquitous demilled SkipJack every security or constable uses. Here at DGMW, it is only one pilot and one SkipJack per shift. I guess that is what you get when an army's primary fighting force is SkipJacks.

It is a one-way trip through a Gate. Our human minds are resilient things, but only to a degree. We can make the transition once from Earth Prime Dimension (EP1) to any Dimension Two (D2) with little difficulty. To step back over from D2 to EP1 is suicide. We have three hundred years of proof from braindead fools.

I step in through the flimsy door that is surrounded by the temp scanner, the handprint scanner, and our ID badge scanner to a small, yellow-lit vestibule. I turn right past the breakroom to my pod and locker. I am just a tad bit early, and I am hoping to get in that quick conversation with Mark before he leaves for the day.

I would describe this remote security office as worse than any amenities I experienced while a member of the NAC military. It has hard, off-white plastic walls transitioning into a yellowish-orange at the base. I assume the walls are plastic so that it can be cleaned with a pressure washer fed with commercial-grade disinfectant. The floor is a hard, recycled plastic tile, slippery as all get out when it rains.

I quickly drop my stinking haptic suit into the sonic washer and pull my oldest remaining one from the rack. It is the suit I was wearing when my leg was injured. My lower left leg does not have the needed sub-dermal implants, and as such, my SkipJack will be limping tonight. Maybe that will save me a bit of pain today.

Yeah, that is not going to happen.

The spaces that house the pods are semi-cubicle areas. You have a small locker/rack system similar to a gym's locker room to store your day gear, and a small, specialized sonic cleaning machine for our haptic suits. It is still called a "washer," go figure. Then you have a six-foot wide tube that is the pod. You step in, and your feet touching the floor powers the haptic suit.

The pod floor is hundreds of small ceramic metal bearings curved into a concaved dish shape. As you walk, run, lift, kneel, and stretch, the haptic suit records the motion of your body. The pod interprets the amount of force, velocity, and distance. That data is broadcast to a low-orbit satellite wireless to the SkipJack. All in all, it is an efficient way to do work with less stress on the human body.

As I put on my old military haptic suit, I see the old wear pads and patterns from years ago. These are expensive pieces of kit. There is no way my commercial haptic suit could look this good after a similar term of service. If it were not for my damaged leg, this one would be far more useful than my current off-the-shelf suit.

The best available commercial haptic suit has upwards of sixty points of haptic input. A military version has upwards of three thousand. Commercial units are adjustable for the user by adjusting a slider system during fitting. They can be reset and reused by new individuals. The downside is commercial units only work in a pod.

A commercial haptic suit system can cost a pilot three to six months of pay to purchase. A military issued haptic suit is 3D-woven and printed onto the owner during a sedation cycle. The military haptic suits match up perfectly to the small sub-dermal implants for positive suit function. The military units allow for broader use of SkipJacks.

SkipJacks can range from four-legged dogs and cats to six-legged spiders and pack mules, to chicken-walking heavy support infantry, to standard humanoid troop units. They also include most of the necessary utility SkipJacks for build-ing, digging, lifting, and transporting anything the combined Compact Military (CM) needs. There is one catch: suppose something happens to break that haptic suit's function—for example, having your lower left leg savaged. The suit is now useless to the military, as are you. 3D-printed haptic suits are incapable of being retrofitted to a new pilot.

It has been five years since I wore my issued haptic suit. It is a bit tighter than I remember. It is not just at the waist; my shoulders, arms, back, and thighs are all stretching its fabric taut. Proof once again that I am not in my fighting trim anymore. It is on my body, and for tonight, it will work.

I exit the cubicle my pod is in and pass the empty pod cubicle for our non-existent, third-shift guy. The third-shift guy should be taking the weekend night shifts for David and me on a rotating basis. We have not had one since I started here at DGMW. It made the suck of night shift worse. We get a transient SkipJack pilot in three out of four weekends a month. I continue walking past David's pod cubicle with a little shake to get the haptic suit to settle a little easier on me.

I see Mark's door open, and I blurt out before Mark can spin the conversation down a path I do not choose. "Mark, you got a second? I need to talk to you, let us do it in your office." I see Mark start to open his mouth for something as the distance between us closes. I continue as my hand touches his shoulder. I apply tiny amounts of pressure to go back into his office while saying, "Thanks, Mark, it will not take long. I know you are going out in a few."

Mark seems a little dumbfounded. This is the first time I have not let him get a word in. If I let him put that word in, or drag me off-topic, I never regain control of the conversation. Jacki will be rightfully pissed if that happens. I will be upset. I realize I am losing my edge on the stunned Mark as he takes that massive breath to start his obfuscation talk. "Mark, I have been here for two years. I have not called out. I take the extra weekend shifts without complaint. I need to make a move to the day shift. David is long overdue for his posting to a job like yours. I want to start a family, Mark, and I want to have a chance with Jacki. I need to make that move," I say. I watch Mark's eyes and face react to my statement.

An obscenely loud exhale, a dozen eye blinks, a gasp, another couple eye blinks as Mark seems to come to terms with what I said. Mark is not such a bad guy. He is 165ish centimeters, mid-sixties, balding, with more weight around the middle as a desk jockey typically has. He is good at general administration in so far as he excels at never really screwing up, keeping the status quo, never rocking the boat, nor allowing waves. His utter lack of ambition has made him the perfect person to manage remote gate security at DGMW.

Mark seems to gather himself and, with some hesitation, asks, "Feeling a bit nostalgic today, Ray? That haptic suit looks good on you. Is it your anniversary of mustering out? Oh, what I wouldn't give to have three of you prime vets with your suits." Forcing a smile, he continues, "Hey, you have any buddies? There are signing bonuses and finder's bonuses for talent right now. Tell you what: I'll draft a FEED message, and you send it out. We can split the finder's bonus. Won't that be good? Good, okay. I have to be going." His confidence spools up as he talks.

As I am still blocking his door, Mark only makes it that half-step before his brain tells him I am not moving. I put a bit more steel in my voice. "Mark, stay on topic. I have brought this up a number of times these last few months. I need to know the answer. I can go pilot a SkipJack anywhere."

With a wheeze, he turns around, heading towards his small desk chair behind the pre-turn-of-the-century government surplus desk. He places his thumb on the security pad. The wafer-thin sheet of a screen pops to life as he resignedly answers. "Okay. Okay. I am on the topic, Ray. It's not looking good. I can't put you on the day shift. Hell, the demand is so high right now, I can't even get weekend replacements for the next three months. You and Dave are going to have to split a 24-hour duty every weekend."

That startles me, so I reply, "What do you mean, demand is so high?"

With a wave of his hand, he gestured me behind his desk. "Look, Ray, I wasn't kidding. Do you know any old military guys with the ability to pass the security checks to get this job? We are that short. You know last year we hit one thousand private Gates in the Compact. We should be running a five-guy schedule. Remote sites like ours never had more than three. Well, that is worse now. I know we have added several Gates since last year.

"What happened yesterday is not going to help, Ray." Mark pauses when he sees my confused look. "The CFO sent out an inspector two months early. He was here all day yesterday. He did our yearly inspection four months early. Look at this, Ray." Mark points to his FEED screen. "Our Gate passed inspection with top marks in every category. Why would we need a third pilot, when two are doing the best job possible?" Mark slams his fist down in frustration. "I was forty minutes late to see my wife last night.

"Every security contractor is buzzing for bodies. Even the weekender pool has been assigned to permanent slots company-wide. I have no one available for the weekends. All the larger Gate systems have priority over our minimum staffing levels. It does not look like we will get our two open positions for our Gate."

Mark's voice is a burbling thing. There is not a lisp, but the words do not have the clear enunciation old troopers like me need. I simply have too much hearing damage to make out his rapid-fire words without some serious contemplation.

"There has to be something. The company is growing like crazy. Mark, explain to me why I cannot get one of those day slots? Even if it is not the Dillon Gate, surely the Bozeman or Missoula Gates have an opening? Yeah, my commute would have been longer, I can deal with that." I am probably more forceful in my questions than necessary, and Mark shrinks back from my tone and volume.

"Ray, the company is growing, and it is doing well. Even with that growth, we lack people by forty percent across all our Gates. Since we are at the minimum here, the company won't transfer you out till there is a third person here. Because any new hires will go to other needed slots, we will not see a third person until all those positions are filled." Mark continues, sheepishly, "Ray, it isn't just our company. We have the third highest number of Gate contracts. We offer the highest monthly salary because we focus on remote sites. We offer the second-highest sign-on bonus. We offer finders and referral bonuses. We mirror the industry, though; the numbers are still close to that forty percent vacancy."

"Mark, you are telling me I am stuck here on nights? That my only choice is to find another job?" I was starting to heat up. I know it was not Mark's fault. This situation is just wrong.

"Ray, I am saying we are all stuck. Our security contracts only let us move from position to position when we have a replacement." He pauses and meets my eyes directly. "I was supposed to retire the year you signed on. The NAC security clause, the one we both signed when we took these jobs, does not allow us to just leave without cause. I can't retire. David doesn't care; he just comes in and does his thing. You, well, you were a godsend. You replaced, well, you know." Mark whimpers.

"You mean I replaced the Gate walker? John? Jim?" I sigh.

I have no idea that Mark is two years over retirement, but I know that David is just clueless enough not to care. I realize this is likely why the previous guy walked the Gate.

Mark says with a bit of a stammer, "Jesus, you replaced Jesus." With a bit of a pause, "His grandmother comes here every Friday. She raised him, I think. She is the lady that brings the food on Friday evenings at shift change."

With a big exhale and drooping of his head, he sighs. "Ray, I can't change it. I can't get you out of it and I can't get me out of it. It's a prison term if I try to leave myself. My wife has been in the hospital for five months now. She caught that flu while on chemo. I don't know what to do, Ray. I just want to see her every day. I tried that first week, you know. They found me at her bedside.

"Consolidated Gate Securities United (CGSU) told me that I used my vacation for the year. If I did not return to work on Monday, CGSU would file charges to prosecute me. I'm a civilian, Ray, prosecuted for leaving my post, I have never been in the military. Now, I can't leave. They check my login and usage. I get responses on the weekly transit reports. They require me to be here, Ray. I must be with my wife. I sleep there now. The nursing staff lets me." His agony is at the very edge of his voice. Mark is about to lose composure.

Shit. That is a heavy burden to find out. I say, "Mark, I am sorry if I came on too strong. I apologize. Jacki and I, well, we want to start. Her nurse's indenture ends in a few months. We want to start a family shortly after."

With a swallow and a sigh, Mark says, "Ray, it's okay. It's helpful for me to get it out. I needed to say it. With you and Jacki thinking about it, you need to know it. Look, my wife is waiting. I will try, Ray. I will." I hear the tone in Mark's voice and know that not much is likely to change.

"Thanks, Mark. Give your wife my love," I reply as I exit his office towards my pod. I am a few minutes late and I am sure David will be gone.

I round the corner into my pod and go through the pre-check. The lower left leg fails in all but the most basic heel up, heel down, heel left, heel right function. I will have a long night. There is a big difference between me and most pod-based pilots: they are limited to piloting from a pod, while I can pilot remotely with only my haptic suit and a reserve battery pack.

Because I was able to successfully dump my will, or as I like to call it, my mindspace into a SkipJack at will multiple times during boot camp, I was watched. When my time came, I was snatched up. There are a few of us out there that can pilot off a reserve power cell in our haptic suits.

Only military suits like mine have those power cells. I have never met a reserve pilot who was not CM-trained. Even then, folks like me, we are rare, numbering in the hundreds out of a five million-standing CM military personnel, let alone those tens of millions of civilian pilots. If I wanted, I could parade-march right along with my SkipJack all night.

CGSU's official policy is pod-piloting only. I will stand my twelve-hour shift in this pod. The connections made, I start my shift. The thrill and joy of piloting never fades. Even in a pod, I find it relaxing. Having this skillset brings happiness to my soul.

***

C1 S3

Twelve hours later, I observe David's SkipJack exit the bay as I finish switching the Mag-lev tracks for an incoming freight arrival on the day shift. I make my way back with a wave and head to the storage shed's SkipJack docking station. As I exit the pod, I grab my clothes from my locker. Thoughts of Friday night invade my mind. Jacki will be off, and I am looking forward to being able to spend time together. I do not know how she is going to take the news.

Exiting the community ride share, I tab the payment stud with my thumb.

You pre-pay for the next week's rides. As I limp the short trek to the door, I realize my lower left leg does not hurt as much. Not a lot less, but enough to notice. I have a better range of movement, better flexibility. I touch the door handle and remember I left my commercial haptic suit in the wash. Cursing at my eagerness to get home, I pray that Jacki will like a guy in uniform—okay, a stinky jumpsuit. I open the door.

Jacki is there. She is all of 170 plus centimeters with curves. Nutmeg-brown skin, her braids loosely hang as she reclines in her chair talking to her sister in Virginia District. She waves. "Hi, Ray, I will finish in a minute, sugar."

I walk back to the shower, stripping. I put the haptic suit onto its hanger on the back of the door. I start my routine for the shower. I spend some time looking at the more-than-reasonable flexibility and range of movement my foot has. I suppose you have good days and bad days. There is not much in the artificial myomere bundles to rub out. Odd. I must have unconsciously been babying my leg all night. I chuckle at the zombie-like, shuffle-walk my SkipJack must have displayed.

Exiting the shower, I find food, glorious food, almost ready. Jacki has set the table for us. I am not big on cooking or eating formalities. Jacki is very particular about food, and how and when we eat. If I am not there, she leaves me a plate. Jacki finishes her FEED message with her sister as she plates the food.

We sit down for meals on a military regimen: every six hours. She has said it is how her family did it in Virginia District. This morning, tonight for me, was more soy, always soy. It is what we can afford. Since almost all large-animal meat production has moved to the D2 iterations, its costs have drastically risen.

I tried to raise chickens a few years ago, and Jacki named them. We had eggs, until she found out the chickens could hatch their eggs sometimes. Then we had chicks, and they got named. A year later, when it became too much to handle, we gifted them to a local family that needed the chickens more than us.

"So, Jacki, what is on the plate this morning?" I ask as I begin to salivate. She tried inverting her meals for me, but she says dinner for breakfast is just wrong.

"A variation of Matar Paneer. Not soy, real Paneer." Jacki's eyes sparkle. "I picked it up on the way to the community ride share stop last night." She knows I grew up on real meat. She knows I would love to be able to buy more of it.

Unfortunately, I could only arrange a bit through our Gate. Even then, it is wildly expensive.

I sit down to the tomato and onion dish. I am about halfway in before I feel sated enough to talk to her. With a *get it over with, break the bad news*, I say, "I spoke at length with Mark." Adding a pause out of dread, not anticipation, I continue, "It does not look good. There aren't even enough pilots to fill weekend spots."

I watch her hesitate as the words came out. I see the shoulders set. My answer is not the answer she expected, nor is it an answer she wants to hear. I continue relating the conversation with Mark in detail. She sits like a stone, listening, adjusting. I am coming to an end of my explanation by describing how Mark had been living nights at the hospital.

She takes a deep breath and then says, "I can't believe you let him spin that story about staying at the hospital at nights." She seems to have hung up on that point. Her voice is picking up inflections and a specific tone as she continues, "I know he has been at the hospital; I have seen him heading up to her floor. I checked in on them the first few times I saw him. That doesn't mean you can't get on day shift." She is almost entirely into the windup.

I caution in a calm voice, "Jacki, there isn't anyone to take the night shift. There is not anyone to take weekend shifts for at least three months."

"Dave can take the weekends and nights. You don't have to, you were military. You deserve to have seniority. Dave doesn't do shit." She is now at a full roiling boil as she speaks. This conversation is not starting off well.

With a chuckle, I reply, "Yeah, Dave is a waste, does only what he must. He, however, was hired before me. He has been there longer. There is no preference for military service in seniority." I speak as calmly as I can. I am trying to deflate the coming hurricane Jacki is spinning herself into.

Jacki whirls, hands in the air, whipping at the direction of the demarcation zone where I work, and the careless fling of the hands adds to her verbalization. "Those two are just gaming you."

With extreme caution, I state, "It isn't just about Dave and Mark. The whole company is lacking people. The security contracts we signed do not allow any of us to leave post until there is a replacement. Sure, Dave and I could theoretically switch, but we could not stop. We cannot just leave. They have Mark boxed in two years past retirement. They practically dragged him away from his wife's bedside. No matter what, Jacki, I am required to work, and it will be weekends for the next three months. What would you have me do?"

With a slap on the table, the conversation came to an end. "Ray, you tell Dave. You work it out with Dave, you make it happen. If there is to be an us, you need to make this change, you got that?" She stands, turns mostly away from me, hesitates to point her finger at me. "I am not kidding, Ray, do it. I deserve more."

Right then and there, I felt the tension in the room shift, as Krakatoa blew its top. There is a level to her voice I had previously never seen or heard.

"I am going to my sister's for the weekend. I will be back in time for my Tuesday shift. Ray, you better be on days by then. Good job, Ray, this is supposed to be our weekend. How could you screw this up!"

Bam! The jolt of the door slamming shut brings me back around. I am so stunned, I did not even notice she had had bags packed, had them near the door, or that she walked to the door in her speech. I hear her pulling a bag down the concrete walkway as she keeps her tirade up.

I will. I do not know what I am going to do. David will not easily give up his day shift. I will ask, I will urge, I will bribe if I must. Drained, emotionally numb, I head to bed. While walking down the hallway, my left ankle spasms. I start to fall. I grab the rail in the hall corridor. As I am holding myself there, I feel the throbbing I know so well. It is not a good day, after all. I make the rest of the trek to the bed in a lurching limp. Thankfully, the military teaches you to fall asleep within seconds of closing your eyes. It is a skill learned via sweat, blood, tears, and hammered into your head by drill instructors via nightmares.

***

C1 S4

I awake late. I dash out of the bedroom and to the bathroom for a shower. I jumped into my sweaty haptic suit. I will have to take single-seat rideshare to be at work on time. I move past the hallway, past the food and dishes all over the table and counter. I chuckle: at least Jacki would not get mad at me for that. I can clean it up in the morning after work.

Maybe I will save some of Abuelita's food she brings on Friday evenings. I hear the ping from my FEED and the ride share is here. Man, I smell, my stench will be worse on the way home. With a surprisingly smooth gait, I make it to the micro mag trike. Okay, it is more like a tiny MLR with a second seat. Micro-micro compact?

The driver cannot be more than eighteen. He accelerates off, weaving through traffic, never speeding, and never breaking the law, just not obeying the spirit of the law at all. To my surprise, I am there even earlier than usual.

I touch the pay stud, stagger off and out of the seat. I take a moment to stretch. As I am doing a turn, I see Abuelita, Jesus's grandmother, wave as she is closing her door a block down and across the street. Huh, I did not know Jesus had lived so near the demarcation zone. I make my way to the office door and through the pointless security. I am positive a good wind or even Abuelita could break through this door.

Standing in the vestibule, I turn to see David already out of his pod. He looks at me. "Dude, is she here yet?" His jowls and voice are bouncing with equal excitement.

With a raised eyebrow, I say, "She's just leaving down the street. Why aren't you in your pod?"

With an exasperated whine, David scolds me. "Chill, dude, I gotcha all caught up. I ain't missing her food over anything. Nothing comes in till one, anyways."

Realizing this is about the best time to ask, I begin to say, "David, I need to ask you something." I am about to finish asking for him to swap the day shift with me when he fades back into his pod space. He is taking his haptic suit off. Oh, god, he is a no-skivvy guy. Pasty, pallid flesh ravages my eyes. "Dave, what the hell, you, you, that's just gross," I say in a higher octave than normal due to my shock at seeing Dave butt-naked in the office.

David pops out of the cubicle after dressing and says, "What, huh?" as he removes an earpiece from his ears, which is something else you are not supposed to do during the operation of a SkipJack. Music distracts, distraction kills.

I am shaking my head at David's lazy attitude to everything. I am about to ask to swap day shift again when he shoves his no-skivvy suit into my hands and vigorously asks, "Stick that in your wash, will you? My second set is still in mine. I'm going to help her bring food. Mark is gone already. Something happened and he rushed out. We're gonna eat in the breakroom tonight, just like when Jesus was here."

With that, I am holding his sweaty, stinky, no-skivvy haptic suit. I am staring at him as he hops out the door and down the three steps into the yard to meet Abuelita. I did not know Dave could survive a hop like that. The unskilled bastard. At least he has sweatpants and a ratty old t-shirt on. Hell, at the end of the night, I am not sure I could, either. Regrettably, I am holding the stinky waste of a haptic suit by two fingers at arm's length. I move to my cubicle and remove my suit. Dropping the hazardous waste inside, I program the unit for a three-cycle setting total of nine hours. Maybe that would be enough. Hanging my suit up for tomorrow, I start to hear murmurs and smell the scent of spice, tortillas, and beans. I turn and make my way to the breakroom.

I find Abuelita chattering about the food over sugarcane disposable plates and cups. I do understand Spanish, but this is some sort of Mayan dialect. I am not sure which it is. David has said it is not Spanish, but one of the twenty-seven known dialects of Mayan.

After Jesus did his Gate walk, Abuelita has continued to come every week and share a Friday meal just so we would deliver a letter for her. I have had quite a few of Abuelita's meals in my two years. They are amazingly good. Shortly after I arrived, Mark put the kibosh on her eating with us in the breakroom.

Mark is not here, and I hope nothing went wrong with his wife. Dave is pointing and asking about the food in broken Spanglish. Just as we sit down, I hear the first blast of rolling thunder, the kind only heard on the plains of Montana. It is a tremendous, three-second prolonged detonation of sound. David gleefully chirps, "Sucks to be you, Ray. Fourteen-hour thunderstorm starts just as you begin your shift."

I do a quick check on my FEED. Sure enough, the storm front should be sweeping from the northeast and rolling back onto itself off the Rockies. Tonight is going to be a long night. As my stomach grumbles, I decide I need to eat, especially with a storm coming. That means the train will not be heading in at one a.m. It also means the opportunity of the Gate losing its temporal lock is higher.

I will be spending my night running the SkipJack in the rain from one monitoring station to the next. It is going to be a busy night. I laugh at that. There is no way I will know what to do if any of the stations report out of the green zone to either the blue or red zones. Blue zone means the temporal lock of the D2 iteration causes time to pass slower. Red means it passes faster than Earth-prime. In two years, and with ten or more storms a year, I have never seen it out of the green. I doubt it is like the old days, where every storm held the possibility of catastrophe.

The three of us sit down and start diving into homemade food: fresh tortillas, tamales, and some kind of chicken dish. Coming from the upper north of old Alaska, all this is fairly new to me. I ask David to give her my thanks.

Dave responds, "She wants you to give Jesus a letter."

I look at David. "How am I supposed to do that? He cannot come back. I do not even know how to get him a letter. That dimensional earth doesn't even have its FEED network up." I know that within the first forty-five years the Dillon Gate Montana West: D2 iteration, (DGMW:D2) should have its low-orbit network up. We are seven years into that process, as far as I remember.

With an exasperated sigh, Dave swallows one mouthful before putting one of the rolls of tortilla and meat in either hand into his mouth.

Dave mumbles, "Do what I do: tape it to the next train. If Jesus is still there, he will get it. I think he is because I don't know how she can afford to put this spread out every Friday." With a gulp and a subdued voice as he chews, he adds, "He has to be sending her back something right, isn't that what they do? Send something back to their families?"

I roll my eyes at David's ignorance. I do not see it as racism. I see it as the limits of his knowledge showing its boundaries.

I point at the letter and say in my most well-enunciated English. "Abuelita, I will put this on the next train for Jesus. That should be sometime during my shift tomorrow."

Abuelita points the envelope at me and says, "Yes, tomorrow."

"Dave, I need you to swap from days to nights," I say. "Jackie and I are wanting to start a family."

"I'd like to, Ray," Dave says unconvincingly. "I've got league in the evenings. I can't swap to night shift."

"Dave, it is only until Mark gets us a third guy replacement, or you a supervisor slot at another Gate," I say. "As soon as either of those come up, it is back to day shift for you."

"I'd like to, Ray, but I don't want to be a supervisor," Dave says. "You've seen what they have done to Mark. No thank you. I have it nice and comfortable here as day shift lead. I'm staying right here."

It is nearing time for me to head to my pod. I excuse myself and clear my spot. As I wash up, I hear the door close, the wind slamming it shut. I turn to see David at the table, still ladling food onto his plate. He is pulling Abuelita's plate over to his spot. Lord, that man can eat.

I head into my pod and start my shift. Most commercial haptic suits and SkipJacks have a minute or two of boot-up sequences. Unfortunately, my military haptic suit has a longer boot-up due to the extra points of contact from the suit, the user, the pod, and the SkipJack. So I stand there in my pod, and bring up the visuals around the DGMW demarcation zone (DMZ) while waiting for the system to boot up.

The SkipJacks we use for security are demilitarized military MKII trainers. They are not full combat units, just combat-capable without weapons. They are old, probably pushing well past their training service life. They work for walking, throwing heavy Mag-lev rail levers, and checking the functionality of power feeds. They are impressive in their own right. Anything that can pick up seventy five kilos with one arm is remarkable. It takes a well-trained hand not to destroy things. I begin to think of the bent Mag rail levers and realize it is because Dave has become lazy with his power feedback settings again.

As I am waiting for the remaining sixty-five percent of the connections to finalize, I see Abuelita walk past the tracks the wrong way. I swap visuals to follow her with my dropdown Heads Up Display (HUD) goggles. The images come from my SkipJack's ocular mount.

Damn, it isn't in the right spot. I swap over to David's SkipJack visuals. I see the shape of Abuelita walking through the driving wind as the train whips from one side of the yard to the other. She is only a couple of hundred yards from the Gate.

I scream in my best drill instructor voice, "David, she is doing a Gate walk. Abuelita's doing a Gate walk. Get your ass in your pod."

I hear a scrape and a rush out of the breakroom door. I hear him bounce off the hallway wall into his cubicle. "Ray, I am not in my suit. I can't get her. I can't get it going fast enough. Stop her, Ray! CGSU will fire us if we have another Gate walk."

"I will try, Dave," I yell back. What I would not give for a true comms set-up between us.

The Compact Military teaches you a vast number of things. Many, at the time, seem pointless, like how to make a bed with sheets so taut a quarter will bounce. What the heck is a quarter? I know what a loonie is, and my first drill sergeant said it was like a loonie.

I pull my mind back on track. One of the things you learn is that at any point, you may have to "dump" into your SkipJack: force the connections, force your mental self and your mindspace into the SkipJack's command systems. I do not know if a commercial haptic suit and commercial pod could do it. I do know my old military haptic suit can.

I look at my feed. I am only forty percent booted in. I set the primary login as next. When I reach forty-five percent, I have access to the boot-up commands. I open the feed. Through my HUD goggles, I select the primary boot override. I click affirmative at the prompt, click the force connection prompt, click affirmative, click on the one hundred percent feedback, click the affirmative.

Imagine having your whole body in a pins and needles state while jumping into ice-cold water, and having your head compressed from all sides by a vast weight. That is the beginning of forcing a connection by dumping into your SkipJack. It is not unheard of to have veteran pilots black out during repeated dump training.

I fight the wave of pressure on my mind. I see the dark halos come to my eyes as my brain struggles with the sensory input. I start chuffing breaths just like I learned in basic Skipjack piloting school. Chuffing breaths forces oxygen into my brain. I clench and flex all my muscles as I run through the dump sequence.

It has been at least five years since I have tried this. Within what seems like minutes but is only seconds, my eyesight returns. What comes back is the weight, like I am carrying an extra me compressing all around my body.

I select from my feed to go to battery power. This is the part that separates me and my skills as a pilot from all but less than one percent of other pilots. As the selection confirms, and the mental mass of my MKII becomes mine, I change my mindspace to reserve piloting. Piloting in a pod is one thing. Your SkipJack mimics your exact movements. Piloting via reserve is a level of complexity that few human minds can manage.

"Ray." Dave's weak voice makes its way to my mind. "Get her back. If we have another unauthorized Gate walk, we will both be in big trouble."

My mind-spaces are devoted to my SkipJack when I hear, "If we get her, I will move to nights."

I devote a separate mental space to the left eye, which is allows me to see where I am walking in real life. My right eye sees the SkipJack's visuals in the dropdown HUD. As soon as the start-up completes, my SkipJack jumps from its docking station. My left eye sees me pass the door of the security office, and the right eye swivels the SkipJack head to find Abuelita. Damn, all I have is a goggle set-up. The rain blurs the picture. It is just a wall of falling water. With the HUD controls up again, I swap the right eye over to thermal visuals. I can see a faint glow. It has taken me too long. Abuelita is further along than I thought.

My left eye is near worthless from the wind and rain whipping against my HUD goggles. I do not have my full military helmet to protect my eyes. You can take the haptic suit, and you can pilot with the suit, but you need the helmet to sight and fight. When a pilot musters out, the suit is part of their payout. The Compact keeps the helmet with its heads-up display and encrypted communications suite (coms).

I line up my SkipJack with my estimation of where Abuelita is as compared to where I am. It would be much easier to work in a straight line. I start it forward. As the parallax of the two images merge, it became easier to guide the SkipJack into a smooth gait. Once I am lined up and seeing through the ocular port of the SkipJack, I drop down both HUD lenses to view through the rain in thermal. I can dash forward now. I am putting all my human strength into moving the SkipJack.

As a pilot, you have to move something with approximately 350 kilos of walking or running mass. The haptic suit boosts what you do to the unit. It just does not help you. When you pilot at ten percent like that fat bastard David runs at, it does help you because it is only requiring ten percent of your strength input to move. The issue with piloting with high feedback is that you often over-pilot a SkipJack. Every movement must be precise. Pilots force dumping into the SkipJack do not have that option. I start my run and I put in every ounce of effort. I am closing in on Abuelita. It will be close, and that added uncertainty spurs me on.

The downside to running as a 350-kilo mass is that you must stop that mass. All that strength to get up to speed must be used to slow down. I cannot just run at her full tilt. I must reach her at what would be normal human contact speed. If I try to grab her any faster, I could seriously injure or kill her. Neither would likely be useful for me getting on the day shift. The SkipJack struggles to slow things down on the wet concrete. I revel at the way my left leg is holding its own. Five years since the injury, five years of it not being stable. If I had wood to knock on, I would be pounding on it.

I am short of Abuelita by a few steps. She slows as she approaches the Gate. I see her look back in terrified horror at the SkipJack. The fear blooms in hot patches in the SkipJack's thermal vision. I can understand, as she is seeing a two-meter monstrosity with five ocular lenses, two glowing organic green, one vibrant red, running at her.

The MKII demilled units are vaguely humanoid. The closest thing to humans a SkipJack has is the dubious honor of having four fingers and one thumb on each hand. Imagine these hulks thudding through your home in the night and pulling you out. Given her age, it wouldn't surprise me if she has seen that in the last Central Mexican Authority revolution.

My metal plate-covered arm reaches out slowly and catches hold of her sweater as lightning flashes overhead. As I firm up on that grip, the thunder rolls. Damn, that is close, just outside the sound shadow or quiet zone of the lightning. My SkipJack's left arm is reaching to grab another part of her sweater. Abuelita twists, and in a twirl, slips free of the sweater.

I am nearing my SkipJack. With a quick flick, I open the left eye back to human vison on my HUD goggles. Crap, the rain is hard to see through. I orient my human body a couple of degrees closer and move my perception back to the right eye HUD display. Moving the SkipJack closer, I grab out and miss her arm.

Behind me, I hear another SkipJack coming at full tilt. Man, I hope David does not barrel into us at full speed. I refocus on her. She is just steps from the Gate. Once again, I get the SkipJack close, this time on her left side, and reached out with my right arm to take her left wrist.

I have her. She stumbles, almost falling, but stays upright. She scrambles feverishly to free herself from my MKII's grasp. Then, David's SkipJack hits mine. It is not fast, it is not harsh, but that 20 centimeters of bump throws my perception for a loop. My SkipJack twists on the wet cement. The sudden movement in my right eye that was not part of the directed movement of my left eye shifts my brain into neutral for a second.

With effort, I make it back on track. David's MKII has a grasp on my Skip-Jack's hauling clevis, and my SkipJack is holding on to Abuelita, who is still somehow standing. I start walking my human body to her as David's SkipJack begins to lose its footing. He is leaning backwards too far, and his SkipJack's footing goes out in front of him.

The fall pushes the whole group forward. I am standing in inches of water, in between several sets of Mag-lev tracks. I grab out with my human body to pull on David's SkipJack. At that moment, I realize I had made a terrible mistake by not focusing on piloting. I turn my attention back to my MKII visuals, looking through the SkipJack just in time to see Abuelita reach out and touch the Gate.

I feel the intense pain of electricity.

White fire fills my vision.

Chapter 2
Recovery

C2 S1

I remember half-rousing to a soft glow at night. I would later learn that it was just a darkened room. I misjudged the light because my eyes had not opened for a long time. I have a great deal of discomfort. My throat is raw, my lips cracked and chapped. My nose burns when trying to breathe through it. My skin is numb. I realize my whole body is numb. There are twinges of soreness, hints of burning, and subdued pain. I understand that I am on pain medication. I remember waking like this after my injury to my left leg.

I lay there for a while, ruminating about what could be, before drifting off again. I know I am alive, and that means the fight is not over. Only when the cold of death comes is the battle over. Memories of the cold and its unforgiving nature strike me hard. I remember those first days alone, those first nights as a very young man. I remember what saved me was a plan. Sleep comes for me then.

I am awake again. Noises intrude into my mind as I keep my eyes closed. My eyes are stiff and sticky, layered in goop that prevents me from opening them more than a sliver. Someone will be along to help in a while. I am still numb, and while I can sense my fingers and toes, the sensation of touch and movement comes from a separate place.

What I need now is a plan, a process. Yes, I need to develop a plan. Whatever I am on for pain medication is making thinking slow and ponderous. I need to understand better what happened. I can set my goals when I know the severity of my injuries. I fall back on my childhood mantra. I could not verbalize just yet, so I shout it in my mental space.

Day one, cut the wood; day two, chop the wood; day three, stack the wood. I repeat it to myself. That mantra from such a naive young boy comes back to me. Like then, I will learn, somewhere I had made a mistake. All is not lost, I am alive, I have a chance, and I will learn from that mistake.

A person, who I assume is a nurse, enters the room. The light level rises a fair deal. They begin to talk to me in a raspy, firm but quiet feminine voice. "Hello! You've been in an accident. Your recovery is going well. You're at Community Dillon Regional Hospital."

I make a tiny, coughing sound, which is about all I can do for now.

In response, I hear her go, "Hmmm."

It is as if she has spent years yelling at the top of her lungs. Her voice has a coarse, grating sound that just seems unable to get over a specific volume. Her reply is just under the level of a polite conversation.

"I'm Nurse Brinx. I'll be your day shift nurse. I figured you were awake a little earlier this morning." With a bit more rigidity to her tone, she continues, "Now, you're a strong man. You need just to relax so I can clean your eyes, nose, and mouth. I'll get you a few ice chips and water after. That will make breathing and speaking much easier. Do you understand? No fidgeting, no moving."

I cannot quite understand her comments as a whole unit. There are too many words strung together for my drug-addled mind to parse any meaning from her statement. It takes Nurse Brinx two additional explanations for everything to sink in. Whatever I am on is like walking through waist-high mud for impeding thoughts.

I have some time to digest that long fusillade of instructions, and I exhale a bit of air in response. I try to nod, but there is already a firm palm on my forehead, holding it steady. I feel dampness at my left eye. My body is still so numb that I do not recognize the touch of the hand until I feel the moisture at my eyes.

My head is gently pushed left and right as she works. Nurse Brinx continues to explain what she is doing. All I want to know is where Jacki is and if she had been through already today.

"The Doctor will be in to explain things to you soon, as you're a bit more coherent," Nurse Brinx says. As she finishes wiping my mouth and nose, she whispers in that ripped voice, "All right, I'm going to be back in a few with some ice chips for you. You take a rest. You look exhausted already."

With a final double-tap of beeps, I drift back to sleep. I wake to Nurse Brinx bringing in those ice chips. She helps put a few in my mouth. Oh, that cold, that glorious, biting coolness that soothes you. After the first few, I croak out "thanks." My voice sounds odd to my ears, almost as if that 'thanks' had half its letters stolen, just in the speaking. I nod as a second and third set of chips are placed on my lips.

Nurse Brinx asks in very well-enunciated whisper, "Now, how is that? Can you tell me your name?"

With a murmur that seems to take all the breath in my lungs, "Raylan."

I do not know why I speak my full name. I have only repeated it on forms and papers; never to any other person since that day when I was thirteen. "People call me Ray." That takes it all, every ounce of air I have in my lungs. Imagine a vacuum removing the air as you speak. My power to verbalize leaves me that quickly.

With a firm look and a frown, "Well, Mr. Ray, what's your last name?"

I respond with a scrunched brow, and a great deal of thought, as I do not think I can explain it in the amount of air I have in my lungs. "Just Ray." A long, few seconds of shallow breathing pass by. "No last name." That effort takes it out of me. I sink back into the thin firm mattress.

Her gaze softens as the rasp issues forth. "Okay, Mr. Ray, do you know how old you are? Where you live?" It seems Nurse Brinx was a former interrogator in a past life. Her gaze brooks no disagreement.

With an effort, I smile. Oof, that hurt my cracked lips. I have a firm hold on my joke. I cannot let it go. "Yes, and yes." That last word comes out with a wheeze and a tiny cough. I wink to let her know it is in good fun. I guess my smile, wheezy cough, and wink make it look more like I am having a stroke.

In a flash, she grabs my wrist. While taking my pulse, she asks, "Are you okay, Mr. Ray? Your pulse is fading. Oh no, you're dying."

My eyes go wide, pupils expanding, heartrate shooting up as I hear a soft, paper-thin chuckle in response. "Two can play that game, Mr. Ray. How about from now on, you stick to answers and I will stick to nursing? We'll leave the jokes for the attorneys."

Relief floods me as I realize Nurse Brinx, master prankster, got me. I smile weakly and look at the ice chips cup again. She gives me a few more chips and says, "I'll send in the Doctor when he arrives at the hospital."

I ponder that. Why is the doctor not in the hospital? Why am I in a private room? Why am I seeing only her and this doctor, no other staff? I have a lot of questions. I try to remember.

I remember seeing Abuelita moving in the driving rain to the Gate. I remember the heat glow of her form through the rain and wind. I remember catching her arm, only to see her heat glow spin out of my grasp. I remember a brief flash of her face as that spin came midway around. This image was not a heat-soaked rendering, but a face drained of color because of the cold rain. Her face had a smile, one that only those set in their final moments of resolve can have.

***

C2 S2

There is a knock at the door, and this drops me out of thoughts and memories. I blink rapidly as the lights are turned even brighter. Bright lights have always been extremely harsh on my eyes. Now that I am just about staring into the light fixture, it is rather annoying. It must have been clear that it is uncomfortable as shortly after that light recedes down.

"Excellent response to light. Wonderful, wonderful. Nurse Brinx tells me you are a bit of a prankster, Mr. Ray," says a thin dark man in a doctor's coat. With a warm smile, he continues, "Let's have none of that now, though. I have a lot to go through." His voice is central west, Great Lakes District, and it carries many of the old Canadian inflections in it.

Before he can get rolling, I asked in a much louder voice than I thought possible, "Abuelita? Is she okay?" My question seems to elicit a frown from the doctor.

In a reliable voice, the Doctor replies, "We'll get to that, Mr. Ray. My name is Doctor Peter Alverez. You may not remember me."

He continues looking me over clinically. I can focus on him better now. Old—he is old. His skin is much darker than Jacki's. His eyes are a wrinkled softness that carries generations of compassion. His round wire glasses are an affectation, maybe? Almost no one chooses to wear glasses anymore with the available eye surgeries. Finally, a thick, white, densely curled beard.

"I am the one who worked on your left leg. Do you remember?" Doctor Alverez asks.

I scrunch up my face as I try to remember. I have no memories of the first accident. I am still fighting through the mud to think and remember. Nor do I have many memories of my first surgery to fix my left leg.

Dr. Alverez's voice pulls me back to the here and now as he continues, "No worries, I shouldn't have expected you would, as I was only there for the surgery. Someone else did the post-surgery care. By looking at the sad shape your lower left leg is in, I'd say no one bothered to continue physical therapy. We shall fix that this time."

It is hard to focus on his words. They are all there, but in the background, as if heard on a speaker from the next room in my mind.

"Abuelita, is she okay, did she make it back?" I ask.

It is my first full sentence since waking. I deliver my question in a reliable and firm tone of voice, one I rarely used outside of the Compact Military.

The doctor, now in a rolling chair right next to me, sits bolt upright. I hear a third voice from the doorway. It is male, so not Nurse Brinx.

It is a sputtery, lispy tangle of lips, jowls, and tongue as it says, "All right, then, that is my cue, Doctor. I have a bit of legal business to conduct with Mr. Ray, uh, Ray, um. Well, Mr. Ray. He has regained faculties, as we have discussed.

Please leave the room, as I am his legal representation and his attorney for the moment."

With an exasperated tone, Dr. Alverez replies, "Mr. Jenkins, you ambulance-chasing toad. I told you I will make the determination of when he can have visitors."

Before the angry doctor can continue, the attorney splutters in that awful voice, "Dr. Alverez, *Virginia vs. Plantagenet Industries* states that when mindful enough to ask specific questions relating to legal matters, the client must then be provided said legal counsel. Mr. Ray has expressed as much, asked as much. Please excuse us."

In a very firm growl, Dr. Alverez says as he closes the distance on the attorney, "Mr. Jenkins, Mr. Steven Jenkins. If his heartbeat so much as goes up by ten beats per minute, I will have you dragged from this hospital, shuttled in front of a presiding Judge in the nearest Community jurisdiction that will do it, and charged with torture."

The doctor closes the distance between him and the attorney so that they could rub noses if the doctor were not 200 centimeters tall. Mr. Jenkins is a full head shorter. The man is nearly as wide as he is tall, it seems. The attorney is flat up against the door.

"DO" *pause* "YOU" *longer break* "UNDERSTAND?" Dr. Alverez asks in his baritone voice. The noise of his question reverberates down the hall.

I see Mr. Jenkin's shadow gulp on the doorframe. His Adam's apple and chins are still quivering as he croaks out a quiet "yes."

This situation is not good. Anyone who receives such a threat and capitulates so quickly will stew on it for years. Today will come back to haunt me, I am sure of that. Steven Jenkins will blame me. I will pay the price for Dr. Alverez's protection. I groan audibly, and that breaks the tension. The doctor stops staring at Mr. Jenkins, and he turns towards me, searching for an excuse to end the meeting. I look at Mr. Jenkins. Doctor Alverez nods in affirmation and walks out.

Jenkins is standing there with his back pushing the door wide open, his briefcase in front of him. I can see a small stain spreading out where the briefcase meets his slacks. Yep, this is going to bite me in the ass for sure. I need to think, so I let my eyes slide mostly closed. Bare slits remain open, only open enough to see his form.

I do my best to adopt a sick person's speech. "Close the" *long pause for effect* "door, Mr. Jenkins."

The effort of sounding like a sick man is not as difficult as I had envisioned. With a click and a loss of light from the hallway, I know the door is closed. I keep up the ruse as I say in my tired voice, "Sit."

Like a puppy, he crosses the room, holding that now peed-on briefcase to his crotch in an awkward gait. This man is going to lord this over me—not today, at least, then possibly in a week. Oh, I can only guess at how much Mr. Jenkins is going to bring the suck for me to embrace. I know it will come; men like him never forget.

As Jenkins opens the briefcase on his lap, he says, "Mr. Ray, Consolidated Gate Securities United would like you to know that your injuries sustained while on the job will be covered under employment contract up and until the point you regain function to the level you were at when injured."

With a breath through his nose that stops halfway, he realizes he is sitting next to my not-yet-emptied colostomy bag. He exhales, scrunches his face, takes a breath through his mouth and swallows hard. A hint of green pokes at the fleshy spot by his ears and throat. Jenkins might lose his lunch.

"I have all the necessary FEED message forms for you to sign," Jenkins says. He pulls up his FEED and scrolls through something. "I just sent it to you. Please sign and return it."

I am more than miffed, but I try not to show it. His voice, the slurred "S" sounds, the over-enunciated "P" sounds, and the falling "L" end up grating through my mind.

I turn my head slightly and looked at him with the one eye that responds. Clearly, the medication for pain is fading, as turning to view Mr. Jenkins is painful.

"Mr. Jenkins. Do you see my hands?" I ask, my voice quaking. I take a few long breaths. Speaking is becoming more comfortable, but I really cannot say a lot at once. Still keeping my very sick man ruse up, I continue, "I do not, I cannot move. I will not be" *another couple of moments breathing* "signing anything until

I can read it."

Gasping for air and sucking it in as fast as I can, I am starting to lose my breath. I can hear my heart pound in my head.

"I have no access to my FEED until they allow me to move," I say with some difficulty.

The last four words are a series of gasps. I see his eyes flicker to the heartrate monitor. My exertions must have sent my heartrate up. He looks as if he expects a dozen men to charge in and beat him down prior to dragging him out the door. Jenkins settles back, and after a few seconds, his confidence grows. His face calms into a smile that comes only to his lips.

I have seen that smile on people before. It is the smile of someone who is only happy when hurting another person. I detest people who enjoy delivering pain to others.

With a long look through his FEED, he begins to flip things over to me.

With a wicked tilt to his smile, he says, "Ah, there we go, Mr. Ray. I have covered your medical, your contract. If you have any questions, feel free to reply via the files transferred to your FEED." That smirk on the lips grows until it reaches the corners of his eyes. Jenkins continues, "Now it is my final duty, regrettable duty..."

I swear quietly to myself; we both know he is regretting none of this.

"...To inform you that CGSU terminates your contract. Dillon Gate Montana West District of the North American Compact did not survive the three separate lightning strikes. DGMW is scheduled for dismantling. Your injuries were a result of the effort to save one 'elderly Abuelita,' preventing her from perpetrating an unsanctioned Gate walk. CGSU holds you not responsible for her death. Currently CGSU does not hold you responsible for the loss of Dimensional Lock on Dimensional Gate Dillon Montana West D2 iteration and the loss of some 27,000 souls."

I can see that smirk widen as he tells me the extent of the loss. His indolent, popping voice reverberates in my mind. My heartrate starts to rise again. I do my best to take deep breaths and to return my pounding heart down to normal. I know at that point that one day, Mr. Jenkins and I would stand toe to toe and have a conversation about what he has done here.

"CGSU has been unable to determine the cause of loss of dimensional lock at DGMW," Jenkins continues in that grating, condescending tone.

Once again, he pauses to unfold that smirk upon me. He knows full well that I felt the weight of those eventual deaths upon my shoulders.

"With that termination, you are to return any CGSU property you have on your person. All your personal effects have been collected from our local office and shipped to your residence," Jenkins says. The spluttering speech is becoming more excited and pronounced as he reaches some sort of personal gratification from this interchange. He continues, "I have forwarded the appropriate notice to your FEED. I have therefore notified you as required by law." As he finishes speaking, his voice turns from officious to mocking.

With that, he rises. He walks to the door, opens it, only to see Nurse Brinx there. She glares at him and snarls, "Mr. Jenkins, what have you done to my patient?"

Steven Jenkins straightens his rotund, basketball-shaped body and responds with a thin-lipped smile as he continues in his mocking splutter. "I've done nothing, Nurse. I've informed him as required by law. You should be careful with him. Mr. Ray spit on me."

Jenkins lifts the corner of his briefcase, to show a little wet stain. He brushes past her and down the hall, out of sight. A weight of weariness crashes down onto my soul. I am aware of Nurse Brinx looking at me from the doorway. I do not have the strength for another struggle, particularly not with a mind as sharp as hers. I close my eyes completely. Sleep comes nearly as quickly as if I had been in basic training again.

***

C2 S3

I awake the next morning. The nursing staff does the sponge bath where they can, changing my various bags, and I am allowed to sit up. It is not a lot of elevation, but enough to ease some of the tension from trying to view people while lying down. Within ten minutes of them finishing, Dr. Alverez arrives. He turns the lights down to a comfortable level, closes the door and pulls up the chair from yesterday.

"Now, Mr. Ray, I'm going to talk and do some tests." He says with his previously heard voice, the voice I understand to be his doctor-patient communication default, "Do you understand? If so, simply nod, we will move on to speaking later." With a nod, it begins.

He starts with function tests of my eyes, eye movement, and head movement. He is tilting parts of me this way and that way. What comes next is shoulder movement tests; the left has a much larger range of travel, the right less so. We work on elbows, wrists, hands, fingers, thumbs. From there, he works his way down each leg to the toes.

Finally, he sits back down, looking through his FEED, tapping inputs here and there. With a sigh, he looks up and says, "I am going to talk for a while. When you want me to pause, raise your left index finger."

I nod and keep my index finger down.

"Mr. Ray, as I said, we've met previously. I did the surgery on your left leg several years ago." He taps my left foot gently. "You may not remember that. For the sake of simplicity, I'll start there. You have a myomere lower leg. Initially, it was from the ankle down only; I replaced your foot bones with myomere-infused bone and myomere muscle groups.

"Regrettably, I couldn't save the bones just below the knee. When it became clear I couldn't save the lower leg calf and foot muscles, I printed additional myomere muscle and myomere bone replacements for those also. Part of the reason I was able to do this level of work was the fact you were a military SkipJack pilot."

He looks me in the eyes and waits to see if I raise a finger. To be honest, I have questions. I do not want to stop him and sidetrack the man. I have never really received a sufficient answer as to what my leg prosthetic was. My wool-gathering is taken as consent to continue.

"Being a military SkipJack pilot is the only thing that gave me enough industry contacts to make a functioning lower leg and foot for you. Years later, here we are again. So why *are* we here? Well, since you were my previous patient, the serialized leg pinged my office. When I saw the injuries, I came out personally," Doc Alverez says.

Again, I have the impression that he is waiting for me to raise that finger, to voice the dozens of questions. Yet, my thoughts of why, how come, what for, must have taken more time than I thought.

Alverez continues, "See, you're the first full bone, muscle, vein, nerves, non-skin prosthetic transplant of a myomere group. Because you were military, it never really made the news FEEDs. Moreover, there was supposed to be a system in place to care for you after the surgery, so I never had cause to check up on your progress. In any event, it's likely the military would've prohibited me from doing so.

"Lo and behold, I get a notice almost five years later you are working as a SkipJack pilot at a Gate security office. Honestly, that's way better recovery than I expected one to make on their own. Again, when I saw your injuries, I knew I needed to make the trip. No one here could have cared for you like my staff and I can." He waved a hand at the room at large. "Hence the private room and the agreement that your nursing staff remains consistent. Your care is part of my deal with the hospital. I'm taking on some patients for them who would otherwise go elsewhere in exchange for being able to treat you. No, it isn't illegal, but yes, it is unorthodox. Technically, I'm a visiting physician and surgeon teaching here for the duration of your stay, three days a week. Keep that to yourself, if you please."

That pause again. Okay, now I have questions. At the Veterans Administration (VA) hospital, they told me I had a muscle-only prosthetic. Doc is implying it was bone, nerves, veins, *and* muscle tissue, which is a lot different than just muscle. It means my left lower leg is not a prosthetic in the genuine sense. I am also the first. I know I do not have the frame of reference to understand what that means. I hear him clear his voice to start up once more. Understandably, I am not at my full capacity for the conversation, and I keep missing these chances to ask questions.

Dr. Alverez straightens in his chair. He takes his glasses off, his baritone voice rumbling forward. "Mr. Ray, this is the unpleasant part. I have a good reason to go into our past relationship. I need to convey to you the reason I'm committed to your recovery. Please nod if you understand."

I likely do not completely understand the full severity of what he is saying. In fact, after Mr. Jenkin's conversation, I know I do not fully understand. Yet, I provide the requested nod.

"I took some liberties with our prior arrangement by saying you were an ongoing patient, using the previous surgery as an example. Your girlfriend took exception to that, rather badly. As I had not been allowed to be your doctor during your post-surgery care, I didn't know about the poor physical therapy the military provided you. She made some rather good points. I countered with my offer to the hospital and a signed contract for your care. Within ten hours of your arrival here, I began." His articulation of the issues seems clear enough. I have the impression a lot is left out, though.

That pause again. This time my left finger went up. "Jacki," I whisper.

He looks at me and smiles and says, "Let's focus on the medical first, and then I'll see if Jacki can make it up here before or after shift."

With another tab through his FEED, he begins. "I'm going to put this as plainly as I can: you took at least two lightning bolts to the right side of your body, starting from the left shoulder, across the collarbone, and traveling down the right arm and leg."

There is a slight pause for me to register this bit of information. The possibilities and realities of what my life might be like start to collapse in my mind.

"When lightning hits a body, it tends to travel along blood vessels and nerve endings first. In your case, blood, nerve endings, your sub-dermal connection points, and your haptic suit. When those get flooded with electricity, your bones, muscles, and fat carry that electrical load. They have a much higher resistance to electrical current," Dr. Alverez says.

"In short, they cook. The bones in your collarbone, right arm, most of your ribs, your pelvis, and right leg down to the toes were unrepairable. Your fat content on that side of the body was lost. The muscles on that side of your body were lost," Alverez continues in a clinical, well-enunciated voice.

I lay speechless, too stunned to lift that finger. I begin to realize how severely injured I am. I remember those first days, terrible cold as a teenager in the wilderness of the Brooks and Ogilvie ranges. I remember I must find out what happened, so that I can plan. Cut wood, split wood, stack wood.

"I had to split the skin to relieve the tension and swelling. I then removed the destroyed bones, muscle, veins, and nerve groups. I won't bore you with the details," Alverez says. "We used some skin on the least affected portions of your left side. We were able to grow new skin from that base and transplant it in stages over on the right side. I then used some of your left side's first-generation myomere bonded muscle, bone and nerves to 3D-print essentially half a skeleton for you.

"You're five days out from the last surgery. Your surgeries have taken over five weeks. You are showing amazing control of this new half of you: blood vessels, bones, tendons, nerve groups. The skin, for the most part, is yours just grown on a 3D-printed form," Alverez explains, and his explanation rattles my mind.

Am I even human anymore? I frown as I realize the cost: Abuelita, 27,000 lives from the dimensional Gate loss.

Dr. Alverez continues in a more somber tone, "You're not out of the woods yet, but your skin is healing, and your system isn't rejecting the 3D-printed parts. I didn't think it would, as your body hasn't rejected them in the past five years. Hence why I went to the trouble of using your myomere first-gen prototype systems that I developed."

I do not raise my finger, but try at a single raised eyebrow. Alverez chuckles and smiles back at me.

"Your first-generation myomere is more robust than any current system in the world for 3D body sculpting. Speaking of which, this brings us to what I couldn't do. Scars and fat: you have a lot of one, and very little of the other. Your skin is bonding to your musculature. That bond is going to look gruesome by today's aesthetic standards of beauty. At some point, you'll need to consult with a 3D body sculptor or, as I remember them, plastic surgeon, to repair that."

There is a long pause. I have more time to respond to Dr. Alverez this time. He is giving me leeway in how long I have to form a thought. Finally, I raise that finger and whisper, "How long till I can walk?"

A smile plays on his face in reply, and Alvarez says, "You're a go-getter, aren't you? Well, to be honest, you've taken to the surgery very well. Your stitches are healing at an excellent pace. Even after that, it will be tight until you regain full range of movement. That process will be slow. Your ability to already make the mental connections for moving your new parts is just shy of miraculous. I think that's because you've had prior experience with the same system during the moderate recuperation you managed with your left leg." He pauses, thinking to himself before continuing. "At the current rate, I'll guesstimate three to five weeks before I'd let you out of bed for any length of time. Part of that is coming off the feeding tube, bag, and making sure you have no infections or rejections of the transplants."

A small smile plays across my face. "If you cannot run, walk; if you cannot walk, crawl; if you cannot crawl, it is because your buddies are carrying you to your grave." Or so I remember from that old sci-fi show. There is not a doubt in my mind that I will walk again. I now have a plan. Recuperate, do physical therapy, walk. It is time I get started. "When do I start?" I say with an assurance I have not felt in a long time.

A broad grin shows on Dr. Alverez's face. "My friend, we will start tomorrow. This time, I will have proper physical therapy for you. It will entail small movements first. You have a lot of scarring that is healing. It will be very tight until you gain your full range of movement."

With a second of thought, his brows knit together. It is the first time I look at the man. I have a general sense of him earlier with Jenkins; now, though, I could examine the man who had rebuilt me. Thin, his white-trimmed beard a vivid contrast to his dark skin, and round glasses in an era of routine laser eye-sculpting surgery. Narrow shoulders, and slight build overall. Like those photos you saw of pre-SkipJack soldiers, he is lean, muscled, with no extra anything.

I will not call Alverez's face kind; I will call the culmination of all his physical traits kindly, and all of that in stark contrast to the threat he leveled on Mr. Jenkins. Putting that in with the image of Dr. Alverez, I realize there is some steel in him. There had to be, or maybe he was myomere. To negotiate a deal with a hospital for my care, to negotiate with Jacki and win. That brought Jacki back to the immediate issue.

With a double pat on his knees, he stands, remarking, "Rest now, Mr. Ray. I know you have a lot going on in your head. Tomorrow, I will introduce you to Franc. Yes, his name is an anachronism. He chose the old Swiss money as a name. I think I can have him here by tomorrow. He will be your personal physical therapist until he gives you the all-clear."

After the doctor leaves and the nurse completes her check-ups, I have a little time to contemplate my situation. I am hurt; no, I am severely injured. I am not held liable for two or three random lightning bolts destabilizing the DGMW. Nor am I held liable for the death of Abuelita. A severe case of melancholy hits me over the losses and I drift off to sleep.

***

C2 S4

I wake from what seems to be a very restful sleep to the sound of a concrete block of a basso voice.

The massive man before me says, "They tell me you were a soldier once. My name is Franc, like the old Swiss franc. I'm a nurse, and I'm your physical therapist. If you dare call me Nurse Franc, I'll physically therapy you." A short pause, then, "Do I make myself clear?" He adds pauses between each word, extending each pause to emphasize the last word.

My eyes open fully, and I tilt my head slightly to take in the man. He has a dozen skin shades, if he has one. He is a walking bit of human camouflage. My nurse is a man who has seen real war, not the SkipJack piloting war I know. I look him over carefully. Hands the size of plates, arms the size of my legs, or leg. A torso so broad that ancient bodybuilders, the Mr. Olympians, come to mind.

Franc has close-cropped hair and a face that matches is voice. He notices that I must swallow to speak. It is a trade-off: do I show the weakness of swallowing, or do I be weaker still by acquiescence? I need my voice. I need to muster those years in the CM. This is a test of wills.

"MOS?" Franc asks, before I can ask about his Military Occupation Specialty. Without a flinch, a twitch, I give the simple reply of, "0161."

Franc scrunches up his nose with mock concentration while trying to guess. It is old, very old. It is a joke only a few of us SkipJack pilots would get, and only a man who has been around my unit would know that joke.

"Postal Clerk? Marine Postal Clerk?" Franc says with incredulity so thick, you could sweep it away. I am blessed with a basso grunt, but his eyes twinkle. Franc is not fooled in the least. "Franco-Prussian Foreign legion, corpsman, a long, long time ago. I am here because Alverez asked. Piss me off, and I will leave."

I realize this man is not an employee of Dr. Alverez. Whoever he is, he has a bond with the Doctor. He is here as a favor, a hefty one if my guess is correct. If the Doc, who has put me back together, called this large of a favor in. Well, I am going to make use of it.

"Let us begin," I say with as much finality as I can.

What begins next is a short, concise lecture on scar formation, how it happens, why it happens, and how Franc is going to combat it: stretching, massage of the scar pad, retraction, lotions, and various other methods that I am sure will mean pain.

We begin. The first day was finding my movement limits as stitches are still in and places are healing. It is a gentler process than one might gather from Franc's demeanor. As those scars heal and the stitches come out, it becomes a daily run down the pain ladder, then back up again. For all that, Franc knows his stuff.

As we are finishing up our third session, I have a chance to ask him about his service and only receive a grunt. The moment passes as Franc turns to the door when it opens. There stands Nurse Brinx, frowning. She looks Franc straight in the eye with zero give. Franc the unmovable object versus Brinx's unstoppable motion. To my surprise, it is Franc who nods first.

In his basso grinding voice, he says, "Nurse Brinx?"

In her solidly firm, do-as-I-say head nurse raspy whisper, she replies, "Mr. Ray has a visitor." A vision of Jacki coming to see me dances through my mind.

Franc nods. He does not speak when a grunt, point, or nod will suffice. He is not stupid, just careful with his words. In the evenings, I have seen him reading at the nurse's station. He reads periodicals like *Psychology Today, Physicians Handbook, Diagnostic and Statistical Manual (DSM) 42,* or *Dental Work Today.* I have even once spied him reading what I assumed was the most recent military field manual on piloting a SkipJack.

He completes a final set of stretches and rubs under her gaze. I do my best not to show pain, and Nurse Brinx does not buy it. Once done, he folds the small towel he has and picks up his tiny bag. I realize it is not a tiny bag, but a corpsman's bag. I begin to understand his size as he moves to the doorway that Nurse Brinx is standing in. She is less than half his size.

Her gaze never leaves mine as she says, "How is his therapy coming?"

He still looks at her in his way. With his whole upper torso turning towards me, he looks at me, then turns ponderously back. I have the sudden insight that he is doing this as an affectation. His real movement will have been more smooth, lithe, and supremely faster. With a final look at Nurse Brinx as she backs out of the door, Franc says, "Exceptional."

I breathe a sigh of relief I did not know I had been holding. I can endure the pain of physical therapy. To me, it is work. All work is work. Today, instead of piloting a SkipJack, my job is physical therapy. Tomorrow, it might be cleaning the toilets. Work is work. The last thing I want to do is lose my access to Franc.

In my short three days with Franc, I have been able to hold my cup of ice chips. Yeah, it is left-handed, but even so, I am counting that as a win. The restraints are left off my arm now. I can sit up higher, straighter in bed for more extended periods. I can run the bed controls with my left hand. To me, that is the first step to walking. I have a list, a goal. My mind turns to Jacki as I hear a knock at the door.

***

C2 S5

I look up to see Mark MacCalister there in the doorway. A pain spikes in my chest. I have not realized how much I have missed Jackie, and I grasp how much I have been looking forward to seeing her. Something must have shown in my face.

Mark says, "Bet you didn't expect to see me here."

I am taken aback by the violence behind Mark's voice, and I look into his eyes. Mark has changed. He was always massive, balding, fleshy jowls, and an extra chin or two, but Mark has lost weight and likely has not had a haircut since I saw him last. He is wearing jeans, a shirt, and a button-up sweater, none of which looks like it has been laundered recently.

"You survived, you son of a bitch," Mark growls as he moves into the room. "First, you tell the hospital that I am sleeping in my wife's room, then you convince them to transfer her to a long-term care facility four hours away."

With an effort, he takes some deep breaths. His face is red, and there is spittle forming on his lips. "You killed David in his pod, you killed the Gate, you killed Jesus's grandmother, and you killed 27,000 citizens in Dillon D2," he says. His rage is growing, and his voice scales up in volume exponentially. "The worst of it is, you had me arrested, and you got me fired. They held me for questioning for nine days. Morgan died while I was incarcerated."

Mark is now spraying spittle everywhere. His body is hunched over the foot of my bed, his voice a full, bellowing scream, his face so red it almost touches on purple. He takes a few deep breaths, and as he does, I hear the nurse's station go into action.

"Why, Ray? Why would you do all that? Why did you turn me in? Why did you have my wife moved? All because I could not put you on day shift?" Mark pleads.

It is at that point that an arm reaches around his chest as he leans over my feet. I watch as a second arm wraps around from the other side. Then a second later, Mark is wrenched from the bed. I watch as his still-pudgy fingers go first red, then white as he grips the bedframe with a strength only the enraged who have lost their mind have.

"You are responsible, Ray, and I don't care what the company says David did. This, this is all on you, Ray!" This final accusation is screamed at me as he is manhandled out the door by the two security guards. Nurse Brinx just looks at me, her mouth pursed, re-evaluating me, it seems. I have moved from unfortunate accident victim to conniving murderer.

At that point, I have nothing left in me for the day. Having those deaths brought up, being accused of them... I have wracked my memory a dozen times. All I remember is grabbing her sweater and seeing her spin in the thermal image. To human sight, it was a mass of a soaking wet, determined old woman. That is the extent. I need to talk to someone, and I want to speak with Jacki. She will help. Why does Mark think I ratted him out?

Then the connections hit: Jacki's pre-packed bags, our fight over not being on day shift. There must have been a FEED message to the hospital stating that Mark was staying in a patient's room. The transfer to a facility a few hours away. That explains why Mark left early the day Abuelita arrived.

I know for sure that I had not made any such FEED message or report. I also know I had only told one person: Jackie. I had never considered Jackie capable of that kind of petty thing, but perhaps she was, as Mark rebuffed her plans. With a sickening feeling, I realize the type of human I had almost started a family with. I have no proof, and I know I would likely never get any, but the pieces fit.

***

C2 S6

I have time to contemplate the new layer of crap I find myself in as I doze off. Upon waking, I find the doctor back on my fourth day instead of my sweet-hearted physical therapist. With his entrance, he proceeds with his tests, remarking how much recovery I am showing. Nurse Franc is the right choice. At that, I grunt. Mumbling to himself as he issues small requests, he proceeds to poke, prod, inspect, and reveal.

With a mighty exhalation, he says in that officious doctor's voice of his,

"Well, Ray, you're looking good. I would normally say that I wouldn't expect nearly this much progress after a simple four-day absence. Franc is quite right: 'Extraordinary, remarkable,' were the terms he used. You're learning control of those muscle groups, and those scars are healing nicely. Your range of movement is getting better and better. In fact, I think you'll be right on time for the feeding tube removal." At that last statement, his baritone voice picked up a cheery note.

To me, this is great news, still being a little dry from sleep. I need a pick-me-up. The previous meeting with Mark and my thoughts on Jacki have been on my mind all night. I lick my lips and ask, "What is next after that?"

With a slight smile, he chuckles, then with that doctor's voice, says, "Well, you're ready to get after it, aren't you? Here's the thing: you must heal first. Then you can have a FEED system put back in. If you plan to pilot SkipJacks again, you will need to undergo that surgery after a healthy recuperation. Modern medicine is good, Ray, but it doesn't create miracles."

He opens his FEED, and I can see the display of a calendar. Dr. Alverez starts to mutter to himself. While still looking at the FEED system, I hear, "Six months, if all goes well...yes, that's the earliest, I should think. Two months for the feeding tube removal or thereabouts, then another four months for FEED system implants." Looking back down at me, he winks and replies, "I think you and Nurse Franc can manage that."

Six months or more without a FEED system? The Compact's FEED system is integral to everyday life now. FEED units pull energy from your body's movement to operate. The whole FEED system laces under the skin of the dominant arm. It is the visual and auditory entertainment system. It provides you access to broadcasted data networks and streams. The utilitarian functions like banking, payment, and data transactions happen via the stud on the back of a hand. Not having a FEED system is going to be a hindrance to my recovery.

I hear the sound of two boulders grinding. I turn my head to see Franc standing there with a smirk. Oh, shit, I am going to pay for hearing "Nurse Franc." With a slap on his knees, the doctor stands to recuse himself from the room.

As Dr. Alvarez passes the door, I squeak, "Close the door, please," only to see that grin on Franc's face widen to teeth-baring smile. Damn if he does not have a set of perfect, pearly whites. I move my gaze to his eyes, to see that his smile also touches there. Oh, shit, shit, shit.

The pain, to my surprise, is not more that day. It is just longer. What has been an hour-long session is now three hours long; four days later, it is six hours. Hours and hours of physical therapy leave me drained emotionally and mentally. During the seventh session, I breach some sort of internal hurdle.

The new myomere parts of my body open the taps on all the free nerve endings that act as pain receptors. Dr. Alverez stops by to let me know that I have been at ten percent capacity before this day. Now I am operating at full nerve capacity. In my opinion, he seems just a tad bit too excited, too joyous over that prospect. Franc, though, does not show anything. He works. He pushes me physically and mentally. He knows when to cajole, when to prod, when to poke, and when to back down and let me come to that decision. I keep at it: cut wood, split wood, stack wood. Keep the cold at bay. Make a list, do the work.

The staff removes the feed tube right on schedule these many weeks later. Slow and steady, I continue to make a recovery. I am eventually allowed to sit in a chair and walk with aid. Then little by little, I start to get back on my feet. Every morning, I wake up, realizing that my previous poor effort to control my myomere left leg might have been the reason I was to slow that night. Knowing that, had I worked harder at integrating it into my life instead of hobbling about, I might have been able to save David and Abuelita. I am not sure what I could have done for the 27,000 citizens of Dillon Gate Montana West D2.

I redouble my efforts. Franc often tells me to slow down, go slower, to learn the limits, only to be nudged past them later that day by Franc himself. Okay, he never really says any of that. He implies it in the grunt or the hand on the arm that extends too far and lifts too much.

By the day they have discharged me, it has been twenty-four weeks since I woke up in the hospital. I still have not seen Jacki, nor have I inquired. I will find out sooner or later. Franc has declared himself done about a week before my discharge. I am not at full motion for an average human, but I am also not making use of Franc anymore.

He has shown me the movements, the exercises, the scar tissue rubs, and the ointments. At this point, he just stands and watches. I am mobile, I am eating, and for all that, I am so done with my second trip to the hospital. I feel like I have a handle on where to go, and after signing physical copies of my paperwork, I summon a Community medi-share ride. I need a handicap version, as I am not sure I can make it in and out of a stepped van.

In time, I arrive home. Nothing has changed on the outside. All the Community block homes are, in my opinion, depressing. It has smooth, gray cement walls, seventy-four square meters of space with a total of four windows, and the Community mows the grass. I make my way to the door. I am dreading the confrontation with Jacki. I am not looking forward to the fight.

I need to end it. I need space to recuperate. I am not sure what I can afford. In the worst-case scenario, I will go to a Community bachelor room. All this is rambling about in my mind when I touch the doorknob. A blast of memory hits me. I never did the dishes from the night she left. Oh, hell, I am going to pay for that. I twist the door handle to enter.

The door is locked. I twist my palm to pull up my FEED and remember I still do not have a FEED system. I stumble down the steps and walk half a block to my neighbor's house. My neighbor's wife works at home. I knock politely. The voice from the other side of the door asks what I want. With a brief explanation of an industrial accident, no FEED, she agrees to call the super to let me in.

Only when the door deadbolt slams do I realize that maybe she knows I worked at the Gate, or that my injuries seem like more than an accident. I slowly make my way back up to our blockhouse. An hour later, the super walks up, and none too nicely moves me aside. He taps his FEED to the door and leaves. Not even a response to my "thank you." I genuinely am a pariah.

I walk in. On the floor, I find a box from CGSU, with the label "personal effects." I almost trip over it. It cannot have been placed a centimeter past the door swinging open point. As my gaze climbs up, I notice the furniture is gone, and the living/dining area is a bare, fake wood floor. The floor is not even swept.

I find a used sliver of soap in the sink and my sonic toothbrush in the toilet. I walk by the half-office; all my clothes, which were previously there, my memorabilia from my military time, my manuals for SkipJack piloting all gone. I hobble into the bedroom. That makes three items. Jacki was kind enough to leave me the mattress, cut with a knife, its springs and coils sticking out. I dodged a bullet on that one. I take a bit of time, make a turn, and head back into the LDK. As I pass the kitchen, I see a taped envelope on the fridge.

"Ray" is on the front. Written is too simple a word. It is carved into the envelope by the use of a pen. I take those few steps. Reach out with my right hand. *Always push those boundaries, Ray, grow. Cut, split, and stack. Do not fall prey to resistance anymore.*

I grab the letter with my right hand, and I transfer it to my left. I force my right hand through the process of opening the envelope, pulling out the note, unfolding the Dear John letter, and then I begin to read. I lean my back against the vestibule between the kitchen and the rest of the LDK.

"Ray, you jerk, all you had to do is get on day shift. All you had to do is have ambition. You did not even try. You did not do that, and you ended up killing two people and closing a Gate because of your stupidity. My sister was so right. Nearly five years I wasted on you, two in recovery, two or more in living with you in this shithole Community. By the way, Ray, I donated all your stuff. I sure as hell fixed you just like I fixed your boss. I met someone on the Tram back from the Virginia district. Johnathan and I have taken a position away from you and he is a Doctor. Go to hell, Ray.

P.S. I left your dinner in the fridge.

P.P.S. The blockhouse is now in your name. I had to pay the six-month rent to do it, so I emptied the rest of your account."

I take a deep breath. I dodged a nuclear missile on that one. I force my right hand to work with the left to refold the note to put the letter back in the envelope. I stick it back on the fridge. Six months. Last I heard of Jacki was just after I woke, but before my feed tube had been removed. I have two to three weeks in the blockhouse before I must move. No cash, nothing to sell. Well, that just bites.

I chuckle, already knowing what I am going to find. With the laugh still on my lips, I open the fridge, realizing too late that it is off. I find the rancid dinner takeout trays shoved in. In my state, I cannot make it to the sink to throw up. I laugh and laugh as the smell of the rancid food forces me to vomit.

I dodged a world-ending asteroid. I do not know how I did not see it. It is plain as day now. I put the brakes on that rational thought. I knew exactly how

45

I had not seen it. I was wrapped up in my pity party, too self-centered, too much needy me. I was willing to accept her help, her aid, and I never grew out of that victimhood. At least two people died for it. Three, if you count Mark's wife, Morgan. I am not going to put her death on me, though. That was all Jacki's petty vengeance.

With a sigh, I crawl my way over to my box at the entry door. I am hoping there are things in there that can help me clean up the vomit. If I must, I will use the sweats the hospital gave me when I left. I do this slowly. Being on my knees is one of the more painful ways of movement. I take it very slowly. I peel the tape off the box, and inside I found a list of personal effects.

3 Unwashed haptic suits

1 New haptic suit

2 Clean haptic suits

Well, I am not destitute. If I can sell these haptic suits, I can afford to stay here maybe six more months if I do not spend lavishly and only pay the rent. I am pulling off my sweatshirt while I kneel on the floor. I kind of crawl-walk over to the previous vomit. I proceed to use the shirt to pile the disgusting bits into a pile in the sink. I then stand up and begin to work on the fridge. Hours later, it is wiped clean. Oh, it still stinks, there is only so much you can do with a toilet-scrubbing toothbrush, a bar of soap and a flimsy sweatshirt.

I make my way to the shower, tossing the stinky sweatshirt in the wash. It has plenty of soap on it. Set the sonic cleaner to six cycles. Eighteen hours. I shower, and I notice for the first time that the left lower leg does not bother me. I smile. *Cut, split, stack.* I make my way to my mattress. I flip over only to find that side had also been sliced. I shrug, lay down on the floor. As I fall asleep, I thank the raven in the sky that I dodged that supernova.

Chapter 3
Return To Work

C3 S1

I rise relatively cold and early. I drop the remainder of my gifted hospital clothes in the sonic wash. During the shower, I do my regular check of scars and sutured areas. My left side from the calf up looks normal, my face looks worn, my hair dark, limp, and straight. My facial hair is thin and meek, a testament to my heritage. I look at my brown eyes in the mirror and say, "Cut, chop, stack." I will shower to warm up, put in my time doing exercises and stretching, shower again, and dress. I can make my plans for the day during the exercises.

Shifting back to the mirror, I realize I am much paler than I was in the past. Until the scars fully heal, I need to be careful of the sun. I turn my gaze to the right side of my body, the side where I had been burned from the inside out, where the fat, muscle, and bones had cooked. I looked at the ravages of being hit with more than one high-voltage bolt. I should not be up and walking, and I should not have the speed of improvement I do. Seeing my new and old skin patched together in almost tiger stripes, I wince. Looking at the vertical scars used to relieve the pressure of the high voltage burns still makes my stomach flip in loops. I had done my research about the damage I suffered on the hospital's loaner standalone FEED unit.

I turn slowly, using the opportunity to pivot on my new right leg, using my new hip, twisting my new torso, so that I could turn on the shower with my new right arm. I still have to check the temperature with my left hand. The feeling on the right side has been off more than once. Catching a glance at my body, I start at the disparity between left and right. I have never been overweight, but the more than six months in the hospital has caused both water retention and the loss of muscle on what remained of my left side. The right, by contrast, looked like it had been vacuum-sealed to the myomere muscle fibers. My new skin sucked to it in an almost superhuman fashion. While it may have looked good in, say, a comic periodical, it is inhumanly wrong. Doc Alverez is probably correct. At some point, I should seek out a 3D body sculptor.

Moving over, checking the water, I begin my shower. The left leg, even for all its past pains, is now somehow more whole and less demanding. The rest of my body does not feel complete, and the damaged parts are slow to react. I bump into things, step a little short, or too long. I reach for items and miss them. It is strange to see and feel the difference between muscle on the human left and the myomere structure on the right. With the shower over, I make my way into the LDK.

My morning exercise consists of stretches and bodyweight exercises. I finish the session and the day by rolling out scars with hard little balls and using lotions to lessen the tightness. By the time I finish, I have a plan. I need money and I need to go to my bank. I likely need a new ID to prove to the bank who I am. I need to pay bills. I have no idea where Jackie left me money-wise, rent-wise, or even what bills she paid. There are things I need to do.

First, I should put an ad up for the haptic suits. If I downsize from this blockhouse, I might be able to pull in enough for all of them on the used market to afford another fifteen to eighteen months. That could greatly help with my recovery. The best place to do that is at the Community Center, with its free-use terminals in the library. I will need to acquire a replacement ID. I am not sure ID is given out anymore, with the standardization of the FEED implants. The bank should be next to figure out my financial situation. After that, I need to figure out food.

I know the Community Center and the library are six blocks straight into the circle. My bank is three blocks past that, two blocks over. I am unclear where the Community licensing offices are. I will have to investigate that at the Community Center.

Thinking about it, I am not sure I am up to a ten kilometer walk to the center of town, as I have not eaten in eighteen hours. Dr. Alverez had cautioned me that myomere requires a lot more food intake than usual. The central nervous system works overtime to provide the energy it needs to operate. At the same time, I have no choice. I have no other options. With my mind made up, a direction to start, I start my day.

I gather up my gifted clothes and put them on. Slip-on shoes, blue sweatpants, a thin gray sweatshirt. I am clean, clothed, and as able as I am going to be. I exit my house, knowing I am going to have to get the super to let me in again or loan me a FEED fob for the door. Making a left, I walk up to the corner and turn once more left into the center of the Community of Dillon Montana West.

I remember doing marches many years ago. A ten kilometer movement with a full ruck should be done in under two hours. I start my walk as dozens, if not hundreds, of people leave their blockhouses one after the other to be picked up by their community ride share (CRS) groups. Each of them stepping in and sitting as the CRS moves off. I chuckle as I notice no one talks. No one acknowledges each other, just like my old ride share.

I wonder how much "community" is in our communities. I keep at my task; I walk. When I stop, I lean against a sign or the occasional tree. I do my best to keep my pace. At first, things loosen up. I feel like I can do the walk, no sweat. After the first hour, my little shuffling steps became shorter. I make more mistakes. My shoulders hunch. I am beginning to have pain receptors flare-up in small agonizing spikes all over my right side.

The flashback of those first days alone, as a kid, flare up in my mind. A cold blast of early spring air whips through my thin gifted clothes. With a midstep pause, I straighten up and pull my mind from the wandering it is doing. I orient my mindspace into control, into working with my new body. *Cut, chop, stack.* One plan at a time.

49

I take it slower at first, my mind deliberate in its motions. I treat this as I would piloting a SkipJack. I make preset movements in my mindspace; it is a systematic queue of instructions that must happen for each step to be successful. As that process clicks in the queue, the next preset follows.

The pain is still there, but I am standing straight, making my small steps, looking forward. The improvement is noticeable. I have issues. I stumble, nearly falling on my face because of a split piece of sidewalk that is sticking up. I recover, stand up, and restart my queue. I am honestly surprised when I step up to the curb of the Community Center and see the Community library building right across the street. That buoys my spirit considerably. Pushing through the doors a few minutes later, I follow the receptionist, much more slowly than she would like, to the FEED terminal section. We return to the main desk when she realizes I do not have the required FEED system to login.

The explanation of why I am missing a FEED system takes longer than I wish. The receptionist summons the manager. I pull up my right sleeve to the elbow to show them the damage to the arm. With that, the manager lends me a FEED fob. I repeat, stating under oath that I understand that they track all traffic, all browsing history, all purchases verified, and all printings sent to the proper authorities. I understand this is how it is, but they try to make it seem like it is a huge thing. I simply smile and agree.

If they only knew how much the Compact tracks their FEED systems and what is reported to the Compact, they would rip the systems out of their arms with their own hands. The fingers of intrusion by government, cooperate, and municipal services are literally under the skin. It is, however, modern life.

I complete a few searches on the FEED terminal using my record-everything fob while musing on the issue of FEED systems. Most folks have a rudimentary FEED by age six, as they start their education. My first FEED was installed when I inducted into the NAC military. I grew up where there was no option of FEED systems.

It amazes me that in ninety years, the FEED system became so ubiquitous with life, it is nearly mandatory for a normal life. The fact is that you do not have to have a FEED system, from what I am finding out on the terminal. Every Compact system has a non-FEED user option. It seems that three percent of the population have their bodies reject the FEED systems. However, the public perception is that criminals and indenture broken tags do not have a FEED. For the criminal element, FEEDs are turned inert in prison. The people who have an indenture broken mark often have the FEED removed so that people do not find out they broke their indenture. Ah, I am beginning to understand why the library staff gave me the stink eye.

I chuckle at that. I look like hell, and I am wearing a very shabby set of hand-me-down clothes. Then I scare them into loaning me a fob by showing them a destroyed, tiger-striped arm. I could be a man on the run, a criminal from the law who is one step from being caught. Maybe they think I am a reprobate so vile that I broke my indenture and suffered a medical issue when I had some back alley hack remove my FEED system. Sigh.

Having found the government office for licensing in my search, I also discover I will need some form of proof of who I am or submit to a Biometric and DNA scan to prove it, at my expense. I groan. It looks like the bank is my first destination.

I finish writing my ad on the community thrift page of the FEED system. "Haptic suits for sale." I list the make, version, and estimated use. I put my price out there in the Standard Compact currency of Credits, (SCC.) I am hoping for a decent sale. It will go a long way towards my rehabilitation. The more I can devote to healing, the faster I can find a new job. For interested buyers I leave instructions to stop by the blockhouse tomorrow.

With that done, I head to the bank. The bank is three blocks or three miles in the other direction. My bank is a relic from when Jackie and I first moved here. The bank had been on the way to the hospital from our temporary blockhouse. Thinking about the bank now, it is nowhere near our current place. Since I have no FEED system, I think it best to go to my original branch office.

I find myself keeping to my walking presets. If I let my mind wander, I will stumble or fall. I must then redouble the effort and get up and walk again. My need for food, and my time being out in the cool air, is showing. I make it to the bank a good while later. I step up to the viewing terminal. Bank offices never have real staff anymore. I explain my issue to the virtual teller and three different managers. I even show my arm multiple times. Finally, the branch manager steps out from the back of the building's office space. I am non-plussed to find out it is the first virtual teller that I spoke with.

Mrs. Davis is a solid lady in her seventies. Her hair is starting to gray. She has crinkles around the corners of the eyes, just turning into wrinkles. She and I have been over the issue via the video conference. To enter the facility, I need to step through the x-ray machine. The lights went from green to red. She blanches. Then she gasps. Then she does this mouth open and mouth closed thing I had only ever seen fish in aquariums do.

With a slight stammer, she says, "Mr. Ray, I can certainly see your issue now. What remains is that I cannot verify who you are. We would need a DNA test to prove that. That payment is upfront, Mr. Ray. Do you have the funds for that test?"

With a sigh, I step out of the scanner and sit on the bench against the wall. I have not yet crossed into the backroom office as had been implied by being scanned. I think, seeing what has happened to my body in x-ray form put a little more than fear into the branch manager. She still seems visibly shaken.

With my elbows on my knees and my face in my hands, I reply, "I doubt it. Mrs. Davis. I was released from the hospital yesterday. I found a Dear John letter on the fridge and the blockhouse cleaned out of everything except for my toothbrush." With a tremulous voice I didn't know I had, I continue, "The note said she cleaned out my account. Before leaving the hospital, I asked for my personal effects. ID fob, insurance fob. The staff informed me that in the accident, everything had pretty much melted..." I paused, "to me." Okay, so I am playing it up just a tad.

Mrs. Davis seems to soften quite a bit. I sort of feel bad for hamming it up, but the thoughts of how Jackie left me would only send me a couple of ways, neither of which I could afford to have in the bank branch. I will sort that out later. For now, the priority is to sort out my finances to get my bank fob.

I ask, "Is there an option for those of us who cannot have a FEED installed for medical reasons? My Doctor, Dr. Alverez, is a visiting physician at the hospital. He says it may be up to six months before I can go in for a FEED system implant."

Mrs. Davis brightens when she says, "Well, yes, there may be something I can do about that. This situation is a medical issue and that makes it much simpler. Come on back, Mr. Ray. We can get you past the security questions and issue a temporary fob for medical reasons.

"Due to Compact law, I am not allowed to ask or inquire as to your situation medically. As to Compact law, you are within your legal rights once confirmed to be Mr. Ray to request a fob."

I can hear the smile in her voice as she rounds the two corners to her office. I am still struggling to get up. I do not move that fast. Clearly, this woman can out-walk me just about anywhere.

As I pass through that scanner a second time, I hear her whisper, "The things that bitch did to that boy."

I reply, "I am sorry, Mrs. Davis, I did not hear you. I walk pretty slow. Give me a second."

I enter her small office. I would not have even known it was an office. The back wall looks like a living room of a tidy blockhouse. I chuckle on the inside at the clever ruse. In under five minutes, I passed the questionnaire screening. Soon, a new fob would be printed out for me. She and I are about to go over my financial situation after removing Jackie from the account.

It turns out I am not broke, yet. I have a medical leave filed on my behalf, which paid out half my full-time pay. My last paycheck went through. Like Jackie had said, she had used all my savings to pay the six-month blockhouse rent. Even then, she must have had to kick in some of her own. Which means, I have damn little in the account. I will need to downsize my living accommodations soon, maybe back to a cheaper singles blockhouse. I shudder at the thought: a bachelor room in the Community barracks. I would need to talk to the super today or tomorrow to give him the required notice. So, at the start of this month, I had a small sum. I do mean *had*. Jackie did not pay our bills.

There are several outstanding. Knowing I must pay those to be able to lease a new flat, we spend an hour paying the power, water, sewer, trash, and our mutual FEED bill. Sadly, our bill statements are intertwined, so yet again, I must pay for her. Mrs. Davis is happy to break the ice on the FEED messages and get Jackie taken off the power, sewer, FEED, water, waste, and Community cohabitation licensing.

Mrs. Davis also speaks with the director at the Community Government licensing office. She greases the way for me just a tad. I will have a place to sit and go through the process with the assistant manager due to my "medical" condition.

With all the bills paid, I now have under 200 credits. That will not go far. Looking at the banking statement, we surmise the medical disability payments are over. The last one was paid out yesterday for an irregular amount. So, no more help there. It looks like I might have enough to get a replacement Government license/existence ID, as I like to call them. That will allow me to rent a singles blockhouse. With a very heartfelt thank you, I leave. Mrs. Davis locks her office doorway and presumably returns to tele-banking inside the branch.

I think about taking a community car share as I leave the building and realize I still do not have a FEED system to order one. Even if I want to, I do not have the capability. Walking, it is. Being in an uplifted mood helps only so far, as it distracts me from paying attention. I return to my walking checklist. After a while, I make it to the Communities' government licensing offices.

I walk in, and I know this place at a glance. We have all been to the government office of licensing hell. A central dais with a counter and a gatekeeper to the row of individual counter slots, all of which seems to have someone there, but no one is working. I speak to the person at the center dais, who directs me to the back of the row of counters. There, I wait for nearly an hour. I must stand or lean on the shelf of the counter, as the only place to sit is the floor.

A lanky guy walks up eating a sandwich. He turns his card over to reveal the name: Illias Diven. I slowly move over and twist in front of him. I ask for the assistant manager. I am explaining that Mrs. Davis had cleared a meeting with the assistant manager for me.

Illias tilts his head to the left, crumbs falling out of his mouth. He opens a big smile. "Dude," he says with a wave at every other teller at their counter, "we are all assistant managers." I watch as the crumbs hit the counter from him talking while chewing. The alarm bells of "oh crap" begin ringing in my head.

I steel myself and put on my most gracious voice. It is difficult, as I am well into twelve miles of walking one day out of the hospital. I have been here for an hour only to find out that I could have made my way to any of the other counters.

"Mr. Diven, I need a new ID fob. I am unable to have a FEED system due to medical reasons."

I had been schooled on the use of this wording by Mrs. Davis. I am hoping it would knock down barriers. Illias is staring at his sandwich and moves with a slow shake of his head while overly gratuitous lip-smacking reaches my ears.

"Sorry, we cannot do that. You have to fill out Forms 467 and 493 and mail them in with payment for a replacement," Illias says. He reaches behind him and, without looking, pulls out two forms, both with four pages attached. He pins them under his left elbow while biting into the sandwich again. "Here are the areas for you to sign and fill out. You will need proof of identity." He is dribbling crumbs still as he highlights sections on the forms. With a quick slide, he moves them to me.

Then he yells, "Next." I am not moving. I look at the form titles. "Transfer of ownership," "Legal Partnership of a service industry business to a parent corporate licensed entity."

I look back up and say, "You are mistaken. I need forms for identification replacement, not these."

I receive a cold stare from Illias, then as the queue behind me fills up, I hear groans and muttered whispers. Mr. Diven has just turns his name card around, and it says, "Lunch."

Going back to the center dais person, I again state my needs. The person looks at me again. Yet again, they point to Mr. Diven's counter spot. I reiterate what Mr. Diven had said to me and show the burly attendant the paperwork given to me. With a grunt and a roll of the eyes, the forever frozen wheels of government lurch forward an centimeter. My two forms vanish from my hands and are replaced by three more, from cubbyholes directly under the dais the attendant orchestrated this farce behind.

Mimicking Mr. Diven's highlighting scheme, the attendant, who I am not sure is not more robot than me, slides them across the counter in front of me fanned out like a magic card trick. The first pad is a replacement for the Compact ID form. The second pad is authorization to scan my DNA and pay for it, and the third form is to deliver the new ID pending DNA scan to my residence and pay for that.

The formless attendant twists in the dais listening to another questioner, and promptly hands my previous two forms to the gentleman asking about matrimonial licenses, while pointing at what I now know to be a random attendant behind the counter.

It takes me a fair bit of time to fill out the forms. I must switch between left and right-handed writing to complete the three. When Mr. Open Mouth Chewer returns, I slide the completed three forms to him. He looks the first over, the second over, and the third over.

Mr. Diven asks for my hand and tries to run a FEED payment on it. He becomes frustrated. In that instant, I place my temporary banking fob on the counter. With a puzzled look, he scans that and grunts. He is losing more crumbs as he chews. As I am looking at my banking fob, I now have under fifty credits from my near-200 credit balance. I sigh. Food, maybe? I feel a pinch as a stamp-like device pierces the skin on the back of my right hand.

"DNA test will take ten days or less, and you should receive your new ID, delivered to the address provided in fourteen days total. The ID will match the name tied to the DNA, not the name submitted by the form. NEXT." Diven's mouth dribbles out the words along with bits of his lunch.

I slowly turn and start hobbling out, and I am becoming exhausted. Also very hungry. As I am walking, I hear a sheaf of papers slide on the counter, a scratch of a highlighter, and "Next," followed by a short clunk of a nametag plaque turning around. It seems government licensing never changes.

Darkness is setting when I pass a small shop. It is a little bodega; a corporate subsidiary to the Bale Family Corporation. I notice their sign advertising tortas, so I step in and inquire about the price. It is not bad. I order three tortas, one for now, one for breakfast, one for dinner tomorrow. I am unsure how much walking I would be doing tomorrow. I return home much later than I had expected. On the off chance I can get in, I try my banking fob. Sure enough, it meshes with the door ID, and I can go inside. That night I put my clothes in the wash and food in the microwave as the fridge Is still not running or clean. I eat my first torta. I complete stretches, drink water, lots of water, and take a shower.

Sleep comes to me quickly. It seems when you are healing, rest is easy.

***

C3 S2

The following morning after my wake-up, shower, exercises, stretches, and second shower, I was about to heat up my second torta when I receive a knock on the door.

I open it slowly after hearing, "I'm here about the haptic suits?"

A small, lithe man stands in front of me. He has short, black straight hair, and brown eyes like mine. He seems a bit out of sorts. With an abundance of life to his voice, he asks, "Are you Ray?"

"I am," is all I get out.

He lets out a breath, and he says, "Tough neighborhood, man. No one likes you. You know that?"

With a chuckle, I respond, "Yeah. I am getting the cold shoulder lately. I dodged a bullet with a breakup recently. I think they are more invested in my former girlfriend than me. I am Ray, and you are?"

He gives me the onceover as he does a little bounce up and down on his toes in the fresh morning air.

"Eiven, Eiven Chen," he states this in the same deadpan tone of a movie star.

"Come on in, Eiven," I say as I back away from the door.

He is faster through the door than I am at backing up. Whereas Mrs. Davis yesterday was fast on purpose when walking, Eiven is just boundless energy barely contained. I reorientate myself to him and do a quick shuffle on my feet in order not to fall. I catch myself with my left hand on the wall for support. I swing the door shut and must continually turn to keep up with his wandering around the LDK.

I ask bemusedly, "Eiven, could you stand still, please? I have just returned from the hospital. You are hard to track and keep up with."

"Chen, I like to be called Chen," he quips as he pauses and resumes his movement. "Damn, you ain't kidding, she cleaned you out. You did dodge a bullet," he says, somehow making it into the kitchen with his head in the fridge. The gag that comes from him is punishment enough.

"Ray, what's that smell? Not the fridge, but the other one? I rushed over here and didn't have time for food yet."

I can hear him sniffing behind the partition. If it will sweeten the pot, why not?

"It's a torta from last night. It is on the counter, have at it." My stomach grumbles quietly in protest. "I have haptic suits to sell. How many you want?"

I could hear the "mmm"s and gulping. To my surprise, I heard Chen drinking from the tap. He must have noticed that Jacki took all the glassware also. Mouth full, he answers, "One, for now. I got a lead on a buyer. Just show me that it works, and we can negotiate."

Uh, oh, I had not thought of that little problem.

With concern I respond, "Chen, that's going to be a problem. My accident, the one I mentioned in the listing, fried every sub-dermal input in my body. I can't use them anymore. That is why I am selling them."

Chen pauses in his bites. Swallows audibly. "Damn, I need to know that it works, man. I'm not a SkipJack pilot. I know my buyer, and he is going to want proof." I realize Chen could not be more than nineteen or twenty, maybe younger. I can see the youth and inexperience in his actions.

I think for a bit; if Chen has a FEED system, he can reset the sliders to base zero, which is the starting point for anyone looking to fit it to their sub-dermal implants.

I answer slowly, testing the waters. "I have an idea, Chen. You can set the sliders to base zero. Doing this will make the haptic suit neutral per se for anyone about to put it to use. That way, your buyer can tailor the suit to their pilots' needs right then and there. Kind of a selling point. Try before you buy."

"That's not bad, mate, that's not bad." Again with the faux British affectations. "Tell you what, you help me do that, and I'll offer twenty points."

I audibly choke. Twenty points, Chen was only offering twenty points on what I had asked. I was not out of money yet, I had enough for a few days of food, and two weeks left on the lease, give or take.

"Chen, I appreciate it, but man, I am unable to do that. Right now, with my injuries, I am unable to work. I need the credits to live. The least I can go for is eighty points."

"Let me see the suit, walk me through the reset. Then, we will talk," he mumbles as the last of the torta goes down.

I retrieve the box of haptic suits and my old certs that had been on the walls of my pod room.

Chen looks at the certs as I lay them on the counter next to him and says with some skepticism, "Are these real?"

I look at the dozen or so certs and sigh. "Yeah, the last of the wood ones were five years or so ago. The newer clear plastic ones are all civilian certs."

I lay out all the haptic suits divided by mine and David's. Six total.

To my surprise, he picks up David's stinky one I had not cleaned yet. "So, you are really one of them?" I can tell he is making a statement and not a question. He was examining David's former suit. "Okay, dude, what am I looking at? If we want to sell these, I have to know how to do it, how to speak to it?"

In that flash of a statement, I know Chen and I would get along well.

We get down to it. When we finish going over what the suits are, how to reset, program, use, and describe their options, few enough as they are, we start talking about the price.

"Here is what I can do, Ray. One, right now, I have a buyer for one. Big guy, so I need this one," he states, holding up David's stinky one. "I can sell the stink, it will help, trust me. I also know their budget; they ain't going to go for eighty points. It's thirty points over their budget. They're a small mom-and-pop place. The best I can get is fifty points. That is me selling the hell out of it," he explains in a rapid-fire staccato as we both sit cross-legged on the floor.

Hours have passed. I do not know Chen had eaten both tortas, the one in the microwave included, until my stomach growled fiercely. He claims to be ravenous also. He orders on his tab four times the amount of food. Enough for me for two days. He also has that little bodega deliver cleaning supplies for the fridge. While I am teaching, he had his head in the bottom of the fridge tinkering. Sure as hell, the damn thing turns on. He pops out, telling me a fuse had blown and he jury-rigged it for now.

I remember guys like Chen in the military. Everyone knows one: the scrounger. That guy you could order to round up air support and he would come back with an air battalion from another military to help. I like him, but man, fifty points on my asking price. That is a hard blow. That will not cover another three months in this place, even though I am moving.

I am mulling his offer over as he says with a softer voice, "It gets worse, Ray. I got to make something on this. I can flip this today, but I can't make nothing. The best I can do credits-wise is thirty points." He looks at me. I can tell he knows it is way less than they are worth and way less than I need. He continues after my lack of a response, "I can help, though. You need it. You need stuff: a bed, clothes, bedding, a glass for water. I can get that for you, at my cost." He realizes what he said and winces. "A little above, maybe."

This idea has quite a bit of merit. I cannot afford new items. On top of that, I cannot put everything together or assemble it. I tell him as much. Then we get down to haggling. Then serious haggling. There is not any animosity in the bartering. We are just two guys playing the game. When we finish, I receive thirty points of credits on my banking fob. I put in an order for basics: a small futon-style bed, sheets, blankets, three sets of clothes, a collection of dishes, pots and pans. A two-person table with two chairs. Finally, and what had been my sticking point, a few old-style games I remembered from growing up. The games Operation and Perfection, to start, neither of which was I very good at as a child. I also asked for poker chips, several decks of playing cards, pens, and paper. He lets me know it would be a few days on some of the items. Others should be here by the end of the day, tomorrow at the latest.

When he leaves, it is almost dark. I have spent the whole day going over the suits and haggling. I am as exhausted as I was the day before. I now have some funds, no debt, food coming in, furniture, and tomorrow is a new day. I start work on the fridge first thing. I need to clean the stink out of the fridge. Funnily, the smell did not make me want to vomit anymore. It is as if I could shut it out.

I spend hours cleaning the refrigerator: getting the mold out, the slime, then the oils, and then, cleaning all that yet again. I realize when I look outside it is well into the middle of the night. That bit of news, that bit of assuredness from making that first sale, stabilizes my future in the short term. It has given me that first bit of boundless energy to see this out going forward. As I hit the shower, I realize how I am content for the first time in a long time. I am doing this. My failure could be my own, but much more likely, my success would be my own.

With my stinky hand-me-down clothes tossed into the washer, I head to the bathroom and shower. Afterward, I lay out on the floor of the bedroom. Again, I am asleep in a minute or less, as if I were still soldiering.

***

C3 S3

The promised goods trickle in everyday until it is all here. I start adding my games into my exercises, walks, and stretches. I learn to cook. Okay, I learn how to put things in one pot and put it on the heat. Only a few things I cook can be considered edible.

In other parts of my daily life, I am having issues. Perfection the game is a bitch. The delicate muscle control is complicated and very hard. The game Operation is not any simpler. By my first check-up on Friday at the hospital, I have destroyed one whole deck of cards. I am, however, becoming very good at "52 card pick up" off my smooth, fake wood floor.

Nurse Brinx sees me that first Friday and lets me know the order of things. "You'll see me three Fridays in a row and you will see Dr. Alverez every fourth Friday."

Her poking and prodding are not any more comforting than with my physical therapist, Franc. She checks my range of motion, my walking speed, my oxygen, pulse, blood pressure, searches for signs of tears, bleeds, or bruising, and all the while being cold and clinical. Finally, I could take no more.

"When did Jacki leave?" I ask with a bit of deference in my voice. She has her nose in her FEED and likely answers without thinking.

"About three days before you woke up from sedation. Jacki was here with you the night you came in for about an hour. She had arrived back from her sister's when you were first injured."

At this point, I think Nurse Brinx realizes the cat is out of the bag. She stops. Breathes through her nose, sitting straight up.

"This is between you and me, you understand?" she says, not even waiting for my reply. "She conned or convinced Dr. Johnathan to agree to the hospital paying out her remaining indenture the week you were injured. Jacki and Johnathan..." She mutters the last Johnathan with a bit more warmth than I had thought she would. It seems like Dr. Johnathan was well-liked here. "Well, anyways, Jacki and Johnathan took a contract somewhere else. They didn't tell anyone. Johnathan was working the day they announced you were to be allowed to wake midweek, which was a Saturday. Monday morning, they were gone. Both contracts were fulfilled, both in a contract elsewhere. Johnathan was always a bit stupid around younger nurses." Brinx's last statement comes out a bit reprovingly.

"She killed that lady, you know? Mark, the man you had to drag out of my room, she was his wife. Jackie's the only one I told about Mark's wife, and I was the only one that Mark told," I say quietly.

Brinx takes another of those long inhalations through the nose and seems to deflate at the same time.

"You know that's not proof. I investigated it after that man was here. Dr. Johnathan is the person who complained. He put it forward to the regency board, and he also later put forward Jacki's indenture payoff. He was already off indenture. So, when they agreed, they were both free to contract elsewhere on their own. I have FEED messaged him, no answer. It isn't proof, Ray," Brinx says. "It is likely." She makes that last statement in total defeat. She is a senior nurse admitting that one of her Doctors or contemporaries had made a grave error.

There is a third inhalation through the nose. "You keep well, keep up your therapy, work on those exercises, eat well, and for God's sake, get some new clothes." I look down at my hospital freebies. I chose the most expedient thing to put on and or take off. I do not have the luxury of spending money on extra clothes to wear to the hospital, nor do I have money for CRS there and back. So, time to take the fourteen-kilometer trek home. Thankfully, today is a bit warmer, with less wind. It should be a nice walk.

Weeks two and three fade behind me. At the beginning of week four, Chen helps me move my few things across town to a singles blockhouse. It is a thirty-seven square meter block apartment on a tiny lot. I am closer to where my first temporary living was when Jacki and I moved here. It is small, a 1DK, as they call it.

Chen stops by frequently just to chat. We are becoming fast friends. We end up playing a lot of cards and poker, the manipulation of the cards and chips being great practice for my new hand. The only major point at the end of week four is the disappointing news from Dr. Alverez on allowing me to get a FEED system. It would not be able to be installed until specific goals medically had been met. Not just physically, but medically. There is not enough epidermis for it currently. When I press, Alverez puts it in as kind of tone as he could. "Month five or six."

***

C3 S4

I start the Saturday after my doctor visit in a bit of a mental slump. Chen stops by and asks if I want to make a few credits. A local shop needs someone to look at their pods, suits, and SkipJacks. The problem is intermittent, and they do not want to pay the union rate again. They contacted Chen, thinking it may have been the new suit they bought. Chen thought of me, who seemed to know more about this than anyone at the shop.

"All we got to do is agree on a split," Chen says.

"All you have to do," I reply with a chuckle. "I have to figure out what is going wrong."

"I got us the work," Chen says. "Fifty-fifty."

I give Chen a wry grin. "Eighty-twenty my way," I say.

Chen's eyes narrow, and he smiles. "Sixty-forty your way."

I stretch out my hand and we shake. The bargain is sealed.

The trip over goes smoothly. I notice the problem as soon as we arrive.

I ask the owner, "You are running on a local mesh grid, not Low Orbit Satellite Systems (LOSS), so you can avoid the fees, correct?"

The man squints his eyes under his cap and nods.

"You have birds nesting on several of your mesh grid broadcasters," I say.

The man follows where my right hand points and grunts a surprised acknowledgement. Sure enough, with a five-minute reboot of the system after relocating the nests, the shop has their units up and running without a hitch.

The owner is named Boss. I am not what he expects. What he expected to be a costly day is not. Chen is none too pleased that the take-home is so small, but then, Chen is Chen.

I watch as Chen steps forward with the Owner and begins the sales pitch. "How about you hire my guy on the weekends? I know he can get this system running better than new."

The owner looked at me and asks, "Can you?"

I take another look around, watching the SkipJacks as they move and the workers in the pods.

I answer with confidence, "Likely so. You seem to run a shorter staff on the weekends. That is good for me, as I do not move fast. I do, however, know that guy's suit over there is way out of spec. That the SkipJack over there is losing charge too fast for this time of day and that the four pods I see in use are not transmitting motion as efficiently as they should be.

"I would recommend starting with tuning the haptic suits to each wearer, no more swapping back and forth. Even if they must wash it every day, it is still better than operating at base settings. Then we will move on to the SkipJacks themselves and get their preventative maintenance (PM) done," I say with a pause to give a bit more thought to the steps needed afterwards.

"Next, get them back to baseline parity before tuning them to your metal fabrication needs. Finally, work on the pods. You do not have them enclosed, but out in the open. So, there is a lot of cleaning and maintenance to be done to get them where they could be."

Boss frowns, as if I had called his wife ugly while he caught me in bed with his daughter. A growl of "Hmm" leaves his throat. "I will try you today and tomorrow for a start. Show me the benefit of a tuned haptic suit." Then, after further thought, he asks, "What will you need?"

"Each pilot up to an hour or two for tuning, and Chen. I cannot do any of this without him. So, it becomes two men at that hourly rate. What I can say is if you are not happy by Monday evening with these suits calibrated to these SkipJack pilots, I will return my portion of the wage," I say, my confidence evident in my voice. I am happy to be here, doing something I enjoy.

The man, with a hand of tanned leather, leans forward, spits in his hand and says, "Deal." I return the gesture. The rest of the day is a blur. Chen pulls the pilots off work, resetting the suits to the SkipJacks factory zero. We then spend time tuning the feedback, inertia, tension, grip, and stabilization for each pilot available that day.

Four pilots are not a lot, really. In the CM, I would have done twenty-five or thirty in the morning. The CM would never let them operate this far out of specification, though. So, four in over six hours of nonstop work seemed reasonable to me. I read the data displayed on Chen's FEED system. I do the mental math, and Chen inputs the changes via his FEED system. Tomorrow we will move on to the SkipJacks, as no one will be working on Sunday.

"Chen," I say, "tomorrow is more repair work than calibration."

The following day is just as full of work. We have the place to ourselves, other than the owner, who watches us like a hawk from his office. Each of the nine SkipJacks must be set to the Follow function and moved to the repair bay. I guide Chen on how to start and interpret a diagnostic readout as they begin a thorough deep-clean and lube.

Even though these SkipJacks are task-specific units, as opposed to the de-milled semi-human units I had piloted, much of the main design is the same. After all nine are cleaned and lubed, Chen and I go over the diagnostics for each unit. When examining everything, I realize we can get six running as new over three weekends, with one down each weekend till the third weekend, with a total of three down after that, or all nine running at about sixty percent of new.

With a final swig of my lunch beverage, I look at Chen. "Time for us to see the boss," I say in the warm, late spring day.

Heading to the office, the Boss meets us at the door. As we all walk back to the SkipJack bays, I start explaining the underlying issues. Then I highlight the problems with each SkipJack as we pass. Finally, I look at the Boss and say, "Let me know what way you want to go."

Taking off his Scally cap with his hand of well-tanned leather, the Boss reveals his bright white pate. "I ain't but running six guys. That is all there is call for around here now the Gate is gone. How long can those three extras be used as spare parts?" Boss mumbles out the question.

I inwardly wince. Three dead, 27,000 lost, and now a Community of lost jobs on my shoulders.

"I will use every functional part of them I can, and if they don't have it, Chen will source it before I ask for new," I say evenly.

The Boss stops looking at his nine SkipJacks. In a brisk tone, he says, "Gimme da six of them, then, as good as ya can. How long will they be down?"

Breathing in, I reply with a bit of thought. "Best bet is to get a start on the first one next weekend. We will finish out today, taking the parts I need off the other three for the first one. I just need someplace to put the parts so they don't walk off, if you know what I mean."

Boss turns back to me, his tone very firm. "My boys already dun told me the suits are as good as gold. The repair bay is yours now. None of my boys will mess with the mechanic." As he turns away, he stops after a couple of steps. "My boys is good boys. You keep your grubby mitts off the two you ain't met yet."

There is a clear command, as he stated this last part. I stare him right in the eyes as he squints at me, flatly replying, "Boss, I am here for work. I very much need this work. I am not the type to play tricks on working men, and your boys will have no complaints of me."

He tilts his head and states, "Are you slow, boy? The last two is my daughters. You keep your mitts off them. I know what you did to that Gate."

Stunned, silent, I just nod. Chen looks at me, to the Boss, and back. Chen asks, a bit surprised, "What Gate? You mean the Gate, Ray, what is he talking about?"

"Chen, now is not the time," I sigh with my hand in the air, knowing the time would not be later. The time had already passed, and I hope I did not ruin a friendship over not telling Chen. I am wrong, "Sorry, Chen. I am the SkipJack pilot who survived the lightning hitting the Gate as it went down," I say dejectedly.

I turn as I finish my statement to see Chen look at my eyes, then watch them travel down my arm to my hand and its desiccated flesh. I watch him lower his eyes to the ground, then make up his mind.

He raises his head right at the Boss and says very firmly, "Boss, we understand. No making time with your girls. Ray and I will be on our best behavior."

In that instant I am no longer a lonely man. Chen's simple declaration solidifies our friendship. I would always look out for Chen and Boss. Some people may hold it against Boss for airing my laundry in front of Chen. I do not see it that way at all. Boss probably guessed that Chen did not know and wanted me to clear that air now. If he had a problem with me working there, I would have never set foot into his foundry. I could not have been more relieved.

We finish removing the parts we need for the first SkipJack overhaul, and even some of the parts for the second overhaul the following week. We label and bin the parts, and organize everything in the three-sided, run-in shed that houses the pods, SkipJacks, and the lone repair bay. As we are finishing, I hear quietly from Chen, "Ray, did you, I mean..." Very long pause. "Did you...well?"

I turn to my friend, who has kindly waited until I could sort out my thoughts and feelings.

"Chen, I don't know. I have one image from that night. Me grabbing Abuelita's sweater and her spinning out of it. But that is not right, it had to be my SkipJack. That is the honest, complete truth. I woke up six weeks later. I was released eighteen weeks after that." I smile. "I met you the next day. Thanks for being here, Chen," I reply warmly, a smile hitting my eyes.

Chen looks down. "Thanks, Ray. Thank you for not dodging that."

***

C3 S5

We hire a CRS back to the general area of my single blockhouse. I get out, and Chen continues to his place, wherever it is. I realize I have never seen Chen take a CRS before. This is the second time that I know of, and the other was also this weekend. Chen, like me, seems to keep his cards close to his chest.

I settle into my single block that night. I am too tired, too emotionally drained to make food. I sit at the table alternating, trying to learn how to spin a pen with my right hand or dance a poker chip. Then, there is a knock on the door. That surprises me, and I am not expecting Chen at all. I stand, aching way more than I realized.

Reaching the door, I am about to say, "Hey Chen." Instead, it comes out as "Hey, Sam" even before the memories hit my mind. I recognize him instantly, even though five and a half years have passed. He is less lean, still seemingly too good-looking. He is the guy that drew the attention of every lady at every bar, club, or venue we had ever prowled.

I watch Sam look at my face. We are staring at each other when he breaks that silence with, "Thank you, Ray. I was never able to say it before."

Sam's voice has not changed. It does, though, carry equal parts thanks and regret. It takes me a moment to gather my mind.

"Come in, Sam," I croak. "You are not who I was expecting. Please come in."

Sam glides in as I back up and out of the way. Boy, am I feeling it, being on my knees and legs like I was today. My skin is still thin, with no cushion of fat, and limited stretch. I am sure I am going to have some injuries tomorrow. I wince audibly as I pass him, pointing to the table.

"Please sit, what brings you by?" I ask.

Sam sits in my tiny folding chair. He is way too tall for my small table. His long legs stretch out, arms almost encompassing the little two-person table as he leans forward onto it. Sam idly picks up a poker chip and started to fiddle with it in a disturbing show of dexterity.

Sam takes a moment to look at the chip, and in a mild voice of remembrance says, "Just a tad more than five years, man. I want to say thanks for saving my life. I know it cost you your career." He starts playing with the chip again. He continues, "I never heard it, you know. Even augmented by the ear pro in the helmet, I never heard a thing." A long breath in and out. "I am sitting there doing our nighttime watch on our workup. Bamn, man, a ton of bricks hits me. My plate carrier had scratches in it, right through the polymer spall material. My stomach was not so lucky. The rear claws raked me as it tried to bite at my neck."

He chuckles. "The order that attached us to the Scandi Commonwealth and telling us to do the work up in full gear. Those neck protectors," he says, shaking his head in memory. "That stupid material meant to stop fragmentation from hitting the neck. Well, it had gotten a hold of that and was shaking the piss out of my head. If it weren't for that ballistic panel, it would've broken my neck, Ray. The whole while it's shaking the piss out of my head, I can feel one paw dig its claws into my shoulder. In and out, trying to get a better purchase. The other is peeling flesh from my right arm. I'm right-handed, Ray. I couldn't move it much. I tried, Ray. I tried. Something snapped, then. The buckle, or maybe it just came loose. The next time it flipped my head and shook me about, the helmet went flying. My head hit a rock, I think, Ray. I was out at that point. I don't remember anything after that. I tracked down a few of the guys when I got out of recovery. You, you..." Sam trails off for a moment.

There is a lot of pain there. I can see a kaleidoscope of emotions pass his face: fear, pain, anxiety, humility, and humiliation. There is a minute or two of silence.

"The boys told me they heard you growl to challenge it, Ray. They said you tackled it, knives out. The two of you fought down the hill, rolling, biting, and kicking from my watch post. Two hundred meters down the hill, Ray, I went back and lasered it. You fought rolling, kicking, and stabbing till you hit the ledge where our unit had had the bivouac. They said you growled at it again when it tried to flee from all the guys in the squad. They said it turned to you and growled back. It had knife wounds all over it, Ray.

"It rushed you, and you met the cat right at the edge of the ledge. They said you tried to dive to the side, and it caught your leg in its jaw. That as you both went over growling, yowling, it was raking, scratching, and biting as the two of you tumbled over and over. The men got me off the hill fast. Up top, well, you know it was above the tree line. It was easy for a tram to land. You and that cat, Ray, you fell over a kilometer down into that stream-run gully. It took two days for them to locate you and two more days to get you down to a spot the tram could come in and land."

Sam sat there, pausing in his memories. He looks me in the eyes, and with more sincerity than I have ever heard, says, "Thank you, Ray."

I look at Sam, who seems better now, like he had just exercised this demon from his soul.

"You know, Sam, that hurt like hell," I quip. "I lost my left leg." With a long breath out, I slapped him on the shoulder. "I was there, Sam. It is dead and we are not. We get up, we cut wood, we chop wood, we stack wood." In a softer tone, I continue, "I was there. It is done and gone. Plus, the way I hear it, I tasted so bad it crawled off into the woods and died."

Sam laughs. He skips a couple of breaths holding back the tears only men who have been there would know. We both had more than a decade on the same team. We had faced all kinds of evil with our SkipJacks. I wonder if that was Sam's first-time facing death as something other than a metal behemoth of war.

I ask, "We had been all over the world, Sam, and we had fought in nearly every environment using SkipJacks. Was it the fact this was your first time facing it without a SkipJack?"

With a tight-lipped expression, he replies, "No, I have faced people, things, dogs before. An attack hit my first op in another squad. They turned the dogs on us before our SkipJacks came in to mop up. It wasn't that. It, well, this is going to sound stupid.

"It was the silence. It could stalk me in complete silence. I've checked my biometrics. My helmet audio was set to a heavy amplification for picking up sounds. The fact that it could stalk me in silence, pounce and tear the living shit out of me...and I could do nothing. It immobilized my arm, Ray. Both of them eventually." He pulls up his left, long-sleeve shirt to show a series of scars from the bicep to the wrist. Then he unbuttons the collar of his shirt to show his right shoulder. I see five or six sets of claw punctures dug into his shoulder near the joint. When he sees me looking at his scars, he says, "It first tore the tendons in the right arm. Then using its claws, it kept stabbing them in until it could cut them at the shoulder of the right arm. How can a fucking cat do that, Ray?" he asks in all seriousness.

That is an excellent question. How could the cat know to hit a human that is dodging low and to the right? Enough to knock their dodge out of the way, then have enough sense to grab the leg as we both fell. A cat that big shouldn't have been on the Faroe Islands. I shake off that line of thought. I had fought it, and the beast had died. I roll up my right arm on my loose sweatshirt.

"We match now, brother," I say.

I don't think he expects that at all, given the reaction on his face. We eye each other as we are unable to contain the amusement. It turns into a full-throated laugh fest. It takes the two of us a few minutes to calm down. We are nearing the end when there is a knock. Sam motions me back down. He walks over and opens and speaks through the door: "It is well. Could you bring us something suitable, and the gift? Gift last, if you please."

He returns to the table. Sam examines me in the same way I study him. He has shifted after that laugh and a changed man sits before me. Gone is the Sam that was here ten minutes ago. Now he is the Sam of more than a dozen years in the military.

"Look, Ray, I saw your name in the FEED reports. There was no photo, just the Dimensional Gate Dillon Montana West story. The tag line was, 'Did Ray sabotage the Gate'? I know only one Ray, and the lack of a last name almost solidified it. I had a line on you at your old residence, but no one was there when I stopped by. Later, I learned you were still in the hospital. I've been away for a couple of months on Family business. Today is my first time on this side of the continent since then. I will also be leaving tomorrow and will not be back for maybe three to four months. So I made the time to come here tonight," he says in complete openness.

I thank him for stopping by. We talk about his time after he was injured. He returned to the Family business, and was at their beck and call. Sam spent the first weeks of the recovery in Central Asia. After that, he moved to the Virginia

District for over a year. His first real work for the Family was in the Mediterranean and Brazil. Recently, he has been working in the India subcontinent.

I relate my story at the VA, Jacki, and working here. I mention what I remember of that night; waking up, coming home, even show him Jacki's note. We share a good laugh at the bullet dodged. His FEED pings. Sam stands up and walks to the door. Three people come in, one wearing a driver's cap, coat, and gloves. The driver directs two others. The livery staff lays out a table with napkins, plates, silverware, and wine glasses. Then the food comes, and they quietly assemble it on my counter. His driver asks us to wash up and be seated.

As I am returning to my seat, I see the plates. These are not just any dishes. The plates are superb bone china with the Jankowitz family crest.

"Kick me. Sam Janks," I say out loud while shaking my head. "Samuel *Jankowitz*." I had the pleasure of saving the youngest son of the world's most influential family from a fucking lion and never knew it.

Sam sits, primly pulling the napkin on to his lap. "Ray, you're the first to know." He then inspects the wine presented to him and nods. "When I chose the military, the Family legally changed my name, removed me from the rolls, and stuffed Samuel in a cloister in some monastery."

With a luxurious sip, he continues, "When I was injured, a failsafe I didn't know about triggered. An 'errant son' recall program kicked in. The Compact Military ties to my Family are deep and vast. They yanked me out, discharged me, and put me into recuperation with the Family. In fact, I was in the UK being worked on in surgery when the CM search parties found you. That's where the Family's doctor met my evac tram. It took me a few years to break away from Family obligations, work, and life to track down and piece together the story," Sam explains. His working, his tale, is in the voice of a business titan.

As he finishes, plates are laid before us by the staff. How the hell do you find liveried waitstaff in Dillon Montana West? It is an excellent five-course meal. To top it off, it is prime rib. The livery staff plates twenty-four ounces of real beef for me. I eat two twelve-ounce slices. Between the hors d'oeuvres, soup, salad, main course, and dessert, I am full. Sam...Samuel just watches in amazement as I pack it away.

I explain, "I eat a lot. The reconstruction takes a lot of power, and food is the power source, as the good doctor says."

Samuel starts chuckling. "I bet, I bet." With a breath between wine sips, he says. "I'm looking into this Gate scandal for you, Ray. When I saw your name, I knew you did not sabotage that facility." He looks me straight in the eyes.

I stare, my mouth agape, doing the now internally-famous Mrs. Davis fish imitation. "What are you talking about?"

Sam starts, blinks twice. "You don't know? Ray, they think you did it. The whole Compact thinks you cut off that Gate." He slows down, and takes a breath. "The Consolidated Gate Securities United attorney Scot Jeremy, or Steve Rankin."

"You mean Steven Jenkins?" I reply.

"You do know him. He's running around saying you admitted to doing it. That in his many meetings with you, it's clear you planned it out," Sam replies, hands up in the air.

"Sam, I have only met Steve Jenkins once. Even then, it was only for a few minutes the day that I woke up. The Doc...he chased him out of the hospital room. I have had *no* communication with him since," I say.

I remember that little man, the one who had been humiliated and made powerless. Just as I thought, I am now going to pay for that man feeling belittled.

Sam sits back, brings his wine to his lips, lowers it, and looks up. He sits there, very much like he would do when working out a deployment problem. Finally, he takes a drink. "Can you tell me the names of the hospital staff, your old co-workers, and your former love interest who seem to have kicked this whole thing off? I'll put some guys on it, Ray. I know people who can drag the truth out of that cat you killed," Sam says, outlining a clear way forward.

With a thought, I start at the beginning: Jacki wanting me to move to days, Mark explaining why that is not possible, Jesus doing the Gate walk before I took the overnight shift and David being a slovenly mess that only did half the work he should. Abuelita coming every Friday night for notes for Jesus. Nurse Brinx, Steven Jenkins, Mark's visit, and Franc as my physical therapist.

At the mention of Franc, Samuel pauses in taking notes. He looks at me over the top of his FEED, and asks, "Big guy, sounds like gravel, 'I am a Nurse, call me Nurse Franc and I will punch you' type of guy?"

73

I chuckle. "Yep, eighteen weeks of his tender loving care. Dr. Alverez set me up with him. Honestly, he pushed me further and faster without injury than I ever would have been able to do on my own."

Samuel is just sitting there, making my now-famous fish mouth impression. "Ray," he says slowly, "Alverez is my *father's* personal doctor and best friend. He doesn't take patients."

At the mention of "father," the driver snaps his fingers. All three are out the door. I hear them start singing as they walk down the road. Samuel turns back from looking at the door and stares at me.

"Your doctor for this accident is *Alverez*? Thin guy, white beard, round glasses? The sixth member to sit at the Family table?" Samuel takes a breath and spreads his fingers, counting off as he speaks. "My father, Stewart Junior, number one; eldest sister Eliese, number two; brother Darien, number three; I am number four; youngest sister Trish is number five, and Dr. Peter Alverez is number six."

I look at him, pivot in my chair, pull off my sock, stick my left leg out, and put my calf on the table.

"Yes, he whipped up this myomere leg about five years ago," I say.

I put my foot down, letting it drop with a heavy clunk. I lean forward and stand. I pull off my greasy, oil-stained sweatshirt. With a matter-of-fact tone, I say, "And this myomere body twenty-four weeks ago or so. I saw him on Friday for my check-up."

Samuel gasps. I know it is horrendous to look at, and then I realize it is not a gasp of horror. He is in shock. "Ray, put your shirt and socks on. Do it now, before they come back. Who knows about this, that you're half-myomere? Everyone, Ray. I mean everyone," Samuel insists.

"Well, Jacki knew about the foot, but did she? I mean, I am not sure I ever told her it was myomere in the same sentence as 'it is a repaired leg.' She knew it was repaired and would always tell me the scar tissue and scars on tendons would be the reason it always hurts. Then there are the people at the hospital: Franc, Brinx, Alverez, other nurses. I do not tell people about the surgery. Just mention the industrial accident and them seeing my hand is enough," I explain with a good deal of caution.

"Good, good. Ray, no one has made a working biometric myomere. My father and Dr. Alvarez have been after it for decades. Longer than I've been alive. Were you and Alvarez or you and Franc alone when you spoke about myomere? Were the other nursing staff there?"

Taking a minute to track back through my memories, I reply, "Myomere was only mentioned one or two times: the first time I sat with Alverez after waking, and maybe one other instance shortly after that. I do not believe Franc ever mentioned it. I believe he knew, but thought it was beneath him. The rest of the staff treated me as if it were a burn to the flesh."

"Never repeat it, Ray, ever. Never repeat it. Never show it, never comment on it," Samuel says. He looks at me again. "The cost of what he did, Ray, is worth more than running the Dillon Montana West Gate for a hundred years. Ray, I know." His hands go up, forestalling my objection. "I know the Dillon financial statements. We owned it, remember. It made good money."

He sighs. I can hear the livery staff returning while singing.

"I'm going to have to leave, and I don't know if I can get enough time to return earlier than three to four months. I'll try. I'll get some investigations going, and I'll put some attorneys in Jenkins's way. Knowing that CGSU couldn't field a full staff here will give me a place to put some leverage. Keep your head down, say nothing, stay out of trouble. Get better, get well, get back on your feet. I wish I could do more, Ray, I do," Sam says.

There is a knock on the door, then they enter swiftly upon Samuel opening the door. The two liveried personnel pack up the table and dishes, storing any leftovers in excellent containers. They put them away in my fridge, labeled. They leave behind two other choices of wine and three choices of beer on the counter.

As they finish, the driver steps back to the doorway with a seventy-five by seventy five centimeter box. It is a box wrapped in a military spec camo pattern, with matching bow. He hands it to Samuel.

Samuel steps towards my little card table and sets the box on it. Looking down at it, he says, "This brought me so many nightmares, Ray. Nightly for five years, seeing you, telling you 'thank you.' I know I'll sleep better tonight, brother."

With a quiet nod, Sam turns and walks out the door. I am tired and have had a bit too much wine. I hobble over and shut the door. I am too weary for anything else tonight and I can shower in the morning. I have been on my legs or knees for two days straight.

I step over to the futon, full of food, wine, and memories of good friends. I strip down. I fall on my futon in its couch form and feel it slam to the floor. Shit, just my luck—I broke it. In under a minute, I am asleep, just like I was sitting on a mountainside halfway around the world.

Chapter 4 Fun, Friends, Family

C4 S1

I rise the next day and feel like it is my first day out of the hospital. I can barely move during my exercises, and my flexibility is horrible, as I am tight everywhere. It takes me three or four cycles of my stretching to be able to reach full extension.

When I drop my soap in the shower, I can barely grasp the bar. I even have troubles grasping with my left hand. I sit on my butt and trap the damn bar of soap between my two palms to be able to pick it up. After that, I cheat and use a hand towel to wash. If I drop the soap, it is much easier to pick up with a washcloth.

I fill my days with games and stretching. I improve from the tightness in my muscles and skin. My time with my games is laughable. I have only ruined one deck of cards up to this point, but the second is well-used. After today, I am into my fourth deck. I do my stretches, exercises, and games all day long. I feel like I have slid backward in my recovery. I take the following two days to reestablish my recovery routine.

My check-up at the hospital goes smoothly enough. Nurse Brinx comments on the backward trend I display. I let her know I started helping in a yard fixing

SkipJacks in an advisory capacity only. I add that last part as she glares at me. With a stern glare of disapproval, she reiterates I am not to be in the sun, am not to be working. I am to be recuperating and doing my physical therapy.

Nurse Brinx has never tried to pay the rent in recuperation credits. Nevertheless, I listen, and to the best of my ability over the next three weeks, I practice. The food that Samuel had provided lasts me a week and a half. I portion it out into much smaller meals and then eat those daily.

Saturday and Sunday work with Chen goes well. We will soon be bringing all six SkipJacks back to baseline. Then we work on getting the pods at baseline. Chen is starting to get a firm grasp of the different components and systems. We still have many weeks of work once the SkipJacks are at parity.

My time working at Boss's foundry is some of the healthiest recovery and recuperation time a soul could get. I do not know if I will ever pilot a SkipJack again. I suspect I can make a nice life for myself as I find out that I am a hell of a troubleshooter and mechanic on SkipJacks.

As Chen and I come around to the finish dates of all three parity base projects, I start to instruct him in the necessary tuning of all three systems together. This is when Chen's innate talent begins to show. Chen just has a feeling, a knack, an inner guidance that allows him to make logical leaps of intuition. I would have to slog through, do each step, and then test and verify. More often than not, Chen's hunch calls it correctly from the get-go. Sometimes we have a little tweaking here and there, but not much. What I am able to do in a ten-hour day, Chen is able to do in three to five hours.

My fifth monthly appointment with Dr. Alverez rushes up to me. I have had plenty of time to grow, expand, learn, and dial in my skills. With the weekend work and the occasional sale of a haptic suit through Boss's shop, I have eaten consistently and regularly. My life is very spartan out of necessity.

I have gained weight, put on human muscle again, and I am feeling good. I have even done a shuffling jog to one of the SkipJacks to help Chen swap out a part. Boss has put in some cash to get the seventh SkipJack up and running as a spare, so we are working on that unit. Boss's "boys," as he calls them, are filling orders as fast as his teamsters can deliver them. That is not to say that he is doing well. Boss had to let go most of his staff, and close two shifts. His little foundry does not have the pre-Gate collapse levels of business. It is his boys and a small crew on day shift. Chen and I work on the weekends.

Boss, though, is happy he was able to keep some of people employed and they have credits for food when a lot of locals do not. I am beginning to see how much the Community of Dillon's economy revolved around DGMW. Boss lets Chen run the little repair bay on the weekends for other SkipJacks in the area, as not many other businesses can afford to send their equipment to a union shop.

There are a few clients at first, and those few keep Chen and I busy on the weekends between Boss's projects. Chen is going to be a first-rate SkipJack repair guy if he hones that hunch of his to an art. I had a suspicion that if I leave, Boss will keep him working full-time, opening that repair bay for other services during the week.

I still do not have a FEED unit yet. Doc Alverez has cleared me for a FEED unit, but it turns out Jenkins had another nasty twist. CGSU, and by CGSU, I mean Jenkins, is refusing to pay for the FEED unit unless I sign the paperwork that he thumbed to me the first day we met in the hospital—which I can only do via a FEED unit. Specifically, my FEED unit coded to my DNA and biometrics.

I am not sure when I will be able to get one. I might be able to afford a comparable unit to what most people have if I work six days a week like Chen. I am not working the kinds of hours required to pull in that level of credits. Getting a FEED unit put in for the first time as an adult is not cheap. Upgrades to an existing FEED system are much cheaper, hence why most parents put one in when kids are small, and the initial cost is small. All I can do is keep my head down and earn enough to pay for my needs. It is not lucrative, but as Boss says, I am fed, housed, and clothed. Cut, chop, stack.

***

C4 S2

It turns overcast late Monday evening. I have been fiddling with the game Perfection for five evenings straight. I am almost able to get ten of those pieces in the thing before the timer pops. No, that is not a world record. It is, however, a benchmark for me. I hunch over the table, trying to get them all in, when a knock sounds at my door. That abrupt sound about startles me right out of my shorts. Just as my nerves are calming down from that, the Perfection buzzer goes off. I am again abruptly startled enough to bump my tiny table.

I rise, stepping on a few little pieces and wincing something fierce. Doing a shuffle-hop to the door, I open it to find that Sam is here again, this time with just the driver. I invite them both to have a seat inside. The driver declines. I ask if he wants anything, realizing he is not a driver, but a bodyguard in disguise. Once again, he refuses. Then it clicks: the face, the hair, the height...he is a Nepalese Concordant Gurkha. With Samuel inside, I close the door, walk over, stepping on more pieces with my feet, and sit down.

I reach down to pick as many up pieces up as I can, saying, "Hey, Samuel. Sorry, you caught me doing homework."

He raises an eyebrow and says, "We," waving his finger in between the two of us, "definitely went to different schools."

I chuckle, almost falling over trying to get a piece under my seat. I bravely stay the course and retrieve my nemesis, still laughing.

Samuel takes the bait and asks, "Okay, Ray, what's so funny?"

I snort again. All the pieces are on the table now. I am curious about my brother-in-arms, to be sure.

"I will play a game with you for the answer," I say.

Before I finish speaking, Samuel is whisking up the fountain pens, notebooks, inks, poker chips, and cards into a pile and is eager to get at it.

"You're on, brother. What's your best?" he asks as he straightens out the pile into a semblance of order next to him.

I reply, "When I was a kid, about nineteen to twenty. If I practiced, about twenty-two to twenty-four."

Samuel smirks and asks, "And now?"

"Ten," I reply. I do not put any heat into the word. "I am working on ten."

I have seen the scars on my brother of mud and blood. Samuel knows what

I am doing. My precise motor control and memorization are all jumbled up. It affects my placement of the pieces, which means this is my homework of a sort; cut, chop and stack. It comes down to putting in the time needed and treating this as work. My mind knows how to do it. My body does not.

"Okay, then, here I go. Be prepared to answer." He pulls the game over to him and starts. I get up and find a couple of the beers he had left from the first visit. I am not a big drinker. I will, but I do not ever remember drinking alone, and I certainly am not going to start now.

I watch Samuel study the board and place the pieces as the timer ticks down. I wonder if I look that goofy; tongue partially sticking out and not quite getting the right part to the right spot.

As the buzzer hits, I pronounce, "Thirteen."

In triumph, he accepts his beer as I sit, and he rounds everything up. I bring the game back over to my side of the little table.

I ask, "Double or nothing? Thirteen is the number to beat."

He clinks my bottle with his own as I line it all up, press the board down and turn the starter dial. Without thinking about it, I leave the bottle in my left hand. I continue to pick up pieces and put them in, and the damn buzzer gets me again. I am startled out of my seat, spilling a bit of beer.

Samuel laughs so hard at me being startled and my beer spilling he is unable to say the number straight. I am pretty sure I have beaten him. Then I hear it: "fifteen."

I whoop again, a five-piece increase over my previous best score. I think that sets Samuel off even more.

After Samuel calms down, he says, "One question each. I'm not sure I can pay much more than that. You play for keeps." After I stop laughing and we clink bottles again, "In all seriousness, there are some questions that are Family business, and I can't answer those."

I look him in the eye, we clink again, and I say, "I would not ask those."

Samuel nods and leans back. "We are over forty now, Ray. Our days of shitfacery and stupid things are over. Yet here we are playing a game meant for children and enjoying it."

With a sigh, he looks up at the ceiling. I have seen him do this many times; it is his way of planning, organizing, and laying out his line of approach. Samuel Jankowitz is no man's fool. Lighthearted nature aside, he has been one of the best remote SkipJack pilots out there. He, like me, stayed at the top of his chosen field till he could not do so anymore. Having never really thought of it, we left the top of the mountain and our profession the same day.

As Samuel leans forward again, he asks, "What was so funny, Ray?"

I clink his bottle again. "Last time you told me your name. I still have only one, but you ought to know it. It is Raylan, not just Ray." He looks at me, puzzled, and nods. I keep going in an offhanded way. "What was funny is your assumption that not only did we go to school, but different schools. I found that hilariously funny."

Samuel looks at me, really perplexed. "Did you go to one of the half-dozen schools I attended? Do you remember me from then?" he asks.

Samuel's questions elicits another round of laughter, and I nearly blow beer out my nose.

"Samuel, I did not go to school. I was raised in a mountain valley so remote that there was no school. It was just my parents and I until I was thirteen. I saw a total of five people my whole life until I was seventeen," I say with a soft smile as I describe how I grew up.

"No effing way." Samuel is working up to another comment. I politely held up my hand.

"My parents built a cabin in the old Alaska territory, now Nunavut, and I grew up there. They taught me from as early as I could remember," I explain and take a long series of breaths, slow deep ones. I have never spoken about my life pre-military, not even to Jackie. I continue, "My mother, Susan, came from the Nunavut district of old Canada. I get my love of nature and the outdoors from her."

"My father was named Joshua. He was an old Alaska coastal native. I am pretty sure my aptitude for SkipJacks comes from him. He loved everything mechanical. I know both had paid their indentures off. Mom had been a chemist of some sort, and Dad had been a mechanical engineer. I was taught by the best I could have ever had. We lived a straightforward subsistence life. I was taught from my father's and mother's college textbooks when I was thirteen," I say, and we clink nearly empty bottles to show there are no hard feelings.

Samuel sits there, looking at me for a long minute. He starts to say something and stops. He looks up. He then spends another minute or two categorizing that plan of his.

"Six schools for me," he finally says. "Two elementary, one middle school, two primaries, then the military war college like you."

Samuel holds up his now-empty bottle, pointing to where I had retrieved them. I nod in response.

As he retrieves the drinks, he says, "It isn't that I was a hellion, just not, well, only a hellion. I knew I would be a soldier, Raylan, I always knew it. As I became old enough, I began to plan that out. My Family, capital F, is kind of known for their planning abilities, as you can guess. At about ten or eleven years old, I became serious and made soldiering my goal. I knew I would not be allowed to enlist in the CM if I told anyone in the Family. So I did it myself, in my head. I never wrote it down or spoke where my FEED could pick it up," Samuel explains as he hands me a bottle, and we clink again as he finishes.

I respond, "Then we are not that much different, you and I. Both war college grads, both living in our heads as kids through our teenage years."

Samuel frowns. "You, brother, had your parents as teachers. I had private schools, mistresses and masters of my life and education."

I think Samuel must have seen me wince at "parents." He stops, the bottle halfway to his mouth. Eyes widening, that little cue was all he had needed. Samuel had lost none of his discernment in the last five years.

"Raylan, why did you stop homeschooling at thirteen?" Samuel asks it in a whisper, a whisper that one could politely decline to hear. When he sees me take that deep breath through my nose, he sits up and sets his bottle on the table, already aware the time for jokes is long gone.

"I had only seen five people by the time I was seventeen. Two were my parents, a third was the tram pilot who delivered supplies before the spring thaw and after solid snow in the fall. The spring weather was early and warm those last few weeks, but the pilot made it in," I explain.

I have never told this event to anyone, and I craft my tale carefully, as it is nearly beyond belief.

"My parents took the snow machine and sled to pick up the supplies. On the way back, they went through the ice," I say.

This time it is my turn to look at the ceiling and take some time holding back the pain.

"I knew something was wrong, as it was dark, and I had no way to get where they were without the snow machine. 'Stay with the shelter, so you don't get lost,' I thought. It was well into the night when there was a thump at our door."

At this point, I have tears in my eyes as I tell my story. "My mother had walked covered in ice, with frostbite on her limbs. She hiked the trail with hypothermia that long distance to our cabin. I think the snow machine pulled my father under, and that possibly she was in the sled at the back. She might not have been over deep water.

"When she arrived at the door, nearly all of her clothing was encrusted in ice. She died right there in our cabin. I never found my father. That next summer, when the water cleared, I saw the snow machine at the bottom of the lake."

I take a few more breaths as the tears clear and say, "From thirteen to seventeen, I lived, studied, trapped, fished, cut, chopped, stacked, smoked, and repaired. In the spring of my seventeenth year, a new tram pilot flew in on a bush tram. He was there to drop some fishermen off at what was supposed to be an abandoned cabin."

"That cabin was ours. It turns out the pilot who normally delivered supplies up and retired after that spring delivery. He did not think to let folks in the nearby village know of this family out in the bush. The only reason our cabin was on the map was that my father marked it on the old Fish and Wildlife map in the Community Hall. The guide happened to see it and put it on his list to try out for clients.

"The Community tried to put me in a foster care home with a bunch of people I did not know. They tried to stick me in a remedial education system because, clearly, no one could be self-taught," I say, and I can tell my bitterness at that point in my life is coming through. "I turned eighteen that fall. I went to go and enlist to get the hell out of dodge. I was unable to because I had no proof of formal schooling. The enlistment sergeant stood with me before the tribal council judge and vouched for my ability to take the general education certificate, and to enter the Compact Military."

Looking down at the rim of the bottle, I say, "I passed, received that certificate, and went to boot camp a month later. I have not been back. I still remember his name: Sergeant Nehez."

I look back up to see Samuel staring at the ceiling. I am not sure what Samuel is thinking, as he seems contemplative.

Then Samuel says emphatically, "Your question, and make it a good one. Damn you, Raylan, it had better be good."

I am unsure why I ask, but I do not hesitate. Hell, it is not like Samuel would have anything but a periphery knowledge, anyway. Yet, without really giving it thought, I put forth my most pressing desire.

"Can you tell me what happened that night?" I ask. "The night the Dillon Montana West Gate lost dimensional lock?"

I do not think I could have surprised Samuel any more if I had slapped him. He looks at me, then stands and pulls a FEED fob from his pocket. He sits back down.

"Raylan, I've seen what's on that and I'll watch it with you, if you want. It's the real reason I am here tonight. Not to trade stories or play games. I came here to give you that. You just pluck it out of the air as if," Samuel says. After a small pause and inquisitive look, he asks, "Raylan, what are you?" He grabs a bottle for him and me and he opens them. "Did you open the present?"

I stop halfway through a sip. No, I had not. It is in the cupboard near the fridge. I shake my head no and point to the fridge area with my right hand. Samuel rises, and after a minute of opening doors, returns with the gift. I had cleared the game off the table. He sets it very gingerly in front of me.

Patting it twice, Samuel says softly, "Open it."

With reservation, I do. I pull that ribbon off gently, tear that CM camo paper with care. I split it at the four corners of the box lid. Slowly lifting the top, I look inside. There are a few things in there. The flattened head on woolen felt of a dark cat, some form of lion? The flattened front paws and 2 helmets. I look up at Samuel with a question in my eyes, as I lift the first helmet out.

On the side of the helmet, "Janks" is stenciled in off-hued green to the color of the helmet. It has everything on it, ear-pro with sound amps, HUD face shield, mic, even had the two cameras attached just above the ears. I set it aside with reverence.

In doing so, I notice several sets of gouge marks above and almost on top of the helmet. I pick it back up and move the flat cat skullcap to it. Sure enough: that would have been the lion's first attack. Straight to the top of the skull. I set both aside.

I pull out the final one. I see the name on the side: "Ray." Similar spacing, slightly canted, just a tad different color. On it is one ear cover for ear-pro/mic/sound amplification; both cameras are there. The wide-angle lens camera is cracked and seemingly broken. The HUD Goggles and face shield had broken into pieces at some point.

I cannot remember if I was wearing them. I seem to have a knack for ending up in a blackout fight. I notice the mic is hanging by only a couple of wires. I notice gouges across the helmet, I try the paw on them but cannot verify that the cat had caused the damage. I set it down.

Samuel says in a clear, warm, and caring voice, "When you can get your FEED system back up, submit the bill to the address FEED contact in the box. They will set you up with as secure a FEED system as we can manage. Your new FEED system will link to the two helmets. Watch the footage, Raylan. Look at it. Study it."

I see the strain on Samuel's face. There is something there that has haunted him for a very long time.

In his best Colonel Janks voice, he says, "Then find a way to burn those helmets. Do not let anyone else have access. I implore you as your brother in arms, watch it, and destroy it. I'm the only other person ever to have seen these videos, Raylan."

I can do that. Boss's foundry yard has an incinerator.

"Ray..." He slides the DGMW's Gate yard FEED fob footage to me. "Then do the same with this. Father gave this to me personally. Watch all of it," Samuel says, his tension drains from him.

I can tell Samuel does not have the stomach for keeping himself at that stress point any longer. Something had eaten at him for the last five years.

"At the end of it, there is an analysis by myself, father, and Dr. Alverez. Watch it in completion. Then destroy it. Let no one have it," Samuel says. "Finally, Raylan, there's an address to FEED message if you would like a job, sorry, not a job, a life, Raylan. We want to offer you a life. One like you've never seen before. The details are in the offer. If you call, I know you will accept. If you don't..." Samuel finishes that statement with a shrug of his shoulders and the following words: "I'll do all I can from the sidelines."

Samuel has communicated the warning very well. He stands up, turns, and heads for the door.

"Ray, one last thing. I could use you. I need a guy to watch my Family's back. I, we, the Family, need a guy who can do things on his own, who can go places others can't. We need someone who can operate for maybe years at a time without direction. I know you would do well with us. I must leave, Raylan. If I talk to you, I talk to you. The heat over this Gate collapse is hellacious. I hope we see each other again," Samuel says, and his tone is one of acceptance, of the past, surely, and maybe the future. He opens the door and walks out. It closes very softly behind him.

I sit there. I finish my beer and look at the bottom of the box. Sure enough, there is a FEED number. I will need to use the Community Center tomorrow. After returning everything to the box, I put the fob from the Gate under my sonic washing machine. I shower, stretch, roll out my scars, then lay down on my flat futon.

***

C4 S3

I am up, showered and stretched early enough to be waiting for the Community Center to open. I pass through the gauntlet of statements about my untoward nature of using the Community FEED system. I receive the temp fob and ping that FEED contact on the note. With a quick series of exchanges, I now have an appointment at the hospital that afternoon. It seems as if Samuel has pulled some strings.

I make my way over to the hospital, a slight spring in my step. All FEED systems come with a monthly bill. It will, however, make the majority of my transactions less conspicuous. At the hospital, I am greeted and sent back up to my regular office. I sit down on the crinkle paper, taking my shirt and sweats off as asked. A nurse I do not know comes in and takes all my stats.

Then she says, "The visiting nurse will be here shortly. He has just arrived and is washing up."

I recognize the vibration on the floor. It is like a mythical tyrannosaurus rex walking down the hall.

Before he turns into the hallway, I say in a very conspicuous voice, "Great to see you again, Mr. Franc."

I hear a stutter step before I see his bulk close off the light from the doorway. He is wearing regular light-blue and teal scrub pants. On top, though, he wears a new scrub top. I am pretty sure he put it on there to make me laugh. I am not going to laugh. It is not going to happen.

He walks up to me in his little rainbow rubber duckie shirt and tilts his head down to me.

"Ready?" Mr. Bedside Manner is back.

I lay back. He takes the time to wander over to his sink and tray. He washes up again. It is a four-minute wash. He gloves up and puts a facemask on with a clear plastic visor.

Franc then says, "Local," proceeding to swab me down with a liquid that feels like the dead Nunavat winter bottled. My arm, shoulder, pelvis, right leg, and chest go numb. He lifts out a plastic envelope and unfolds it eight times. It looks like six feet of filaments attached to a larger than standard stud interface.

Franc peels it open and demands, "lean back, look up, shut up."

Which I feel is drastically unfair, as I only said hello. I lean back. There is a pinch and a poke on the arm. My chest feels a little more pressure, as does my upper thigh. Then I smell the platelet glue, and the laser cauterizer as it warms up. Within a second, he traces out the lines, and I catch the scent of my flesh cauterizing. Twenty-five minutes total, from start to finish.

The first nurse comes back in and states, "Okay, um, Nurse Franc gave me this. I assume to give it to you. Nurse Franc doesn't talk much, does he?"

The nurse has this boundless energy and a happy gleam in her face as she talks about Franc. The pamphlet is a long list of things to do, an even longer list of suggestions, and one item of do not.

I say to the nurse, "Oh, Franc and I go way back. Super quiet guy."

I make my way down the list on the pamphlet only to find the single "don't" on the list is, "Don't fuck with it."

I am beginning to like Nurse Franc as I much prefer his no-nonsense nature to Nurse Brinx. I am re-reading the pamphlet when I hear from the diminutive nurse, "You're all set. Please see Billing on the way out." Her voice is so chipper and has a ring like a bell to it; her voice is the exact opposite of Franc.

I walk down to Billing. Franc is there, a tiny stubby of a pen in his hand. It is half of one of his fingers long and about a third as thick. He signs some forms. Lifts a string on his neck; the string is damn near as thick as a rope, and puts the pen into a little cap. Then he turns the necklace to look at a watch face.

Franc says in that voice of gravel grinding on granite, "Lunch Time."

Out of the back pops that chipper bell-voiced nurse. They walk side by side towards the cafeteria. The nurse begins chattering away like a songbird, and every so often Franc looks down, and I swear there is a smile on his face.

I walk up to the counter and tell the receptionist that I was just down the hall with Franc, as there is no way in hell I am going to say Nurse and Franc in the same breath.

The receptionist hands me a Non-Disclosure Agreement (NDA) form and says in a clinical voice, "Mr. Ray, Nurse Franc signed for your bill. Here is a receipt for your records."

With that, she thumbs me my first FEED message in over a year. I look through the NDA. It seems if I need an upgrade, service, or remove the unit, I only need to FEED message the same number again. I turn to where Franc walked to the cafeteria. I can see his bulk at a table, his back to me. The song-bird Nurse sits squished up next to him. I chuckle. I sign the form. I decide I would rather be struck by lightning again than have Franc remove the FEED unit.

I return home. I am stiff, but not painfully so. I sit at my table, Samuel's present in front of me. I start with Jank's cam coverage. My FEED unit takes a moment to connect with Sam's helmet. This FEED unit of mine is a wonder. I am able to increase the viewing window to an imposing fifty centimeters wide, forty-five centimeters high. This is a significant upgrade, compared to the Military FEED unit I previously had.

Sure enough, there is no sound before the cat landing on him. I hear just nighttime ambient noise. There was not even a yowl. I watch as Janks's cameras are hammered to the ground and turned over as the cat tries to get at his throat. The cat tries to bite and rip that neck ballistic panel off.

I do not believe it is trying to shake him, as Samuel speculated. In my opinion, the cat is trying to rip off that neck coif to get to Sam's throat. I watch the beast look at its two front paws, one after the other, and realize that it is deliberately trying to disarm Sam. The cat even tilts its head under its chest to look at its rear legs as it savages Sam's stomach and groin.

The head moves out of view of the camera only an instant before it returns right back into view and strikes again at the ballistic collar panel attached to Sam's plate carrier. The cat savagely tries to rip through it. The beast shakes the collar so violently that the buckle on Sam's helmet breaks. A moment later, the helmet flies off Sam's head.

The near-feral salivating beast drops Janks as it hears a competing feral growl. Sure enough, it pauses long enough to yowl a warning before I tackle it from the side. Through the helmet's wide-angle camera, I see tidbits and snatches while it is in night vision mode. The quality of the video is flat and without depth. I do watch myself hitting the cat in the right front shoulder.

I review Sam's footage three times, each time becoming more and more sure of my supposition. I finally put it back in the box and retrieve my helmet. I start the FEED video and I forward to the point where I am about to notice the cat. I back up a full two minutes and watch and listen. I swap back and forth from night vision to normal mode.

Sadly, these helmets did not have the impressive thermal cameras of a Skip-Jack. I view it five or six times more. There was zero indication of an anachronistic feral cat on the prowl. There are few large cats remaining in EP1, let alone any existing on the Faroe Islands. It should not have been there. I keep the footage rolling, and I watch the beast hit Sam. It is at the edges of my helmet camera's field of view.

Back then, I might have been looking elsewhere. My memories from that night are hazy, and I have the impression that I was trying to focus on where the movement started, not where it ended up. The image shakes as my former self starts toward the struggling pair of combatants.

There are a pair of sounds. It is a familiar sound; I have not heard it since that night: two old brass snaps being unclasped with a *snick-pop*. I do not remember intentionally reaching for my knives, but I had. Somewhere on the mountain, I lost those two knives. They were double-edged Applegate/Fairbairn blades that once belonged to my father. I had started using them daily after my parents died. I can almost feel them in my hands, even after all these years.

As I watch myself cover that last bit of distance to Sam, I hear the moment I let out the growl of my own, and it surprises me. It is deep, throaty, and a clear threat to the beast on top of then Major Janks. The cat turns and yowls back a response to my challenge.

I hit the cat, and I think I surprised it. It seemed to hesitate for that fraction of a second as my screaming form hammers home into it. I have two views of this fight. The left side of the cat is covered by the standard camera lens. I watch my left arm repeatedly striking it in the chest, as the boot knife slips in and out. My right hand, I am assuming, is on the other side attempting to do the same type of damage.

The beast begins to buck and rock as I power it off Sam. My mind spasms as what I remember, what I saw in the regular lens, and what I am seeing out of the wide-angle blends into a patchwork of memories. I pause the FEED vid as flashes of images hit my mind-space. I see memories, I know they are memories, but I feel as if I am there. I slide to the floor in confusion. When I look down, I see sections of dirt below instead of the hard tile of my blockhouse. When I look up, there is the overcast dark sky of that night years ago instead of my flaking blockhouse ceiling.

I ride a wave of pain as my mind forces the imagery back apart and into separate memories with their own distinct mental videos. White-hot spots bloom behind my eyes, and the pain blossoms in my head. I squint my eyes closed and press at them with the palms of my hands. I find myself on the floor of my blockhouse sometime later. The headache pounds at my temples and the base of my neck when I try to open my eyes. I manage to peek one eye open and turn off all the lighting in the blockhouse. A few minutes later, I dim my FEED video display.

The FEED display is poorly lit, but with my pounding headache, I cannot afford to tweak my FEED brightness settings. The cool tile floor sucks some of the heat from my pounding head, its coolness providing a mild relief to the throbbing pain.

I start my FEED vid. The constant rolling and tumbling play havoc on the camera's light sensors as the beast and I roll down the hillside. I watch us both hit bottom in a ball of patchy fur and plate carrier armor. I have both knives still in my hands. We have come to rest on a small ledge where our unit has its bivouac.

I watch myself roll up to a crouch, boot knife version in my left hand, normal weighted Applegate in the right. There is a shake of the helmet that causes the images to blur together a bit in my mind. This sends a spike of pain through me again as the memories try to merge.

I start the FEED vid again. There are unintelligible voices of my squadmates in the background. My recorded breathing drowns the voices out from the camera's mic pick-up. I hear myself growl, "Help Major Janks" before stalking closer to the beast. I pause the video when I see that the right side of the cat has six punctures and several wide and long lacerations. The cat turns a circle, looking for an escape path.

This is not a normal beast; besides the wounds, it has fleshy nodules under the skin. I see his left side. Three punctures with blood flowing freely. The lungs on this cat should be full of blood. As heavy as it is breathing, there should be streams of misty blood pouring from its wounds with every breath. Most of all, it should not be standing.

I hear my second yowl, a copy of the one from earlier. Again, it seems to be confused for a second, almost like it lost its mind and regained it. We are charging each other a fraction of a second later. The cat fakes me out. It lunges to meet me face to face, only to duck its head down and to the left. While the beasts head is low to the left, that right paw hangs in the air.

I retrieve the paw from the box. I take a moment to study it. Resuming the video, I hear and watch us connect. Connect is too mundane a term for "slamming together with the intent to kill." The paw lands at the base of my right collarbone, its claws hooking into my neck's ballistic panel and dragging me off-balance. Claws and teeth flash from the beast. I watch the cat duck its head a second time to avoid a thrust from my left hand. In retaliation, the beast clamps on to my lower left leg. I watch as my boot knife finds the soft part of the cat's stomach.

I notice that my right hand seems ineffectual as the cat drags me under it. I hammer the beast in the breast, but it seems as if I am only punching it. After the third viewing, I notice my first strike lands true enough. The force of the blow causes the old double-edged blade to crumple and shatter as it lands home. I watch it three times more. The knife splinters in my hand, right at where the blade meets the hilt. That is enough for the beast; the cat pulls me over the edge. I fight to stay on the thin ledge with my compatriots, and the cat loses its footing on the scree when it finally pulls me free.

I do not have nearly the advantage I did the first time down the mountain. The cat seems to be above me, then below me, but not really in any reasonable striking distance of my left hand. Then, as we roll, it loses its grip and we part. We search each other out during our rapid descent and when we find each other, we scramble back together. We fall into the tumble of claws, fists, teeth, and blades again at the first opportunity. I right myself and lunge at the feline menace. Face to face, that boot knife sinks home. The blade slips perfectly into the left eye socket.

I pause it, watch it again and again. I look at the badly weathered and flattened bit of the cat's head on felt backing. I look closely at the left eye. Sure enough, there is a centimeter-long gash where the knife slipped off the bone and into the eye socket. I continue the video.

The cat keeps fighting, scratching, clawing, and biting. Somehow, it has hold of my left ankle again and is pulling me down the mountain at a run. I notice that my helmet's wide-angle camera no longer works. Its video feed is dead. I scroll back to see it happens just before I stab the eye. I return to watching where it was dragging me by the foot. I watch my head tilt back and my arms reach out, grabbing at anything, a tree, a bush, a stout clump of rocks in this scree. I hook my arms around something big enough to pull the large cat up short. The beast loses its footing on the steep scree, and sadly, I lose my grip.

This time, I land badly on top of the cat. In the FEED vid, I hear the audible crack in my legs as they break. My body goes still at that point. The video does not show the cat right away; there is a rocking motion as it scrambles out from under my unconscious form. A minute or two later, I hear munching, then gasping and wheezing. Then I see that bloodied, semi-dark tan shape pass my head in three ever-larger circles.

Ah, it had lost its sense of direction with one eye poked out. Then it just stumbles and starts shuddering violently. That is when I am sure I have crux of the issue. I understand what Samuel was getting at.

The spasmodic shuddering is not something you see when you kill an animal, and it is not something that happens when you kill a person.

This is something far more sinister. It is a level of violent muscular tremors that only comes from one type of death. It is what you see happen when a SkipJack pilot dies from a seizure because they are forcibly disconnected from the SkipJack they are piloting. The SkipJack and Pilot will shudder and twitch violently to the final pulses of haptic suit's input. Someone piloted a mountain lion and sent it to attack the youngest son of the Jankowitz family—the son who had been incognito inside the CM for more than fifteen years.

***

C4 S4

I am in need of a shower. My body is coated in the sticky sweat that only happens when you have gone through a traumatic situation. My thin, secondhand clothes cling to me and the migraine builds as I open my eyes wider. In a few minutes, I move from the laying on the floor to my knees. From my knees, I stand hunched. With every step to my bathroom comes a wave of mental pain that nearly drives me unconscious. I enter the shower and strip while the water washes over me. I am careful not to pull any of the glued and cauterized areas. I look at the fresh row of scars from the FEED system.

All modern FEED systems are of the reverse root type as opposed to the older, charged battery devices. The root network covers my shoulders, chest, hip, and my right upper thigh down to my calf. It is stiff because of the platelet glue, but I feel only a little pain when I touch it. Wherever Franc learned his craft, he learned it well. I bet that after a month, I would hardly see the lines of my FEED system quilted into my skin. I dry off and put on some sweats. Tomorrow, I will dump the helmets in the incinerator at the repair bay and watch them burn. It is time I put that past horror behind me. I began to steel myself and my will for the next video, even as my headache rages.

I have no need to watch the third FEED vid tonight, as part of me dreads doing so after what I just watched and its implications. I am not looking forward to facing the loss of 27,000 lives in DGMW:D2. In the short two hours it took to watch those previous videos, the world has just become a much darker and scarier place. I now understand Samuel's nightmares about the forces behind that cat.

There are differences, though. I remember the events in this video, as they are fresh in my mind. Even with what little I do not remember, there is a small sense of detachment. The world has told me where I failed, where I have screwed up. I have been living with the repercussions of the Gate's failure for nine months or more. I let my FEED unit connect to the fob Sam supplied.

An image pops up, a rendering of black and white tinged in the blue of my FEED display. The image is from the camera over the SkipJack shed at the edge of the DMZ yard. There is a bluish-gray dot exiting the trailer. It moves at a hobbled run. I watch myself dash from the upper left corner of the display and, at the same time, my SkipJack heads straight out for an intersection line.

I see us line up in almost a straight run for Abuelita. My heartbeat builds, and there is a whoosh-whoosh sound in my ears. The headache also builds as I push back on the memories, doing my best to keep them separate, to split them apart before they stitch into one multifaceted memory.

I watch the SkipJack reach out and grasp Abuelita's sweater. I overlay the fear I saw her face in this little FEED vid. There is no way I can see such detail from this camera angle; I pause the vid and forcibly separate my various points of memory again. The pain in my head forces me to close my eyes and hold my palms to them. The pressure is nearly unbearable. The FEED image picks up again with my SkipJacks mechanical hand closing on her sweater. Abuelita spins out of the sweater.

The race between the three of us is back on. Abuelita hobbles forward as my body continues to hop-run towards her. My MKII lunges forward, grasping at her a second time. The fear on Abuelita's face that night blooms in my mind again. When I wake, I am on the floor. There is drool on the tile, and I feel as if I have the world's worst hangover.

I know if I hesitate, I will never start the FEED vid. I start the vid from where I left off. I watch those last crucial seconds until David's SkipJack plows into mine. When the two MKII's collide, it allows Abuelita to reach for the gate. I watch myself attempt to pull two 225 kilogram SkipJacks by hand in a series of violent jerks.

My left arm at my side, right arm locked onto the service clevis on the back of David's SkipJack. David's MKII unit is frantically trying to backpedal while on the ground. That effort by David pulls my SkipJack backward. I watch my head turn back only to see a flash of light, and all four of us are gone. Abuelita, my SkipJack, David's SkipJack, and myself have all just vanished. Steam or mist rises from where we stood. I keep watching in amazement. The yard is empty. I am straining to find myself on the screen and looking all over the yard.

In a moment, I see myself. The twinkle of the Gate catches my eye. I am walking out, holding a wet and limp Abuelita in my left arm, and what remains of my right. I stagger about eight steps. The first of the SkipJacks emerges from the Gate. The second follows even before the first is all the way through. I watch the SkipJacks follow me those improbable eight steps. Maybe somehow, I have brought both units to heel. Wait: the MKIIs shift and walk to their docking/charging stations.

The Compact, the world, really, has stringent rules as to the autonomous functions a SkipJack may have, which is to say, zero functions. How then did they return to the docking stations?

I watch it again and pick out something on my piloting goggles. I zoom in on my FEED display. I see, through the rain, that my goggles have two HUD displays overlayed on its glass. Am I piloting both at the same time?

It is just then as both MKII units reach the edge of the SkipJack shed that a second bolt of lightning hits my right side, arcs from me to the closest Gate stanchion, and everything winks out. Including the camera on the SkipJack shed.

I watch the FEED vid twice more. I try to zoom in on myself as I go into the Gate and come out of the Gate. It is a fruitless hour as the wind-driven rain only provides glimpses and snatches of imagery. I move on to the breakdown analysis of the video. In it are Samuel on the left, Dr. Alverez on the right, and a man that I guess to be Samuel's father in the middle.

The summary of the break down is simple and pretty much as I had guessed the hour before. Three simple impossible items:

First, I walked a Gate, then walked back over. No person has ever done this, as it strips the mind's self from the body. Countless others have tried to cross back over since the first Gates opened. They emerged without any faculties, their conscious minds ripped from their bodies. Walking a Gate is a one-way trip.

Second, I survived at least two direct lightning bolts, all in an area that should have had many more items with less resistance for the lightning to hit. Every year, Dimensional Gate facilities take dozens of direct lightning bolts and direct them away from vital infrastructure. Yet, that night, every one of those systems failed.

Third, after a lightning strike and a severely damaged haptic suit, I piloted, likely via preset commands, not one, but two SkipJacks. The trio in the FEED vid spend a great deal of time showing me the up-link connection to my haptic suit and its data usage as soon as I emerge into EP1. My visual cortex carries the balance of the uplink to the pair of MKIIs. Apparently, I was looking through the MKII ocular systems as the second lightning bolt struck.

As further proof of the unique happenings that night, Dr. Alverez begins to describe another oddity. Samuel interrupts and thinks he can explain it better.

A brief visual of the top-down layout of the Gate pops up. Things like the Gate, Abuelita, me, and the SkipJacks move in real-time. Something is off, like the image is askew. I have walked that yard nightly for two years. The MKII SkipJacks have preset commands when you remote pilot them: essential preset functions to aid in piloting, preset functions like a ninety-degree intercept with a remote pilot. A function is something the system can complete. I was not running at even forty-five degrees. I was running closer to a twenty-five degree rational curve course. Neither Samuel, Alverez, or Stewart Jankowitz had ever heard of anyone able to pilot a SkipJack on reserve battery, at one hundred percent load, while running a separate complex intercept track.

Samuel understands the complexities as much as I do, and he goes on to say that the Family inquired discreetly about the theoretical need for that intercept track ability with one of the Families military contacts, our old Force Recon commander General Jermaine Diomedes. The elite teams under General Diomedes command asked when they could test said preset.

The Family reiterated it is theoretical with current equipment. General Diomedes had put those groups on to running a few field exercises and forwarding the data to him and military scientists. The data that came back was not good, useful, or helpful. The human mind could not walk straight and pilot diagonally via a complex curve at the same time, not with some serious enhancements to the SkipJack functional coding, and certainly not with a de-milled MKII.

Then General Diomedes's people went on to say that not many could run with a ninety-degree intercept track while on reserves. In a pod, sure, running the ninety-degree intercept is cake. There was a lot of computing power taking the load off the human mind and perception. The pod straightens and interprets the perceived and wanted path of the SkipJack.

There is a minute after the summary where Sam smiles, points to the side of the FEED vid, and I see a note with another FEED contact number. I am to call when I have destroyed all the items. I replace the FEED fob under the washing machine. I head for the shower again. When I get out, I pull the FEED fob out. I move back to the kitchen and stick it in the microwave. I set it to cook for three minutes. It is only a few seconds before it is slag, and the kitchen starts to smoke.

The helmets are too big, and I doubt I can get away with more nuking before the blockhouse's fire suppression system kicks in. The rest, and what remains of the fob, will need to go in Boss's incinerator tomorrow. Then, it looks like I get a new job, a career, and maybe even a life.

Chapter 5
Company Man

C ompany Man

I meet up with Chen at Boss's foundry. He is a little surprised to see me on a weekday.

I need to be as straight as I can be with Chen after the last time. Letting him know first is the best option. I continue at a slower pace. Lifting the box, a bit higher, it clunked a little.

"Chen, I have a job offer down in the Virginia District. Something behind a desk doing a little paperwork, if you will. It is not much, but it will get me by. I do not think I can pass this opportunity up. It will keep me fed and in a single block." I say it as quickly as I can.

"These are some old odds and ends. I am going to use Boss's incinerator, if I can," I explain.

Chen seems a little gobstruck. I can see he is a bit hurt and apprehensive. I have been here to back him up on all those hunches and guesses that did and did not pay off in the repair bay.

"Thanks for telling me, Ray. I'm glad for you. I am. Look, Boss wants this Seventh unit tested. I gotta get back to work," Chen says.

Like me, I think Chen does not have a lot of friends, and me leaving suddenly probably hurts. I am about to say more when Boss's voice breaks over the loudspeaker, calling me to the yard office.

I turn, shuffle over the many sets of Mag tracks in the yard of the foundry. The office is not huge, but it has enough space for him and the break and bathroom areas. Boss meets me at the doorway. He does not look pleased to see me. He looks at Chen, then me, and I guess he is expecting an explanation.

I say, "Boss, I had to tell Chen first. You were next on the list. I have an offer down South, behind a desk doing some paperwork." I watch his expression soften a bit. "I stopped by to let him know and to ask to use your incinerator. I have this box of some odds and ends of my former life that I want to put to bed. As long as I am starting over, I want this all behind me."

He motions me in the direction of the incinerator. We walk, and he says, "You got the better part of two thousand credits I owe you. Chen wanted me to start paying you directly instead of your split. He's on days, and finally making enough for him and his little brother and sister."

I pause and look at him. "I knew Chen had a story. I felt it was not my place to ask." With a sigh, I continue, "He never asked mine, so I did not want to pry."

Boss lets loose a grin and his teeth show. "Both of you are tight-lipped bastards," he says with a nod back to Chen. I turn to see one of Boss's "boys" talking to Chen, who is now sitting with his head in his hands. Boss's daughter has her hand on Chen's shoulder. My head snaps back to Boss. He smiles. "She took a liking to him that second weekend when you both fitted the suits. Asked me if she could take him out. I told her if he made it six months, she had my blessing." He laughed. "The boy was too scared to talk to her when she approached. He has a few weeks left. I think I'll let him know he's got my permission."

I say, "Chen has come a long way. He knows your Foundry SkipJacks in and out." I have put a bit of thought into an idea. I had planned on negotiating with my last haptic suit, but maybe I can do more than just the reference and repair manuals. "What he does not have is a wide base of knowledge. I will not be here to give it to him, and frankly, I am limited in my own knowledge. I can give you a list of things that he can use to learn from." I pause, trying to sense out his willingness. "He needs a good dozen reference and repair manuals,

101

a 3D imaging tester set up, and about a half-dozen union level-one SkipJack repair-tech classes."

Boss stops midway, with a bit of a faltered step. "Boy, I ain't got that kind of money. Even though he is doing well, he isn't even at twenty percent of my companies' business yet." He pauses. "I know things are a-changing, I know I have to change with them. I just don't have the funds to do all that now and keep the boys working."

I look Boss in the eyes and say, "Use the first thousand or so that you owe me for the real deal reference and repair manuals. Get the most recent stuff you can. Do not skimp, and spend more if you must. Put whatever you need credit-wise towards a 3D image tester. It does not need to be big, just feature-packed. I have a few I think would do the trick on my list. Anything left, put towards as many level one SkipJack type repair-tech courses as you can get him signed up. He needs a foundation in the basics. Not their upper level. With that, the 3D image tester and the reference manuals, he can sort out almost anything. If those funds run out, sell this last haptic suit to fund whatever you can." I pass him the last haptic suit from under the lid of the box.

Boss only glances at it. He shakes his head in the direction of the incinerator area. "Get me the lists on the way out. I'll get as much of it as I can before the union boys cut him off." He grumbles.

I nod, picking my box back up, and head over to the incinerator. Boss's incinerator is a multi-step tool. You drop stuff in the top, off a short flight of stairs, into a cutter gate. Those little bits that fall out the bottom travel by conveyor to the actual incinerator. The burned material goes up as ash. The metals travel to a ceramic flask. From there, the centrifuge kicks on and spins the metals into a small ingot.

At the top, I toss in the mountain lion paws and head. I had thought about keeping them. In the end, I decided not to. I realize that if they held evidence, I cannot have it near me for this next phase of my life. Then Major Janks's helmet drops in. It bounces a couple of times before a portion of the ear pro/mic wiring catches and pulls it in. My helmet follows; it catches in the cutter teeth right away. I toss in the box, and soon, I see a steady stream of bits heading to the small incinerator door. As my last act of a past life, I toss the microwaved FEED fob onto the conveyor belt as the chips pass.

I stand there for an hour as it runs its blast cycle. What comes out the other side is sludge and about a loonie sized chunk of some metal. Satisfied, I head to the front gate. I thumb the list to Boss's FEED as I leave. I wave at Chen as I trundle by. He waves back, then sticks his head in the SkipJack again.

I feel low about leaving Chen. Yet, I know that I need to move on. I have a fair bit of recuperation behind me and maybe a new opportunity will help me heal even faster. My time in the Montana West District (MWD) is at an end. Sooner or later, the folks in the Community would cotton on to who I am, maybe even leap to conclusions about any role I had in the Gate collapse. Samuel offered me a place to get well, a bit of protection from those seeking to use the Gate collapse for their own ends. I simply cannot take Chen with me, and he has obligations and responsibilities here. I hope I will be able to stay in touch with Chen over the coming days.

***

C5 S2

I meet the ride to my next phase of life that afternoon. I leave the MWD with the clothes on my back and a duffel of a few mementos. My blockhouse super has a client who did not mind the few things I had left in the single blockhouse. I am on the tram the whole night. We are going to land in the Blue Ridge Mountains of the Virginia District. I chuckle at that. Growing up in the valleys between great northern mountain ranges and living in Montana West District had set the stage for mountains. These barely rate as hills.

I step out of the tram eighteen hours later and into the woods. I am stiff, sore, and in desperate need of some food. I look around and breathe in the pine-scented air. I notice Samuel standing next to a small flight of logs laid into the ground to act as steps. I walk over to him and do my best to work out my stiffness. With a quick shake of the hands and a pat on the back, we start up the stairs.

I make it precisely three steps before I fell flat on my hands. I am that tired, and pains and aches are rippling from every end of my body. Sleeping in a tram in one spot, with no way to stretch that myomere skeleton of mine is now showing its consequences. I slowly get up. I accept Samuel's hand and we began walking up the rest of the way.

I know I have improved drastically in my last six months. I have done amazing things, according to all the doctors and nurses. Yet little things like that slick, canted step trip me. I must stretch daily for an hour or more in the morning to limber up. It is hard to put into terms sometimes. My mind knows what to do, and it is the body's betrayal that does me in.

I completed some metrics with Nurse Brinx just before my last six-month check-up. It is not like directing a SkipJack, and it is not like holding your breath. It is more like willing your left arm to draw a square, and the right arm to draw a circle. I have the coordination of a six-year-old child. I have the mobility of a 120-year-old man. Nurse Brinx was very pessimistic about that ever improving. Like I said before, I prefer Franc.

We step up a small flight of real steps to a wraparound deck. This faux cabin is brown, a pretty good 3D printing of a classical wood cabin. The door swings open, held by a grinning Dr. Alverez. Samuel and I step inside. They give me a brief tour of the cabin. He shows me the impressive one-way windows that line the far wall of the living space overlooking the valley. Alverez coughs; it appears it is time to start work.

"You are here to finish recuperation in a much more stringent way. Under the far deck is a door to a complete workout area. Meals are part of that plan. They will arrive frozen once a week based on the goals of that week," Alvarez says in his no-nonsense "I am the Doctor" voice. "You're working for the Family now, and for the foreseeable future, part of that work is getting well. You've made outstanding progress on your own; yet, that progress is less than it could be, by a large margin."

With a look to Samuel, the doctor continues. "Samuel says you're a military man, that a solid day's PT and food at specific times is nothing to you. That's good. You'll be taking meals at very certain times. Don't skip a meal and don't leave food on your plate. It'll mess up the metrics I use to oversee your recovery." Dr. Alvarez pauses. "Workouts will be provided via your new FEED implant. Due to your iconoclastic nature, please keep all FEED activity set to anonymous. It's not foolproof even here. And finally," he says, with a bit of warmth, "we'll start tomorrow. Please eat today's meals at the scheduled times prescribed on the box, though."

Samuel steps forward and claps me on the shoulder. "Ray, we can't stay, sorry. Follow Alverez's plan, and he'll get you back up and running. As a note, I have your FEED set up to send all incoming messaging from Attorney Steve Jenkins to an attorney hired by the Family. Don't play into his hand with a response. Let our attorneys deal with it. Read them, if you wish. If you feel you must discuss something, reach out to your attorney—he should have sent you his contact info. Steve Jenkins is comedy gold right now." He chuckles, shaking his head in mirth. "Just know your attorney knows how to keep him at bay. Let him do his job." As he steps past me next to Alverez on the front porch deck, he promises, "I'll check in when I can, Raylan."

With that, I close the door when the tram leaves. I look around at my new home, and the kitchen is off the lefthand side of the door. It is a very generous "U" shape. On the far back wall is the sink and a refrigerator. By the door is the area to store the dishes, a two-burner stovetop with hood, and a small baking oven. To the right of the sink is a little bit of counter space with a breakfast bar sticking out from the cabinetry. There are a pair of wooden stools to go with the breakfast bar.

The opposing side of the wall of windows leads to a doorway, with a futon near it. My bedroom is spacious, almost as large as the main room. One-way windows cover the same wall overlooking the valley below. Just off the bedroom is the bathroom. It boasts a glassed-in shower with a seat, a toilet behind another door, and sink behind yet another. It's an Asian-style layout for a bathroom system: three separate spots so that three independent people can use the space at the same time. I wander into the final space, a little nook with a small built-in desk.

I step out the door and continue down the front steps. I walk around on the concrete path to the bottom of the cabin. Turning left, I look at an identical door to the one above. I stumble in to see an open-floor planned room with dense matting on it. There is a stationary bike, a rowing machine, a five-station weight bench, medicine balls, and four-inch hemp ropes attached to the wall. I find a small stack of dumbbells on the right side of the door. On the left in a corner is a pod with hand bars around the inside, likely for me to get used to walking and running.

I am about to try the gear out my new workout equipment when my FEED system pings: my two p.m. afternoon meal. The FEED message tells me which meal it is in the stack by QRC code. Thankfully, Doc had included simple reheating instructions. Next to the FEED notice is a timer: I have that long to eat.

Back up the steps I go, making full use of the handrail, returning to the kitchen. I do not finish the baked chicken and heritage beans before the timer goes off. I do, however, eat it all. The doctor had said we would start tomorrow.

It is hard these first few weeks. I start at three meals, then four, then top out at six meals a day, five during the day, one at night. The meals consist of lean proteins, functional carbs, and some fats. My body is in "go" mode always. I am working out, or stretching, or doing drills for dexterity and manipulation of my new body. I shower two to three times a day to get the myomere to relax enough to continue. My physically weaker human side becomes more reliable, more flexible, and just as capable as it ever was. Myomere me, as I like to call the right half, struggles to keep up. Improvements are noticeable, even at the end of week one. Having tailored food, rest, and workout regimens are paying dividends.

As my recovery progresses, the struggle is keeping my left and right sides in balance or close enough for government work. I work at it; I devote myself to it. "Cut, chop, stack. You do it every day, or you run out," as my father used to say.

I buckle down and focus. This is worse than my time in basic training and harder than my time in learning to pilot remotely during Force Recon (FR) team selection. I am alone, like I have always been. I push myself every moment of every day. This is a fight, a battle in my mind, and I am well-trained to do this kind of work. My FEED system is my sole taskmaster. I have no group of recruits to hold me up. I have been here before and I know that hump will come. There will be a day when all I want to do is throw in the towel and walk away.

The day comes a week later. I slip in the piloting pod and bounce my head off the handrail. I land on my shoulder as my collarbone rams into a support stanchion of the pod. I spend hours in unbelievable agony. Thankfully, that side of my body is myomere bone, muscle, and tendon. Myomere would not break from a simple fall.

The nerve endings are new, fresh, and my body is still learning how to incorporate those signals properly. The pain is more like hitting every funny bone in your body all at once. I am in the shower for an hour, and I use my massage therapy ball to knead the knots out of my neck and shoulder. My tears are flowing as I curse my stupidity, and this clumsy nature I am afflicted with. I will not lie: the self-pity has free rein on my soul.

My FEED pings, and like Pavlov's dog, my stomach rumbles. I know that it is afternoon snack time. I do not even realize I have left the shower as I pull the cold cut and fruit snack from the fridge. I am naked as the day I was born when I finish eating. At the sound of my FEED buzzer, I stop my pity party and move on with my work. It is time to cut, chop and stack. The mass of bruising on my head and collarbone are the only reminder of the fall. I will keep going, and I know I am now on the other side of that hump. I do take a break from working in the pod, as I pushed myself a bit too fast.

Dr. Alverez meets with me every other week. He does the same tests Nurse Brinx has in the past. Alverez also calculates to see how much weight my human side has gained, and how much muscle it has managed to grow. We go over the dexterity drills and the manipulation tools I have available. In time, we start working in the pod again. I start by walking while gripping the bar, then fast walking. There are falls, bruises, lacerations, skin torn off my knees, and split lips. Injuries galore happen when I simply do not do something well enough, soon enough, or precisely enough. This is my time here, all of it long fourteen-hour days, everyday.

The evenings are mine to enjoy. Most nights I read books from my FEED system. For light literature, I return to my war college roots: *The Book of Five Rings, Art of War, On War, The Prince, HagaKure, History of the Peloponnesian*

War, The Unfettered Mind, No Second Place Winner. When I need a break, I study every SkipJack operation manual and repair manual I can get on my FEED system.

When I feel up to it, I keep up with increasingly deranged messages from Steven Jenkins's attorney. He is trying to serve me papers for stealing the six haptic suits. When Mr. Jenkins cannot find me, he goes on the FEED networks shows, all to describe how I am part of a cover-up conspiracy to shut down private contracting for the security of Gates. In other messages from my attorney, I receive FEED video of his news interviews about how I am a rogue government agent hell-bent on destroying the compacts infrastructure.

My favorite conspiracy of his is that "I was sent to destroy CGSU in an effort to push greener and more holistic Gate keeping practices," and that my "destructive efforts have tabled a fantastic piece of legislative work by a House of Commons (HOC) politician." I do not respond, as doing so will only clue Jenkins in that I am out here. Whatever my attorney or my attorney's office does, it sure sends Jenkins into a spittle frothing fury. I leave them to it.

***

C5 S3

I am at my second six-month check-up, a year after being released from the hospital. Doc is sitting before me here at the breakfast counter. His eyes are gleaming, his smile broad and happy.

With genuine warmth, Dr. Alvarez says, "Ray, you've made tremendous progress. I'm clearing you for a new sub-dermal system." Doc smiles again as he leads me on a lengthy description of the new haptic mesh implant. "Instead of three thousand pinhead-sized implants, you'll have a myomere mesh grown between your skin and muscle. It will take about four days in the tank." I recognize the excitement behind Alvarez's glasses. He expounds on the process more. "You'll lay down, suspended in a solution for the surgery. The new system is a continuously variable sub-dermal mesh. It's on the lines of 200,000 active sub-dermal inputs at once. It feeds a new haptic suit that we are printing to match you during the surgery."

I am paying close attention to Doc now. I remember the bump from the training civilian level sixty sub-dermal inputs to the full 3,000 of a CM pilot. At the time, I felt like a whole new person. I wonder how piloting with a continuous mesh system will feel.

Doc keeps up his report. "Ray, this is a pods' level of data processing you could only dream of while in the military. You will be as effective on reserve battery as most military pilots are in a pod."

That is quite the claim, and Doc has my full attention as we wander down the hillside to the new workout room. Doc shows me the crew as they start updating the workout area. My area is no longer under the cabin. It is down the front doorsteps and into an old-style barn around the corner of the hill. I will still be on fourteen-hour shifts for the next three months after the sub-dermal mesh is up and running.

The barn has a functional pod, one designed to work with my new set-up. There are fifteen bays for individual SkipJacks. Man, oh man, am I in heaven. No military ones, but we have SkipJacks that replicate small cats, spiders, dogs, large cats, large dogs, construction, demolition, pack animals, security demilitarized, and even a bird. The latter I never cared to pilot. Three bays stand empty. One bay is for repair and construction; another is a sonic cleaning bay. There is a 3D image-testing station with a half-size screen. I familiarize myself with the barn in the evenings leading up to the surgery. I want to be able to get back to piloting as soon as possible. This little bit of hope, of once again returning to what I know and love, lifts my spirits considerably. If I work hard, I will once again be able to pilot a SkipJack.

The surgery is a success. Doc keeps me sedated and suspended in a tank with a breathing mask. A slit at the abdomen and the first patch of the mesh inserted, and from there, his systems are feeding the myomere and guiding it as it grows the mesh between the myomere muscle, human muscle and the skin. As Doc explains, the mesh was not genuinely growing. It is a 3D replication of the original mesh via the thirty insertion points over my body. I revive four days later and spend a day and a half turning back to human from becoming a raisin. I eat, rest, read, and eat. It takes a week or so for the skin to adjust to reality again.

Then the fun work starts. I still am not at a hundred percent, but damn if I am not close. When I put that haptic suit on and pilot a SkipJack, I can move like the wind. Everything comes back. All those years of training, workups, deployments, even the mind-numbing security patrols flood back into my mind. It is almost as if the last twenty-four months have not happened.

The cat and dog piloting are first, as they generally are. Four legs are much more stable to learn on. Within that first week, I am moving on to the spider. Even though it takes me the whole week, I think I do a pretty good job mastering it again. Whereas four legs are more natural, eight legs are alien to the human mind. It takes a bit of time. I regularly come back to this spider SkipJack, just to keep up my level of confidence. I move on to piloting the big dog next. I spend a week with it, also.

The most significant difference between the little dog SkipJack and the big dog is size. Think of it this way: have you ever worn pads and a helmet and whacked your head or pads on a doorframe as you move from room to room? I must relearn the size of the dog SkipJack. It is not something that one understands as quickly as one would think.

I hit a snag with the big cat. I start my work-up fine, working through its paces and movements. I have my first issue after a very long first day as dusk is hitting. I am piloting my way back to the barn. I pass over a ledge that is in some shadows and jump the large cat SkipJack. Something in that shift from a ledge to shadows sends my mind reeling back.

With that leap, I find myself in a fight with my memories. My memory and the cat I am piloting begin to brawl in the undergrowth of the Appalachian southern pine forest. The large cat I am piloting takes blows from my memories of that fight years ago. My memories are stabbing, growling, tumbling, and rolling. The cat I pilot while being stabbed yowls, bites, claws and rakes me as we roll on the needle-strewn earth

I snap out of it. The cat SkipJack makes the jump to the side, it seems. Looking through its ocular mounts, I see a swath of devastation where my mind fought its own memories. I return to the barn and put the cat in its docking station. I spend an hour of my personal physical workout time, plus dinnertime, reviewing the video. It looks as if the cat lands and pauses. It does not attack an imaginary Sam. It just pauses. Then it is hit from the side and starts tumbling, rolling, thrashing, kicking, and biting all around that devastated area. The total time of the fight is not more than two minutes long.

I rise and move to the fridge, after the fifth warning that I am late for dinner. I replay my memories of hitting the piloted cat. It is a perspective shift, one I have no experience with. I keep replaying it, over and over. I fall into the memory the first few times, reliving it again and again. A migraine blossoms as I keep punching the memory forward.

I feel a hand on my shoulder. I look up, as I did not hear Dr. Alverez come in. The door is standing wide open. The Gurkha bodyguard that Samuel usually has with him is in full battle rattle. He may not be a SkipJack pilot, but he is all business as he clears the house, the downstairs workout area, and I hear his comrades clear the barn. They nod to Alverez and take up positions around the porch and property. I look back to Dr. Alverez and thumb him the video from the FEED. I do not say much. Samuel said he was the only one besides me to see that video, to suspect what he and I both do. Part of me wonders if I should keep this private, but the rational part of me knows I need an unbiased mind to look at the situation.

Alverez watches it, replays it. The tall doctor moves about the living room for nearly a half hour, then he sits.

"I repaired Samuel's arm, shoulder, and stomach when he was trammed to me in London," Alverez says quietly. With a long breath and a small kind smile, he asks, "This was that fight, wasn't it?"

"Yes, at least my side of it," I say, while looking at food. I have only eaten a few bites. "I snapped myself out of it. I knew it was not accurate. Not that it was not true, or real, but that it was not accurate." I force myself to eat and to chew. Looking at Alverez, I say, "It was not only my memory, but it was also real in that instant. My brain shouted that it was not accurate...that it was past and gone."

"Hmm," Dr. Alvarez says, and there is a lot of hemming and hawing as he thinks it through. "Do you think it would happen again?"

I am halfway into my food now and I finish chewing that bite. "Since I sat down here, I have been pushing it to the front of my mind. I have packaged it together and devoted my mindspace to reviewing it. Replay after replay. I am slugging it forward, again and again, time and time again. It nearly got me the first few times. No, not got me," I say, looking from my food to Dr. Alvarez. "I nearly fell into that role a few times. Now...well, now I can see the inaccuracies faster, almost instantly. Now I can prevent the viewpoint from shifting. The perspective from shifting." I take a bite of food. "In my mind, at least."

Dr. Alverez looks at my downturned face, watching for a tell of some sort. "Would you be willing to try again tomorrow? Are you willing to pilot a large cat again? Is there a need, or would you like supervision?" he asks with a great deal of caution.

I look up, force-swallowing a bit too early to speak. "Yes, I will be back at piloting a cat or a dog. I have always preferred the bipedal to the four-legged SkipJacks. No, I am not looking for supervision." With a sigh, I push the food away. "I can manage this, Doc. It will be a challenge. Knowing you came means a lot. I will work on it. It is something I must face if I am to be the kind of pilot I used to be," I say, putting forth a bit of reluctant confidence.

Dr. Alverez watches me for a moment and nods, stands, then pats me on the shoulder before he leaves. When I hear the tram leave, I hit the shower.

I am back at it the next morning. Back in the cat: running, dodging, climbing, jumping, deftly weaving in and out. I stumble upon a small group of white-tail does. I take my time and stalk them, working out the kinks. I give them a great chase. I have no interest in killing, just becoming better.

I almost regress on the third day. This time as I land from jumping off the log, the perspective switch is slower, as it must wade through mental barriers I have put up. I push my mindspace right back at it. It takes a significant effort to wedge my will, my mindspace, back into the cat and move it off in a different direction. The cat scrambles out of the hundred-year-old pines in a series of sideway bounds. I have no further issues with my memories and piloting mixing together in a toxic manner after that. I even pilot the large cat at night once for a few hours. I do not think of myself as cured, but aware. I would always have to be aware of the trauma I had suffered.

From there, I move on to the pack animals. There is a kind of Mag-lev sled puller. It is most like a bull or horse-type SkipJack. Usually, you set them to heel mode and daisy-chain them together with cables. They often tow Mag-lev sleds or Mag-lev Rollers (MLR) over terrain that has no locomotion track system. For example, some SkipJacks work well on steep, high-elevation mountains, quarries, or high temp massive foundries where it is too hot for humans. I wrap both work-ups in under a week.

Finally, I am back to my bread and butter. I love piloting bipedal SkipJacks: construction, demolition, and demilled units. I hope to spend the longest time here. I work with all the available humanoid SkipJacks for five weeks. I swap back and forth to do this or that series of training.

What I call training is building a deer blind on the side of the hill near a pond and gazebo I found. I may never use it, but the construction practice of putting up four shaved pine poles, building a platform on top, building a small set of walls to put on the platform is a fantastic achievement for me at a year-plus out of the hospital.

Then there's the bird. I call it "Squawk." We get along about as well as male turkeys and turkey hunters. The perspective shift to flight is always the hardest for me. I simply prefer flying a drone, as drones are more straightforward and less of a pain. I finish the minimum qualifications with Squawk and kick his butt to the curb.

***

C5 S4

I return one afternoon from a physical walk to find Dr. Alverez waiting. I am not expecting him for a few more days. We discuss my tests, my current scores.

"Ray," Alvarez says with no inflection of his doctor's voice, "My boy, if you're not as good as you ever were, you're damn close. You're on track to be an outstanding pilot. I had concerns before the mesh implant. I didn't think you were quite ready. You had plateaued and had not crossed the Rubicon yet. Samuel argued vociferously that you move on. I relented." He chuckles. "In three months, Ray, you've made more improvement than in the previous twelve."

I smile at him, then grin. "Groundwork, Doc. It was all the groundwork. Without that, your help, and Franc's encouragement, I would not be here at this stage now," I say evenly. "Also, piloting is what I enjoy doing the most. You never met me during my time in the CM, but piloting is what I lived for."

The Doc looks at me, confusion in his eyes. "I've never found Franc to be any kind of encouraging. Knowledgeable, more than competent, and supremely efficient, but not encouraging," he says bemusedly.

Grinning, then laughing, I say, "Doc, I do not want to see Franc. That is all the encouragement I need."

Dr. Peter Alvarez stays for dinner. We chat about this and that. His family is grown, and his wife has passed. He has worked for the Jankowitz group for the better part of sixty years. Contrary to popular opinion, he is not Stewart Jr.'s physician. He is the Family's medical problem solver, as he puts it. As we sit and chat, he asks me to grab two fresh glasses and a bit of tap water in a third. I bring them over as he delivers a bottle to the table. With a twist of the bulbous container, he shows me a glen scotch whiskey of eighteen-year vintage. He pours generously. We add our water to open the nose a bit and clink glasses.

"To a recovery well done," Doc says. It is a fantastic nightcap.

The next morning, I am fiddling with the large dog SkipJack when I hear a tram spool up its engine nacelles for landing. I stow the dog and exit to find Samuel heading up to the cabin. With a near skip, I make my way back to the cabin.

Meeting Samuel on the porch, we head inside. "It is good to see you, Samuel. How has work been?" I say.

This is the first time he has been able to make it back to the eastern North American Compact (NAC) since I arrived.

With a hint of a smile in his voice, he says, "Not nearly as good as your work, it seems. It's almost like you heard you were about to get three days of leave. It's amazing how you're getting about now."

Laughing, I say, "Yeah, you caught me early. I still spend an hour or so working the kinks out later in the day. The stamina is good, energy is good. The muscles, human and not, are showing their age at about the time it gets dark." Smiling, I continue, "I received a clean bill yesterday from the Doc. He says I am as good as I ever was." Samuel and I both laugh. "It took me a while, but I found it. That is a phrase from a song my dad used to play."

Samuel looks at me and smiles. "You look good, Raylan, really good," he says. He gestures to the stools at the counter that serves as the table. "I uh, well, the Family is having its holiday party tonight. Big 'F' corporate Family, not little 'f' personal family. We, all of us with seats at the table, will be there, along with business partners, potential partners, and VIPs from most places around the world and politicians and members of the House of Lords (HOL)." Samuel looks about the small cabin and shrugs. "I came to get you. Father thinks it's time to bring you in and get your work started." I think I hear a bit of relief in his voice. "It will pull some of the weight off me, Raylan. Father will let you know the details."

I quip jokingly, "Now look who needs that three-day pass."

That receives a short snort from Samuel. "Raylan, the family doesn't know what we did. That goes for the big 'F' and small 'f' family. They think I was that postal clerk. Franc, I think, knows better, but he's said nothing about what you and I were. He told them I was a postal clerk when Darien asked what I did in the military. It stopped me from answering, and you know as well as I do that most don't know how our MOS was hidden.

"You should have heard it, Raylan." He clears his throat to make it more profound and raspy. "'His MOS was 0161.' When Darien, my older brother, asked what that meant, Franc deadpans." Samuel clears his voice. "'Postal Clerk Enlisted.' In front of nearly fifty of the family's most influential guests, plus our normal Family corporate subsidiaries. Dead silence filled the room."

Samuel says with a smile in his voice, "I kid you not, Raylan. The four-piece orchestra stopped their music. They resumed playing three times as fast and loud. Prior to that, I thought my Father may have had suspicions as to what I did, but after that, I knew I was nothing more than a postal clerk to them.

"As for the injuries, they think I fell off a hill while camping, or skiing on leave." He slows and sighs. "Let them think that, Raylan. They...well, they just won't get it. They have no frame of reference to understand what kind of work we did."

Nodding, I completely understand Samuel's point of view.

I point at myself and say, "I tell people I was a SkipJack mechanic. It has only come up once or twice. I know the feeling, Samuel. I will keep it simple."

"Thanks." I think that is the most relieved I have ever heard Samuel sound. "I hear you got a new sub-dermal. Is it good? Is it true that it's revolutionary?" he asks, his eyes bright as he sits at the edge of the stool. His right hand shivers with faint tremors of his own trauma that still needs work.

I laugh. Back to shop talk. Samuel had always been as good a SkipJack pilot as our team had. We have always sought that little edge, so it would not be kind to hold back.

"Samuel, there is no comparison. Remember going from the training sixty to 3,000 sub-dermal inputs? Yeah, well, that is like..." I trail off as I try to come up with the words. "Shit, Samuel. There is no comparison. I feel like the dog, the spider, the bull, even the bird. Samuel, do not ever get one—you will not be able to stop piloting. The suit, oh, hell, the latency out of a pod is almost zero. With the feedback at fifty percent, it is like walking. With feedback at a hundred percent, Samuel, I could have pulled to heel those two demilled units," I say as I wave a hand at the units down the hill.

Samuel stops me, then points at the FEEDs in our wrist. We are fully aware of the small FEED terminal in the half-office. With a shake of his head, he lets the conversation go, and so do I.

He stands and says, "Crap, we don't have much time. Get showered and some clean clothes. We'll get you trimmed and in a monkey suit for tonight when we get there."

After twenty minutes, we are off to a party, with a capital P, it seems. He runs me through the family members: Darien, his brother, Eliese, Darien's older twin sister, and his much younger sister Trish. He says out of the four, Trish is the socialite, the perfect miss Southern gal. She declined a date tonight and has bemoaned the vultures that would undoubtedly be around. "I offered you as her arm candy, Raylan, and Trish accepted," he says, looking at me and smiling.

"Um, I do not know about that," I say as I flip through hairstyles on my FEED that the stylist has sent me based on my face shape. I tap one just to get it over with, only to find a stream of monkey suits. Samuel chuckles, reaches over, spins it like a wheel, and touches one. "Thanks, I think." I grimace.

"No worries, Raylan. Trish is young and pretty, intelligent, and kind. She won't steer you wrong. With you near her, the vultures will leave her alone. Mutually beneficial. It isn't anything more than that," Samuel explains. I catch the side-eye look of an older brother.

"Thank God," I say in honest relief. "I do not need you to set me up."

Getting prepped at the venue is, well, unique. In boot camp, all applicants are marched in their skivvies in a line through a room purposely kept ice cold. Ostensibly, this is for physicals and shots. The process to put me in a monkey suit is about that embarrassing. I am standing in my briefs while getting my hair cut by a dude standing on a chair, and my face shaved by a lady tall enough to cut my hair without the chair.

During those indignities, a second lady proceeds to measure my arms, legs, waist and chest for the penguin suit. At first, they all stare at my body's appearance. The tiger striping effect of the grafted skin had lessened only a bit. My sub-dermal mesh had evened out the difference from normal human physiology on the left side to, well, abnormal human on the right. My right side just barely loses the word "freakish" from its descriptor. Within an hour, my face and hair are finished. The clothier wants to display the scaring and striping on my arm, figuring me some great war hero. I politely decline with a glare that leaves no ambiguity. I mentally thank Franc for that lesson in stoic determination.

An hour later, my suit is complete, freshly made, and 3D-printed. No seams, no stitches. I am in for a treat: facial makeup, hair styling, and a slew of people to dress me. It is an experience, to be sure. I am wearing a bowtie, vest, jacket, shoes, and cufflinks. One of the attendants brings forward an archaic selection of watches for me to choose from. I skip over the wristwatches and pick a vest pocketwatch and bone fob. I look at the mirror. The man that scrutinizes me is my father. I have not seen Dad in twenty- five, twenty-six, maybe twenty-seven years. I am stunned. I ask what day it is, as I have long ago stopped paying attention.

"December third, sir," one of the men brushing the suit flat and clean of imaginary lint replies. December third. My birthday. I am forty today. I have my mother's ear shape and my father in the bulk of my features. In those areas, I am just a little softer on the edges, more like my mother.

I step back from the mirror when I hear Samuel's voice as the door opens. He walks in wearing a similar suit. On his arm is a young lady about half a head shorter than him, maybe an inch shorter than me. Blonde wavy hair. She is wearing a stunning, black bare-shouldered dress. She must be Trish. What I had not contemplated is that she would be half my age. That would have been nice of Samuel to mention.

They stop a few feet from me. Samuel says, "Trish, this is Ray. Ray, this is Trish, my lovely best-looking sister."

Trish, in a cultured accent of undefinable ambiguity, says, "Sammy, you better watch it. El will make you pay for that." She steps forward and off to my right side, slipping her left arm through my right. "Oh, Sammy, he is so much better than the picture you showed me," Trish says while looking at us both.

I stammer. "Wait, what picture?"

Samuel turns and has made it to the door before replying, "The photo I have of us in Barbados." My face flushes, which is difficult, extremely difficult for me to show.

In that same voice from before, Trish chimes in, "Don't worry, Ray, it is a picture from when you arrived at the cabin. Though I would love to see the photo of you guys in Barbados. Who knew our little postal clerk was such a wild guy?"

I am flustered and I know I am out of my league here. "Trish," I begin, conversationally, "I need help; I am so out of my league here. Not just you, as lovely as you are. I found out about this less than five hours ago." I pause for effect and lower my voice. "Trish, I have never been to a party."

She spins in front of me, grabbing both hands. "Ray, Sammy trusts you, and that says everything. I think he would go postal if any of the vultures here tries to get their clutches on me. Tonight, Ray, you are my knight in shiny new armor." She lets go of my left hand and continues, "I'll twirl us around." She demonstrates, lifting my arm into the air. "I'll introduce us, provide the small talk, and seek your opinion. Then, Ray, you give it even if it sucks, *especially* if it sucks. Even if it isn't what they want to hear. "Don't worry, Ray, I'll back it up with some spoofy logic." Another twirl. "We'll have dinner and sit across from each other. Watch my cues on what I do, and simply do the same." She takes a step back and looks me up and down. "If we do this well, Ray, neither of us will have anyone nosing around us for scraps for six months." She says with entirely too much glee.

I smile. "I think, Trish, you are my kind of devious. How did we meet, and what are your plans?" I ask with that same glee she has displayed.

Trish, with a huge grin, says, "I so owe Sammy for this one. Well, Ray, I go to a private secondary uni for financial banking. How about...we met during my summer internship." She coos that last bit as, evidently, this is her game to play. Her arm is back through mine. We head out the door, down the hall, devising the story to keep the vultures and their turpitude at bay. It is clear she has no interest in any kind of romance. The letdown is polite, and honestly, a significant relief. I am not emotionally ready for that kind of thing. As Samuel said, she needs to keep the vultures away. A forty-year-old battle-hardened veteran would likely scare off just about any one of them.

We are announced at the main ballroom as we stop to enter. No one cares, and no one looks at me. With Trish on my arm, we move from one polite small talk to another. I play it safe and keep my comments as benign as I can. I do not make waves. In between bouts of pointless chatter to whom she calls vultures, I find out that she loves horses, yachts in the summer, and skis in Europe during the winter months, when school allows.

Trish has a thing for financial banking. She wants to go in that direction of the Family's path. She would become the first one to do so since the Jankowitz Group became involved in Gates. Trish is smart, polite, kind, and a joy to be around. She is hoping she can build up the hedge fund side of the family's business again. It has always done well, and Trish has dreams to be the first to grow it since Stewart Jankowitz Senior passed away. She sees the Gate side of the business as stable and having room to grow. The Family owns the single most significant number of privately owned Gates in the Compact.

***

C5 S5

A little over an hour in, she leads me to a hallway, stating, "Daddy's ready to see you. I'll drop you off at the secretary's and come collect you for dinner." We take a couple of turns down the hallways that are all lined with dark wood. We stop as we enter an oval seating area. On the left is a semi-circular, chest-high desk. Behind it is an avatar of beauty: long, straight black hair, a classy, wide-strapped black dress, eyes the color of morning coffee. If I guess correctly, she is as tall as I am. She has a beautiful oval face with a pointed chin. With a gesture, Trish sends me over to the seating area on the right.

I weave my way over and sit in the chairs, which are an uncomfortable three inches too low. I decide it is deliberate. In front of me is an oval coffee table made from a mishmash of darkly stained woods. It has plenty of magazines on it, all seemingly telling the person sitting how vital the Family is to everyone.

I move my eyes back to Trish, to see her chatting with the secretary. I return to my inspection of the table. I stare at the corners, the perfectly flush seams of wood that meet in the middle of the ovals. There are six different types of wood. There is not one seam out of place. Not one is sticking out or recessed too far. I have a distinct impression that it is all hand-fitted together. Maybe it is as much a puzzle as it is a table. That would imply it could be taken apart and reassembled. It flabbergasts me, and I have no clue why.

As smooth as a canticle, a voice says, "Made by Daniel Pinker, master cabinet maker over one hundred years ago. There are six types of now-extinct earth prime wood in that table. That was purchased at auction for 22,000 credits just to match that couch." That voice steals my breath away, if ever a voice could do such a thing. "Stewart will see you now, Mr. Ray. Please follow me."

I rise, and I follow. I am still in a daze at the secretary's voice as I enter Stewart Jankowitz's office. The Father of the Family. He rises from his desk of equally rich wood and comes around to meet me. We shake hands. He motions me to sit in one of a set of chairs across from his desk. Stewart is older, and I know he has been working with Dr. Alverez for at least sixty years. He seems in good vigor and carries himself probably better than I had up until recently. That siren call of a voice sounds. "Stewart, Mr. Ray, may I get you anything?"

With a gentle shake of my head, I decline. Stewart does likewise.

Stewart says in a basso much smoother than Franc's, "I think you're the first military friend of Samuel's the Family has met." He pauses. "I do mean friend. Samuel has made that clear, out of the dozen or so years you knew him in the military. Over the time of your recuperation, you never sought his aid. You never leveraged that friendship." He paused again. "When Samuel pressed me to offer you a position during your recuperation from the camping accident, I declined. I had sent you Dr. Alverez. He had done his magic. I thought that payment enough." Mr. Jankowitz takes a long pause and a mighty inhalation. "I need to apologize. I should never have left the job half-done. After Samuel's return, I devoted my mind and time elsewhere. Your initial injury and its subsequent care fell past my concern," he says with remorse.

I start to open my mouth, to say it was not necessary, when I see his hand raise to quiet me.

Stewart Jankowitz explains, "Alverez was wroth with me. He almost resigned when he saw your name come up in an alert the second time. All his patients become coded to him. Anytime they're injured, they get sent to him, or he goes to them. That's how he fixed up Samuel in London. He's my greatest confidant and closest friend. I let him down, Mr. Ray, when I let you down. That's not how the Family operates. You are a friend to my son, a patient of my best friend, and I forgot you. For that, I give you my deepest and most sincere apologies."

He lowers his hand. I take that extra bit of time to think it through before responding. "Thank you, sir. That is very unexpected and welcomed. I appreciate the extent the Family has gone to for both my recuperation and safety."

With a sigh, Stewart says, "Thank you, that's very gracious, Mr. Ray. This room is secure: six inches of lead floor, ceiling, walls, and doors. The only other place nearly as secure is your cabin. It, however, can still have an issue with being overheard via your FEED. This is as secure as we can make it without a FEED cuff. Please keep that discretion in mind."

Stewart Jankowitz Jr. smiles and leans back. I am beginning to see how he can control a room of people. He is amiable, self-effacing, and excellent at setting the tone and pace of a conversation.

"You, Mr. Ray, walked a Gate twice. There are no records of another person doing that. Not only that, but you survived two lightning strikes while transiting with two SkipJacks. Transiting a Gate with your perception split when piloting a SkipJack is the same as walking a second Gate, if I've been informed correctly. Mr. Ray, you are currently the only one out of 150 billion people on Earth-Prime who has managed to do either of those things."

Again, I am about to speak when I realize he is laying the groundwork.

"Ray, I own the largest number of private Gates in the Compact. I'm currently able to survey, support, and set up the infrastructure of one D2 Iteration at a time. I'm 238 Gates behind. We're looking for ways to speed up that build time. There is zero infrastructure in a new gate. No survey, no geographic map, and no low-orbit satellites for SkipJack pods to relay signals to the SkipJacks. Right now, it comes down to about seven to ten years for me to set up a demarcation pad with sufficient power and living space to start sending through 3D printers. Seven years just to get to that Stage One point."

Mr. Jankowitz is in full sales pitch mode. "We call that Stage One; 1,000 to 5,000 citizens. The basic function of Stage Two requires 5,000 to 25,000 citizens and takes the Compact a minimum of thirty years. Stage Three constructs independent power, water, housing, and sewer facilities, and an operational mesh FEED network. The Compact has not reached this stage in under fifty years."

I am beginning to see why Stewart is the visionary titan of the corporate world.

"We've been working on a system, a plan to train surveyors. We think we can significantly cut that time down by using the new sub-dermal mesh, new haptic suits, new SkipJacks, and a new set of MLRs. Each of those surveyors could set up a localized wireless mesh for SkipJacks, allowing me to send in un-piloted

SkipJacks from this side, and have the data run through a data trunk to the localized mesh.

"We hope to have the demarcation point and Mag-lev tracks set up within thirty-six months. The second thing would be for the surveyor to survey the best area for settlement. Right now, the first initial settlements get abandoned. Abandoning a settlement makes the wait for creating those new homes, businesses, and other venues significantly longer. Suppose I could put it in the right place the first time? I would save a ton of effort by the colonists," Stewart says.

"Finally, Ray, the last thing is to set up a balloon orbital survey to do high altitude radar, laser imaging, and track atmospheric conditions. Many of our first towns have severe setbacks due to weather. The weather in D2 worlds is not always like here. Much of the time, it is far wilder. A weather warning system for the colonists is necessary," he says. His sales pitch weaves through a series of FEED images that he calls forth from the display on his desk.

He takes a moment to think that over, then continues, "There's one big issue. It's a two-year training program for a competent SkipJack pilot. If I want a pilot that can do the ten or fifteen types of SkipJacks and tools that might be needed, add a half dozen more years. It is upwards of another year to train someone to set up a remote power station and a localized data mesh network. Toss in another year for training someone to read maps, release the balloons, connect them to the mesh, and then find the best site for the first village. I would like it to be within five kilometers of the Gate. To summarize: I'm at upwards of ten years of training per single-use Surveyor for about thirty-six months of work."

Now I see the plan. Now I know what I can do for the Family. We get down to brass tacks. We start discussing necessities, tools, methods, SkipJacks, and a system from which to design the Surveyor corps. Well, corps of one for now.

"Ray, I'm sending you the packet of the first twelve Gates. I want you to devise the plan, the tools, and the order of completion for each Gate. Can you get that done in a month?" Stewart asks.

I think it over. It is a tall order, and I am not sure what gear I have at my disposal. "I will give it my best shot, and I will come up with the most reasonable chance of being successful that I can," I say with equal parts excitement and dread.

***

C5 S6

Stewart and I stand up and shake hands again as Trish enters the office unannounced, which elicits a frown of disapproval from the secretary at her desk. I do not have the mental framework to spend the time parsing out what that says.

I pass over staring at Trish to look at the secretary. It has been a long time. I turn my attention back to Stewart as the secretary notices me looking at her standing behind the desk.

Trish gives her father a peck on the cheek and says, "I have to steal Ray back."

How does this family have such impeccable timing? Trish loops her arm through mine and deftly steers me out the door. We make our way back to the ballroom. Now there are stares—long envious stares at me. Little Ms. Trish had just introduced me to her father, the head of Jankowitz Group. Oh, boy, Samuel, you devious little twerp. Whelp, now it is time to fight some vultures.

The vultures come: jealous bachelors who are my age or older working on the third wife, or young studs who are working on moving up in the world. There are numerous Casanovas who are doing their best to separate me from Trish. I play up the injuries. When they do not take the hint, I shake their hands, or I step on their toes with my myomere-reinforced bones. There is no contest.

The whole time, Trish smiles, chatters, and songbirds her way through the crowd. One of the liveried staff steps from a doorway and announces that dinner would be in five minutes. Trish veers us off to a private bathroom that only Family have access to. I stand there like an old, scarred alpha lion protecting his pride. The joke is not lost on me, nor is it lost on the few vultures that try to traverse the path to Trish. I am under no illusion that Trish cannot handle them alone. There was never any doubt in my mind about that. I think this happened to be a great coincidence for us both: a night off from the vultures for her, and a guide through this social maze for me. I am chuckling over her term for these vultures when I hear another voice.

"And which mongrel are you?" it asks. The question pounds at my ears. This voice had a Northeast District of the Compact accent. Whoever is talking laces their question with snide condescension, so I ignore it. "You hear me, sycophant? Which mongrel are you?" With a sniff, he continues, "It never phases any of you, does it? You come here to a party at my home, prance around doing your best to woo a sister. Why are you here, mongrel?" The condescension rolls off him.

I turn, politely smile, and say, "Samuel said Trish needed someone to run interference tonight for the vultures. I owed him a favor. The name's Ray." I speak deferentially. I stick out my left hand for a handshake. Very few people are lefthanded, and it is a simple way to throw most people off. Plus, with the left, I would not have the temptation to crush his hand into a bloody pulp.

He does not even look at my hand, nor does he take it. "So your Sammy's little army postal buddy." With a chuff and a snort, he adds, "This is more pathetic than I thought. Enjoy your night, mongrel, and don't touch the silver." He tries to shoulder into and past me. Little does he know, myomere muscle weighs more than twice what healthy human muscle weighs. The myomere bones are more than three times denser than human bone. I may not look it for 177 centimeters, but I am pushing 136 kilograms. I do not even smile as he reels off my shoulder down the hall. I know that smarts something fierce.

A moment later, Trish comes out. With worry to her tone, she says, "I thought I heard you and Darien talking? Was he pleasant? If not, I will talk to him and Father."

I smile. "Darien was just looking out for you, Trish. He thought I was one of the mongrels or vultures. I took no offense," I say with a bit of humor.

Trish snort-laughs like a pig. She catches herself and does it again. She turns beet red. We wait in the little alcove until she finishes.

"Ray, there isn't a mongrel in the world that could live up to you. You are my big pussy cat," she says as she weaves us back out into the ballroom. She gives me a peck on the cheek, just as everyone turns and looks again, some secretly, some openly, some with only their eyes. They all understand: Trish is off the table.

Damn, this Family is good.

We are sitting opposite each other. I follow Trish's cues on everything: what glass to use, what silverware to use, and so on. I do not clear my plate, as no one else does. I have sussed out that I eat 8,000 calories a day. Leaving food on the plate goes against my desire to feed the myomere inside me. Nevertheless, dinner is pleasant. We talk to our partners on either side. Nice people. One is an executive for a regional bank who is thinking of investing heavily in the Gate systems now that the market had dipped after that man sabotaged that Gate.

The other is a socialite who appreciates the more exceptional arts in life, mostly anyone not ruffian enough to block her son's chances at Trish. The most startling thing is when Stewart enters and sits at the head of the table. To his right is his vivaciously stunning secretary, and on his left is Darien. I do a quick left-right-left-right search with my eyes, almost inconsiderately staring. I am such a slow idiot sometimes. Sure enough, Eliese, firstborn, Samuel's sister, her Father's daughter, and secretary, stands up to deliver a speech. The voice, the simple canto of sound, draws my soul in.

I receive a small, pointed shot to my right leg and hear an almost inaudible "ow." I turn to see Trish wince, and she shakes her head. I exhale. Trish has been a fantastic person for which to be arm candy and I have no interest in being a cad.

I pull my attention back to Trish and smile and say, "I just figured out who the secretary is. Thanks for the warning."

The lady next to me, Mrs. hot and bothered her boy would not have a chance now, snorts wine out of her nose. Not much, mind you, but whatever battleship her son was commanding just went down with that depth charge.

I resolutely pay attention to Trish the rest of the evening. Magically, we are always on the opposite side of the room from her older sister. I learn how to dance, and Trish leads. I do not break her toes. As the evening winds down and the guests are leaving, Trish and I run into Samuel, Darien, and Eliese.

"I'm putting in my order first, Sammy. I get him for New Year's," Trish says. She stands up on her tiptoes and places a peck on my cheek, leaving a trail of lipstick behind, to Darien's apparent chagrin, and an elegantly raised eyebrow from Eliese. Trish moves off as Samuel makes formal introductions, and I shake hands. I offer my left hand for Darien and my right to Eliese. That little switcheroo does not go unnoticed by either Eliese or Darien. Samuel steps in and politely makes our excuses.

The return tram is easy, now that I am out of the bow tie and vest. I feel a whole lot better.

"Trish likes you. That's unusual for her to stake a claim like that," Samuel says with a smile.

I snort and exhale. "Trish and I get along well. She is amazing at what she does. She, however, is not my type. That woman moves too fast, is too quick, decisive, and devious. Oh, it is fun for a dinner party, but Samuel, I could not keep up with her a moment longer," I say in all sincerity.

We laugh, and Samuel takes a breath and continues, "I thought old stick-up-his-rear Darien would bust a vessel when she put in her order for New Year's. For Trish to then give you a peck on the cheek and leave her mark...damn, she wants to tweak his short hairs."

He keeps chuckling while I recount the hallway incident. He almost slides out of his chair when he hears the shoulder-bumping part. I make it clear I am not insulted. After seeing the mongrels, a better term than "vultures," running around and then the adults vying to get in, I let Darien's overprotective nature roll off my back.

With a couple of steadying breaths, Samuel says, "He's always had 'Second-born Syndrome.' He was something vicious to me whenever I was home from school. I idolized him when I was real young, but he, well...Ray, be careful. He has a petty streak in him. I don't think he would do anything against the Family directly, or its interests, of which you're now a substantial part. Yet, he can be petty," Samuel says. His warning clear and carries some concern.

"I will stay away," I say with a smile. "I have four or five months of research, planning, and practice to get done in thirty days." With another smile, I add, "I will not be available for New Year's, Samuel. With what I have on my plate, I do not want to stress over another evening coming up." I look at him directly.

Samuel replies, "I'll let Trish know. She won't be hurt. She's typically skiing in Europe during that time, anyway."

It is late, so I pass on the nightcap and simply trundle up to my cabin. I am stiff, sore, and mentally worn out as much in every way as I had been any five days during the last three months.

***

C5 S7

The next thirty days fly by. First, I try out several mock-ups of how to go about setting up the settlement in the most efficient way. What it comes down to is getting the data trunk connected to the remote power; then putting up the localized mesh system. That will allow the SkipJack pilot's data to traverse the Gate and construction of the central Mag-lev demarcation zone can begin.

At the same time that they're building that section, I will complete a survey forty kilometers in radius around the Gate. I am spiking the base property markers, high-altitude weather, mapping, and relay balloons. Once I have that in place, I will take the data they send and look for capable water sources within five kilometers of the Gate. Nothing huge, but enough to support a settlement of up to twenty thousand. I think the first few will take me nine to twelve months, depending on the climate, weather, and just getting used to doing it. I think after that, I can bring the time down to maybe as low as five months.

I do have some provisos laid out in my proposal. I want to do a work-up before the first few D2 iteration transits, using as close a terrain as possible. I have narrowed the first Gate down and made my selection. It is in the Montana West District. I do this to drop a bit more into that regional economy, as I have played a part in the other Gate's collapse. I also choose it because of the type of material it plans to harvest lumber; Douglas Fir and Ponderosa pines. The D2 would selectively log and replant. Currently, the price of lumber in the Compact is at an all-time high.

After a few years, the lumber from Confederated Blackfoot Nation: D2 will reduce the consumption of EP1 lumber. The second reason is that it will be the new home of the Blackfoot Confederated Tribes. They have purchased the colonization contract, offering tribal membership to those that move to the D2. There are many people free of indenture that have signed on. Many of them have the skills and knowledge to make the new D2 iterations successful. In particular, they have recruited several soil biologists, plant biologists, and arborists who are going to take samples of D2's flora, create seedlings, and ship them back to EP1. Those seedlings would then be propagated by the remaining EP1 Confederated Blackfoot Tribe to replant their Montana West District and Saskatchewan district lands.

Another reason is the Confederated Tribes have a start date that works with my timeline while leaving me enough time for a work-up training period just outside the old Bob Marshall Wilderness. The schedule would be fifteen days to get my gear together, fifteen days to work up, leave and transit the Gate in early February. Thankfully, I have inert samples of just about everything. I understand how everything works, including how the gear is to come online and how it will act if it fails. I will be taking some spares, but once I have the mesh up, replacements can come in as soon as the demarcation zone is up and running.

With my choices made, I forward the plan to Stewart on December 30th at 9:00 p.m. I am on time. I have a concise, laid-out plan, and it is something I believe I can accomplish. I now have a three-day pass that I give myself. I am incognito until January third for some much-needed mental relaxation.

I start the next morning with a jog, a human one. I have been running in the pod, but I want to keep up with doing things as a human, not just as a SkipJack pilot. I eat my scheduled breakfast on time. I shower and then go out to do something I have not done since I was alone as a young man in Cold Foot.

I set some squirrel snares. I had some food delivered a day or two before: corn, beans, pork belly, onions, garlic, carrots, chicken stock, Worcestershire sauce, and some spices. I am going to be celebrating the New Year in style. I check the snares in the afternoon after doing my cooking prep. Sure enough, I have a few squirrels in my snares. I walk my complete trap line and pull all the empties. I only need the three.

After cleaning the squirrels, I quarter them and brown them in bacon bits.

I deglaze the pan with the white wine. At the same time as the squirrel bits and pork belly braise in the little oven, I set to browning the onions, garlic, and carrots in some more diced pork belly. I add it all into the Dutch oven. I put it back in the oven and let it simmer for a good long while. I am a bit dirty from setting the lines, cooking, and cleaning the squirrels. I hop back in the shower and clean up. When I exit the bathroom, I turn the Cabin's FEED terminal to some background music.

I am standing at the open oven door when there is a knock on the front door. I place the Dutch oven on the burner, open the door with a mitted hand, and proffer a perfunctory "come in." I hear the click of heels on the deck, then multiple sets of feet as I try to pull the mitts off while turning the oven off. I turn to see those darn livery attendants setting up a dinner table. At first, I think Samuel is here again.

The sound of the heels out on the deck brings me back around as the livery staff keeps setting up carts with little Sterno burners. I just lean back out of the way. Trish is beautiful, lovely, and an enjoyable person to be around, but that is a road I do not want to go down. I know she has "put her order in for New Year's." I am not comfortable with that. I am not comfortable with that at all, especially after Samuel talked to her.

I push off the counter to put an end to this when I hear the siren sing. Eliese must have stepped away from the door on the deck to place a FEED message. The vision that is Eliese Jankowitz is finishing her FEED message now, and I listen.

"Yes, we're going to speak about the plan soon. I'll get his take on your concerns, Father. Love you, too," Eliese says.

I am frozen, half-pushed off the counter with what must be a very startled look on my face as she walks in. Her long black hair, slightly wavy, a tan jacket, blush-colored blouse, and matching tan skirt that sways as she moves. There is that click-clack as she turns to see where I am. I know in an instant that I have a stupid look on my face by the smile that graces hers.

"I heard your New Years plans fell through," she says. "Since you're done with the project early, I scooped you up for myself. I hope you don't mind?" She asks with a lilt that plucks at my heartstrings.

The hairs, that can, stand on end all over my body. I pull myself together.

I cough and reply with a bit of a gasp, "You just saved me from a great deal of embarrassment and two beatings. I do not mind at all."

With a broad smile, she replies, "You look pretty embarrassed right now, but the other two must be Darien and Sammy." Eliese quips, "Am I right?"

As nonchalantly as my body and mind can be convinced to sound, I say, "Partially. Trish is an awesome lady, it would be horribly embarrassing to have to let her down after all this."

I wave at the livery staff, who are finished setting out the rolling carts with food heating. They leave. Three men, more of those Gurkhas, come in. They do a top-to-bottom search, basement and barn included. Four more Gurkhas appear on the deck and pronounce it is clear.

They soundlessly retreat outside, closing the door. I stand up and ask, "Can I take the secretary's jacket?" I give it my best playful tone.

Eliese laughs and consents. I help her out of it and hang it on a hanger on a peg near the office. I make my way back to the pot and remove the lid, releasing the aroma I have not smelled in a very long time. I turn and ask, "Have you been up here before?"

"Briefly, years ago as a teenager, between high school and college. This sort of became Sammy's retreat. After the accident, he stayed here off and on through the years. We have all sorta just let it be his." With a soft twirl, a spinning whirl of sound that is her voice plays across my ears. "Do you mind if I open the wine?"

At my nod of consent, she does so. I wander to the table to see the same crested plates, but the rolling serving trays are new. I peek at the food under the food covers: roast beef, whole chicken, or duck. Man, am I in trouble.

It takes a couple of repetitions for my brain to hear my name. "Ray, what do you have cooking?" I can see her wafting the vapor to her face with a hand. "It smells delicious," Eliese asks.

Well, turnabout is fair play. I say, "Brunswick stew. I have not made it since I was a teenager, maybe sixteen or seventeen. By then, though, I was pretty much making it with pine nuts, moose or bear fat, and squirrels." I pause, waiting for a reaction as I deadpan, "You are in luck, though. I was able to get real hominy, corn, beans, and some pork belly to go with the squirrels."

By the end, I am pretty sure she thinks I am putting her on. She does straighten and turn to me with that glorious eyebrow raised. Challenge accepted, apparently.

I point and say with humor lacing my voice, "Look above the door."

Pinned to the frame are three squirrel tails. She giggles. I could spend the rest of my life hearing her giggle. "I'll pass. No offense, but dead tree rat is not my thing."

"No offense taken. Shall I call you secretary or Eliese?" I ask, hoping to hell it is the latter.

She takes a minute to move from the counter to the table to pour the first wine. "I'm not sure yet, Ray." Her smile is wreathed in magic. "Let's see how dinner goes."

"Dinner will go well," I reply. "Between my Brunswick stew and your offerings, I will be a happy man. I skipped my meals today in anticipation of my stew. A reward, if you will, for my work. I am now a little over 8,000 calories deficient in my daily caloric intake." I take in the whole setting.

The food could burn, along with the building around me, and I would still be a happy man.

Eliese sets the bottle down. I help her into her seat, and we continue to discuss things while her food comes back up to temperature.

"You all call him Sammy? Why is that? The rest of the family don't have nicknames?" I ask.

"Samuel is the only one to go off and do his own thing. He only came back because..." and with the wine glass in hand, she puts air quotes around "of the accident." She explains, "When he returned, it was as if he was still eighteen in our eyes. None of us knew him. We hadn't seen him in person in, oh, fifteen years or more. He pops back up in London, injured from some ski camping accident while on leave."

She turns her head, tilting it down like a bloodhound who just caught a scent. "That's how you know him, isn't it? You were there when he was in his accident." She pauses, looks to the side and taking a sip. "No, that isn't it. He was a postal clerk. You were a SkipJack pilot. No, you would not likely have been friends." She turns her one eye to me to see if I would give it away.

I learned long ago never to interrupt intelligent people when they are puzzling through something.

She spins and crosses her legs to face me. Eliese is pointing with a finger while holding the wineglass. A smirk of victory is on her face.

I can hear the anthem of triumph in her voice as she says, "You were both SkipJack pilots. That's why he's no longer afraid of Darien." She lets out a short whistle. "There's more to it, I am sure." A thoughtful pause, then, "You wouldn't be doing this project if you were a run-of-the-mill SkipJack pilot, would you?"

I look at her and say, "No, I was unique as any man in our unit, and your brother Sam was as good as any one of us on any given day." I inhale, then exhale slowly. "That, though, is as far as I can go. It is his story, not mine."

The tension leaves me as I inhale and exhale again. Eliese is astute, and a very keen problem solver.

"Eliese, Ray. Please call me Eliese. I won't pry any further," she says. With a tiny sip for a pause, she purrs, "Shall we dish up? How about we," a wink and a lovely smile strikes me fully in the heart, "start with a stew course first?"

I give her my best-lopsided grin, stand up, and fish out two tin bowls that are entirely out of place with the family's bone china. She pulls some rolls from one of the heating carts and tops off our wine. I return, placing the chipped and dented, blue and white speckled tin bowls on her gold-rimmed family crested plate.

As I sit, I look at all the silverware and say, "You will have to forgive me, Eliese...without a guide, I do not know what spoon to use."

I watch her face as it beams, and the bells of laughter roll forth. With one hand, she retrieves a spoon. She pointedly covers her mouth with the other. She waggles the spoon for me. With that cue, we start dinner. In between bites, she starts reciting my plan from start to finish. Eliese outlines every asset, every person, every tool, every supply, every date, and backup date.

By the time we move to the duck, as it is a duck, we are covering the possible sites for the colony, and we use what drone footage we have available to review. Eliese includes contingencies for weather-related issues, as it will be February when I make the transition. We talk about what gear I will need outside of what

I have listed. It comes down to guns. Unlike when my parents had them, the Compact strictly regulates them.

Come to think of it, I am not sure the firearms my parents had were legal, either. However, I had one as a teenager in Alaska. I did not know how illegal it had become. I rattle off a couple of rifles I would like. I ask for the Compact's standard Military Carbine and a thousand rounds of ammo. I choose a lesser-known caliber for my hunting rifle: 6.5x55 Swede. I pair it with 500 rounds of ammo. The straight-pull 6.5x55 Swede will take down moose just fine.

I give a couple of suggestions for small rimfire rifles with 5,000 rounds. Finally, I name a defensive handgun with 500 rounds. I choose to go with the venerable 454 Casual my father had always favored. I find models, ammo, cases, scopes, and prismatic sights for them. I thumb that to her FEED. She responds she will get it cleared with the Blackfoot Confederated Tribes.

Moving on, I keep returning to the fact I will be working in winter. I am concerned about traveling with a SkipJack pack animal version in snow. I have snowshoes, but that would not help much in two meters of snow. We table that part till the work-up and Eliese will investigate options.

The roast beef is excellent. I have four servings, compared to Eliese's one. We finish the walkthrough and are chatting about life.

I ask, "So, why the secretary ruse?"

Eliese covers her mouth with fork in hand as she finishes chewing.

"Honestly? Darien. He's always been sore that he is not firstborn. Hell, you've met Daddy, Ray. Do you think he gives a second thought as to which of us is firstborn? Darien started calling me 'the secretary' because he thought it belittles me," Eliese says. "I decided to be better than him, and ever since I was fifteen, I work harder. I take work more seriously, and I listen more, I manage more projects. I kick his ass every time."

She stops and takes a drink. We are on our second bottle of wine now.

"I graduated from college early, then finished my indenture early. I returned to the Family first. I had been working here for about nine months when Darien finished his indenture and came back home. I gave the secretary the day off, took his FEED message to Daddy, and made him schedule an appointment. Every time he got mad, I hung up. When the appointment day arrived, he had to sit in that little settee," Eliese says with a laugh. "I picked that settee just for that day, you know."

With another chuckle, she continues, "Darien was pacing back and forth. He even tried the door. He finally sat down. I let him get about three-quarters of the way relaxed and then said, 'Mr. Stewart Jankowitz will see you now.' I then played the same role I did when you were there. Whenever Father meets someone new, I play that role." Her hands lift to touch her shoulders, and Eliese says, "I am now my father's gatekeeper. That oval space is now my office. The doors were open when you were there, but they usually are closed with my name on them."

She sighs and lets out a long breath and looks up. "Father had those doors put in that very night after Darien left. He put my name on them. The next morning when Darien came in for his second appointment, I had been at work for two hours. He had to make an appointment with my secretary to get through. He tried barging in, but Father walked out and told him I was his successor, period. Then showed him his office three doors down. The very one I started in."

I am speechless. Something like that takes a lot of grit to pull off. I do not doubt that what started as sibling bickering had egged her on. She stepped up to the plate and took a swing.

I bow my head and say, "Deftly done, to put years of hard work together, combine it into an instance where you could define how people should view you. You then capitalized on their choice, great or foolish."

She freezes, turning half sideways, and looks back at me. "No one has ever realized that before. Most think I was just a bitch."

I grimace. "I dated a bitch once. She got my boss's wife transferred to a facility where she died in under a week. After the accident, she donated all my stuff and ran off with a doctor after convincing the hospital to pay her indenture early. Because of my boss's wife's transfer, the boss was not there at work. He was traveling to be with his wife four hours away."

Eliese's smile calms into a cool, flat-lipped look. I know it is bad form to talk about exes. This is about me and my broken nature. Eliese might know some of the details, but not all, and she should know it if this, whatever we might be, moves forward.

"My co-worker let off work early to eat food brought by an elderly grand-mother. She stuffed him so much he could not get back in his haptic suit in time to stop her from Gate-walking. I tried to reach her in time, but she Gate-walked. I was then hit by lightning twice. They arrested my boss for not being at work, the old lady was dead, and my co-worker was braindead. All of Dillon Gate Montana West D2's 27,000 lives were cut off when the dimensional lock was lost," I say with a bit more venom than I should have. "That is my definition of a bitch."

I take a long drink as I hear, "That's a no on a Mrs. Ray, then?" I laugh. I laugh hard enough to ground out those months of pain and anger.

I smile. "Thanks, Eliese, I needed that. For now, no. I...well, I have a lot to learn. My injuries were substantial. I have a new opportunity before me, and I have a chance to pilot SkipJacks again. I am different physically and mentally now. I can do this." I wave at the table, then to her. "I can spend time with someone so lovely as you. That...that is healthy for now."

My smile broadens, hitting the corners of my eyes.

"You see, Ray, that's how you should let down Trish in the future." She gives me a wink. "I'm Family, Ray, and I always will be. Most men don't...well, it doesn't work. I much prefer this." She waves at the table and me.

I lean forward, and we clink glasses. The night goes well. I learn that Eliese had focused on business and accounting in uni, with a minor in math. She completed her indenture for one of the big three accounting firms. She put in the extra hours and paid the indenture out early. She isn't a wild child, and she loves being a policy wonk. She can manage multiple projects as well as anyone. Her real strength lies in bringing new people together and forming a cohesive team.

I tell her stories of my days in bootcamp before moving into SkipJack pilot-ing. I feel my childhood and my time in the FR teams are a little too much for this first conversation. Our conversations carry on until the very early morning. We have long since retired to the futon with a blanket for her and the floor for me.

The sunrise is very near when Eliese says her goodbyes. I realize that in a single month, I have had two beautiful evenings with ladies who were worlds apart.

I take the time to clean up my mess. The livery folks had removed what they brought in. I take a shower and lay down on my futon. Her perfume lingers on the cloth, and it sends me to heaven. I am out and asleep for eighteen hours. When I rise, I get back to work. I have a message from Eliese outlining the project is a go.

Three days until I leave for the work-up site.

Chapter 6
Dimensional
Survey

C6 S1

This time, I am not traveling in Samuel's fancy personal tram. I am in a much more functional and ubiquitous heavy lift tram (HLT). The tram is crammed with stowed cargo and gear. I have a nice comfy jump seat of webbing material. I chose to ride with the equipment I will be using. I look back at the SkipJacks with me, stowed and locked down in portable docking stations. I have the following SkipJacks with me: spider, two large dog models, two construction units, two demolition units for clearing the ground, one standard demilled sentry, and four of a new six-legged SkipJack.

I call the new pack animal model the Donner. When I first saw this new six-legged pack variant, I cannot help but think of Caribou. The broad inward curving toes, followed by two stabilizing rear dewclaws made for some very wide sure footing. I bring up the specs on them: a thirty-two-hour powered use cycle at load, twenty-four-hour solar and wind charge cycle. Their specifications include a whopping 275 kilograms of weight-carrying capacity. To match that carrying capability, they can pull 635 kilograms of drag load.

The Donners have built-in panniers for food, equipment, and supplies. What is not to like? Down at the bottom of the SkipJack is a description of an aggressively tuned follow program. These SkipJacks will walk in each other's footsteps. They will follow me, at a set distance, while pursuing my preset paths. This portion of the Donner programming will be interesting.

Our mil-spec pack SkipJacks are relatively dumb. They can follow you, sure, but you turn a sharp corner and it will stop. You must take wide swings around obstacles for it to keep to your movements. Most pilots run a tethered lead, daisy-chaining to the mil-spec models, and pull a quick release when needed. Still, if this new follow program does not work, I am going to hate it. Reading further, I do find that they leave me the tether option. If all else fails, daisy-chaining it is.

I move on to the newly supplied HUD goggles. I have them stowed on where the push to talk, (PTT) would generally be on my chest rig, as I am not likely going to be using a PTT in a new, unpopulated D2 iteration. The new goggles auto-dim for sunlight, have a modicum of low-light capabilities, and multiple HUD displays for each eye. This feature allows me to switch eyes for SkipJack ocular vision modes. I can use one eye for normal viewing, and the other for lowlight. I keep the chest rig and dump the hard ballistic armor.

I have integrated a front pack and a heavy pack for the rear. I will carry the necessary gear in one of those two packs, things like my emergency shelter, water purifier, salt, medical equipment, five days' worth of food rations, three days' worth of clothing, camp shoes, toiletries, compass, one small drone, and so on. My handgun will be in a leg holster, a five-shot, 454 Casull by the venerable Bowen Arms. I have one set of boots on with spares packed, a replacement vintage Boker boot knife on one leg. The right side of my chest bears a stout, single-edge, nine-inch blade for regular use.

I start by looking around and decide I cannot put it off anymore. This shakedown needs a lookover. I look at all of the loadouts for the four Donners. Part of the issue is how to fit these things in the panniers and to balance that load equally, front to back, side to side. Weighing as much as the Donners do, and carrying an additional 275 kilos of gear, proper weight storage is critical.

I spend some time looking at breaking up my load outs. I use the first Donner to store power supplies and localized mesh gear. I task the second Donner to carry my food and personal items. I store the SkipJack docking stations, charging equipment, and tools in the third Donner. The last tows a sled that has cases of the high-altitude balloons, the balloon spikes, and mesh spikes.

There should be a resupply once the data trunk is in; barring any unforeseen problems, that will work. The initial load outs will keep me busy for the first three months with the mesh installation and settlement site survey. Putting one over a five-kilometer square area will be a chore. By then, I should have the data trunk running from the EP1 side. Then they can send over a resupply. The EP1 SkipJack pilots can finish the demarcation zone. If they are running behind, I will have plenty of other work to do.

We land in a remote area of the Confederated Blackfoot Tribal lands, a few dozen kilometers from the old US and Canadian border. It is an area called Big Sky Community. There is not much but SkipJacked wheat or potato farms here now. As it is February, it is butt-ass cold out, and I will have a nicely cleared area to do my work-up. It all starts well. We land, and everything is un-stowed from the trams. I pull the SkipJacks to heel in the order I am going to walk the Gate. This task takes me a good deal of time.

Pulling SkipJacks to heel is a mental fight. Each time you pull one to heel, you drop a portion of your awareness into and onto the effort of controlling that SkipJack. That awareness sets it to follow loosely on you. Think of it as a mental daisy-chain. Good pilots can pull to heel two SkipJacks. Great pilots can pull more. Sam once pulled six on a bet and was in the hospital for a week as result. I settle for pulling them to heel individually, then daisy-chaining them together.

I practice a theoretical Gate walk in hardpacked snow sixty centimeters deep. I roleplay the theoretical unpacking and mock-up first steps into the Gate. Then I practice packing it all back up every day for two weeks. I have a small three-person crew with me. They provide immediate shelter and food. I typically make the trek about five to seven kilometers from the camp they set up, then act as if I had transited, only to march back into the bivouac for lunch. After lunch, I walk out the other side of camp to do it again before dinner. It goes well. The spider is not worth a damn in the snow, and neither are the dogs. As a result, the dogs trail last, with the spider carried in a pannier on the third Donner. That put the third Donner decidedly over the weight limit, which, in turn, has a reasonably noticeable effect on its power cycle times at load.

At night, I set up the remote charging stations for the Donners. During the nighttime, I run up a balloon carrying a wind-power charging device. Thankfully they are reusable and somewhat durable. I am not sure how well they will do in the thunderstorms that come down from the north in this area. During the day, I try the solar power generation. That twenty-four-hour charge cycle period is overly optimistic. One of my crew, a tech for the Donners, tells me to use both systems at the same time. Sure enough, the combo of solar and wind during the day brings me within charging specifications. My time at the work-up site ends. We make our transit via trams to the Gate.

***

C6 S2

We arrive at the Gate's DMZ. The landing area and a narrow strip of the demarcation zone are kept mostly clear of ice and snow. Everything else has sixty centimeters of encrusted white death. The area directly in front of the Gate's archway has some heat bleed through from the D2 side. For about twenty-five meters, the space is bare concrete. I gather my SkipJacks to heel and set them to follow mode as my crew and I do our final checks. I spend a day restocking, checking for broken items in need of repair. Finally, on my scheduled day, I transit to another Dimensional Earth iteration.

I willingly walk my Gate.

I have some small amount of concern as I walk the Gate, though not as much as I thought I would. I have made it through a Gate before, and I know that surviving the Gate walk with my mind intact exists, at least for me. I have kept myself focused on my work and the required preparations for the Gate walk. Separating the fear from my work allows me to move forward to do this thing that no mortal man is supposed to be able to do.

What is it like to walk a Gate? I can say this: at least when the temporal lock is in place, there is no sensation. You are here, and then you are there. The temperature is zero degrees, with thirty KPH winds and sixty centimeters of snow across the EP1 DMZ. Once through the Gate, I am into forty-five centimeters of melting snow and clear blue skies at twelve degrees Celsius. Indeed, this is big-sky country. I keep my little troop of SkipJacks moving forward. When we are all through, I pull them all to heel. I look around and find my bearings.

Pulling on my goggles, I remote-power the demolition SkipJack. I spend the better part of what light is left in the day, about two hours, clearing the area for the pod. I have a bit of time left and run the demolition unit into the night. I clear a small area for my shelter under high output LED lights. I will focus on my accommodation this evening, then set up the pod and hopefully clear the space for the remote power generator tomorrow.

It seems there is some time discrepancy, a lag, between the two worlds linked by this Gate. I came through the Gate at 7:00 a.m. EP1; the D2 time is around 3:00 p.m. I am nowhere near tired, but I know I will be. I stick to doing my basics. I set up my shelter, using the demolition SkipJack to make enough logs for a lean-to. It takes another hour with the construction SkipJack to hang HOLEDs and to set up the lean-to. A construction SkipJack, with its powered hammer, makes hammering eleven-inch nails through logs a cakewalk. This lean-to is mostly an initial windbreak. I can set up another sometime tomorrow, then a third lean-to the following evening.

I put up my pop-up hard-sided shelter in the lee of the windbreak. I soon find a place to hang and store much of my food. By the time I am done, I have put in nearly nine hours. The cold night stiffens me. I go to work, starting a fire and heating some food. It is 1:00 a.m. local time when I finish. With that, I turn in.

The next morning brings glorious sunshine, and birds are singing everywhere. This new dawn is most strange to me, as there is not one mechanical sound. There are no high-altitude trams, no community drones monitoring the area, just wind and birds as they start their trek back north. I stoke the fire and make some of my groats for breakfast.

I set about re-inspecting things in my area with my own eyes. The power generator needs a bit more work before I can place it to power the pod. After that, I will start to crank out the work. By 5:00 p.m. D2 time, I clear space for all my SkipJack docking stations. I place the power generator which powers the pod and docking stations. I take the last forty-five minutes or so of light to set up the two remaining windbreaks from the lodgepole pines. It is not fancy, but it is keeping the wind off tonight. I can see the clouds in the north; they will sweep this way eventually. With everything buttoned up for the night, I retire. Tomorrow, I decide, I may straddle a tarp over the three windbreaks. I put a small table there and a chair. Sitting on the ground continually is a pain.

Over the next few weeks, I map out and mark the extremities of the mesh system. I clear the land as needed, which is me piloting the demolition SkipJack logging those five square kilometers of DMZ. I log for half the morning before piloting the demilled SkipJack to hook up the logs to choker cables from the Donners. I pilot the Donners to pull the logs to a staging area.

Logging on a large scale like this is quite a bit more work than I had anticipated. I am clearing this demarcation zone so that the mesh system has the most comprehensive coverage possible. I start methodically working from the Gate to each extremity in half-kilometer increments. I then trench power cable sections to each series of mesh stakes in line.

After those first weeks, I need a break. I decide that as soon as the mesh is wrapped up, I can start on the survey for a settlement location. I will also do some hunting as I go. The holes are complete, the trenches dug, and the fiber cable power cords laid. At this point, I am glad one of the demolition SkipJacks has an auger and a trencher attachment. The other has various replaceable tools. I start by placing all the poles in the trench, using their self-leveling feature to keep them standing straight. I drop expanding fiber cement in the holes, securing them in place. When power connects, the data trunk should be coming through shortly after.

I figure I am closely on target for my original mesh completion date. I have learned a great deal. It takes a ton of work to set these sites up. The mesh is in place, and the data trunk will come any day now. It is time for me to start the settlement survey in the morning. I am going to have to look at different spikes for future Gates. This version of spikes simply takes too much work. They are also semi-permanent.

***

C6 S3

I prep the rest of that night. Stowing most of the unneeded gear from the Donners, redistributing their weight, and getting my mobile camp gear ready. This is the part I have been dreading. Each of the Donners carries or tows a supply of mesh repeaters. I will need to string these along to keep piloting SkipJacks. I sight in my rifles and prep them for ease of access.

I begin Phase Two the next morning. Moving over two kilometers past the square mesh area, I start the search for a settlement zone. I send up my drone to seek a good aerial view. I do my best to overlap the zones and maps with EP1. The closest I could come was an area up by the Community of Lethbridge Montana West District of NAC. With that as my guide, I head south and find a reasonable spot.

I take the time to stake out its boundaries so that its northern border just touches the Southwest edge of the demarcation zone. This place has a river, wood, and plains nearby. It is as good as one can hope for in the five-kilometer limit. I spend those six weeks marking out plots and boundaries based on the initial settlement plans the Confederated Blackfoot Nation (CBN) has provided. I keep working on ways we can bring this timeframe down. I should not need to mark every single plot for the construction crews.

I chuckle at the name as I spike out their new community. The Compact does not allow the use of "nations" by the First Nation people. The NAC will not stand competition. Accordingly, all the First Nation peoples are tribes, according to Compact law. Also according to Compact law, the tenant of a D2 iteration may call it whatever they wish. The Confederated Blackfoot Tribes of the Compact Earth Prime purchased this D2 iteration and call it Confederated Blackfoot Nation Dimension Two (CBN:D2). It is an act of defiance that the NAC will grind its collective teeth over for decades.

There are a few elk and mule deer. I know that I will need the meat for the beginning phase of the balloon spike and release. I use the straight-pull rifle to take one of each. It is the better part of a day to skin, part out and hang the meat to age. After aging, I will spend another day or three salting it, turning it into strips, and smoking it. Then into one of my food panniers it goes. I supplement the more substantial game with smaller rabbits, squirrels, and grouse for my daily needs.

It is interesting, being the first human in this D2 iteration. Nothing has ever seen a human; the deer and elk are more intrigued than afraid. It does not necessarily make spotting them easier or finding where they are, but it is enjoyable. As the month comes to a close, I finish my settlement markers, denoting the individual lots and property lines as laid out by the settlement elders.

I move slowly back to my base camp, working as I go. I need a resupply and some time to let things air out. I need to clean up my gear and my Donners. I figure it would take me a week to repack everything for the long walk around the initial settlement, staking in markers and releasing all 314 minimal FEED, weather, mapping balloons. I like these spikes more, as they are self-cavitating pitons that easily drive into soft or hard ground. They tether the balloon until it reaches its full height. Once there, it merely cuts free and launches a second wind-powered charger. The original balloon and the base spike communicate wirelessly over the planet. Its data latency is terrible, but it gives real-time weather and mapping updates.

I return to find that no data trunk has come through the Gate yet. I do find bear tracks. This bruin has been in the main hard side shelter. It has made a mess of things, but nothing drastic. There is only a sleeping cot, stool, and flooring in there. It seems it was confused when it pushed in the flap, and the flap closed. Likely it tried to claw its way in and out. The bruin knocked the hard siding off the shelter trying to get out, finally ripping the self-closing flap open to make its escape.

I hang my dried meat in its pannier up in my food storage area, which looks like the bear's second home. His tracks are everywhere. This bear has put territorial scratches on the trees marking its territory. Of course, I piss all over the trees. I keep my 6.5 Swede with me and wait for it to return. I have a few days of laundry, packing, bathing, cooking, and rest due. I wait. I know a big guy like this is going to make his rounds. He will not stand idle to any newcomer in his area. In the mornings and evenings, I put myself up on top of a makeshift tree blind, one that gives me a good overview of my base camp. I have an even better view of my food hanging from trees 500 meters away from my hard side shelter.

Sure enough, old Griz comes through the third day. He smells me at the shelter. I can hear him chuffing all around it. He goes in the three lean-tos and back out again. He moves as if there is not a thing on this earth more capable than him. Individually, there likely is not much that could stand up to him. I almost feel sorry. I am not going to leave this bruin here for the new settlers to tackle as our Earth Prime has few predators such as he and I.

I watch and wait.

He settles at the base of a tree I peed on. I can see him sniffing and snorting that spot with his nose. He shakes his head and stands, reaching even higher than his last claw marks by a few inches and starts gouging out his territory.

The round hits him just behind the elbow, piercing through his ribcage, maybe about two inches above the sternum. It drives through a rib and left lung. By the time it has hit the heart and right lung, it has fully expanded. It exits the space between two rib bones, coming cleanly through the other side.

I hear the bruin's surprised grunt after the shot. He continues his territorial marking down the tree for a few more inches. The old guy returns to all fours and starts to wander off. There is not a spooked reaction, nor a response to dash off because of pain.

It is a clean kill. I watch the blood exit the lung area as he walks. The fifth step, he slumps. I cool my heels and watch him and the field for the next thirty minutes. I prep while waiting by powering up the demilled SkipJack to hook him up to a Donner. I tow him over to a large log I have placed at about twelve feet high across two trees. With the ropes already through the snatch blocks, I hoist him up and lash the line to the tree.

I release the Donner and put it and the demilled back on the docking station. Under the light of my HOLEDs, I get to work, skinning, dressing, deboning, and setting the cure salted meat aside for curing the next day. Dinner is old Griz loin. I season it with Alpine Touch, a spice combo I had come to love while living in Community Dillon. A Montana West District company, that is almost a couple of centuries old.

While smoking the bear the next day, the data trunk line comes through. I forward its data cables to the portable power system that links the data trunk to the mesh system. I am finishing shaving when the first Mag-lev carts come through the Gate. I hook up all four Donners and pull it to the pre-determined landing area before I set it on the ground.

***

C6 S4

The next morning, I pilot the three dozen SkipJacks out of their docking stations in the Mag-lev. I place the SkipJack docking stations in the now-designated SkipJack yard and hook them up to both the power and data.

I have always been told you cannot pilot a SkipJack through a Gate, as that is how David had ripped his mind from his body. It is possible I might have, but that does not mean I want to try doing so again. You also cannot deliver power of any magnitude through a Gate via a continuous form—for example, no power lines or power transmission cables.

Some special team Eliese uses discovered that you can pilot SkipJacks through a data trunk, which is somewhat of an outdated tech and not used often in EP1. While I set up a power in the D2, my EP1 team will deliver a data trunk and then provide a group of capable pilots in EP1 to do work in the D2.

Sure, they are limited in the space they can work, but they are here and ready to work. I hear the SkipJacks most of the night. The EP1 pilots think they are starting at 7:00 a.m., which is 3:00 p.m. my time.

I am up and on the trail the next morning. My Donners are packed. I have my gear. I suppose I could have told them about the eight-hour difference in a FEED message. The truth is, I am the only one here. There are thirty-six pilots on the other side working in three shifts for the next four to five months, at least. They have a job to do and so do I.

After putting a few miles behind me, I prepare to stop for the day. Using the Donners as a windbreak, I eat a late, bear steak breakfast on a beautiful open meadow. After a restful nap, I finish a couple more miles. I sleep well that night. I hear a few wolves just before morning in the distance. A pack seems to be testing the old bruin's boundaries.

The next day proves challenging. I must cross a marshy area. My 136-kilo body and the added weight on the Donners are not capable of crossing the area easily. I fly my drone all around the marsh, and the swamp is not a "let us walk through it" thing. It seems like this is a natural spring a couple of miles wide in either direction. The spring eventually becomes a creek, that leads to a stream and eventually connects with the other rivers near D2 Lethbridge.

After backtracking about a kilometer, I lay out markers from the drones' live video FEED on my HUD. Hopefully, they will keep me out of the swamp mess. I trek back towards the DMZ, then south to avoid the whole marsh area. It might allow me to hit the forty-kilometer radius and start my balloon spiking from there. I hike back about six kilometers and south four kilometers or so to the circumference point. I am once again at the eleven-kilometer point when I camp for the night. More bear steaks for dinner, and I add some dehydrated carrots, onions, potato, and celery for a vegetable stew base. That night, the wolves are a tiny bit closer.

My evenings are not unproductive. I have plans to make. With Stewart's eleven remaining Gates, I begin to parse out the needs and necessities of the next few choices. It is not quick. I have 428 kilometers of mesh spikes and balloon releases to do. Each of the next five possible D2 gates has its own issues. I incorporate changes to the problems I am facing here in each new plan.

I spent too much time putting in a permanent demarcation zone and settlement layout. Construction crews can do it faster. That needs to change. The solution could be to get the work crews in sooner and have them complete the work. Thirty-six SkipJack pilots can more effectively build this out in less time than I can. I ponder how to make these plans more efficient night after night.

I am using my FEED system to review options at my disposal. Suppose I can find some company to combine cavitating pitons and a mesh spike system. That would eliminate much of my time in the demarcation zone.

Every night, the wolves come a little closer. They must have caught wind of the food in my packs or crossed my trail. I wish I had brought the demilled SkipJack with its better night vision and thermal capabilities, but like a fool, I did not. There are nights I have to sit watch when I need the sleep. There is also the side effect of wolves chasing the game away. I have concerns, as my stock of dried, smoked, or preserved meat quickly diminishes under my severe appetite.

I am now south of where the city of Magrath would be in EP1. There are a series of valleys and coulees surrounded by woods. I have been lucky so far, in that I have been able to sleep in a meadow or at the top of a small knoll. If I am stuck in trees next to a river valley or the coulees, I am going to get torn to pieces. I fly the drone the next morning and find a set of small hills rising into a rocky formation. I pull some jerky and start laying my bait on to the ground.

I continue as much as I can on my walk, staking my balloon spikes until I must make the hard turn toward the rock outcropping. I pull the Donners to heel at the base, with one of the mostly empty food panniers open. I take my time laying out my sight lines, my markers for distance. When they come, they are just shadows in the waist-high grasses and flowers.

I am in love with this beautiful, custom rifle shooting the 6.5 Swede. Its glass is clear, and the ranging feature confirms my lasered distances. Soon, the last wolf crosses that 125-meter mark. I let the first of the wolves have it.

Starting from the back, the first goes down. I cycle the straight-pull bolt and drill one that is perpendicular to me. The third shot flies high over a moving wolf. My blood pressure is up, and I can feel my heart pounding. The fourth shot hits one as it is fleeing. I top off the fixed mag in the rifle. I can see the two remaining wolves hunkered down about six hundred meters out. I orientate the drone and my line of sight. I shoulder the rifle and look for the depressions in the grass. It takes me a while to realize they are in a little swale hidden from my view. I can wait.

Forty minutes later, they begin to move. I follow them in the swale using the drone. They are looking to swing a wide path to get to the Donner. With a thought, I drop down the HUD display on my left eye. I dump myself into a Donner and I use preset commands to remote pilot it.

The Donner rotates, sixty degrees to its right. It proceeds to walk 120 meters forward. The others are daisy-chained together. Lord, I am such an idiot. I wait. Nothing to do but wait. I put them in a spot where I have excellent coverage. Again, these wolves are canny and thoughtful. They sense the change in the Donners' position.

They rewind their way down the swale. I am about to curse them when I see them cross on to the hill, coming at the Donners from what would be an animal's blind spot. My first shot is a little rushed.

I take the trailing one in the spine behind the front shoulder, stopping its progress but not putting it down cleanly. I cycle the bolt and finish the wolf. The remaining one now has a hold of the SkipJack's throat area. It is hanging on, scrambling at the chest with its front and back claws. The Donner is doing its best to deal with the added eighty kilos attached to its ocular containment stem.

The Donner has six legs, each with broad padded toes. It does a fantastic job until it is pulled sideways by the shaking wolf, and the remaining three Donners plow right into it. It struggles to keep its footing. The last of the Donners hits the first and the hit pops it up onto only three feet on one side. The Donner falls to the ground, spilling food from the open pannier all over the ground. My shot hits the wolf in the ribs. It dies latched onto a meatless beast.

That is all six. I grab the rifle and head down. I lean the topped off rifle, barrel up, against rock while I deal with the Donner mess. Hours later, I have it sorted out. The damn wolf killed my Donner. His bite didn't, but the other three loaded Donners popping into its side destroyed two of the three shoulder actuators on the right side.

The fault is mine for not unhooking them from the daisy-chain. I have spent the last dregs of daylight hours getting my gear and foodstuffs from it. The three remaining Donners are now slightly overloaded, about thirty-five kilos each. I am not too concerned, as my load will become lighter each day. As of now, I am twenty percent of the way into the staking of the balloons in the territory. Already, my FEED has been picking up weather mapping info. That will become better as the number of balloons increases. I set up camp away from the downed Donner, and the wolf corpses.

That night I inspect the rifle while cleaning it. The 6.5x55 Swede is the firearm I have interacted with the most. As a young man in wilds of the Nunavut District, I had my father's Mauser in 6.5x55 Swede. It is what kept me fed from the ages of thirteen to seventeen. While examining it, I notice fine hairline cracks in the bolt upon cleaning, and everywhere I keep looking, I find those cracks. They spread pretty much on every metal surface. I oil the straight pull, stow it, and pull out the rimfire. It is a synthetic stocked model sixty and is tube fed, very much like another rifle I used when growing up alone. I keep it next to me, along with the 454c revolver. By my estimation, I have between thirty-five and forty days remaining if I make seven miles a day, doing seven drops each day, then a couple of days back to the dimensional Gate.

I realize I am well into the eighth month of being here. The weather has been changing considerably. I think I dropped at the end of February, D2 time. That puts me here in October. I do not want to be here dropping balloons and driving stakes in November or December. I have done enough wintering over in my teens.

If anything is to light a fire under my rear, it is that thought. I have let time slip by. I do not want to remain here in a remote area over winter. The idea of over wintering with one rifle down settles in, and a different type of fear hits my soul. When I wake the next morning, I have a new resolve. Cut, chop and stack.

I drive, stake, let loose the balloons, and walk on. Even so, over the next fifteen days, I manage seven miles a day. Blazing a path in virgin terrain sucks. It is hard. My weight does not help, nor does keeping to a more or less circular route. Even in the prairie grass, I pound deep depressions into the ground with every step.

I take some time as the first skiffs of snow fall at this elevation to put my packs into the Donners' panniers. I go as light as I can. I stow the rimfire. The bolt shatters one morning when I try to take a shot at a second prairie chicken, a Sharp-tail Grouse. I choose to carry only the handgun. The weight of the carbine will slow me down. Since the wolves, I have had zero issues with predators.

***

C6 S5

Days later, I ford a stream early in the afternoon. That means drying and cleaning my revolver. It is laced with hairline cracks, also. There must be some sort of defect engineered into civilian arms. I am already down both my knives, as they have chipped away over these many months. It would not surprise me in the least if the NAC government mandates that.

I stow my pistol and sling my carbine for the last three days of staking and ballooning. I move off my radial hike as the final balloon connects to the mesh system. It takes me two days to return to the DMZ. I return to find initial construction crews, and settlers. I had heard the 3D blockhouse printers pumping out new lodgings a day and a half back. As I walk in, the three Donners following me, I attract as large a crowd as a new D2 settlement could provide.

The Elder in charge, Daniel Standing Elk, introduces himself. We stand eye to eye, though he carries quite a bit more muscle mass on him. I am a leaner-looking man, not a lighter man. I think Daniel is itching to ask me, as most lower nations people want to do.

I head off his unasked question and say, "Name's Ray. My mother was from Nunavut territory. My father was from around Tok, old Alaska." I pull my goggles off, shaking out my platted black hair. "I just wrapped up the last of the survey two days ago. It has been a long nine months. I would kill for a shower. Tell me you have a shower," I say a bit wearily.

Daniel smiles warmly and responds, "Another Cannuk, eh? Ya, we got a shower. Say, was it you who took down that brown bear?"

I chuckle and say, "Point me at that shower, my friend. I need it, and I have about a day's worth of packing up to do, then I have to move on." I do not want them to know I am going to Gate walk. They will do everything they can to stop me. "And Bruiser there? The old Griz? The one I tanned and left in the hard shelter? Yeah, I was the only one here," I reply in good humor.

Daniel seems to warm to me a bit more. "Look, the showers are just next to your old hard shelter. The shelter, well, it's kinda the changing room now for the showers." He states, "Don't worry, though, I got a place for you tonight. And, Bruiser, is that what you called him? Well, we cared for him. We'll make sure he gets returned."

I smile as I looked at Daniel. "Bruiser needs to stay here. We took the land from him; let us not take him from it." I walk towards the portable SkipJack docking bays. "Let me get the Donners put up and showered, and then we can talk."

I shower, dry, wash my clothes, and generally clean my gear. I pull some of my stored clothes from Donner, sniff them, and shrug into them. I see Daniel and four others waiting. They must be the acting leadership council of the current settlement: three women and two men. They are hosting a dinner for me. I tell them of the food in the panniers and one of them FEED messages someone to retrieve it. The walk is five kilometers to the Nation's hall. The main hall is pretty much where everyone is staying until the utilities are completed and set up. They have a second and third power generator and mesh system running. Men in pods are working, prepping, clearing, digging, and finishing 3D-printed buildings. Dinner starts at 8:00 p.m. D2 time. I can see six men working on ladders to attach Bruiser to the wall behind the council seats.

Dinner, conversation, chairs, utensils...hell, I have been eating out of a single cracked and leaking pot for almost nine months. It is something to handle. It takes a great deal of effort to try and drown out the noise. The chatter of other people is fantastic to hear and terrifyingly loud. All that aside, I am happy to see them start a colony.

Daniel introduces me to the owner and foreman of the logging company, then presents the person who would be collecting grasses, turf, trees, and all the flora that EP1 has lost in this region. The business of propagating those plants

153

to send back for reintroduction is new. I am not sure that endeavor will be as successful as she hopes. I cannot fault her for trying, and the trying still needs to happen.

I sit across from Daniel at the cafeteria-style tables. I tell the story of Bruiser, of the wolves, and how one had taken down my primary Donner. I also explain to them where to find the wolves and broken Donner. I thumb my maps, data points, points of interest, geological stakes, and balloon release points to him. He promptly sends it on to the elders.

Daniel then inquires about the Donners. I explain about needing the wider feet in winter snow, and their carrying and pulling capabilities. After a quick consult, the five elders add the two worn-out ones to the survey contract. He is taking them off my hands. They have a small SkipJack repair bay. I am confident any half-competent repair bay staff can get the work done. I would be leaving with just the one and my other SkipJacks.

It is loud at night. There are ninety people in the building, with segregated family sleeping areas, single male, single female. I exit after the first ten minutes of mumbled whispers and snoring. I spend the rest of the night in my tree blind with the quiet. I am packed up and ready by the time everyone has headed in for a communal lunch the following day.

Daniel walks up next to me. "Where are you surveying next, Ray?" he inquires. I think he knows it will not be in this D2. I watch his eyes and his body language; in the end, I take that leap of faith.

"There is a fishing conglomerate that wants a port in the Northeast District. The Gate comes out at the historic New Haven area. I am heading out today. I will have a few days downtime, then a refit, and work up in the Northeast District EP1."

I look at Daniel as he takes it in stride. "They have a similar system they want to put in place about re-introducing extinct or endangered fish into EP1 fisheries, which is also a good market product right now. Fish prices and seafood, in general, are very high. It seems like a logical choice for my second Gate." I say with a smile, "I'm a Company man now, Daniel. I go where the work is."

Daniel replies, "So it was you who picked this as the first test? What if you can't go back?" A serious tone resonates in his question.

I look at the big sky country, the bright blue clear sky that only an impending winter can bring.

"Yeah, I picked this Gate. I was given twelve possible Gates. CBN is the first. I chose this to help the local economy after the Dillon Gate Montana West D2 collapsed. It also helps a Nation. It helps reforest a Compact. That is enough, I think," I say. I turn back to look at Daniel.

He is staring intently at me, looking for a lie.

"I'm not worried about walking the Gate, Daniel. I have already been through the Dillon gate and back before I walked through the CBN: D2 Gate," I explain.

I pull my goggles on, drop both SkipJack lenses, pull them all to heel and set to follow as I start walking forward. Before I hit the Gate, I raise the dropdown lenses and disconnect from piloting. I can walk Gates, but I still did not want to try and pilot through one.

I step through the Gate into more fucking snow. There is well over a meter of it here in EP1. The heat from the D2 side has bled over to the EP1 side again.

I stand in a small circular patch of wet demarcation concrete. Outside of this small fifteen-meter area is a meter of hardpacked snow and a meter of fresh powder. Geez, this EP1 world sucks. I drop the left lens, daisy-chain the Donner and construction jacks, and have them bust me a route to the security shed. It is five hours till the snowstorm lifts and the tram that has been waiting for me can take off. I stow and square everything away. I fall asleep in the webbed chair and do not wake till we land at the cabin.

I unlock all the SkipJacks and pilot them to the docking stations in the barn. I pull the hard-sided gun cases and head to the cabin. I am emotionally and physically beat. That webbed seat is hell on a myomere back.

Chapter 7 Thap! The wedding

C7 S1

I trudge up the hill to my little cabin. I have three cumbersome hard-sided gun cases banging against my thigh containing the two destroyed rifles, the carbine, one small pistol case containing the inoperable Bowen 454C, and what is left of my knives. I need to have a safe installed in the workshop down by the Tram landing area.

It has been a long tram ride back to the Virginia District. I rested a little, but I am mentally and physically beat. My shower and bed are calling my name. It is well into the evening, maybe 9:00 p.m. or later as I make it up the log-lined steps of my cabin. I would look at the time via my FEED, but I would have to juggle cases. Right now, it is bedtime. I need a shower, and a long night's sleep.

I struggle with the door handle, kick it open with my left heel, and back through, trying not to get stuck in the doorway with the cases. I let out a little expletive about having to carry these cases. NAC rules and regulations on firearms are clear, and utterly stupid.

I hear my siren sing from behind me as the scent of her perfume hits my nose. The hair on my arm rises in response to my senses picking up Eliese being in the same house as me. Pain and weariness fade, starting in my addled mind. I cannot figure out what I like more, the voice or the scent.

I hear her song, my siren's voice, as Eliese says, "Would you like some help, Ray?"

Both, I decide. I love the scent and Eliese's voice. She quickly moves past me and shuts the door. I move to the corner and put the gun cases down. It is not as if anyone can open them, as the hard side cases are specific to my biometric FEED system. Even if they could, well, the weapons are all inoperable now.

Stepping back and standing straight, I turn to see Eliese: Wow, just wow, black hair, black jacket, white blouse, black slacks. Just gorgeous. That is when the smell of the food hits me. Her family's crested table is laid out for our dinner. The carts are to the side, aroma driven back by her close presence to me.

"What, no Brunswick stew?" I ask with a grin. My stomach receives a treacherous signal of food from the nose and lets loose an avalanche of a rumble. I guess more than eighteen hours in a tram will do that to you. My nose catches another scent: wood smoke, stale breath, sweaty, half-washed clothes. I am rancid. I say, "Shower?"

With a twinkle, Eliese replies, "I am not barefoot, so no to tree rat soup." She wiggles her foot on the heel of her shoe to show it off. With a feigned plugging of her nose and a wave of her hand, she adds, "Please burn the clothes."

I am considering it. These clothes are the very best of what I had left after nine months. The haptic suit is threadbare and encrusted with dirt. The boots are long since toast, with holes in the heels, toes, and sides. Myomere feet eat through socks and boots. Burning it all is a solid yes.

I laugh on my way to the shower. I pull some fresh clothes out of the closet cubby. Sliding the bathroom door closed, I use clippers to remove the bulk of the nine-month-old patchwork of a beard, finishing the shave in the shower. I ended up using a scrubby pad to wash in the shower. The grime is that pronounced. Nine months of sponge baths and cold-water swims just does not cut it. Even the shower at the demarcation zone had been cold water and perfunctory.

I brush and floss my teeth, something I was able to do every day in D2. I dress in a long-sleeved shirt, cargo pants, socks, and my workout shoes. I am nowhere near as classy as Eliese, but I think she knows that. I also think she does not care.

I hear soft music from the office's FEED terminal. It is November now, so the classic holiday music is playing. I like it: the tunes are light, with no expectations. I had a lot of time to think while walking in the D2. I am going to go slow. I have a life doing what I could only dream of doing. I do not want to go back to piloting security SkipJacks, nor do I want to complicate this life with a soured relationship. I like Eliese, but for now, this will do.

I exit the bedroom to see her sitting cross-legged on the futon, waiting with a glass of wine and my blanket for warmth. She stands as I enter, walks over to the table, retrieves my drink, and hands it to me. She moves as if possessed of Aphrodite herself. Feminity, power and grace.

I reach my glass out for a toast and declare, "Happy Holiday season, here's to a great November, a wonderful evening, and a successful settlement start."

Her face only shows the briefest puzzlement before she replies, "It's September, and the music is what the holiday tunes are originally from." She smiles. "It happens to be my excuse for playing it year-round. I like it." The smile deepens to her eyes. "Let's sit, Ray, get some food, eat a bit. I heard your stomach earlier."

I pick up a bowl and lift the lids. I find the soup, some sort of Asian dish—Eliese later tells me it is Thom Ka Gai. I make four bowls vanish into thin air. That sates me enough to talk, as I dish a fourth helping of everything else.

I puzzle the question forward in my mind and ask, "September? I was in D2 for nine months."

Eliese smiles, takes a breath, and dives into the explanation. "There was a time-slip while you were in D2. It would have been about six days after you entered. The slip ran for about eight days. D2 moved two months ahead over those eight and a half days. I...we caught it." she says with a soft smile.

Eliese lets that sink in, then continues. "It took us a couple of hours to figure out the 'ratio slip,' which is what we're calling it, and eight days to double and triple-check daily. Then in half a day, we brought it back to parity. By that time, well, you were well into getting things done."

I take the time to ponder that as I continue to nibble on food. "The data trunk did not arrive on time." Realizing the "ratio slip" was the reason, I continue, "What might have caused it? I spent a few years watching and monitoring the temporal locks. They are pretty foolproof."

"A directed malware attack on the Gate's power fluctuation systems. For example, the software that keeps the temporal lock steady. The change was not drastic. It was a directed attack, though. I think whoever attacked the site thought it would be slight enough that we would not notice," Eliese says. With a small sip of wine, she adds, "After DGMW: D2 was lost, we looked over everything, and I mean everything. That is why we dismantled it. We took it apart and reviewed every function. There is no way that lightning should have made the Gate lose lock, let alone temporal lock. It should never have reached the Gate. There were over forty systems in place to redirect lightning strikes, Ray. FORTY!"

Eliese's left hand holds four fingers up, and her eyes are bright and clear. I bet she has been working at the edges of this problem since the malware attack on Confederated Blackfoot Nation's (CBN) Gate. She sets her glass of wine down and rests her hands in her lap.

"We increased the capabilities of the whole Gate system's backend. We can now monitor a Gate's temporal ratio slip down to one day on the D2 end. Before, it might be as much as a three-week disparity when examined. If the person just went by the Gate's temporal lock icons—blue, red, green, and not the software in the office—the temporal slip ratio could be as much as three years for an uninhabited D2 iteration," Eliese says.

With a series of taps, she brings up FEED displays to show me the info she is relaying. "For some reason, once there's a person in a D2, it becomes much more stable, ratio slip-wise. It can still be affected, but not as easily."

I let that sink in as she eats a bit of a noodle dish that she calls farmer's noodles. While I plate up seconds, I ask, "Was there temporal slip on DGMW:D2?" I continue with, "Do we know who tampered with the CBN: EP1 Gate?"

Her expression becomes serious. "No, and no. DGMW: D2 confuses us. CBT: EP1 Gate...well, we're looking into it. We did a five-month review on all lines of attacks via the Gate systems. We've hardened them with recommendations from external experts, then tried to secure them more with our own internal mechanisms. We can't plan for everything. We do think we've closed off the remote temporal slip and crashing of all the Gates' power regulation systems."

She leans back. "The Family has added a series of redundancy protocols and initiated them across all our future Gates. We can't promise it won't happen again, but we do think we've made it exceedingly difficult to repeat. Since you were tangentially involved in both Gates, we've started with the next Gate system. After that, it's an upgrade to our older Gates first." Eliese reaches for her glass and sips.

I take my time; that is a lot to take in. It seems like the Family has that end pegged down as far as one could. Our adversaries are not going to give up on the malware attack. As that is not anything I can control, I will leave it to Eliese and her people.

I muse out loud, "Is it possible to control the ratio slip?" I am not quite sure where I am going with this train of thought. I drum my fingers on my leg. "I mean, that worked out pretty well by knocking two months off my EP1 timeline. If we can control the slip, we could minimize the EP1 time it takes for the Family to start a settlement."

Eliese raises an eyebrow. With a lilt in her voice that I am beginning to recognize as excitement, she says, "Now *that* is an interesting thought. We have an issue, though. One of the new pieces of kit we put together, based on the reports you sent, is a Mag-lev Roller (MLR), and the Donners are required to pull it. You drag one to each edge of the five-kilometer DMZ."

She takes a breath. "Basically, you unfold the sides and the back. Next, you plug in a one-kilometer mesh stake system and then connect it into the data trunk. The sides are the SkipJack bays, and the back is the remote power source. Once connected, EP1 pods will pilot the SkipJacks in the temp mesh clearing and set up the permanent mesh network.

"They expand on their own. It should take just over fifteen days for them to build out the five-kilometer demarcation zone, and another seven or eight to clear and spike up the settlement spot you pick. There will only be thirty-six, eighteen in each MLR. It will cut your initial set-up by almost a full three months. We have a hard limit on SkipJack pilots. We can do thirty-six SkipJacks and two 3D printers on a single data trunk line. Each 3D printer is about a full sixteen Skipjacks' worth of data on the trunk. We would need to push through a second trunk for more pilots. Right now, the cost factor for that is too high."

I smile, as that is good news. My least favorite part about this job was SkipJack logging and clearing, closely followed by setting up the mesh network. I ran over by almost a month on both. To say it is tedious is not enough.

While ruminating this plan together, I say, "I have been thinking about that. That part of the survey was certainly my least favorite. What I am getting at is we need the mapping and weather monitoring first. There were days where work was not possible because of the lack of that information. I am planning on recommending that we complete the staking and balloons just after setting up base camp.

"If I do that, I can use the updates and mapping data to pick a more suitable settlement location. It will beat using the drone," I say. "Once I have the mapping data, I can return, set up the demarcation zone, and get them rolling, then finish any projects that are needed, and Gate walk.

"As to the Gate walk, I would like to be the only one in the D2 iteration. I do not want to be seen Gate-walking by people, even by accident." I smile. "I have given this a great deal of thought. Only one person saw me leave last time. I did not have the impression he would tell anyone. Suppose there were a bunch of guys piloting SkipJacks when I walked. Who knows what they would say?" I ask. "I am not sure I want that kind of attention so soon after DGMW's failure."

I look to Eliese. Her lips are pursed, and she is looking intently at her FEED display.

Eliese clucks with her tongue before she says, "We are contractually obligated to allow them in to start work just after you set up the temp mesh." She looks at me and smiles, and after giving it some thought, she says, "I like your idea; the concerns are valid. I'll be more mindful of this during the next contract negotiation. What I can do now, though..." She trails off in thought as the FEED keeps scrolling and moves about with a wave of her manicured fingers. "I can put them on a preventative maintenance upgrade to the Gate just after you walk the Gate. That will only cover about half the time allotted for the spiking and balloons. You would have to return in time to set up the MLRs by..." She breaks off again.

Evidently, she is working out the possibilities of this as she sips wine. "Is a three-day window enough for you to clear the demarcation zone once you set up the MLRs?" she asks.

Before I can answer, Eliese pops to her feet. She steps from the table while using her FEED system and starts pacing the room. Obviously in deep thought, I can hear her talking to herself. "What am I thinking? If we ratio slip after you Gate walk in, it doesn't matter. I can ratio slip you till you've finished the balloons. Then you'll have enough data to stake out the settlement. We'll slip the trunk in at the same time you enter the D2."

Eliese pauses to turn to me with a raised eyebrow, checking to see if I am following along. When I nod, Eliese says, "When you're back at base, you can FEED message and we'll lower the ratio slip. There will be a delay in our messages getting to you, but yours should come through in a timely manner. Though I still have only about forty-three EP1 days after you walk to work with."

Eliese is fantastic to watch as she tackles a multifaceted puzzle like this. She chips away at the edges of the problem until only the solution remains.

I sit there watching, eating as she works her end of the issue. I have said it before: do not bother intelligent people when they are working. I hand her a glass of the second bottle as she paces from the entry door between the setup table and food trolleys to the full row of windows overlooking the valley. A couple of passes later, I collect her high heels from her as she walks by. It is a good thirty minutes before she has it all sorted and organized.

"There, it's workable. We'll have to shift some of your SkipJacks so you can initially carry more. Four Donner SkipJacks won't cut it. We made some improvements to the Donners V1s while you were in D2. They're about eight percent lighter overall, but they still have the same tow and carry capacity. The panniers are better suited to their shape while being designed for your specific mesh spike design," Eliese says, while still pacing back and forth.

As she passes my seat at the table, she stops to blow me a kiss and keeps walking, still using her FEED system, working on another portion of the plan. She makes it to the door and gasps. She sets her glass on the counter by the two-burner stove and puts her hands over her face.

"Did I just blow you a kiss?" Eliese asks in a very soft, embarrassed voice.

I want to laugh, but right now is not the time. Without humor, I reply, "Yep, you can go back to working it out now."

Eliese lowers her head, shakes it in her hands. She throws her hair back as she straightens, opens the FEED back up, grabs the glass and continues. I work with her on the process of adjusting things, scrapping some supplies, and changing gear. It takes us hours of planning and confirmation to nail down the best set-up for this next Gate. The only real thing I put my foot down on is the firearms.

I pull out the guns from the cases and show her the damage. She adds weapons to her research plans. Over the next couple of hours, we cut a lot of dead weight out of the panniers and my packs. We remove many of the casual clothes and add more socks, boots, and haptic suits. Less repair gear for the SkipJacks or shelters. I will just drop a Donner over repairing all but the most basic of problems. I will build a shelter, if necessary. During the summer, my sanctuary was most often a rainfly tied to the Donners.

It is 3:00 a.m. before we take a break from planning. Eliese is back on the futon, and I am reclining across from her in two of the chairs brought by the livery staff. We are chattering away. I tell the story of the wolves and of Bruiser the Bruin. I mention Daniel Standing Elk and the elder council. I express how optimistic everyone was and the kind of energy they seemed to have in CBN.

Eliese tells about her side projects. She is making my stay in D2 more efficient and more comfortable. She says she has a gift for me. She hops up, pads over to the counter, and brings back a box from behind the counter that I somehow failed to notice.

Okay, Eliese is a commanding and demanding presence in a room. Your mind, your eyes, and your attention gravitate to her. I decide to give myself some slack. She skips over and drops the box lightly into my lap. I look up at her, and she starts tapping the floor with a stockinged foot. The heels were the first thing to go while pacing and working. "Well? Open it, Ray!" She is very exuberant in her request.

She is beaming with energy over this. It is in the same style of container that Samuel had given to me. I pop the lid and pull it off. I tilt the box to my face and look at it quizzically. Mini snowshoes? No, that is not quite right, not enough. Marsh shoes! How did she know?

"How did you know?" I ask with a puzzled grin.

"We pulled the data logs once enough of the balloons were up. We saw you had hit some sort of barrier. We matched the area to a historical account of a marsh around Lethbridge. It was pretty much the first thing that was drained by farmers. We knew that the Donners could not make that, or you. So, we started two projects: Donner lightening and you. Peter Alvarez shot down my idea about putting you on a diet. You clomp around like a horse. You know that, right?"

I stifle a laugh. I want to get a word in edge-wise, but Eliese is too excited and happy for me to break her train of thought.

"We came up with those marsh shoes, a titanium-myomere blend. It should attach to just about any boot you have. So what do you think?" she asks as she waves gracefully at the shoes.

Now is the time for payback, so I blow Eliese a kiss. Eliese turns fire-engine red. Hands to her face, she slides back to the futon and, with a bit of laughter, says, "You're horrible Ray!" She giggles. It is not like the snort-laugh of Trish. I love this laugh for Eliese.

I say, "Thank you, Eliese. These mean a lot. I see that you took the time to understand what I was doing and how best to help me. That, I appreciate." When I look up from my marsh shoes, I continue just as the sun tops the horizon, and the windows auto-lighten to let the morning light through the glass. "I do not know how to express that enough. Seeing you here tonight, this morning, it, well, it has been the best night of my life." I pause. "Blown kiss aside, I am still working through a lot, Eliese. I think there could be something...an *us*. The kiss...well, that made those nine months, or seven, worth it. Thank you for that, and the marsh shoes."

Eliese's face is hidden in her hands. She peeks out between her fingers, gasps, and turns fully to the windows. "Shit, I call the first shower." She is gone before I can object. I get up as the door slides shut to the bathroom. I turn to the cubby of a closet and pull a towel. I knock on the slider, and it slides open, out comes a pile of stinky clothes with the comment, "Burn them." The bath towel disappears and the door closes.

I take the clothes down to the workout room and dump them in my hamper down there. I have mended my clothes since I was thirteen, and I will repair these also. I start my workout for twenty, then thirty, then forty minutes total, before

I hear the water turn off upstairs. I give her ten more minutes to get ready for the day. I should have given her twenty after that. She exits the bathroom a good while later.

Eliese is putting earrings on and holding her shoes in one hand. "Your turn," she says as she switches ears. "You have an appointment with Alvarez in two hours, an appointment with Father at the house at 3:00 p.m., then Family dinner at 7:00 p.m. Capital 'F' Family dinner. Just the Family, Ray."

Eliese pauses at the door, then turns to me and takes a deep breath. "It was the best night I've had in a very long time, Ray. I like this. I don't know if I can do more. This," she says, and she gestures at us with a wave of shoes, "is good for me, and you're officially my first, second date in fifteen years."

She winks, blows me another kiss that sends me and my sun-darkened olive skin fire-engine red. By the time my heart makes it back down from orbit, Eliese is gone, taking my tram. Good luck with that jump seat, Eliese.

I hit the shower as I am short on time.

***

C7 S2

Dr. Alverez is in good humor this morning. I am more flexible and showing better coordination than when I had left. My tests have all gone well. I am still five feet ten inches, but now weigh a whopping 145 kilos. Alverez speaks up when I look at the scale. "Your myomere is growing, so to speak. Your myomere system will require plenty of minerals to reach maturity. That's why you have such a massive appetite. You did quite well in your nine months of our eating regimen. I'm betting that has a lot to do with the wild game you focused on," he says in his Doctor's voice.

I suspect that he is pausing for me, so I reiterate the bulk of what I had taken and eaten. I am amazed at my recollection. I bring up that his prepackaged supplies ran out just at the last week.

Dr. Alvares nods, opens his FEED terminal next to him, and says, "Well, Ray, I wish all my patients listened as well as you do. I am going to change things up a bit for this next trip: more focus on trace minerals and general nutrition over variety. You seem to be willing to eat just about anything without complaint."

I laugh. "After taking down camp, walking seven miles through forest, back-tracking, spiking balloons, and setting up camp, one-pot meals are about all I care to make."

"Okay, then," Dr Alvarez says, and turns back to me with a soft smile. "Let's talk about this temporal slip, or the ratio slip, as Eliese likes to call it. I have my opinions based on your tests, but I don't want to share them till I have yours."

"At first, it felt like I was being torn apart. It was agony," I say, keeping my expression straight.

"Horseshit," the Doctor says, laughing.

I chuckle and say, "I had not a damn clue till I got back." I look him in the eyes. "Seriously, Dr. Alvarez. I noticed nothing going through the Gate. One instant you are in EP1 and standing in sixty centimeters of snow, with blowing winds of over thirty kilometers per hour, and then I was in forty-five centimeters of snow with completely different topography, and it was almost four degrees warmer, with sun and no wind.

"However, it was eight hours later than when I left EP1. I arrived at D2 around threeish p.m. No feeling, no change." I pause, pulling up the memories of Gating out. "I left Daniel Standing Elk next to the base camp, pulled the SkipJacks to heel, connected them via the daisy chain and disconnected from piloting. I left at twelveish, on an eighteen degree Celsius clear, Indian summer day. I stepped into more than a meter of snow, nearly fifty kilometer-per-hour winds, and had to daisy-chain the SkipJacks together to punch a hole through the snow to the security shed.

"It had to be 4:00 p.m. EP1 time when I Gate walked back, so there is a bit of time advancement because of the ratio slip. The snow kept us locked down for the better part of five hours. It took a few hours to get everything stowed in the tram. When the tram took off, weather patterns put us in an eighteen-hour flight path. I was bushed from being in the snow and stowing things in the tram.

We had a three-plus hour layover because of that same storm. I sat in that tram as it charged till we lifted off back to the cabin. I want to say that I slept on the return tram, but I would be lying. I had very little chance to rest. The whole tram flight back was a mess."

I pause, holding a finger up. I very carefully ask, "If we could control the ratio slip, would you oppose that?"

Dr. Alvarez sits back, looking at me intently. "If you provide me the documentation, testing, and retesting multiple times, I can see giving it a chance on this next one. Any ambiguity or fudging the numbers, and I'll put an end to it. You are far too valuable to the Family now, and there's no use putting you in harm's way," he says while giving me an even penetrating stare.

I wave that off and say, "Eliese is handling that." I sigh as he pulls out a pair of glasses and his old bottle of whiskey from his cabinet.

"Honestly, Doc, wait? Is it even noon?" I ask as I pull up the time on my FEED. Sure enough, it is noon. We clink glasses and begin talking about nine months away from people and how that time away affects me.

"Fundamentally, Doc, I do not care. I have work to do during the days. In the first few months, I reviewed and planned the next few gates. I study the equipment that I can make use of and other things outside what the Family provides through its corporate holdings. I then started reading and listening to audiobooks. I felt like I had contact," I say.

I pause and explain, "I am...well, I have been alone for long stretches before, Doc. Nine months is nothing compared to three years and 267 days." I have no idea how I pick that number. I think about it and I believe that number correct. With a bit of astonishingly quick math, I figure out that I am correct to within three to four days either way.

Doctor Alvarez looks at me funny and asks, "What do you mean?"

I spend the next hour explaining how I grew up.

Dr. Alvarez frowns, his bushy eyebrows furrow, and he asks, "Your parents...what were their names?"

"I only know their first names. Joshua and Susan," I say.

His face goes still for a moment, and he takes a long slow swallow from his dram of whiskey.

167

"Did you know them?" I ask.

"I don't believe so," Dr. Alvarez says. "Names and faces are hard for me to match. I don't think I know of anyone by those names."

A liveryman knocks on the office door. He is here to collect me and to take me to the Family estate. I finish my whisky and say my goodbyes.

***

C7 S3

The tram sets down on a broader landing pad than when I was here with Samuel. A small shallow MLR connects and tows the tram into a hangar facility. The livery agent directs me to the door at the side of the hangar. There are nine personal trams. Not the utility trams you see all over the Compact, but personal ones.

In the Compact, where personal ownership of property is nearly unheard of, the display of nine trams for personal use is a statement of wealth and position. As we walk by, I notice the registration tags on the side start with JFC. That explains it, then; these are the property of Jankowitz Family Corporation.

The costs to build the hangar, maintenance of those trams, let alone the expense of those trams, boggles my mind. The money I have toyed with over the last nine months is like nothing else I have ever experienced. When Eliese shared the expense report of my survey, I found out that one Donner I abandoned after the wolves attacked was well over 200,000 credits. My pay as a security guard was 30,000 credits a year.

The liveryman and I walk down a series of hallways. We pass offices, cubicles, and staff as we go. I ask, "Surely we are getting close?"

The livery agent replies, "Sir, this is just the staff area for running the Residence complex. We will be entering the corporate building for the Jankowitz Group offices before our final destination: the Family's residences."

We pop out of the building, cross a courtyard about fifty meters wide, and enter another hallway. A moment later, we start to pass a gym on the left side. It is glass-walled, equipped with a bunch of workout hardware, a boxing ring, free weights, and everything a workout room should have.

Darien is practicing his punches with what looks like his guard. One-two, one-two, one-two-three-four. He pauses, catching us in his peripheral vision. No, not us—he catches me out of the corner of his eye as we walk by. He deftly jumps the ropes and meets us at the other door to the workout room.

"You may go, agent," Darien says, turning to me as the liveryman exits through the door. "So, mongrel, back for more scraps? Don't look surprised. I never forget a face. Let me guess. You ran out of money from whatever you pawned?"

Darien steps closer. He is slightly taller than me. Darien is not as intimidating as he thinks himself to be. He glares at me, as only a bully would. He pushes forward, bumping his chest against mine, but he finds more unconcerned resistance there than he expects.

Darien's voice rumbles. "Sammy's not going to..."

"Darien, back off!" Samuel shouts.

His voice rings loud and clear in the long hallway. I have heard Sam speak in that voice many times before. It is a voice that comes with being in command of the lives of men. The statement bounces off the glass walls, leaving it oddly clipped. I sidestep Darien. I turn to see Eliese and Samuel with their guards. As I look at Eliese, a tiny flicker of Eliese's finger releases my tension.

Samuel is already halfway to Darien, just as tall, immensely more imposing. In his voice rings with every drop of sweat, every tear, every milliliter of blood he has ever given in the service of the Compact Military. His nose taps Darien's until Sam has Darien back up against the wall.

With the simple phrase of "never again," Samuel conveys the truth in two small words. Never challenge me, never call him Sammy, never try to bully anyone in this house again.

Darien's back is against the glass and is just a hair slow.

"Sammy, you don't have it, postal clerk," Darien says mockingly in a vain attempt at condescension.

Samuel just puts his left arm on Darien's chest and pushes. Not hard, not a punch, but a show of force.

"You are always such an idiot, Darien," Samuel says.

Darien's breath starts to escape him. Darien realizes there is enough pressure to prevent him from pulling fresh air into his lungs.

"You know that 0161 MOS that Franc always turns into a joke? Did you, in your infinite wisdom, ever look it up? No?" Samuel asks.

Darien's face is turning tomato red. I watch his guard frantically trying to take off the sparring pads.

Samuel is on a tear as he growls, "Let me give you a hint, you simp. You know Ray is a remote SkipJack pilot. Did you ever look up the MOS for a fucking remote combat SkipJack pilot in the Compact Military? No? Let me impart a little bit of knowledge into your thick head. It is 0161. Postal Clerk is an inside joke."

I watch Sam, my brother of blood and mud, the Force Recon trooper Sam releases the pressure as Darien's face starts to turn purple.

"The old NAC Marine Corps commander, who started the SkipJack Program for militaries around the world, has a sense of humor. That is where 0161 came from, you little shit," Sam says. Samuel releases him fully as Darien's guard steps between them. "Back the fuck off, my brother," is Sam's final command.

It is over. Samuel's guard steps forward. Darien's guard turns to cover him as he gasps for air. I follow Samuel. Within seconds, the five of us are heading through the halls and corporate offices to Eliese's office. Not a word is said.

***

C7 S4

Samuel turns to Eliese and, with masterful control of his voice, says, "I have a little prep to do yet. Sorry for holding you up." He turns and goes back down the hall, his own guard, a Segundo, as Samuel had called them, following. I look at Eliese. She smiles, takes a deep breath, and walks us in.

"Sorry, Mr. Jankowitz, Samuel was held up for a moment. We apologize for the delay," she says as she straightens her dress. "Would Mr. Ray like anything? Mr. Jankowitz?"

I feel a little bit dry-mouthed after the whiskey and altercation. I reply, "Water, if you please. It has been a busy morning." With a nod from her and a "the same," from her father, Eliese glides to a corner wood-covered cabinet and pulls out two bottles of cold water. Returning, she opens both, places them before us on Stewart's desk, coasters and all. Then she sits in the chair to my left, pops her FEED up and nods to her father.

"Ray, I want to thank you for taking the risk of walking a Gate again. I know that can't have been an easy thing to do. It takes a unique kind of valor to engage a project such as that."

I look Stewart Jr. in the eye as I nod. When someone compliments you for a job done, shut your yapper and nod. Honestly, I had not given walking the Gate a second thought. I knew and understood in every fiber of my being it was possible for me, as I had already done it.

Stewart continues, "You single-handedly shaved nine years off the first stage of that project. If you are willing to do this again and manage these openings in the same fashion and vigor that you have displayed so far, we have a place at the Family table for you." I notice Eliese's head snap up in shock; her eyebrow lifts for a second before settling back down into her secretary's mask. "Let's talk over this Gate walk, and then you can think over the offer." He thumbs the offer message to my personal FEED.

As we discuss and evaluate my recent survey of CBN:D2, I begin to thank the heavens for Eliese showing up with dinner last night. Had we not talked it through till late in the morning, that discussion prepared me for this interview. Or is it a meeting? I am unsure if or what my place is here in the Family Corporate structure. I thought I was going to work with Samuel, but I have only corresponded with Eliese.

Eliese is my Siren, certainly. I would have looked like a bumbling idiot without her help. She chimes in with stats and costs, and the first numbers on propagating rare plant life to be sent over from the CBN:D2's greenhouses. CBN is setting up logging camps and portable lumber facilities, and will be expecting shipments to begin in earnest next spring after the lumber is kiln-dried.

Stewart asks, "Will you be willing to take on the next Gate project?"

"I have a pretty good schedule lined out. With the new MLRs and Donner V2s, we can cut the time considerably, to be sure," I say, bringing up what Eliese and I had worked through last night.

Stewart smiles. "That's what I like, a guy on top of a project. Did you even sleep last night, Ray?"

I know I am caught out. How do you answer a question like that? Let alone from the father of a lady with whom you just spent a fantastic evening. I go completely red.

"I...uh, well, I..." is all I can stammer out.

Stewart and Eliese do not fail to notice this. I almost open my mouth a second time when Eliese straightens up, tossing her hair back like she did last night.

In a clear aria, she says, "I had dinner with Ray last night, Daddy, and we covered a lot of business. The plan for the fisheries Gate needed some fine-tuning with Ray's input."

Eliese thumbs him an expanded version of my file.

The look on Stewart's face is bewilderment. I think he remembers me with Trish at the holiday party, and now he is readjusting that mental process. He looks at me, then looks at Eliese, then at me again. When he turns back to her, I can see he wants to ask.

My Siren speaks clearly and concisely, and with authority only she could bring to bear on the head of the Family. "That was the second of such dinners, and there will be more. Those dinners are my business, and Ray's."

There is no pleading, no "Daddy," no "Father," only a simple end of discussion. Stewart takes a moment to look at her, nods his head, and looks at me, with another nod. Much is conveyed in that second nod. A father's wishes, a blessing, and wrath if that blessing is abused.

I nod back.

"Well, I will look over the adjusted plan. If I have any concerns, I'll let you both know," Stewart says, still a tad off his game. This Family is like magic.

Eliese's Segundo knocks, enters, and states that dinner will be served at 7:00 p.m. sharp.

***

C7 S5

As we leave Stewart's office, Samuel is walking through Eliese's doors. I say my goodbyes and follow Samuel down the hall, around what seems far more corners than is possible, and end up facing a door with Samuel waving at it like it is a prize. He shakes his head in bemusement as it is evident I do not understand why he happens to be waving his hands.

"Open your FEED, Raylan," he says, and I do.

Samuel thumbs the door's contact info and keys the room to my FEED. He pushes open the door.

"This is your new flat when at the residence. It's keyed to you...well, you and your Segundo, Lalbahadur Thapa," Samuel says. He fires off the name in one swift statement. Samuel always had a gift for names and languages. Frustratingly, and in Samuel's way, he introduces me to Lalbahadur Thapa, then says, "I need to get ready for dinner also. I leave you in his capable hands." He backs out of the room.

"Lalbahadur Thapa," I attempt to say, and I know that I garbled up the name horribly.

It comes back at me thirty thousand times faster than when Samuel said it. "Lalbahadur Thapa."

"Lalbahadur Thapa," I say again, just as horribly.

Lalbahadur says, much slower this time, as if him saying it slower will help, "Lalbahadur Thapa."

I repeat it very slowly, trying to enunciate every bit as he did. "La-lb-aha-dur Th-apa."

In perfect regimental English, he replies, "Nah, mate, Thap is fine. I was just tweaking your knickers."

I stick out my hand. I am going to love this guy. "Public Ray, private Raylan." He shakes my hand.

As he shakes my hand, he says, "I'm a Sudedar-Major, you colonial. I outrank you!"

I burst out laughing and slap him on his shoulder, and he takes a half-step to the side.

"Fuck me, boss, that felt like running into a steel door," Thap says.

"I am sorry, Thap. It is, well, a long story, but accept my apologies," I say.

He nods, all business now. "Let's get started. I'm your Segundo. A simple catch-all term, small 'f,' the family name for what we do. I'm your second, your bodyguard, also," Thap says.

I look him up and down. He is about my age, five-four, maybe 165 pounds, not much fat and in great shape. His face is almost oval, with a thin wispy mustache. Thap continues, "You are now my contract during my life indenture."

"Wow, whoah, back up, back up." My mind grasps at the reality of what Thap said. "Explain. Now," I say in clear command, using every ounce of my own command voice. Like any soldier ever in any first-world military, out comes a clear, concise story.

"When the Nepali Concordant wanted a gate; needed a gate to feed, shelter, and clothe our people, the government shopped it around. They went to the Chinese Confederacy, India, the NAC government, Japan, the Russian Hegemony, France, the Germanic Federation, the Slavic Compact, Hellenistic Isles, and the Egyptian Majority. They all wanted, well, to only leave us scraps," Thap says.

He continues, never wavering in the solemnity of his voice. "There was a General who had retired from service to the Crown, and he returned to Nepal. He had an idea. He called together the regimental leadership, then the regiments themselves, and finally the civilian leadership of the Nepalese Concordant. They all agreed. Once again, the Gurkhas would carry this burden for our people.

"Nepal sent its ambassadors to all the nations that had the ability to help us. They laughed at us. We had offered 13,000 men as indenture in perpetuity, so long as the Gate remained running in our control. See, we weren't SkipJack pilots. A few years before, the NAC had revolutionized war yet again. The SkipJacks hit the battlefield. The Nepali Concordant was too poor to do such a thing. Even if we could, it was not our way," Thap says, and his voice is full of pride.

He stops, eyes locking onto mine. He wants this clear between us now, with no ambiguity. "A retired Sudedar-Major was living in the Virginia Metro district. He was at a formal event celebrating the passing of privatization of Gates when he happened to see a young Stewart Jankowitz Senior with his wife. At that time, the Family was untested in international matters. Stewart Sr. listened to that offer.

"Stewart Sr. knew that privatization would be the future. He explained to the Sudedar-Major that he would give the offer all due consideration. The Sudedar-Major was heartbroken. Even though he didn't have the authority to negotiate the offer, he had put his hopes on it, anyway. Yet three days later, he was riding in a tram with Stewart Jankowitz Senior," Thap says.

Thap takes a deep breath, and I hear the thickness in his voice, that little tremor of pride and humility meshing, as he says, "They landed in the Nepalese Concordant. They were escorted into a room with every official member of the army and government. Jankowitz Sr. flatly refused Nepal's offer and outlined the reasons for his refusal.

"He would not take a 13,000-man force to staff, protect, and guard his Gates. He would not rob a nation of its most dedicated and loyal heart. He spoke of knowing the value of our lives. He slid forward a single sheet. He would accept forty in perpetuity, forty Gurkhas as personal guards—Segundos, as he called them. 'Second' had been written next to the word Segundo.

"These applicants to the Forty would be put forward by Nepal's regiments, agreed to by the Jankowitz family—small 'f,' not the corporate big 'F,' and indentured as an individual, contracted to serve a single member of the family. Until the time of ending an individual contract, they would be the family's guard, not the business's," Thap says. He has to steady his voice even more. "One would think us slaves or serfs. However, we serve at our own will. We do not serve anyone else's whims, not even the little 'f' family. We have our own leadership corps, and a group specific to those members with a seat at the Family table. We retire when we wish, indenture paid, be it a single day, or fifty years."

That tremor and thick voice is even more pronounced. "Ninety days later, the Nepalese regiments had submitted their recommendations for the first forty Gurkhas. Among them was the retired Sudedar-Major from Virginia Metro District. He was Jankowitz Senior's contract holder. My father served him until he passed away."

There is a profound silence between us. Thap finishes his report, and he will say nothing more. I stare at him, and our eyes lock. "Moving on," I say in the same solemnity Thap had used.

"Yes, Raylan, I will live here in this flat when we are here, and I will live at the Hill House when we are there," Thap says in that regimental British accent.

"I'm moving? I like my cabin!" I gripe with a bit more force than I had intended.

"I refuse to call it a 'cabin.' As of today, it is officially known as the Hill House," Thap says.

He pauses, waiting to shoot down any objection. Oh, I have them. It is a cabin, dammit.

"I have taken the liberty to change the disposition of the lower flat to a suitable living space for myself." Thap says everything in that regimental English that I am pretty sure is an affectation. "My living areas are private spaces and subject to all expectations of privacy. Your spaces are not." He eyes me now as he speaks, looking to pounce on any of my objections. "I am your Segundo," he says, flatly ending any discussion or commentary on the point.

"Moving on, Raylan. Your tailor has sent suitable clothing to the Hill House," Thap says, with the emphasis on Hill House, "and suitable clothing to the flat at the Family residence. While you prepare, I will lay one out for you."

Thap points to a shower in the little bath off the entry. Shrugging, I step in and close the door.

Thap's voice picks up in volume as the water kicks on. "I am thumbing over your current back pay. The pay has been backdated to the day after you woke. I am told that is the day you were hired after you were let go from your previous employer."

I damn near fall on my ass in the shower when I see the number. I do not think I can physically count that high. If I had a corporate franchise, getting my own tram would not be an issue. While the pay is larger than I expect, and I could afford to buy a modest tram outright if I had a corporate franchise, the pay is nowhere near enough to accomplish that, however.

"Raylan, please don't fall," I hear Thap say in a muted shout.

Damn, do I make that much noise?

"Furthermore, you have a Family account, as you're the head of the Gate Survey Group (GSG). You may requisition equipment and gear for evaluation, testing, and modification for survey missions," Thap says. The wall and shower subdue Thap's voice, yet it still carries through that small hallway and into the bathroom.

He takes a breath and waits for me to shout back a question. I stick to my maxim: do not interrupt intelligent people when they are working.

"As to the disposition of and ownership of the Hill House: that ownership has changed to the GSG corporation, under your leadership. GSG is now a corporate facility for munitions research within the Family's Compact Military wing. All munitions research is limited to the two-hundred hectare live-fire parcel that will be marked off by the end of the week. There is a twelve-hundred-hectare boundary surrounding that parcel. The Hill House is in said live-fire range. Please do not blow up our home," Thap says.

I can tell that the last bit is to see if I was listening. Thap has a dry sense of humor.

"Only the basement, Thap, you can use the trap door," I say in mock incredulity.

"Very good, Raylan. This change allows you to have, store, make, and modify firearms on the premises of that five-hundred acres. This is not limited to handguns, rifles, or shotguns. It includes select-fire weapons, moderators, and militarized SkipJacks. I reiterate: all live-fire must not leave those five-hundred acres. The boundary alert will notify the District's constabulary and the proper NAC authorities if anything leaves those 200 hectares," Thap says.

"Thap, we need a range. Get us a decent range built. Personal and SkipJack, please," I say with a boatload of soap in my eyes.

"Already in the works, Raylan." Thap continues, "Your attire for this evening is ready."

"Wait," I say, as the reality hits me. "I have a corporate franchise?"

I hear Thap laugh and then say, "Raylan, you are the new Seventh seat at the Family Table. Everyone at the Table runs a division. I was paired with you because I'm the most senior member of the forty available to be your Segundo."

It is a few more minutes before I am ready to step out. I towel off, then brush my teeth with the provided sonic toothbrush. This thing costs more than my single blockhouse did for three months. It is going to take a while to get used to this type of life. A knock and a set of boxers pass through the door. I step into them, then out of the bath to the hallway. I follow Thap into a sitting area—a sitting room that is larger than the blockhouse Jacki and I shared. Sheesh, this is hard to get through my head. There are real couches, chairs, lamps, and real books.

A cough brings me back. "I will give you a tour in a bit," Thap says.

I turn to face Thap, and he gasps. He follows my left shoulder to the right one, then down. My right arm is limp at my side. I have seen myself in the mirror. The tiger striping is still there; however, it is more muted, with even skin tones, just one or two shades off from each other. While the mesh helps mimic the fat that humans have, it only mimics the look. It looks like bands of individual, vacuum-packed muscle groups, tiger-striped and with slices through them.

Thap gulps audibly, and says, "You know war, and it knows you."

Thap is not wrong. I have many scars from my years in the FR teams. The damage he sees, though, is a different type of battle wound. He shakes his head, snatches up the dress shirt, and hands it to me. Soon after dressing, he gives me the grand tour.

"Living area, volume low, please," Thap mutters, and mimics the acceptable level of speaking for this area. He then points to the hallway bathroom and guest bath. We walk as he shows me the office.

"This is the FEED terminal from which you may access Family files not directly sent to you by one of the other six seats. It is keyed to you only. I do not have access," Thap explains. His statement comes with a glare, so that I understand he will not accept access.

We continue past a door to the main suite. "This is your room," he says. Opening the doors, he steps in and shows me the closet with clothes, and the master bath. The master has a shower as big as the other bathroom. I glare at him.

"You would not be able to hear me in this one. We are short on time," Thap says with a perfectly straight face.

Grumpily, I let it go. I know the little guy is tweaking my knickers again. We back out and stop in front of the door we had bypassed. "This is my room, and it is private." His bark is a final command.

"Thap," I say with a smirk.

He points at every space in the order he had shown them to me. "Not private!" "Not private!" Damn, he even has the fucking knifehand as punctuation. As he hits his door, that final knifehand points with such rigidity, I can hear his sleeve snap, as if it is a martial arts gi. "Private!"

I look my Segundo in the eye with a wink to let him know I am screwing with him. "I am the seventh in the Family, Thap. I outrank you." That almost teased a smile out of him. "Boundaries are clear as day. Unless I must save you from a hail of gunfire, do not enter. I got it, Thap. I am not the nosy type. Hell, I just spent nine months without talking to a single person. I watch him relax.

With that, he starts to ask a question, and instead says, "Thanks, Raylan."

"I do have a request, Thap. I do not know jack about dinner tonight. Do we have enough time for you to walk me through the procedure of what to use when and work up a plan so I do not screw up?" A little color comes to my face at the embarrassing question.

Thap draws out a pocket fob watch. Nods. "A quick one, Raylan," Thap says. He steps over to a sideboard inlaid with wood. Opening the doors, he turns to me. "Don't just stand there, clear off the gaming table and sit," he says in energetic haste.

I look at the roundish table and back to Thap; it is clear and free of anything on it. Thap looks at me now, and I can see the mental eyeroll as clearly as if he were doing it in front of me.

"Sit, Raylan," Thap says.

I sit. He takes a thin section and flips the top from a felt-lined top to a wood veneer. A brush materializes from the sideboard, and he begins to brush the table, then proceeds to lay out everything. With a clap, the lesson begins. It is too much to take in during this short lesson. We do come up with a system to warn me if I was about to faux pas my rear out of the Family. With time short, we head to dinner.

***

C7 S6

I think Thap's accent is affecting my brain function, as dinner smells divine, from what little scent I get as we walk into the dining room. I am across from Trish again. Our Segundos sit to our left. Eliese is to Stewart's right, Darien to his left. Samuel is to my right, and Doc Alverez across from Samuel.

If I reach for the wrong thing, Thap sends a single buzz to my FEED unit. At first, I think he is screwing with me until I remember my napkin. It buzzes like twenty times as my hand hovers in the air.

Trish takes pity on me, and slowly moves her hand over to where her napkin had been on her side. With a mental click, I get it. As I do, Stewart enters, and we all stand. The rules and steps for these formal dinners are going to drive me bonkers.

"Let's have a toast to our newest member at the Table," Stewart says. We have a toast, about me, of course we do. Me? "Ray is a capable man who will be taking on the Gate Survey Group division for the Family. He's just returned from a very successful, near yearlong survey. Thank you, Ray, and welcome to the Family."

This must be due in part to having recently completed the Confederated Blackfoot Nation Survey. It is beyond my wildest dreams. I know what Thap told me earlier, but it is past my expectations. The weight of responsibility and obligations begins to descend on me. I catch a tiny wink from Eliese; that single reassuring look pushes the weight and worry aside. We drink to the toast and dinner is off.

It is a five-course dinner and is crazy wild on my palate. I have spent the last nine months eating out of one cracked and leaky pot. I remember not to fully clear everything unless I want more to appear in front of me. Between Thap and Trish, I do a bang-up job ignoring Darien's dagger glares at me and Samuel.

The food is outstanding. Not as good as the previous night, but that was undoubtedly due to the company. It takes me a while to understand what Darien is goading himself up to do. He is deciding who to berate first. His father's speech and me now being the seventh member of the Family, as well as Samuel calling me brother, have new connotations. As we wait for the dessert course and something called sherry, Darien clears his throat.

"Father." He pauses, as the bully makes sure he has his audience. "Did you know that little Sammy here has grown a backbone overnight?"

Even Stewart stiffens. A bit of silence hangs in the air, then in a bright bell tone that can only come from the vibrancy of youth, Trish says, "Oh, Darien, brother, it has always been there. You are simply noticing now because it occurs to you that you lack one."

The following silence is so thick that even the staff who enters with the desserts pause, almost causing a staff collision. The staff places dessert plates on the table in absolute silence. The eyes of the servers are not even wandering. Samuel takes an exaggerated bite.

With his mouth half-full, Samuel mumbles, "Oh, this is wonderful. Darien, you should try this. I believe it's called 'crow.' You like to eat crow, right?"

Darien throws his napkin down on the table, stands, and marches out of the dining room with his Segundo in tow. Stewart rolls his eyes as the door closes.

"You two," Stewart says, with a reproving look at Samuel and Trish. He shakes his head. "He should know better than to try that at the table. Trish? Samuel?"

Trish responds for them both. "We'll let him cool off and apologize tomorrow before we head out, Father. I'm heading back to my indenture. Sammy, I think, is off...well, I don't know what Sammy's doing."

"I'm heading to the union San Diego Dockyards (SDD). The fishing conglomerate's fleet production has stalled, for some reason. Their board has asked me to put some weight into it and sort out the production," Samuel says. "I'm betting they are objecting to shipping everything here in pieces to be assembled by a different crew on the other side of the Gate. Possibly, this slowdown is their leverage to allow them to assemble them fully. They don't seem to understand that an assembled ship doesn't fit through the Gate. Making the Gate big enough to do that is not in any way feasible in terms of our contract. They're a union shop, so perhaps they don't care. It seems as if they want the full payment and full workload, regardless as to what the customers' needs are."

Stewart thinks about it and says, "Likely so, and I know that the fishing conglomerate did try and find someone here on the east coast to build them. But when they slotted in their order, the Pacific Crest District SDD came up as the shop in Queue. When that happened, no east coast builder would even return FEED queries."

"Iceland," I say without thinking, and everyone at the table turns to me.

"What, Ray?" replies Stewart. "What was that?"

Oops, my mouth has spoken before my brain thought it through. There is nothing for it but to stand up straight and step into the battle.

"Go to Iceland. Samuel and I were...well, we were on leave in Iceland together just after the Scandinavian Commonwealth relinquished rule," I say. I take a deep breath and say a silent prayer that my hunch is right. "They have a very good, if not modern, shipyard." Another breath, in the hope I do not sound stupid. "While they have their own unionized labor force, they often compete with the unions in the Compact for business. English is the official business language, or close enough for Samuel, the master of languages. They are not much further from the Gate than San Diego. There might be some time lost in switching. Maybe not, or San Diego might back down. It is worth a shot. Plus, Samuel likes the Viking girls."

Trish bursts out laughing, delivering a cute snort behind her hand.

Dr. Alverez quips, "I have medication for that, Samuel."

"Bite me, Ray," Samuel says, with no ill will. "Father, I'll take my leave and make some FEED inquiries. Ray's jokes aside, this may be an option, and it certainly gives me significantly more leverage." As he stands and pushes his chair in, he taps his fingers on the back of the chair. "I'll drop in later after I get some info and bring you up to date on the preliminaries. I'll talk to the conglomerate and read their contract with the union San Diego Dockyards, just to be sure we have an out. Then I'll make inquiries into Iceland."

Samuel and his Segundo prepare to exit the room, and a little laugh draws us all back to Trish.

She asks coyly, "How about you, Ray? Do you like Viking girls? Do the blond hair and blue eyes spark your interest?" She bats her eyelashes, creating a strobe effect with her blue eyes.

I look at Trish and say, "No, not really. They are beautiful, and yes, they are strong. But my people revere the raven. It brings the freshwater to the world in its beak. It is the smartest of all the birds, not just Corvids. It is wiley, strong, and cunning." I keep my eyes on Trish. "I like long black hair and rich brown eyes."

I put as much emphasis on that last statement as I can. Then I flick my eyes in Eliese's direction.

"I have been in a lot of fights, Trish. I am afraid that only a Morrigan will do for me. Samuel can keep the Viking women for himself." I tease her right back; in hindsight, maybe this is not the right way to deal with this situation.

Trish blinks, once, twice, and then she looks from me to Doc Alverez, then at her father, at Samuel, who also stares me. Then Trish, Alverez, Samuel, and Stewart turn in unison and look at Eliese.

"Shit, I guess that was not as subtle as I thought it was," I say in exasperation of my stupidity at trying to play a game I do not know the rules to.

Eliese, with a flaming red neck, black hair hanging over her face, and her face in her hands says with some exasperation of her own, "No, Ray, not with this Family."

With a sigh, Eliese sits up, shaking her hair back from a face still red. She says, "You owe me dinner, Ray, and it better not be Tree Rat Stew again." She turns and smiles to show no hard feelings. "Before you leave again, twice, in fact. I almost forgot about the slip-up earlier."

She stands, pushing her chair in, and walks over to me.

"Let's walk, Ray. Since we are both determined to do whatever this is, you can take me for a walk on the grounds," Eliese says, her song now a sultry play on being put in the spotlight.

I tuck her hand in the crook of my elbow, turn to Samuel, and grin. He rolls his eyes. We are walking out the door.

"Poacher," Trish mutters.

Samuel asks, "Tree Rat Stew?"

The doors close, and the Segundos follow us. I let her lead; we stop by a door, and her Segundo returns with an evening shawl for her.

I can smell her perfume with how close she is, and the clear night air. The stars do not shine as bright as those from a D2 iteration. Eliese talks about life in the family complex. I cover such topics as how my previous blockhouse would fit in the sitting room. Tonight is about us as people, about what we chose to be and what made us. We talk very little about work. She does say that she likes the Iceland idea.

Her presence is intoxicating. Some of it is wine, but most of it is her. It is pushing 10:30 p.m. when I yawn, which reminds me that neither of us had any sleep. We return to her room and I thank her for the walk. This thing we are doing will take a while if it is to become anything. I am good with that.

I hear a kiss blown through the door before it closes.

After the click has finished reverberating down the hall, there is a snort from Thap. "You got a gargantuan pair of bollocks, Raylan," he says, almost gleefully laughing.

I quip, "According to Doc Alvarez, they might be myomere steel-reinforced."

We joke on the walk back to my room. I strip my monkey suit as I head into my non-private room, jacket, shirt, and tie all falling to the floor. I hop on first my left, then right foot as I pull the pants off. Thap is right behind me, putting them on hangers and hanging them in the closet.

Thap sees me looking at him and says, "No privacy."

I put on some workout shorts and move into the living room. I need to stretch. Being up this long, I am tight as a wound spring. Two evenings in the company of Eliese have more to do with me being wound up than anything else. He watches me stretching when it dawns on him that I might not have been joking. There were rumors of experiments, of myomere replacements. It would be insanely Family-level expensive. I can see the realization of what I am spread across his face.

"Morrigan, that is like the Celt goddess, isn't it?" he asks softly.

"According to some, she is the Celtic chooser of the dead. Goddess of the battlefield," I say. I release a grunt, and I breathe as I change positions. "Honestly, Thap, I was wracking my brain for an Inuit Deity that had black hair. I totally failed. Our heritage is more animist, so not quite the same mental framework. Military war college paid off, though."

I lean far over to the left with my right arm, straight over my right ear, pulling all the leg, side, chest, and arm muscles taut. I keep it there, stretching, letting everything release.

Thap says, "You are one scary dude." As he shakes his head and enters his room, he adds, "Goodnight, Raylan."

I return, "Man, just like a woman, lead me around and leave me at the door."

I hear his reply reverberate from his room, including the knifehand gi sound: "No privacy, privacy."

I collapse into the bed over an hour later. I feel robbed that I do not have Eliese's perfume on the pillows like I do at Hill House's futon to fall asleep to.

***

C7 S7

I rise to the smell of food. Once showered, I go to our living area. Food is on the gaming table from yesterday's lesson. Everything is set out beautifully like last night.

"Thap, it is too early for this shit," I grumble as I sit and retrieve a napkin. I give myself a gold star for remembering the napkin. What follows is Thap sitting on the other side of me, with a plate piled high, scarfing down food while continually instructing me in proper etiquette.

The man is tweaking my knickers again. I am not that agitated as I need to learn, so I try. The constant "you're slouching, sit up" interrupts my own bout of face-stuffing, though. Livery staff arrive and remove the mess we old warhorses have left as Thap and I drink some coffee.

Thap pulls up his FEED, scrolling intently, and says, "Raylan, you have six backlogged messages from an Eivin Chen. The most recent arrived yesterday evening while at dinner. It is part of my duties to pre-screen messages for priority. Mr. Chen's, I believe, you will want to address." He gives me a look and sips coffee.

I pull an Eliese and raise an eyebrow at him. "You are neither as good-looking nor as talented at that as she is. I'll continue, then," he says with a good deal of mirth. "Here is a short synopsis; you, of course, can read the messages at your leisure." Taking a long pull from his coffee, he begins.

"Eighteen months ago: Chen finished up the three SkipJacks that came in. He thanks you for all the new manuals. He knows you are the reason he was able to sign up for two classes. The local union hasn't said anything about him taking them. He now has a blockhouse close to the foundry. He was able to get his little sister and brother into it, also. He asks how your new place is?

"Fourteen months ago: Chen lets you know he is dating Lily, Boss's daughter. Foundry is slowing, and the Gate crash has most places not needing Boss's stuff. There is work, but they are down to two workers besides Boss's boys. How is the new job, can't wait to hear from you.

"Nine months ago: Boss's shop is down to just the boys and him. He and Lily are talking about marriage. He is now on his fourth first-cycle training. Most of the union guys have left the area, so training classes are infrequent.

"Six months ago: Boss's foundry is running two days a week. The SkipJack repair bay is keeping bills paid. He is training Lily and her sister Meghan the other four days a week. Things are tight. He hopes you are well. He will still keep messaging. He knows you have issues talking and communicating.

"Three months ago: the shop is doing full-time SkipJack repair. Boss is now pulling work from the Missoula/Bozeman Metro area more frequently. Mr. Chen has only one training coming up. He and Lily are serious. He is thinking of talking to Boss about marriage. Lily wants him to hold off until the economy recovers a bit.

"Yesterday: he asked Boss, and Boss gave his permission. Chen heard a new Gate is opening up north, near the old border. 'When I saw the news, I knew I had to ask then. Boss asked me what took so long. I asked Lily, and we are getting married next weekend. Can you come, Ray? I know we have not talked in a year and a half, and I don't know if you are still alive. If you are, please come.'"

"Thank you, Thap. I have been too focused on recovery and other things. Can you set up a meeting with Eliese? I need to clear it with her before I respond," I reply, deep in thought.

My mind is thinking about my time with Chen, cranking, diagnosing, turning, and teaching. I was scrambling to return to life, any kind of life. To compare that life to my world now is surreal.

Thap gently breaks into my thoughts. "Eliese has a few minutes available now, but she is packed for the day otherwise. I suggest we make use of this time if you don't want to wait till tomorrow morning."

Sitting upright in my chair, I say, "Tally ho, good sir!" Clearly his British accent is affecting my brain.

Thap gives me a crossways glance. "Yippie ki-yay, *kemosabe,*" he says in a horrible affectation of a North American Compact accent. I take the hint and head for the door.

I meet Eliese at her office. The four of us are standing, the space somewhat uncomfortably silent. It is Eliese's Segundo's cough that stirs my mind back into action.

"Eliese," I say slowly. "I do not know how time off works." I decide to try a different tack. "I have a friend in the MWD, and he is getting married. I have been out of touch, but I would like to attend his wedding this weekend."

Eliese looks perplexed, then tilts her head at me. "Why, yes, Ray, I would love to be your plus-one. I have a bit of business to finalize with the CBT: EP1, and by data trunk, their CBN: D2 counterparts. I could tie that up Monday with a quick stop before heading home," she says in a chastising refrain.

I blink. That is not what I meant to ask. I am not going to correct Eliese after four days in her company.

Then it hits me. It is what I should have asked. I understand, now, that we are officially an item, and public functions like Chen's wedding should be as a couple, not individuals.

"I am not very good at this, am I? Thank you, Eliese," I say, with more than a little chagrin.

She smiles and says, "This does not count as dinner, since you did not ask." She winks. "I'll have my Segundo get the travel plans and meetings sorted out once I have the contact info."

The sound of her voice sends rivers of life through my veins.

I pause, hemming and hawing. "Do you think you can conduct the meeting or convince the elders to come to the wedding? My friend's business could use the contacts, and likely so can the CBT." I contemplate as I muse out loud, "I'll make the arrangements with Chen and Boss for them to come, if they can. I would appreciate it."

Eliese nods. "Maybe, if I let them know the leader of the Gate Survey Group is there to attend. They are quite thankful," she adds with a melodic purr and a wink.

She steps back, as it is time for her next meeting, while a couple of gentlemen in suits are ushered in. Eliese introduces me as Ray, number seven of the Family, head of Jankowitz Gate Survey Group. Both men are bankers from Central America. I take my leave and head down the hall. Thap and I hammer out a FEED message to Chen, and one to Boss. Thap is well on his way to being indispensable.

The weather for the wedding is fantastic. Boss rents a small island in a nearby reservoir. We are all ushered to the isle on old-style boats. Warm day, light breeze. Eliese is stunning in a summer dress of cornflower yellow. She matches it with a wide-brimmed straw hat.

Within minutes of meeting Lily on Saturday, Eliese has organized a small group of helpers. She brings about the changes necessary for the whole eighteen-member delegation of the tribal elders and their families to attend the wedding on Sunday. What was originally a twenty-person wedding ends up being attended by close to a hundred.

The venue is moved around slightly on the island. Eliese has everything brought in by tram: food, tents, tables, chairs, and staffing. She takes care of it all. Like a singer of spell songs, she waves and directs in an artful dance only she can pull off.

As soon as I arrive, Boss pulls me aside and says, "Ray, you are Chen's best man. Somewhere, we have a tent to get ready in. Your girl set this whole thing up."

Boss and I find ourselves thrust into a tent where we put on our matching monkey suits. Boss is in good humor; his daughter is getting married after all. It is good to see Chen again. He is nervous as hell, so I keep him focused on me. I tell him of my recuperation at the Cabin and how I work sixteen-hour days.

"I have missed our chats and game nights, Chen. I am so happy to see you and Lily together. I even found a date for today!" I say in mock surprise.

Chen splutters. "Your *date*? She's the Family's second, Ray! You call it a date, RAY! You're dating Eliese Jankowitz." He is getting himself together as his younger brother steps up. The young man might have been eight or nine. "Ray, this is my brother. Evan, he is going to stand right next to you today."

I kneel at Evan's eye level. I ask, "Can you keep something for me, and tug my leg when it is my time to hand it to Eiven?"

I receive a vibrant nod. I hand Evan the little black box carrying the rings for Chen and Lily.

"The pastor will ask for the rings. Tug on my leg so I will not look silly, then hand me that box. I will give it to Eiven." I speak as nicely as I can.

189

Evan puts his fist around the ring box and crams the entire thing in his pocket. For the next couple of hours, I do not think he removes his hand from the pocket.

Chen looks back at me and says, "Ray."

"My full name is Raylan," I say quietly. "My brothers call me Raylan."

Chen pauses, nods, and smiles as he continues, "Raylan, thank you. We lost our parents about ten months before we met. Evan was very young, and I think he is just starting to understand they're not coming back." He pauses and turns to watch a girl in a green and white dress run around. "Christie is taking it better than Evan, but it's very hard for her, also. Lily took to her instantly. Evan doesn't make friends well, though. That's why I am careful about introducing people to them. My grandmother could watch them every once in a while, but her age...well, she can only do that for short amounts of time."

I look at him and quietly say, "I am here if I can ever help. Message me. I have systems in place to get FEED messages now."

Chen smiles as he watches Evan sit in a chair eating a cookie with one hand in his pocket. Christie was chasing one of the girls her age around. "Raylan, they mean everything to me. Your haptic suit sale kept us from being kicked out and them from being taken from me by Community Child Services. I know I drove a hard bargain. I just needed every credit the following day."

I smile at Chen, and with more warmth than I felt in a long time, I say, "I would have given it to you, had I known." I blink rapidly to keep the tears from forming. "Brother, we are here, and we each have our road. We help each other when we can. I would not be here had you given me more than those thirty points. 'We live, we are fed, and we have work. That is good for today,'" I say, repeating Boss's mantra that I learned over those months at the foundry.

Chen's head turns, and he notices the CBT elders mingling with Boss and Eliese. With a quick nod at the crowd, he asks, "How do you know the owners of the new Gate? I know Boss is dancing a jig after the FEED message from 'Pun'?" He turns to me, waiting.

I have known Chen a while, and he is a friend, that rare kind of soul that you be apart from and instantly fall into step with. I walk to the side with enough space around us that I could see if anyone is close enough to overhear.

190

Slowly I recount my recent story. "That is it, Chen, that is my job. I Gate walk, I set up new colonies. I want to help people. What happened at DGMW has scarred my soul."

Chen nods. His eyes are damp, and he gives me a hug. I slap him on the back, as an announcement is made for the guests to be seated.

Evan tugs at me at the right time. He hands me his unblemished and well-protected box. Sure, the other hand has gooey chocolate from the cookies, but it is a fair trade.

Eliese is much better at this than I. As a wedding gift to Chen and Lily, she negotiates the repair contract with the CBT:EP1 elders. They were in the market and found a very favorable rate by avoiding the union shops. To follow up, she bestows a gift to CBT for attending at her request. She negotiates a favorable contract for Boss's foundry services.

I find Boss shortly after. Boss grumbles and complains until he sees his last remaining "boy," Meghan, talking to one of the CBT SkipJack pilots.

My gift to Chen and Lily is a bit less thoughtful, but after I chat with Chen, I understand what his family means to him, so I choose practical in the short term. I give what I have: money. I have not spent any of it. I had Thap set up a fund for Chen's sister Christie and brother Evan, along with Chen and Lily's future children, to have their choice of education, allowing them to seek any indenture they desire. While Chen and Lily are enjoying the wedding table feast and dancing, I run across Daniel Standing Elk. On this side of the Gate.

"Daniel?" I say. "Daniel Standing Elk?" He turns to me and smiles.

"No, I'm Craig. His twin. It is nice to meet you, Mister...?" Craig asks

I smile back, a wave of relief walking down my spine. "Ray. I am a good friend of Chen and Lily," I say as we shake hands.

"So, Ray, how do you know Daniel? Wait. Ray, as in Gate Survey Group Ray?" Craig looks at me with hope clear on his face.

I take a sip of the water I am holding and tell myself to be careful. "Yep, that would be me. How are things going in CBN:D2?" I ask, doing my best to steer the question away from Daniel.

"Pretty good, all things considered. I don't know who your surveyor is, Ray, but..." Craig pauses, unsure of how to give me the bad news. "He has not returned. The tribe is a bit worried. Daniel does his best to calm the council. They don't want to lose a First Nation brother like that. He did so much to set up CBN:D2."

I can see how worried Craig is to give me this news. I gesture to the seats near us. After sitting and collecting my thoughts, I come up with a plausible story.

"Being that kind of surveyor is unique, Craig. It requires a kind of soul that, well, needs redemption. I cannot tell you his name. When we find a surveyor, they are unique to each contract, and they choose if they want to leave their life behind. He did. See, he had worked at the Dillon Gate Montana West at some point. When it went down, people he had known and cared for were dead on the EP1 side or lost on the D2 side," I say and pause to let him ponder that. "Surveyor, as we called him, was the first of a few candidates. I thought he was best suited for the job. I am glad to hear you are pleased with his work. His payment was to walk with the SkipJacks and gear he had left."

I take a breath, smelling Eliese's perfume behind me. Her fingers slide across my shoulders, letting me know she is there. I heard her sing her song once again. "He had an obligation, as he put it, to complete the survey. Then, simply to travel in peace and find those he lost."

Craig takes that with a nod of his head. "That's what Daniel said: that the mended man was simply doing his own walk now." He pauses. "We owe him. Do you know he killed this gargantuan—" holding up his hands to indicate the size, "—griz? Then he just gave it back to the land and the people. The school's mascot will be called Bruins. The guy hangs behind the tribal council." He chuckles. "He even gave us two of his reindeer. Donners. Man, I get requests daily for more of them. They are the single most useful loggers out there. Our guys are selectively logging by Donner, which are so much more powerful than a team of horses, with less footprint than a logging deck." He sounds hopeful.

I take that as my cue and turn to Eliese, holding out my hand for her as she makes her way to sit next to me. After introductions, I ask, "Eliese, is there a way we could bring up the V1 production of Donners again?"

Eliese opens her FEED and says, "I don't think so, we've already moved to V2." With a thoughtful murmur and a series of scrolls and slides, she slowly adds, "The research group is working on V3. We have a slated twenty-four V2s

192

scheduled and those are spoken for by Ray's GSG. I'm adding a variant for V3, calling it the Blitzen. It'll be specific to logging and towing with half of the packing capability."

Eliese looks up at Craig and smiles. "I appreciate the show of support for Lily and Chen, and it was amazingly thoughtful of the tribe to attend so graciously at such a short notice." She looks back down to her FEED, then thumbs something over to Craig. "We have six unused V1 Donners left. They will be trammed and Gated within a week. Additionally, we would love your feedback on the first two of the new Blitzens. When they come out of the research group, of course." That smile of hers and the ballad of her voice cements a bond between us and Craig.

Craig is speechless. He knows the value of SkipJacks. The concessions the tribe made today to the Family and in forging a working relationship with Boss and Chen will come back tenfold. Those SkipJacks, if maintained, will work for decades. He nods and says, "Thank you." The tapping of a mic on a FEED system pops and hisses. Music sparks, and we turn to watch the first dance.

We dance, Eliese and I. She leads, and I still do not break any toes. The weekend is awesome. I am on cloud nine. We stay in our separate rooms in a resort and take a tram into Community Dillon daily.

Like usual, we talk until early morning, one time in the main sitting area of the resort, another on an open balcony on a couch under a blanket. One of us is at each end, sprawled out, feet touching. I learn a lot that weekend. She is as new to this as I am. Her first crush soured her, if not scarred her severely.

Eliese had been at boarding school at the age of fourteen. The boy came home with her for a holiday dinner. He tried to use a sophisticated state-sponsored hacking tool to get into her grandfather's office. It turns out he was almost thirty, had undergone extensive 3D body sculpting in order to appear as a fellow student. He had been sent to school to manipulate her, or her brother Darien. The betrayal shattered her. Not so much the boy, but her grandfather's disapproving gaze and the harsh words that he let slip. He had apologized profusely over his remaining years, but the sting and damage has stayed with Eliese.

She says that she has tried to date and have a relationship. It never lasts until the second date. Then I come, bumbling, looking, staring, inspecting her first and favorite professional purchase, a coffee table. She watched me for twenty minutes. When she told me what it is and saw I was glad to know, she was surprised.

She caught my glances that night and caught Trish's glares, none of which I had ever seen. When Trish openly staked her territory for New Year's, she didn't know what she felt. When my plan for the Gate came through the day before New Year's and Trish was to be in Europe skiing, she took that reservation for herself. She had never done anything like that.

I think we find comfort in each other's company. We enjoy our time together and our conversations cover the wind-up of work-related programs. The give and take of bouncing ideas back and forth puts me at an ease I have never felt just talking to another person. It is a fantastic four days off. When I return Monday evening to Hill House, I have a set of goals, a new Segundo in Thap, and a metric crapton of work to get started.

***

C7 S8

While I was prepping for the wedding, Eliese's research group had sent dozens of drones over and confirmed the ratio slip at dozens of points. They received Dr. Alverez's blessing, and that was that.

My work-up for the Gate transition goes amazingly smoothly. The shift to a six Donner V2 train makes all the difference. It is nowhere near as much a learning curve as the first Gate transition. After the third day of work up, I move the Gate walk up a number of days. I transit the nowlabeled North East Fishing Conglomerate Gate:D2 (NEFCG:D2). The trunk comes through as the ratio slip hits.

I head out after confirming ratio slip via my FEED messages back to EP1. There is a delay on my end receiving messages, usually equal to the amount of ratio slip. Going the other way, they get it just fine. I hammer at my work for the next 90 days. Initially, I should have knocked out the balloons and spiking of them over a forty-five-day D2 timeframe. The issue that came up was simple, and we had never thought of it. Humans had never touched the forest in this D2. It is a thick, beastly brush. Trees that have not existed on EP1 in hundreds of centuries are commonplace here. Flora and fauna are out of time and place, making staking and releasing the balloons more work than anticipated.

I must cut a lot of trees down to get a window in the canopy big enough to float a balloon through. I do daisy-chain a demilled SkipJack for security, and a demolition unit to use for logging, but on reserve power, at 100% feedback cutting down trees I end up having to work as hard as the SkipJack.

There are no presets for felling a tree, at least not with the standard operations programs I work with. I must stop about every fourth or fifth day to put up the recharge panels and wind sails. Recharging, laundry, water purification, all that requires even more logging. Call me Raylan Paul Bunyan. My balloon spiking ends up being closer to a sixty-day trek instead of forty-five.

I start to receive FEED reports from all the balloon spikes I released. I am right at EP1's hard limit of 45 days EP1 timeframe. The balloon survey shows the best places for me to layout the dockyard and the settlement. They are not as close together as we had hoped. It is another 30 days before I finish marking that and staking out all the plots for building.

I have thought of replacing the boundary plot stakes with the temporary mesh ones that are powered by the solar and wind sails. Doing this would allow for an even quicker progression for the podded EP1 SkipJack pilots. I fire off my plan to Eliese via a feed message, letting her know I am a few days, maybe two weeks from being done.

I also tally up the damages. My primary Donner V2 that had carried my gear, guns, and food has gone down. It failed from the same metal fatigue as the guns, and I ask Eliese if her team can look into the issue. The second replacement Donner is close behind. All four of my firearms are kaput, as are my knives.

The marsh shoes now into their 2nd week of use while staking out the docks and dockyard are doing well. It seems the titanium and myomere infused metal is holding up. I ask Eliese to look into the quality and condition of the two

Donners I had left with CBN. I put forward that it might be contact with me, not the D2 iteration that is causing the failure.

I settle into staking and planning. The marsh shoes finally fail in the third week. I have only a few days left, so I fabricate some wooden ones every other day or so. I add the use of long six foot walking staves for balance. I finish the settlement and docks/dockyard layout.

I now only need to return this D2 to EP1's ratio slip. The two must be in parity before I can pull the MLR's into position and get it squared away. I have plenty of food left in the panniers. I had zero issues with predators, in fact, I have only seen a few coyotes and one black bear. Everything seems to stay away from my daisy-chained group. I am sick of the marsh and mosquitoes, and it is time to be done.

The ratio slip between the two worlds finds parity. I set about laying out the two temp grids from the MLRs. One is on the west block of the demarcation zone to set up the settlement. The other is on the North East block to set up the docks and prep the dredges for making a harbor. I finish and take the rest of the day off.

That night, my demilled SkipJack keeps sending alerts to my HUD, forwarded to my FEED. I have a demilled SkipJack to act as a security buffer. It is my early warning system, with both thermal and night vision. It keeps me advised if anything coyote sized or larger comes near. I have been here for nearly 90 days. The most massive predator track I had seen was a bear. I have seen plenty of coyote tracks or the D2 equivalent.

I have not seen any wolf tracks until now. I had kicked on the SkipJacks HOLEDs. The wolf tracks are all around the Gate, and at the base camp is a single set of wolf tracks. I am leaving in the morning, and I do not want to be around a wolf unarmed. I am thankful to be done with this survey. This wolf looks to be a large one. I am out of knives and guns. What I have available is a big walking staff.

I retreat into the hard-sided shelter for the night and wait for dawn. I keep the demilled SkipJack up and on sentry duty. It does not notify me of anything again. In the morning, it is time to pack it all. Donners with their panniers are loaded, and construction and demolition SkipJacks are checked. I break the base camp down and stow it away. When I finish, I notify via FEED message that they can begin transiting the MLRs soon.

By noon, I receive notice that the first MLR is coming through. I use the Donners to pull it into place. I start by hooking the MLR up to the data trunk and the MLR's own power generator. The generator requires me to pop up its solar and wind charging systems. The second MLR makes its debut and is promptly set up on its side of the demarcation zone.

I pull the SkipJacks to heel. I used minimal awareness to bring them to assemble behind me for a "follow" command. It is not a full pilot thing; it is more like a line of kids on a day trip out of school, a loose command obeyed because of internal programming. Pulling to heel is often an issue, as it takes more and more of your attention. The more SkipJacks you are pulling to heel, the harder it gets. In the military, I could pull a couple. Samuel, on a drunken bet, once pulled six. He had a migraine for a week.

I know I can pull to heel more than six now. I had done it at the CBN:D2 Gate without thinking. I have ten here with me, so I put my mind to the task. I try out an idea, one that our Drill Instructor for remote piloting explained we should never do. With a great deal of mental effort, I open a third mindspace. It is difficult to break a long-held static tradition. It is as if I have ripped a mirrored image of my mind. I already utilize two mindspaces when piloting remotely. Why not three, or ten? With caution and care, I open a mindspace for each, pulling them all at once.

It is the dumbest thing I could have done. Sometimes in life, you make a mistake. Sometimes you fail to make connections until something triggers that connection for you. My mistake? I forgot multiple things. First, I forgot about the wolf. Second, I forgot to keep a portion of my mental space aware of what was going on around me. Third, I forgot that the demilled is still on sentry duty. Fourth, I failed to remember someone piloted the cat on the mountain, waiting for that opportune moment to strike.

The demilled SkipJack floods my dropped down HUD display with the warning of a ninety-kilogram canine bullet weaving towards my back. There are issues with this, since it is on sentry duty.

I have not yet collected the demilled unit in the pull and it is giving me an off-axis image, one that my brain takes as the correct axis. Because of that irregularity, my spin to intercept the wolf is off. Instead of twirling away, I twist into his attack. Thankfully, I am a guy with a lot of mass, more mass than anybody my size deserves to have. The force of our meeting spins me to my knees, facing ninety degrees to my right from the direction I had been looking. The wolf tumbles and rolls and has overshot me by a good deal.

When the wolf returns, it comes in low and fast at my leg. I retrieve my walking staff from the ground and solidly slap-shoot it across its front shoulders while I dance out of its way. I wish I were piloting my demilled SkipJack—I would pound this pup to dust. Now, though, it will take me almost thirty seconds or more to dump-pilot this SkipJack as I had in Dillon. In those seconds, this wolf will have more than enough opportunity to rip out my throat.

We circle each other. The beast keeps coming in, testing me for an opening, then tossing itself out of the way. Stupidly, I let it turn me about and I lose my sense of where I am in relation to all the SkipJacks. This is because I left that frickin demilled SkipJack in sentry mode. The demilled keeps kicking me out of the command prompts to turn it off with another warning update.

My side smacks into one of the heeled Donner V2s. That is all the wolf needs: a fraction of a second opening, and its teeth snap at my right wrist. I am clutching the staff with that hand. The jaws start yanking my wrist from side to side, and I release the staff.

With my back to the Donner, there is not much I can do. I start pummeling the animal with my left fist. I start yowling as the pain from the wolf savaging my wrist hits me. Myomere muscle or not, I feel the savagery in this beast. I feel that pain, and when combined with its growling, it hits the hindbrain hard.

It is the new mindspaces that save me, I think. I shove the desire to turn and flee into one of those new mindspaces. I use another to analyze my worsening situation. It is the last mindspace, though, that pulls me back as it remembers. It finds a memory from years ago in the dark of night. I remember that hill, I remember that cunning and vicious fight as we rolled down the hill. I know for sure in that instant this is a piloted wolf.

I swap tactics. I brace my body, and with a grunt of strength, I bring the beast up, hanging off my wrist to my face.

In a feral roar, I yell, "Round two, fuckhead, I got you this time."

My left thumb drives into the wolf's right eye as it hangs, clawing and scrambling at my bloody right wrist. I wiggle that thumb around as the wolf slips off my wrist in a yelp. I have another connection click into place from my fight with the mountain cat so long ago. Pain, or challenge, short-circuits the piloted control for even the briefest of moments.

The cunning bastard has retreated a short distance away. We start our dance again. Now that we both know the stakes of this game, it can truly begin. This time I have a plan. As I pass another Donner, I yank off a whitetail deer pelt I had tanned and lashed to the top of it. I began twirling it on my left arm and letting that right arm hang limp, as if it is too damaged to use.

"Where have you been the last six years or so, you little bastard?" I taunt. "I kicked your ass once, yeah, I know you are in there. I know you can hear me."

We are perpendicular to the SkipJacks, and I have space, I have the room. I time the end of the word "me" perfectly. I lunge with a fiendish rolling growl, starting just after the wolf starts his dash in. The right arm still hangs limp, the left arm cocked. I throw a clumsy punch with my left fist. I miss the wolf by at least a District.

The pilot of the wolf tries to regain the fine control of the wolf as it, and not the pilot, latches on to the deerskin wrapped arm. The second he latches on; I bring every ounce of power in my now-clenching right fist into three blows.

I know the strength and mass I have at my control, as I have worked with this body for over two years now, counting D2 time. I have tested it further when logging here under ratio slip in this D2 iteration. Doctor Alvarez assures me I am human, but I wonder about that sometimes. I am different now. I have some portion of the strength and speed of a SkipJack.

I put everything into the first shot to the soft tissue of the wolf's stomach, aiming for the base of the ribs, right where that kidney should be. My myomere fist drives home. The wriggling of the wolf absorbs some of the blow.

That first blow elicits a plethora of mucus and bile erupting out of the wolf's mouth and nose. It covers my goggles. I do not care.

The second blow lands on the ribs as I growl, "Can you feel it, asshole? I am going to rip you apart."

I feel its ribs crack and crumble under that blow. There is no air left in its lungs. What comes out of its nose and mouth is a geyser of foaming blood.

In a singular mindspace, I stand before a wall. I had built it so long ago that the adult me barely remembers it. I had struggled those first months in the CM. I was too eager, too willing to fight. I was alone, scared, and wary of these other people who laughed and joked at things I did not know. I remember the moment I sealed that part of me away.

It is a few short steps to the wall in my mindspace. I reach out and feel a power waiting, pacing, prowling behind that wall. My hand lands on the wall, and a moment later, my other hand finds itself there, also. I realize it is not power—it is completeness.

I pull one megalithic block down, and as I do, I see a pair of hands push and help me from the other side. As the third block is removed and set aside, a primal sense of ferocity hits me. It is not rage, not unbridled hatred, but ruthlessness, a sense of pure creative fury of cold pragmatism which opens from my darker nature.

The mental stops on being violent that people put upon themselves to live in a civilized world are gone in the meeting of my two natures. My focus narrows, and the scream that tears from my lips is eardrum-shattering. The wolf is starting to twitch. I am not sure if the pilot was trying to force disco, or if I have short-circuited his control of the animal's brain again.

My final blow is a hammer fist to the base of its skull. I catch its head between my right fist and the left arm. As the wolf falls limp, I know I have broken my left arm in that blow. I have held nothing back. My left arm hangs, as the deerskin unravels from it. I drop the security setting on the demilled, bring them all into a daisy-chain as I twirl in circles looking for more attackers. Seeing none, I pick up the wolf's two front legs using my right hand and walk the Gate.

Thap is there armed and armored when I exit. Unsurprisingly, something had snuck by the gate guards last night. It was not man-sized, but it should not have made it through the fenced Gate demarcation zone. Thap and the four Gurkhas had been on standby ever since. There is a call for a corpsman. The corpsman bandages my left wrist, and the arm is placed in a splint and a sling.

Doc will be meeting me tomorrow at his office. For now, the corpsman gives me some pain meds. I do take those. I do not stow the gear or the SkipJacks. Instead, the members of the Forty collect the guns, and we all bundled into the cargo tram. Thap pushes me into the jump seat. When we are in the air, I see Thap issuing commands over his FEED. The Family's guards will deliver my gear sometime later.

The corpse of the wolf is at my feet. I guess I have held its front legs the whole time they were trying to bandage my wrist and arm. I am drowsy, and the adrenaline spike is coming down. Thap pushes some fluids at me, or in me.

I hear from some distance away, "How did he? Why not just shoot it?"

I say, grumbling as I fight sleep, "I punched it."

Thap later told me that I, indeed, am now rumored to have big myomere balls.

We land and the security team disembarks. We are up in the air again and heading back to the cabin, or Hill House. I wake at the second landing in much better shape than I had been five hours before. I look at Thap as we exit, and I see two trams, Eliese's and Samuel's. I turn to Thap. "How do I look?"

"Raylan, you look..." He looks at my wrist and left arm in its sling. "Decent, injured, but decent," he finally says, shrugging. "You smell like shit, though," he adds as we walk up the wooden steps.

Chapter 8 Corn Country, Eat Your Wheaties

C8 S1

Thap and I make our way up the wooden steps, and we part ways when we hear footsteps on the deck of the Hill House. I step up to the bottom of the porch steps. There is a pull at my right hand. I look down to see the dead wolf corpse. My head tilts as I remember why I have this. I cannot take this thing inside. I toss the wolf off to the right. If Samuel is here, I will ask that he investigate its origins for me.

A part of my psyche knows I am more than a bit punch-drunk. With an effort, I make my way up those six steps to the porch. I am stiff and I am sore. Any kind of real fight pulls down the mental barriers you put up to keep yourself safe during exercise and training. I tore down more than a few of my mental walls in that fight.

In dropping some of those barriers, I let loose a nature I have kept walled away for a very long time. I have been mentally repairing that wall during our tram back to Hill House. The pain, the pulled muscles, and the bruises I will feel for days. I start pulling off my chest rig, clipping the HUD goggles to the shoulder pads. As I twist the door open and walk in, I drop what is left of my gear by the door.

Dinner smells good. No, dinner smells divine. I can sense her perfume below the pervasive odor of the food. Both Eliese and Samuel share a look of concern. I am sure my blood-covered clothes, chest rig, and goggles that I dropped on the floor do not help. I attempt a weak smile.

"Heh, you should see the other guy," I quip.

I am more than a little punch-drunk still. A cough comes from Samuel as he points to my face, my hands, and the sink in the little kitchen area.

"Wash up, Ray, please," Sam says quietly, his care and love show in that one request. "For Eliese."

It brings my humanity around and helps me assert control once again. The fog, the haze of being punch-drunk, slides away into those handy little mind-spaces. Now that the punch-drunk haze no longer holds me back; I find it much easier to slide those monolithic blocks in place. Part of me, I will not lie, wishes to let my nature roam free. This is a civilized world, and what has happened today shows me that I am only a guest in it.

I blink at Samuel, nodding. My words almost slurring, I say, "Do me a favor: let us get me out of this in my room. Can you help get me washed up, Samuel?"

I point as much as I can. My fingers are stiff from wounds and clamping on to the legs of the wolf for hours. I head to the little bedroom. I am not moving fast. Shuffling my steps slowly, even taking significant steps, elicits a wince of pain. Boy, the fight with the piloted wolf really took it out of me.

I hear Samuel walk over to the door and pick up my kit and I hear him say, "Eliese, only little bits of food, cut up. You saw he can barely move that right hand. Probably some soup, broth, lots of water, and no booze tonight. I'll get him cleaned up and we'll get him fed. He'll probably sleep after that."

The man that is speaking is my brother in war, Sam, and his words carry a vibrancy of command. It is the way you speak to someone who has never seen tragedy or war and battle. It is how you get them to react, move, and participate without being a hindrance to your own efforts. Clear and calm instructions make all the difference in situations such as this. I feel as much as hear the door slide mostly shut behind me.

"Raylan, you're all messed up. Blood everywhere, on your shirt and pants," Samuel says.

His comment causes me to wobble as I try and look at everything. He has me move to the bathroom.

"Stand there, can you do that?" Sam asks.

I smile, and as if I am a SkipJack, I lock up, arms slightly apart, as much as the pain and sling would allow for the left arm. He walks over to a cubby, pops the door, and pulls out a substantial first aid kit. He then starts the water running in the sink. With shears, he cuts the shredded haptic suit and underclothes from me. Samuel begins with the arms, back, and legs. He peels slowly, cleaning and bandaging as he works.

There is a lot more he could do, but he decides it is better left for Doc Alverez to see and assess. When the shirt is off, I have multiple sets of front paw claw marks from when I had held it to me at the end. It was almost as if the wolf was trying to dig through me. The stomach area took a good deal more damage. Dozens of lacerations from the rear claws and front claws are spread across my torso and upper legs. The pressure from the undergarments and haptic suit has kept the seepage slow. My eyes follow the marks down to my thighs. I am also pretty torn up there.

I see bruising on the skin everywhere; the left shoulder where the wolf had initially hit me and the right shoulder where I was pinned against the Donner are a mass of bruises. All the skin around my right wrist has lacerations and is bruising badly. My torso has little pale purple and black marks everywhere not occupied by lines of lacerations. The compression pants for the haptic suit come off. That is better, but not by much. There are some lacerations and dozens of bruising areas. I most assuredly have been in a fight.

"Samuel, the wolf was like the cat we saw on that last deployment," I say. "'Rabid.'"

It was not a deployment, it was part of a workup for an operation we were about to do. Samuel stiffens, and he looks up from cleaning a leg laceration. He sees my eyes in the mirror. He follows my own gaze to my hand pointing down. He shifts his view to my left foot. The meaning is clear and as hidden as I can make it.

"I left him by the front porch, and I do not want Eliese to see it," I say, and with his nod, I know he will take care of it.

Samuel works on. We have both done this kind of thing before. One of the misconceptions is that pilots only fight using SkipJacks, which is true for standard Compact Military infantry. The standard pilots are pod-bound. Samuel and I are not standard.

As SkipJacks became the go-to battlefield war machines, latency and speed of reaction became king. Us humans moved closer and closer, often with elite units fighting our battles on reserve haptic suit back-up power or in temporary pods. If the enemy locates us, they would come directly to the pilots. As a result, there were always a couple pilots and SkipJacks guarding the rest of the men in their pods.

Sam has done this medic work before and has always done it well. The pain is there, but aside from my fractured left arm, it is manageable. He returns with some workout shorts and an armless workout shirt. He kicks the damaged clothes and gear into a pile. I sit on the toilet as he removes my boots and helps me into the shorts. He works the gym shirt over my head and carefully brings the arms through. I am now presentable enough for Eliese's company.

We exit the bedroom, and Eliese puts her hands over her face at the bruises.

"He's just banged up. He'll see Doc in the morning," cautions Samuel. "Let's get him some food and rest."

I am a bit better and I am coming around, if only slowly. I have less punch-drunk and more delirium in my voice as I joke, "Samuel's hamming it up for you, on my behalf. He just slathered me in makeup." I can see my joke does not allay her concerns. It does elicit a snort at my stab at humor, though.

Eliese sits me in a chair that feels luxurious compared to the webbing jump seat of the tram. She pulls her chair over to me. We begin to eat. She has cut up most things, so I treat it as finger food. The main dish is pasta, but yeah, I am having a hard time holding the fork. I stick with bits of bread dunked in the soup and sliced meatballs.

After a half hour, I begin to talk in between bites. Dinner had been silent and somber until this point. I start going over the report and how much of a success the survey is. I cover the success of the MLR and the temp mesh grid. I mention updating the program for a third MLR to set up the settlement, or simply splitting the initial two MLR's. Staking out the settlement plots with the temp mesh system might be a good option.

I mumble a lot as I eat. Eliese listens, and after a time, she looks less worried as I become more aware and less punch-drunk. It does not take much longer before we are winding into full steam business mode.

Samuel stands and says, "Eliese, I can't stay with him all night. Can you? I have a couple of time-critical things on the burner I want to take care of before dinner with Father tomorrow."

Eliese looks at him with worry on her face and she asks, "Are you sure that's okay?"

I cringe inwardly, as Eliese's voice is a lament of concern. I have brought pain and worry to her.

"He's come back around, but keep him sitting up on the futon. Keep him hydrated and let Thap know if anything changes. Most likely, he is going to snore something fierce," he says.

"He doesn't snore." Eliese says.

Eliese fails to cotton on to her brother's trap until it is too late. If nothing else could, that little slip tuned me in to how much she is worrying about me right now. It only takes a raised eyebrow from Samuel to bring Eliese's mind into full working mode. Her neck becomes a fantastic shade of ruby red in slow motion.

Samuel just winks at her. "Good night, all," he says in a final reply.

She turns to me, not upset, just a little frustration showing on her face. "I'm doing much better, Eliese," I give her a reassuring grin, "I like the V2 Donners and the marsh shoes were awesome." I pause. "Something is going on with me and metals. I plan on broaching the subject with Doc tomorrow. The guns, the knives, the marsh shoes, and a set of Donner's all failed at some point," I say with what I hope is some small amount of agency, as most of my wooziness has passed while eating dinner.

"Well, I don't have much back from the manufactures on the guns other than they received them," Eliese says, and she forces a tiny smile. "So how long will it take you to recuperate from this?" she asks, placing me under the sway of her voice.

I think about it and say, "If Doc can cast me and we swap the shale Gate for the farm Gate in the queue, that will allow me to do my initial basecamp set up over a week in D2. I do not have a lot of concern about the work-up for the farming Gate. The swelling in my right hand will be down by the time I Gate walk. Maybe ten days, seven days if I push it." I mull it over a bit more. "The shale Gate terrain is significantly rougher. The new Donners V2 and MLRs will be much more helpful in the farm Gate. I think that is the one to do next. Plus, it gets me off the map for a while, out of the public eye, so to speak."

I am musing out loud and not being as tight-lipped cost me. Eliese is sharp as a tack. She hones in on my last statement, her eyes focusing on mine like a laser beam.

"What do you mean 'gets you off the map for a while'?" she asks.

Her voice is a lullaby now, coaxing the answers out of me. Once again, I realize I am playing way out of my kindergarten league. Her brown eyes are flashing. Her dark hair is roiling as she catches a whiff of me hiding something. I like Eliese, and I know that I love spending time around and near her. I decide in that instant to walk forward in our relationship in much the same way she had at the Family table. I cannot tell her everything here. I can get the basics out and see if we can talk somewhere more secure.

I puff a breath out. "I have suspicions, Eliese, thoughts, nothing I can prove. That is why Samuel left. He is running something down. That phrase before dinner is when he hopes to let me know something. Samuel told me a general when and where: Family residence before dinner. I have concerns, Eliese, enough that I want a secure place to talk about them. They go back to when Samuel and I worked together."

I look at Eliese and try to gauge how she is dealing with this information. Maybe she is wondering if I am like that boy who lied to her all those years ago.

I continue, "When Samuel found me in Dillon, he was hoping we could help each other. Dillon is not an isolated incident, Eliese. I did not even suspect that till today." I am describing a nebulous gut feeling that the three, maybe four incidents are tied together.

"Ray, I'm—" Eliese starts, a bit of heat in her voice. I cut her off politely.

"Raylan, my name is Raylan."

She pauses and starts a few times. I keep going before she can get her momentum rolling. It will be out tomorrow, anyway.

"I am a SkipJack pilot. I spent twelve and a half years working with Major Sam Janks," I say. I use the name he used in the Compact Military. "By the time I made it into Force Recon, I was in the Compact Military a little over four years. I am just that good with SkipJacks. I was a young twenty-two-year-old kid. We did not go through the same FR class, but we were both new to Force Recon and new in the same unit. We were not best buddies at first. Sam and I did become fast friends. All the men in the unit were friends. For the job we did, turnover is about two years," I say quietly.

I look at her to see if she understands. When it becomes clear she does not, I continue, "By that, I mean injury for newbies, like Sam and myself, is within two years. Either they medically discharge you, or they lay your body to rest. Normally there is but one way out of the FR teams." I smile, letting warmth show through. "We..., well, by year seven, Sam and I were the last two of the of our era. We were the old guys. Command went to him. He is an amazing leader. We fought, bled, and stomped all over the world for the next five and a half years."

I am trying to compel caution in my tone, and patience in my telling of the story. I take a deep breath, hoping the visions of that cat do not come back.

"Something happened the night Samuel was hurt." I let that sink in before continuing. "Our unit was on a mountain doing a work-up for a future operation. I was on my way to relieve Samuel when I stopped the attack on him."

I breathe deeply, as images of the fight between the cat and myself flood my mind, at the memory of the pair of us rolling down that hill snarling, kicking, stabbing. For a moment, I have to hold my breath as phantom pains wash over my lower left leg.

I close my eyes and breathe deeply before I continue, "Samuel and I were both taken out of the fight that night, Eliese." I open my eyes again, staring into those coffee-colored eyes. I whisper, "I do not doubt that we would both still be in the Compact Military today had it not been for that night. Samuel had a protocol initiated, likely from Doc Alverez. Sam was trammed to London, and Doc met him there."

I need to prepare for this phase of the conversation. "My unit found me a good deal later. Because of where I was lying, the unit had to hike me down and then out of a valley. Alverez flew to my location and patched me up. He said he was checking on Samuel when the CM discharged me into a halfway-house medical facility in the Virginia District. My VA student nurse had a few weeks left on her schooling. As I got better, I accepted her invitation to follow her to her indenture offer in Community Dillon. CM troopers do not have an indenture, per se: your term of service *is* your indenture."

I am careful about how I speak, and I do not want Jacki's memory to bleed through in this telling.

"I eventually found work as a Gate guard. I spent twoish years of roaming guard duty on weekends. Catch a tram on Friday, tram to a Gate, and work forty-eight hours straight. I would pilot my Skipjack back and forth the whole time. I would then tram back to Community Dillon to crash for a day or two. I hired on full time with CGSU, and they put me on the night shift at the Dillon Gate by chance. I was to share it with two men by the names of Jesus and David," I explain.

Eliese is listening, her hands in her lap. Her face is impassive and free of any tells that I can see. I worry that I abused what little trust I had garnered with her, and I pray she will understand why.

"Well, you know that story. I lost track of Sam, and I never knew who patched me up. I was cut loose with no instructions on how to heal." With both a mental and verbal sigh, I say, "Jackie did her best, but she had no clue as to how to heal a myomere leg. It is definitely not like a normal leg."

I waggle my drying, dirty left sock for her. "It has caused me a lot of issues over those five years. It was part of the reason I was too slow that night at DGMW." I look at Eliese for a moment, hoping for a sign of understanding. Finally, I say, "There is more, some of it is for Samuel to tell, some I only want to say in a secure room." I finish, my voice flowing with gratefulness. If I am the lucky man I hope to be, I have someone to share my burdens with, and she is attentive and gracious. I realize tension is unconsciously fading from my body as I watch her contemplate my story.

Elise looks me in the eye for a moment. Maybe she is worried about the monster I have become. Her eyes move from my left shoulder to my right, down the battered and bruised arm and back over to my left sock.

"You have a myomere leg? From Doc? That's—that's..." Eliese's voice trails off.

I smile and stick out my foot, and wiggle an invitation for her to pull the sock off, which she does delicately with a napkin. My foot is not the cleanest right now, which is an understatement. Dried blood has flowed down the haptic suit to the sock. My lower leg is coated in dry, flaking blood.

I show her the incisions and the replacement, poking it with the soup spoon. I show her the difference between human muscle and myomere. It is hard holding the spoon, but I do it. I want to share everything. Tonight is my chance. I almost lost my friendship with Chen over holding things back. I will not do that to Eliese. I cannot hold back; she would not forgive me that. Her eyes are glued to my lower leg as I push the spoon on one muscle group and then over to the other kind.

When I stop, I say, "Eliese, look at the arm holding the spoon."

Tonight is the first time Eliese has seen my arm without a long sleeve. How she did not notice during dinner is most likely due to her concern for me as a whole, not a lack of attention. Even moments ago, the enormity of my lower left leg being living myomere encouraged her to skip over the scarred portions of my body.

"I was hurt very badly at DGMW:EP1, you know that. You know that lightning struck me." I see her nod, her chin falling separate from the nod. Realization hits her as I say, "Bones, muscles, and fat do not conduct electricity well."

I see horror bloom in her eyes. Eliese's long-fingered hands cover her mouth, and I know that I must not stop. Eliese would never forgive me for hiding it.

In great care, I describe what has happened to me. "The muscles, my muscles, bones, nerves, and vascular system were replaced, Eliese. My left shoulder, collarbone, right shoulder, and arm. The ribs on the right side, my hips, and my leg to the toes on the right side. It burned the fat, split the skin, charred the bones, fried the nerves and blood vessels. Doc was able to give me muscle and bone, but not fat."

I rotate my arm to show the myomere bundles underneath. Her hands still cover her mouth, and now a little gasp slips loose.

"When I say I am good with this," I say, waving the spoon at the table, "I mean it. You ground me as a human. I am not sure how much human is left. I cannot fathom what I am, for sure." I pause, letting the feeling come through. "The Family, especially you, Eliese, and Samuel, have given me a life."

I pause a moment and let the left foot fall heavily to the floor. There is a loud thunk, like a barbell hitting the floor. Then thunks return from below. Apparently, this is a no-thunk zone to Thap. Eliese sits, peering at me, at my face, which is unshaven and likely swollen. She stands, helping me stand. She gingerly moves me to the futon. Eliese does not say a word as she returns with a blanket. My Morrigan sits next to me as close as that little nurse had to Franc. I am asleep in under a minute.

***

C8 S2

I wake up alone on the futon. I work my way to standing. I am sore and extremely stiff from the fight, to be sure, and my left arm throbs painfully under the movement. I must say it feels good, though, to be alive. I am ambulatory. In my book, it is a step up from my last injured visit to Doctor Alverez.

The lacerations are tight. My right hand is more than a little stiff, but I can move my fingers. I step to my bedroom; Eliese has closed the door. I tap and enter on a five-count. She is in my bed. She has rolled to see me come in.

I mumble, "Bathroom." I wash what I can, which is nothing. She comes in, wearing my sweats. She helps with removing the shirt and wipes me clean with the cloth. Then she applies deodorant for me. Eliese attempts to help me in brushing my teeth, which sends us both into giggle fits. She is an arm mover and

211

I move my head. Giggle fits with cuts and bruises lead to more painful giggle fits. Eliese has called off from the office for today.

Pun, her Segundo, is bringing her clothes, and she will accompany me to the appointment at Doc Alverez's office. Her voice is flat and brooks no argument; I am on thin ice. Very thin, indeed. I decide I will accept whatever time she gives me. I try to make groats, then stomp on the floor till Thap comes around, and I ask him. He sees the bandages from the lacerations we all missed in the tram. I suppose that is enough to entice him to help.

Pun delivers the clothes to my room, looking at me, the giant band-aid advertisement man, as he stands at my door. She comes out in dark slacks, dark blue blouse, and a dark blazer. She points me into the room and has Thap and Pun stuff me into my sweats. Apparently, Gurkha training does not cover doing this to a bandaged man with one arm in a sling.

"Thap, please add this to future Segundo training regimens," I quip.

I am in an excellent mood, and I have a chance after many months alone to spend the day with Eliese. That mood fades as Pun tugs my arm through the cut sleevehole of the sweatshirt and I give him the stink eye. Pun returns the gaze without worry.

We head to Doc Alverez's office. Eliese is on her FEED or in private meetings the whole time. There is calling off, and then there is calling off but still having work to get done. I am not complaining: she is here, and she stayed at Hill House. I do not know if we are in good standing, but I hope so. Pun is a thinner wiry man with a less oval face, compared to Thap. He seems the cheerier sort if you were dead. Otherwise, he and Franc probably get along great.

We arrive at Doc's main office. Pun and Thap decide to hobble me into a wheelchair. I am pretty sure they planned it in retribution for having to clothe me, as this is just embarrassing. It gets worse when Franc sees me. He helps Eliese and myself back to the exam room where the Doc will look me over.

"Stand," Franc's basso voice bellows.

I do not know if Franc is just playing at a good-natured nurse because Eliese is here or if he is doing it because I happen to have been slapped around. Once again, I remove the clothes so that Franc could get to work. He starts by peeling off the many bandages.

"Lie down," Franc says.

I do, boxers and all. Eliese looks worried as he pulls off Samuel's handiwork. One by one, he cleans, then platelet glues, and when needed, tosses in some staples. In contrast to the portrayal of a good nurse paying attentive care, he does not apply a local. Staples hurt. I think that is Franc's payback for me bringing my girl into the office. Like I had a choice. I had opened my mouth this morning, only to see storm clouds and lightning in her face. When he is finished, Franc steps back and says, "Good fight. Who did it?"

I look at him, half up on my right elbow, and mumble, "A freaking wolf." He snorts. Then Eliese helps me sit up as he takes a portable x-ray of my arm.

"It's broken," Franc says. He looks at me, and he knows I am saying, "No shit, Sherlock" in my head. "Doc will set it." Then he starts to unwrap my right wrist. When the dressing is off, he pauses and looks at my face and asks, "You let it chew on you?"

Franc's question has all the recrimination he can muster. He gets to cleaning.

He says, "Nothing is torn, just lacerations of the skin." Then with a grin, he adds, "Your doggy couldn't chew myomere." I almost say it, then: I almost call him Nurse Franc. "Doc needs to see this one, also."

Doc comes in soon after. "Hello, Ray, Franc tells me you were in a scrap." Doc's chipper mood plays through his tone. Doc Alverez looks at the x-ray, then at the wrist. That's when he sees Eliese. That is when he looks at me in my boxers, and the myomere showing through the lacerations in my right wrist, and visibly swallows.

I do not know what is going on at this point. The color drains from his face, and he shuffles a step back.

I hear my siren sing, and it is the song that brings men to their doom. "A functional bone, nerves, and myomere muscle transplant?" Eliese breathes deeply. "Not once, but twice, and when I inquire what kind of man he is after you found out about me having dinner with him, you didn't inform me that he saved my brother's life?" Her tone and volume are rising, and the melody is fast becoming a hurricane. "That he's suffered time after time and is still a kind man? That you've spent four fucking Gates on his recovery, let alone whatever you spent on his surgeries?"

Doc, the man I watched force Steve Jenkins down, pales. I certainly have picked my Morrigan. I see Pun, all five-foot-three and 140 pounds of him, step in front of Franc, who looks into the room. Eliese must sense his presence looming at the doorway. She raises one slim finger back behind her in a warning. She points back out the door.

"I told you, Doc," Franc grumbles as he spins on his heel and leaves. "This one is all on you."

"Yes, you did," Doctor Alvarez says. He breathes in and out. He can see she is on the warpath. "I could say a lot of things, Eliese. He is my patient, or that is my portion of the Family business. I can say many, many things." He swallows again as his voice wavers under her glare. "I said nothing because you two need time. If I said something, you might have moved too fast." He sighs. "You both needed to heal." He is speaking now as a grandfather would to a granddaughter. "Eliese, he is as strong in body and mind as you are in intellect and wisdom. I could not dream of a better man for you than him."

That brings her up short. She lowers her hand, looks at me, then returns her tempest gaze upon Doc.

"Raylan, did you know?" Eliese finally asks.

"No, I had no idea. Really? The cost of four Gates on my recovery?" I say as she sits. She reaches out and touches my left arm gently and nods.

I shake my head no, more than a little shocked at the level of investment the Family has in me.

Doc, now that he can talk shop, says in his best Doctor voice, "More like fourteen, all in. See, Ray, you are not just myomere muscle or myomere bone. You are growing. The myomere is coming into its full size...no, size isn't the right word. Capacity: full capacity. That is why you have such drastic weight growth. No one has ever taken to a myomere transplant so successfully, let alone bones, marrow, muscle, nerves, and vessels.

"I had thought you died with that first foot surgery. The NAC Military would give me no further information on you. When I operated that first time, you had been bleeding out slowly for almost two days. You had no water and suffered from hypothermia on the mountainside. That is why I was so upset and profusely apologized to you when we met in Dillon."

"There have been plenty of soldiers with myomere legs or arms," I counter. I had seen them.

Eliese says, "Those are prosthetics, Raylan. Those come off, are charged and powered by a power cell. You are living myomere, which is integrated into your whole body. Nerves, white blood cells, bone marrow, and epidermis cover it all. That's what the doctor is getting at. You escaped death twice, with myomere surgery. That's why your recent recuperation was in secret, I think?" Her last statement is a question for Doc, who nods in return.

I turn to her as she squeezes my arm. Doc is looking at my wrist again. "The wolf only lacerated the skin. Franc cleaned it very well," he says, as he starts pulling glue and staples. "There's not much a wolf can do to this arm. Its teeth would never damage the myomere here." He pauses after applying the glue and holding it together with a pinched face. "Why didn't you shoot it, Ray? I know you're carrying an arsenal." Alvarez asks with a great deal of incredulity.

As I watch him grab the stapler, I comment between pops, "Well, that is the thing, Doc: metal items seem to become brittle around me." He pauses and looks at me as the stapler pops again. That one hurts. At his gesture, I rotate my wrist so he can put in more staples. "Any metal I use regularly eventually is too brittle to use. SkipJacks with the panniers, firearms, pots, pans, snowshoes..." I go with "snowshoes" so that I do not have to explain the marsh shoes. "Maybe I cause it?"

"I can't imagine how. Do you have samples? I would love to see them," he states as he sets my wrist down and looks at the arm.

I said, "Thap has a few knives, shoes, and pots for you. The firearms are still firearms, and I can't release them off the Hill House property."

He nods. "I'm going to set this. First, I need to numb it." There are some quick shots, and then he leaves briefly to get the rest of the gear. I FEED message Thap and have him give Franc the metal bits.

When the Doc returns, he does another x-ray and sets the bone, then a third x-ray before sticking my arm in a 3D myomere printer. Great, now I get this crap on the outside.

As the three of us step out of the clinic office and into the hallway with Pun, Thap and Franc return from retrieving the samples. Doc ushers us all down the hall to his office. There, we cover my nutrition, my intake, and a regimen of fortified foods that he had put together for me. The knives, pots, and pans are of interest to Franc. The discussion ensues over what could cause the issue. It magically hits noon as Doc wraps things up with a small prescription for antibiotics, along with a stern warning to start them tonight as he passes me a glass of his whiskey. We all toast a safe upcoming survey.

Franc, being Franc, toasts, "Here's to Ray winning a fight with a puppy dog." I am not sure if I am more surprised at the length at which he speaks or the joke.

Thap, being Thap, quips, "It was a big puppy, though," as he thumbs Franc a photo of me carrying the dog into the tram.

I think Franc begins to see why I had the fight I did. Franc sounds almost impressed while looking at the photo and eying the part of the knife he is grinding to dust between two of his fingers, "How did you kill it?"

I look Franc in the eyes and say, "I punched it." That seems to get his attention.

"How many times did you have to slap it?" Franc asks.

Apparently, he is not as impressed as I had hoped.

"Three. One to the kidney, one to the ribs, and one hammer fist to the base of the skull while it latched onto my arm. That is when the arm broke," I reply, noting the failure in the last part.

I watch as he nods, before his basso grumble comes out. "Great strategy: break your arm."

Then I hear it again. Eliese has been quiet for a while. Her voice carries command and obeisance. "Enough, Nurse Franc." I catch Thap's eye, and Pun's. I know Thap is as worried as I am. Pun is deathly pale.

"You deserved it," replies Doc.

I look back at Franc, who only smiles and nods to Eliese.

"My apologies. I carried the joke too far, and too personally."

Franc apologizes to Eliese, but not to me. Jerk. As the thought enters my mind, he at least looks at me.

"Ray has never struck me as anything but a man who works at everything. My apologies, Ray, for the jest," Franc says.

"No offense taken, Franc. If you want to come next time and fight the wolves for me..." My grin shows my teeth as I let the offer hang between us.

Franc lets out a short snort for a laugh.

Doc chimes in and says, "Healing is going to take some time. Six weeks, at least."

We outline our plan and how we are going to bring it up to Stewart at the meeting later today.

"I'll consent to signing off the next gate," Dr. Alvarez says, "after you've had seven days of rest."

***

C8 S3

Eliese and I return to the Family residence by tram. I have my sweats back on. Thap forwards a dozen messages to my FEED. I have a meeting this afternoon with General Jermaine Diomedes. It seems Chen and Lily are doing well. Meghan accepted an offer with CBN as a SkipJack pilot, further tying Boss's foundry to CBN. Work has picked back up enough for Boss to put two of his old employees back to work. Lily is now helping Chen full time. Most of the business for them is repair work. Chen mentions the six Donners V1s made it through the Gate and that Craig is sending a gift to Ray, with instructions to make sure it gets to Eliese.

Personal FEED messages dealt with, I start the real work by diving into the data that the head of the GSG needs to know. Later, I prep for my meeting with General Diomedes. I read the list of messages, organize it in my thought processes, and thumb it back to Thap. I then wade into the details on the most critical issues. By the time Thap guides me from the tram to our apartment, I only have a few things of note left to review.

First, the Family has orders placed for surveys only, about ten surveys at time. They have over 200 Gates ready for survey, some under older settlement contracts. Most still need surveys to be completed. The contracts for surveying a settlement, as we are calling it, is limited to about ten at a time. This is primarily due to that ten-year build-up for Stage One on the D2 side of the Gate.

I have cut the initial estimate survey and build-up down considerably on most. CBN:D2 is a trial. They are ready to move forward with logging and need less support from EP1. That is not the case for every D2 iteration. CBN needs less than the fishing conglomerate, which must build docks, drydocks, and harbors, along with their settlements.

While my nine-month trip into CBN:D2 created the base for a small settlement that was pulling in about a hundred new citizens of their nation monthly, it would still be years for the North East Fishing Conglomerate Gate (NE-FCG:D2) to even consider launching vessels and shipping back product.

I have a few choices for my next surveys: two are shorter-term start-ups, one is a logging enterprise, and the other is a farming via hothouse vegetables enterprise. My final three choices are another fishing conglomerate, a shale oil company, and a mineral extraction consortium. Each of these Gates will take years to set up, even after the initial survey.

My surveys knock off one to five years helps, but there is still an opportunity to tailor things to the client's needs to kickstart them faster. I need to noodle this problem over in my mind for a bit. In the end, I will likely bring Samuel in on this. His outside-the-box way of viewing things could be very helpful. He might even be the right person to problem-solve the Stage Two portion of a settlement build-up.

The other main takeaway is that while my surveys are saving money, the whole start-up venture is still too expensive. There remains a high chance these start-ups go under or default on their contracts with us for the Gate. It is a risky business. We need to find markets besides the Compact for these goods at prices that keep the products moving.

I know this is primarily Stewart's and Eliese's realm. I will see if I can come up with anything they have not. For now, I am going to talk to Eliese about encouraging multiple diverse groups in the start-up. For instance, the loggers still need food and the fishermen still need their clothing. Spreading that risk over at least three corporate groups would lower the initial cost for each group and separate Stage Two build-up.

Other than the initial messages forwarded to me by Thap, I use my FEED terminal in the flat. We take the time to sit for lunch. Our talk consists of how I organize things and the comments I lay out for each. Thap is attentive. He quickly adapts to my workflow. If there is something he thinks I failed to consider, he brings it up. If we need to, we make changes. Lunch winds down as I bring up another subject I have been mulling over.

"Thap, I need a backup weapon, a knife or a gun that is in good condition. It should be something I will use only as a last resort. I must be able to conceal it, and it must pack a punch. If it has range, good, but that is not necessary. It cannot have metal. Robust, Thap, it has to hold up," I say, looking off to the side as I flex my right fingers.

"I'll look into it; I have some ideas. I shall see what I can procure," Thap says, adding to the growing list on his FEED. "Raylan, you need to be ready for your meeting with General Diomedes."

I look up. "Where are we meeting?" I ask. "Jermaine is my old commander. If he is here, then he wants something. Informal would be good; do you have any suggestions?"

Thap is a military man himself and he likely knows of General Diomedes by reputation. In Thap, I think I see a kindred spirit, as he takes a moment to comprise his response. "I think, Raylan, that you have two choices: here in the sitting room or the historical greenhouse."

I contemplate those options a good deal as I shower. It is a tricky thing showering with all these cuts, abrasions, and bruises. Thap has pulled a set of slacks and a button-down shirt for me to wear. It takes some work to get my cast through the sleeve, but I manage. I decide to go with our sitting room, and Thap makes the arrangements before clearing the General for entry.

I meet my old commander as he is ushered in by a Gurkha I have seen a couple of times. General Diomedes is an imposing man: nearly two meters tall, broad shoulders, hands the size of platters. His lined face is so dark you only see the creases of war when he smiles. He is generally a good-natured man who has been in this command for a very long time. Any remote SkipJack unit owes their start to his role with the modern Force Recon. He is ninety years old if he is a day.

I step forward and shake his hand, looking up to him as I say, "Good to see you again, General."

"Horseshit, Ray," General Diomedes booms. "I'm the last person a man in your position wants to see."

I turn as two more men come in, and they start sweeping the apartment for bogeymen and bugs. Within a couple of minutes of silence, they return into the sitting area and nod. One retreats to the doorway along with Thap. The other goes outside the door with the Gurkha that escorted the three here.

"Are all of the Forty Gurkhas?" he asks as he thumbs over his shoulder to Thap.

"Yes, part of the package of being a member at the Family table," I respond evenly. I suspect General Diomedes knows all of this, and he is looking for his opening.

The General sits dwarfing the chair, making the room seem very small. He crosses his right ankle on his left knee. I hope I can do that when I am his age. He sits there staring at me, drumming his fingers on the table.

"Ray, I have a project. I saw your name come across a permit for a weapons research group. I only know of one Ray with the clearances to even ask for such a thing, so I signed off on it. I need help. The MKVs that replaced the MKIVs you and Sam piloted suck ass. We lose too many in a fight. My teams are dying." The General pauses a moment. If the FR teams are dying, then normal pod-based troopers are faring worse. "The old MKIVs are too limited in scope by today's standards: time on station, latency, armor, speed, you name it. A few years back, we got saddled with this boondoggle called the MKV." The general's lip curls.

I nod and look at the problem. I pop up a purposely placed 3D tester, bringing up the eight variants of the MKIV I know to exist. I do not know the specs of the MKV, but I have heard rumors. Jermaine thumbs over five models of MKV SkipJacks as I finish bringing up the specs of the older units I know.

It does not take me long to see the issue. The biggest failure with the MKIV was its time on station, and time on reserve power. That includes the haptic suit reserve and SkipJack reserve. The MKV has increased that time by twenty percent, at the cost of armor, ammo, guns, speed, and survivability. The only two things that make it fieldable is its latency from the pilot, which is half as much as the MKIV, followed by that twenty percent increase in time on station.

The General is patient while I look things over. With a wave, I toss it all away and hand Jermaine the 3D tester puck. Everything I have seen is all classified material, and if he wants me to have it, he will give it back.

"General Diomedes the MKV is a lost cause. The structure is such that it cannot carry more armor or weapons. Its power source is unable to swap out. There is a boondoggle story there, but I will pass on that for now. How can I help?" I ask.

Sitting across from my old commander brings out my version of a regimental military voice. I am sure Thap will give me crap for it later.

He grins. "What I wouldn't do to have you and Sam back. In twenty-five minutes, you see what I've been after my staff to see for three years." He slaps the table with his massive hand. "Ray, any chance you know where Sam went off to? I really want input from both of you."

I smile. I know Samuel is here. I look over to Thap, and he steps into the hallway, messaging Samuel. I return my attention to the general. "Lay out the problem for me. If he has time, I will coerce him into helping."

"Good, good. We have a new MKVI chassis that I'm contemplating allowing into an updated trials program. So far, the Compact Military twats have not touched it. This chassis is from a start-up, well outside the typical CM procurement corporations. They're struggling with a few issues, and if they dump a chassis into the trials, they'll be snatched up by those very same CM twats. However, if they partner with a weapons developer and enter the trials as an unknown, with a complete SkipJack model, then they can license that design to be made if they succeed in procuring the contract."

I see how General Diomedes will get his way, and his MKVI for his FR teams. He will convince the rest of the CM to look one way while I build him a SkipJack like the world has never seen.

I respond with a wide leonine grin as I phrase my question carefully. "Sir, what kind of death from the ground would you like for my team to design?"

There is a knock on the door, and then Thap enters with Samuel.

Samuel is too good-looking to be faked by anyone, even in his suit, and you cannot mistake him for anybody else. Jermaine does a double take. "You both work here?"

I cannot stop grinning. Seeing General Jermaine Diomedes be flat-footed is something I am not going to let slip away. "General Jermaine Diomedes, I would like to introduce Samuel Jankowitz, number four at the Family table. Formerly known as Major Sam Janks."

Samuel and Jermaine are shaking hands. I quickly fill Samuel in and we are off brainstorming. After a bit of back and forth between the three of us, Samuel says, "The MKVI chassis should take the standard weapons from the MKIII, IV, and V SkipJacks. Let's not change that. It sounds like Jermaine is mostly looking for a couple of options outside the current five MKV models.

"We need an Interceptor model that replicates the fast pursuit and fast attack of an old MKIII while maintaining long-range support and extended reserve power. Follow that with an Infiltrator model that's as fast, quiet, can use active sound suppression, and packs close in destructive power against non-SkipJack threats, favoring more towards human adversaries."

Jermaine thinks it over. "If you boys can knock it out of the park with those two options, I can delay the trials another year or so. I'm not happy with the options put forward so far, and neither are my pod-based infantry brethren."

General Diomedes drums his fingers on the table as he ponders. "I need them fast, faster than the twenty-seven kilometers per hour of the MKV. I need an increase in reserve power operation over the MKV, not much, but some. I need the ability to chase or stalk." He is deep in thought as he drums fingers some more. "Can you boys do that?"

Samuel looks at me as he intones, "Ray is the head of the GSG, sir. He's the one to ask. I'm just a glorified pretty boy, a gopher."

Jermaine and I both snort out loud at that, as he is no such thing.

"I think I can, and I have a few ideas in mind, General. Some of these ideas might make a difference in the military trials. Let me give it a go. When I have tested one, I will send you the FEED data for your input. Your staff can forward the details and contracts to my Segundo, Thap."

With that, we all stand.

General Diomedes pauses on the way out and says, "It's good to see you boys again. If I had twenty of you two, this would be a far safer world. Be safe, gentleman. Good hunting." His last words are an echo of every briefing he had ever given us.

The Lion of the Compact strides from the room, a titan, his full, compact military bearing on display. I turn to Samuel as the door closes. He says, "No news yet, Raylan. I should have it tonight. I'm heading out of here shortly to run a part of that down. I'll catch up with you later."

Shortly afterward, Thap enters and starts his clean-up of the mess we did not leave. I think he does these acts just to look busy.

Absently, I ask, "Why was Pun scared when Eliese said 'Nurse Franc'?" I turn to give him my attention.

Thap grimaces a bit as a shudder ripples through his body.

"Doc is the only one of the seven without a Gurkha guard," Thap says. "He used to have a Segundo when he first joined. Now, though, all Dr. Alvarez has is a nurse. An ugly one at that, or so said Pun's brother, Phan."

I raise an eyebrow at that, and Thap grins.

"He taunted Nurse Franc for a good long while," Thap says. "One morning, while Phan and others were sparring in our barracks, Franc walked in. He strides up to the mat. It's a big mat, a regular competition martial arts mat. Franc kicks off his shoes and motions for Phan's sparring partner to leave."

"Franc didn't hit Phan; he never struck him. He lets Phan beat on him till Phan's gasping. Franc stood there blocking, turning, tossing, timing the shin, the elbow, or the forehead to intercept. It was just enough to leave Phan a bruised, beaten pulp. Franc never threw a blow in that hourlong bout."

"Phan spent the next week in Franc's care, where Franc listed every failure. Pun watched it all, as did most of us young hotheads at the time. Franc may be slower moving now, but it just means he will not take a beating now as he did back then. It's the first lesson we teach those incoming to the Forty: Franc, *not* Nurse Franc."

I am deep in thought for a long while before I stand. My mind wanders through the dozen topics I need to take care of as the head of GSG.

"Let us get ready for the remainder of my other meetings today," I say with a nod towards my closet.

EVAN DESHAIS

***

C8 S4

With that comes the effort of dressing my arm and my bandaged wrist appropri-
ately. It is one thing for a titan of the military to see my injuries. It is another for
a titan of industry. I am feeling quite a bit sprier after the platelet glue has stuck
everything back together. I am stiff and sore, moving slowly, but I am getting
about. The left arm is in its thin myomere cast. I slip it through a dress shirt
with some effort.

I arrive on time, and a moment later Eliese walks up with her Segundo. There
is a coolness, an undecided nature to our relationship. I have some explaining to
do, still. We knock and enter Stewart's office. We sit after Eliese plays out her
secretary role. Stewart and I both decline any refreshments.

"I am greatly disappointed in the two of you." Stewart says, his hands folded,
looking over the top of his nose at us, glaring at my arm in a cast. "Cavorting
around, causing a stir."

I do not know about Eliese, but I am honestly lost. Neither of us had cavorted
anything or in any way.

"Don't give me that look. Doc sat in that exact chair an hour ago, Eliese,
and told me you were purposefully 'ratio slipping time between EP1 and D2
iterations!'" Stewart says. He sucks in a breath of air as his face reddens. "Of all
the stupid things to play with, of all the dumb things to do." He points his right
index finger at me. "Putting yourself and this Family at risk over a few months?"

There is no doubt in my mind now: Stewart is building up steam for a good
old-fashioned ass-chewing.

His head shifts from one of us to the other and he is about to start in again.

I put some myomere in my voice to slow down the pace of his rant when I
say, "The problem, Stewart, is my visibility. I am the first new Family member

in just over two decades, and the first real non-familial member in more than sixty-five years. A man the world has never heard of, never seen, or read about. No one knows of my accomplishments. No one has access to my sealed military record. My discharge papers show only my medical discharge. If I am not visible regularly and disappear for nine months at a time, people will ask questions."

I pause, holding three fingers up. Stewart's eyes go a bit wide at my assertions, and his lips firm into a thin line, but he holds for me to continue.

"First, Thap has dealt with these inquires since I was named. I will have to answer some shortly. Currently, my recuperation from," I wave my arm around, "will suffice. The inquiries are in the thousands, not the tens."

Down to two fingers.

"Second, it allows me to complete a survey and be back in usually twenty-one days, maybe a bit more. Me being missing for that long visually is easy to explain if I am still using FEED messages and working 'on-site,'" I say, with only one finger remaining.

"Third and finally. My surveys are not enough. We are cutting one to three years, maybe five, on some new D2 iteration settlements' Stage One progress. We are not building the settlement second stages fast enough, as it will take seven to ten years. By building out the second stage and having me prep the sites for it, we will drastically reduce our clients' costs, reducing the chance of our clients defaulting on their project. If that is going to be the set-up, then we need me to have the availability of ratio slip."

Stewart sits back. I am justifying our screwing with ratio slip, of course, but I know Eliese will likely have the data to back up my assertions.

Sure enough, Eliese's song commences, and she says, "We have conducted ratio slip tests on each of the current five D2 iterations. The first was CBN:D2, then the NEFC:D2, and while Ray was in the most recent, we conducted the same tests on each of the farming, shale, and mining iterations. Each and every D2 iteration has its particular ratio slip."

"We test it thoroughly, through twelve separate instances via drones. If there were any discrepancies in the drone tests, we would not use ratio slip. Decoupling from that D2 iteration would likely be less costly in the long run. We can simply connect to a second D2 that does not have that issue."

I notice that Eliese does not mention the ratio slip for CBN:D2. She still does not know how or who had started messing with the ratio slip while I was in the D2. Eliese thumbs the test data and the accompanying metrics over to Stewart's FEED terminal, which he expands, and the three of us go over it in great detail. Much of it is new to me. They could, in the last D2 iteration, effectively ratio slip me up to five years in a week. That would be a trip. The science is fascinating and mostly over my head. Eliese understands enough to be able to have her team of scientists fire off responses to questions she cannot answer.

After an hour, Stewart relaxes, and seems mollified to some degree. It's clear that this is not over as he says, "I know you, Eliese: you won't risk anyone, let alone a confidant, a paramour," Stewart waves his hand at me, "like Ray, without the kind of data you have. I suppose I'm most frustrated at the lack of forthrightness in keeping me updated on these projects and all the parts. I need not know every detail, Eliese and Ray, but I do expect to know *of* everything we're working on."

I looked at Eliese, and she nods at me. "Well, let me start. I am putting in a production shop at Hill House for working up new SkipJack designs that will fit my needs better." Stewart pauses me.

"Hill House?" Stewart asks with a bit of exasperation.

I hook my thumb over my shoulder towards Thap.

"One of Thap's better suggestions, even though I hated it initially. When the corporation formed, the 'Cabin' ceased to exist. In its ashes rose the Hill House," I say. Stewart nods, and I continue, "Along with the Hill House and shop, I am now a munitions manufacturer, which is a requirement for me to keep arms for the surveys I do. One of those munitions is militarized SkipJacks. I have a few experimental frames coming in.

"Thap and I will be building them up for my application. We are negotiating a contract with my old commander, General Jermaine Diomedes. He is looking for an upgrade to the CM MKV that includes an interceptor/infiltrator style build. I think that is how Thap and Samuel got the approval permitting through."

I raise my left and right arms. The left sleeve covers the cast, barely, and the cuff of the right sleeve remains undone due to the bandages over the right wrist.

"In addition to the weapons, I am looking into the issue of the DGMW:D2 failure. I have not decided where to start and I would like your counsel. Yesterday is the fourth time they have attacked me and the third time the Family has been attacked," I say and pause, giving it some more thought.

"I am planning to pull Samuel in on a couple of problem-solving issues—issues that should only be spoken of here in your office, as you mentioned. The most recent of those is the wolf that attacked me. It was targeting me, specifically. It all started with Samuel's accident all those years ago, and I have some serious concerns. Second, less so, is ratio slip, and how to set up the second stage of settlement prep. Yes, our costs will go up, but I think our default rate by clients should go down by as much as two-thirds." I exhale slowly. "DGMW:D2 should only be discussed in this room also. For me, that is about it."

Eliese takes her father's nod for her to start. "Things I haven't brought up to you as yet: I'm covering science pertaining to ratio slip. It's new ground, and we wouldn't have known about it had the DGMW:EP1 Gate not been one of the first to receive a systems upgrade. I've pulled a few, three, to be exact, members of the Family's science team to work on the Gate's temporal lock, offered them these new roles, and moved them to this District. I put them in a secured site and handed them this project under every Non-Disclosure Agreement (NDA) and legal agreement the Family's attorneys could come up with. Once they saw the possibilities, they dove in," Eliese explains.

"It's not a foolproof situation, but it is interesting. Say we have a D2 with a full settlement; instead of small supplies of fish, we ratio slip, and then the D2 ships us the complete season's worth of packaged product at once. There are ethical issues, to be sure. It might work better for, say, mining or timber," Eliese says.

"I'm working on the unique issue of metal fatigue in D2 iterations. This issue was brought up by Ray. It's more in line with what I do than Samuel or Darien. Doc is also taking advantage of his unique skillset to sort out what might cause it." She smiles. "Other than that, I'm overseeing the production side of the various SkipJacks needed for our contract partners to build out the Stage One part of the settlements."

Eliese pauses and says, "That's a partnership with Darien. Most of the initial rapid prototyping goes through his contacts with the Japanese Mega-Corps." With a frown, she continues, "I'll likely start working with Samuel on the Stage Two plans that he and Ray will be designing."

Slowly, Stewart sits back. He folds his hands on his chest and looks up. "Three attacks for the Family, four for you? The Dillon gate, and this wolf. What was the other?"

"Samuel's accident six-plus years ago, DGMW:EP1, CBT:EP1's ratio slip, and the wolf," I say. I look at Stewarts face, and he looks almost lost.

"Samuel was attacked while camping on leave?" Stewart asks, sitting upright in his chair. Stewart holds my gaze for a second and turns to his eldest daughter. At a shake of Eliese's head, he thumbs a message to Samuel. This story is Samuel's story to tell. A response comes quickly; it seems that Samuel is on his way here, and it will be but a few minutes.

As we wait, I take working with Samuel off Eliese's plate. Thap and I need to start hammering out and filling out GSG staff positions. Now would give us an excellent opportunity to get that rolling, even if it is marginally slower.

Samuel enters, and Pun, Eliese's Segundo, brings in a third chair for him. I give myself a mental high five for remembering Pun's name.

As Samuel sits, he adjusts his jacket and says, "Father, Eliese, Raylan. Some-one piloted the wolf. There are 4,200 sub-dermal implants tied to a kind of 'haptic suit' under the skin." Samuel turns to me and lets his own predatory grin creep onto his face. "Just like the cougar, Raylan. It's primarily a reverse SkipJack. Theoretically, you pilot from the pod, the pod sends its singals to the sub-dermal haptic suit, which in turn initiates the sub-dermal implants, and they fire off the muscle groups."

"According to my acquaintance who did the necropsy, the poor thing was under heavy sedation. The whole thing was horrendously complex, much more so than the Lion," Sam says with a kind of shocked amazement. "The latency is horrible, think MKI, maybe MKII, on the wolf. I can only imagine how bad piloting the cougar was."

I hold up a hand for Stewart to wait. "What was the haptic implant count on the cougar, do you remember? Was there a way to trace any of the origins?" I ask Samuel.

Sam pulls up his FEED and thumbs something to each of us. Stewart brings it up on his expansive wooden desk FEED terminal. The two beasts' necropsy stats are displayed side by side. The cougar has about 2,300 sub-dermal implants, sporting a matching quantity grafted onto the skin haptic patches. The power pack was sewn into the soft tissue area of the stomach. The wolf had 4,200 sub-dermal implants, with a skin sporting a not-dissimilar mesh from mine. Where my sub-dermal mesh inputs are continuously variable, and I still require a purposefully crafted haptic suit, the wolf has a visible haptic mesh between the muscle and skin, with fixed positions correlating to the sub-dermal implants.

I sit for a moment. I am pretty sure that Samuel and I were the only ones to fully grasp what we see. Progression, the birth of a new way of looking at a problem.

I point out, "It is like my mesh, except it is as if the opposition came at the issue from a different direction. That they both thought of the problem and worked out a solution without knowledge of the other's work."

Samuel says, "That's my thought, as well, Raylan. It shows a continuous improvement to the previous design." Samuel points at the wolf, then the cat. "Six years ago, give or take, that cat took me down, and nearly killed you. If it had been the wolf, I think we would both be dead."

I nod. "We are in a race now and we are at least six years behind."

I turn to him as Eliese speaks up. "I would like an explanation, Raylan. I'm due at least that much. You hid this from me." There is a hint of accusation. She expects any and all clarity. I cannot blame her.

Sam pauses Eliese with a light touch to her arm and says, "Forgive me, Eliese; that was at my request, before Raylan even agreed to work for the Family." He looks at his father. "I was never a postal clerk."

Sam begins his story: the Compact Military, war collage, the basic overview of Force Recon. Samuel tells his account of the attack on the mountain. He outlines years of night-terrors that started during his long recovery. They only became stronger after watching our helmet videocams. How finding me allowed him to come to grips with what is out there: a pilot that could SkipJack animals. How he suspects that the cat came for him that night on the Faroe Islands.

Samuel explains how he thought me dead until he was handed the review of the DGMW Gate failure. Samuel finishes relating his story, including his work with the troubleshooting of the wolf's systems, including a dissection of the wolf.

Stewart asks, "War college? I hear retirees mention it a lot. No such college exists. Samuel, we'll need to discuss this in private after this. You should have informed me at the time."

Samuel and I both chuckle at the war college comment. I say, "It is part true, part not. There is not a college for which you can enroll, receive a degree, and pay it off via an indenture. It is...how the Compact Military conditions you. Finish a mission, get a college class, and credit. You still have to study, but between deployments and work-ups, you have pretty much one thing to do: war college. Shit, Samuel finished a business degree, art history, and a couple of others."

Samuel nods to his father. "At the time, I was scared. It took me a long time to realize that I'm not only suffering from trauma of the incident, but the footage viewed a few years later. Before Garung and I went back to the mountain and recovered the cat corpse, and the helmets, I had no clue it wasn't just a big, bad kitty." Then he looks at me and snorts. "The historian over there. His one degree to my four."

Stewart looks at me. "What degree would that be?"

"History. I studied war. Specifically, the days leading up to, and the recovery after wars end. I wanted to know about peace and what it took to obtain it. How far a group must push to achieve victory, then what they should do to rebuild." Slowly giving it some more input, I add, "That, of course, leads down many rabbitholes of tactics, logistics, and support. Each is claiming their portion of the victory." I wave in a broad gesture. "I had grand ideas about making a difference once and for all. With time, I came to understand that it is mostly holding back the evils that constantly poke the edges of humanity," I say, rather morosely.

I begin to see Stewart's tactic. He asks questions to the side of any issue, twirling you around while he contemplates the last answer you gave. This kind of questioning keeps your mind dancing.

"Do we have leads on the wolf?" Stewart asks.

Bingo, there it is: Stewart's central question.

Samuel sits up a little straighter. "The sub-dermals are a generic manufacture and the lot has traced back to five dispersals from the NAC: various old continent countries, the Chinese Confederacy, Japan, Brazil. The haptic mesh is unknown, but its haptic input patches are pretty much the same, and the only overlap is Brazil and Japan," Samuel explains.

Stewart does his twist again, twirling my mind in circles. "How were those two dinners, Ray?" As my head is spinning, I see Eliese's smile hit her eyes.

"Raylan is now up to four dinners, Father," Eliese quips in a very magnanimous tone.

"You better get on that, Ray." He smiles. "Let's call it for today. Samuel, will you stay?"

With that, Eliese and I rise. I exit with her. "Four?" I repeat.

Her long fingers dance in front of her. "The two you owed, the tax on them for not being paid in full, and the final one for not telling me all of this in the first place," she says with a smile as she spins to look at me. Eliese has a sparkle in her eyes when she continues, "Raylan, I expect first class. Unique. After last night, I'm raising the bar significantly above Tree Rat Stew." She twirls as she heads for her desk as I collect Thap and head to my suite.

***

C8 S5

I spend the remaining time going over options on how better to equip a second stage build-out of settlement plans. There is only so much you can do through a single data trunk. Even if we add more, it would almost be SkipJacks working on top of each other. I am wrapping it up and shoving it to the back of my mind as Thap lets me know we have a few minutes to head to dinner.

The dinner is lovely. Dr. Alvarez is back to working on whatever research project my injuries and subsequent recovery pulled him away from. I think he skipped tonight's meal to avoid any fireworks between Eliese and Stewart when they have the ratio slip discussion.

Darien is on a tram flight from Japan. From what I understand, his end of the Family work revolves around procurement and manufacturing. Eliese's younger sister Trish is now well into her indenture, and she is hell-bent on beating Eliese's indenture pay-off time.

For tonight, that leaves Stewart, Samuel, Eliese, and myself. Dinner is fantastic and the conversation is light, as if the overly stressful topic in Stewart's office never happened. We are served another stunning five-course meal. For a guy who cooks one-pot food, each dish is something new. The dinner tonight gives me some ideas, a direction to follow with my first two dates with Eliese. I need to put together something different, as she can have this everyday. I now have some planning to do.

We have finished our dinner and said our excuses as Eliese and I walk down to the library. It is a massive room, one whole wall and ceiling full of transparent panels of protective glass. It allows us to see the stars, the moon, and the clouds. It pales against the stars in D2 iterations, as D2 planets have no light pollution, or much pollution, in general, blocking them. I appreciate it nonetheless. Pun steps to a cabinet and retrieves a blanket for Eliese as we stretch out on a two-person chaise lounge. Our feet are just passing by each other. I like this set-up. Our conversations are now face to face as we look at the stars.

"What did Doc mean by 'you both need to heal'?" I ask softly while watching her stare up into the night sky.

I suppose I could comment on the shudder Eliese lets loose. I do not, as I deem it a private frisson of horror.

Eliese's eyes find mine ever so briefly, with a set of pursed lips as she begins. "The boy...well, the man was named Rivas March. Someone placed him in the private school that Darien and I attended. We think it was for the specific purpose of getting here and making his way to Grandfather's office. It's now Father's office."

I can only imagine the kind of expense it would take to insert a student of wealth and means into the schools the Jankowitz family use. There would need to be a background check, along with vetting of the family's history and standing. It is not as simple as paying the tuition; no, in these institutions, you need be the right kind of people. To place a spy, an infiltrator there, you need resources above and beyond simple credits.

With a pressurized steadiness, Eliese explains, "One night after dinner and most of the Family had retired, he convinced me to show him around. I did. I admit I was smitten. He said the right things a fourteen-year-old girl wanted to hear. He was as coy as one could be with a clueless girl." She tenses and steadies herself again, and says, "He asked about the tram storage hangar. Grandfather had a lot of rare stuff, so we toured the hangar. Then I showed him the living areas, which required me to take him through the corporate offices."

Eliese's hands wring together, and I watch her jaw set. There is anger in these memories, along with shame and admonishment, to be sure, but the greatest is anger. I cannot tell if it is anger at this Rivas, or at herself. Maybe after all these years, it is a blending of both.

Eliese's clenched jaw loosens, and she says, "We had been coming from the tram hangar. Long story short, I had just shown him how to escape."

I can hear the tension, the mistrust, the grievance of her soul at how this Rivas used and betrayed her.

Elise continues, "The next night, he knew exactly where to go. My mother and her Segundo caught and held him for the authorities. The cracking package he had on him was something we had anticipated, I suppose. It set off Grandfather's silent alarm. Mom received it and responded. The Forty turned him over to the District constabulary. Rivas was tried and convicted."

Eliese sits up and grimaces a bit. There is more here, more pain, a deeper more frightening pain. Her eyes go a bit wide, and she looks about the darkened shadows in the room.

"I was told he died in jail," Eliese says. With a significant intake of air, she continues softly. "Grandfather was furious at me. Yes, that hurt, and it hurt more because I was his favorite. I didn't know any better. I mean, I knew we were not supposed to be out roaming the Residence at night. Rivas was here for a full week, and no one knew he was an agent. Grandfather was so upset that I was paired with Pun before I returned to school."

Eliese takes a big shuddering breath and whispers, "A few years later, my mother, Emily, died shortly after Trish's birth. We knew it was coming. Trish was the miracle Mother had hung on for. By that time, well, there was nothing we could do."

"We buried her during my freshman year in college. I was still hard at work, proving myself better than Darien's jokes and Grandfather's only ever unkind words to me," Eliese says weakly.

El plays with the frilled edge of the blanket. I decide I like that nickname for her, El, it carries well and holds the totality of who she is nicely. Out of the corner of my eye, I see Pun motion to the door. He and Thap leave, shutting it behind them. The click of the door starts her story once more.

"Pun took delivery of a message to my FEED. It was a short video: my mother being cared for by a nurse. The nurse was doing this crack your fingers thing. Most people..." She begins to pop her knuckles to demonstrate. "Most people start with the thumb or the index finger and work down to the pinky. Rivas, he had this unique way: he did it all in reverse. Pinky to index. He was always this 'do things differently' guy," Eliese explains, phrasing her words in such a manner, as if her story could resurrect a dead man.

She is almost sobbing at this point. I pass her the pocket square from my jacket. El lets the tears come for a few moments. It is a striking display of vulnerability, that I am almost positive no other man has ever seen.

Eliese dabs at her eyes and nose before whispering, "You couldn't see the face of the nurse, just the back of the head. The shoulders and the hands. The voice wasn't the same, either." There is more dabbing. "He said, 'You don't remember me, do you, Mrs. Jankowitz?' Then he began to help her with her medical pump. As he took her pulse, he watches the timer on his FEED, cracking those knuckles."

"I spoke to Doc about her death and showed him the video. He checked: the nurse had been there for five years, and he relocated after his indenture pay-off that month. He relocated to the Miami district," Eliese says. "Doc looked at her postmortem, and my mother went peacefully. No drugs that were not prescribed, no anything."

"The FEED video wasn't even recorded on the day she died. Doc showed me a copy of the whole thing and not just the clip forwarded to me. It was identical.

I knew it was him, though. I was so sure of it, and I showed Darien."

I hear a hint of anger, a little bitterness in her words, as Eliese says, "Darien just took that opportunity to be an ass. 'Doesn't your boyfriend Rivas do that? You could go see him. I'm sure he would love a conjugal visit.' Then he walked off laughing at me."

El returns to dabbing her eyes, finally blowing her nose into my pocket square.

"I was relieved. He saw it also. Since that day, I have not trusted anyone. Anyone not of the Family. Even then, sometimes I find it hard," Eliese says.

I had told her previously of Jacki, and the kind of damage our soured relationship caused. I saw pure torment in what Rivas had done, the kind of fear and bitterness that would always linger and fester.

I say in all honesty, "I will be as open as I can be. Some things, questions from my time in the Compact Military, I just cannot answer. That goes for Samuel, also. It is why we often play up things like the joke of our MOS being postal clerks. Those who know, know. To them, it does not matter. I know one medically retired guy who writes fiction. His books are lessons in reading the word REDACTED. If you ever have a question to ask, I will do my best to answer. If I must, I will answer someplace more secure."

Eliese graces me with a small smile. I understand trust is her issue. That bogeyman, the cat in the nightmares, are out there. Then my nebulous thoughts swirl and form into a solid mass. I know it, but cannot prove it. The fear of Samuel, the torment of Eliese, the attacks on the Family, they were all because her mother had stopped Rivas March. That might be too much—maybe all those instances relate to Rivas March, maybe no. I keep that to myself. I need not go borrowing trouble until I have some more information.

We watch the stars and make wishes on the shooting stars, or maybe they are just humanity's low-orbit satellites. We start discussing constellations. Eliese tells me her favorite stories of stars and ancient people sailing the wine-dark sea. We drift off under the lights of the place man never colonized.

We are startled awake by Darien being held back by Thap and Pun. His words are incomprehensible as he rages at us in a spittle frothing fury over something. His Segundo, Phan, comes running in, pulling him back as Thap and Pun push him out the door.

Eliese and I are both standing when the three Segundos yank him out of the room. The two of us are fully clothed, sans the shoes. We can hear him in the hall raging about us. First, it is at me for being a mongrel parasite, then it is about Eliese for having horrible taste in men, always picking invaders.

Eliese is red, angry, and starts to apologize to me. I stop her. "We have dinner tonight. It is not the one I had planned for tonight, but I think a change in venue will do us both good. You will need hiking clothes. Be at the Hill House by 3:30 p.m. at the latest."

I am surprised to see Eliese make that little fishy face. She takes a second and smiles weakly, before saying, "I could use a good walk after that. Dinner it is." She leaves with Pun. Thap comes in, a little disheveled, but with no marks or bruising.

Thap starts to speak, but stops himself. Then he looks at the door.

"Yeah, I know. At some point he is going to push it a tad too far," I say with sigh, "I will be the bad guy for putting an end to it."

"Raylan, he's going push it more than a little too far. Pun's worried," he says, holding my attention.

I tune in, and return the concern Thap is trying to convey.

"Thanks, Thap, keep me up to date as you see fit," I say, and then I smile. "I got a date!"

I start telling him about my plans while he puts the details down. Thap says he will work the project through and find me what I need. He knows the spot. It will be ready when we get there.

"You know, Thap, I have not met your family," I say.

"Family for us usually happens after we retire from the indenture contract, only after we train our replacement," Thap says as we walk.

"Is there a special lady?" I ask.

Without any hint of joking, he replies, "All of them," then starts thumbing me FEED messages, updates, meetings, and contact points he wants me to review.

***

C8 S6

Over breakfast, Thap sorts out my plans for the week. It is getting to the point I must start showing myself in public. After all, I am the public face of the GSG. I am still stiff, still wear a cast, and a considerable bandage on my right wrist. Tomorrow, I will start with the face-to-face meetings. Up first is the representative about the shale contract. I am going to be putting his start date off for fifteen days. I am lucky that I have the MLR V2s and the new Donner V3s entering service at that time, so I have an excuse. I will meet with the farming concern after and pump hands and convince them to speed up by forty days. I think I can give them enough reasons to move their start date.

With me starting the hot house D2 early and reallocating resources, we could help them get the majority of their hothouses open for the first spring planting. The new plan will allow them all of the summer months for settlement and field prep.

I have another planned date with Eliese scheduled for the day after. Okay, Thap scheduled it for me. The day after is a meeting with journalists, or what the news here pretends are journalists. That is going to be a pain. Eliese's staff is going to prep me in the morning. I message Eliese to tell her that I have a plan to slap the ones who are jerks.

That garners a long message that I am pretty sure is from Pun. Then dinner that night. Darien will be at the Family residence, so El and I will do dinner at my place again. More meetings for prospective contract gates six and seven. I will spend the next few days prepping for the Gate walk and going over all the SkipJacks. Doc has forwarded me a mineral supplement that I am to work into my diet. Finally, I will be working on putting together the final, fourth dinner. This one is on me, Thap says, so I get to do on my own. I let him know what I am thinking. Pun will not be amused if it puts Eliese in danger. The Segundos get touchy about that.

I am down in the barn working on one of the Donner V2's when Thap lets me know the things I need for dinner are here. I spend the next hour changing and getting it ready. He tells me the path to the spot was cleared by a crew from the residence groundkeepers, and it will be an easy walk.

It is just over two kilometers. The trail is simple, nothing too fancy. I have him deliver the goods there and make sure the spot is ready. When Eliese arrives, you could have mopped me off the floor. She is stunning: A wide-brimmed straw hat, red and black flannel shirt, jeans, and new hiking boots, which are better than heels for this kind of thing. I pull the picnic basket, and we go a-walking.

Virginia District has some great mountain views...well, hills. Nevertheless, the lookouts over the valley over the next mile are a new thing for Eliese. We pass over a small rivulet of water a dozen times while we talk. After a bit of show-and-tell and make a lot of stops to point out trees, animals, and tree rats, we come around a corner. When we do, the slight wind dies off.

We see the same stream feeding into a small pond on the farther side of the enclosed meadow. I motion her over, and we walk the edge of the sluice-gated pond. I point out the largemouth bass, the smallmouth bass, the frogs, and catfish minnows. We watch the cardinals and the other birds. I explain the drumming in the distance is a ruffed grouse. I let her know what the sound of a whippoorwill is.

Oh, I am sure Eliese knows ninety-nine percent of this crap. It is part of the experience, part of us being together, part of talking, walking, and watching. We cross over a little bridge next to the sluice that lets the water out of the pond. We pass over a small area of pasture grasses to a large screened-in gazebo that I had found when hiking during my recuperation. Thap arranged for it to be cleaned. A small portable cook stove is placed in it.

Neatly arranged down by the pond are two lawn chairs, two fishing poles and a cooler of drinks. We put the basket on the table and apply some skeeter repellent. My biggest complaint is that mosquito repellent sucks as a perfume when compared to Eliese's chosen scent. I wish Thap had been able to source one of the CM's bug zappers, as it would have been a lot nicer for this area and tonight.

With some laughter, we make our way down to the pond. She has no clue how to cast, and with a cast, I have some problems. We are bobber fishing, so casting is not critical. We pick up some bass and catfish over the next two hours. Okay, I will be honest: Eliese outcatches me ten to one. I keep tossing them back. Finally, as dusk sets, our first brook trout rolls in. We reel in three more of the little guys. The finest-tasting trout there is, in my opinion. I clean them, and we walk back to the gazebo.

"I was becoming worried, Raylan, you just kept tossing everything back in. What are these guys?" Eliese asks.

"Brook trout. They do not get much bigger than this. They are my favorite trout for cooking," I say.

With a grin at her, I begin to unpack the salad, rice, baked beans, and the dressing for the trout. With a pop, the gas grill kicks on.

Eliese sets up the rest of the table, nibbling on bits as I explain about the trout. "Cleaned, salt, pepper and drenched in flour and cornstarch. Fried in a cast iron pan. Flip once each side. They don't have the internal strength to stick together if you flip them more than that."

The fish start cooking, two on each side of the pan. When I turn the first one, the oposite side is golden brown. Eliese starts dishing the rest up.

"They have these little bones, so pick at it with your fingers." I demonstrate on my first fish. We continue talking as the sun sets and the moon rises in view from the gazebo reflecting in the pond.

"Did you plan that?" she asks in awe.

"I would love to take credit. No, I found the gazebo on a walk before I met you. I did not have a way to fish here until today. Thap made a few arrangements for me. I had a crew clear and clean the trail. A second group did some basic work on the gazebo. I plan on being here as much as possible." I give Eliese a wink. "Do I still get credit?" I ask before I drink my lemonade.

She takes a drink of her wine and returns the wink.

"Half credit, Raylan. I like this; there's almost no noise. The Family residence can be loud sometimes," Eliese says.

We watch the light dim as the darkness hits. Thap and Pun light the lanterns at the entrance to the meadow. I fire up the torch in the gazebo, and we pack up our gear. I gather the chairs and poles and leave them inside the gazebo. I carry the little trash we have in the picnic basket and the lantern in my left hand. We walk back to Pun and Thap.

It is a slower trek back to Hill House, even with the three lights. Eliese catches a glimpse of an opossum and a trash bandit. Tomorrow, though, is going to be a long day. I part ways with her as we make it to the tram landing pad. Thap and I continue with the gear up to the house.

***

C8 S7

I meet with the shale company and the farming concern the following day. There is some give and take from all three parties. In the end, it goes our way. The shale company seems to be okay with the slowdown of fifteen days. I have some concerns over that, and I wonder if we should find them a sister investment company. The farming concern is interested in having the date moved up. I spend the rest of the time talking to each of them about what kind of support their new ventures need from us.

The following day, we have dinner at the gazebo again. Our evening is overcast skies, and this warms everything up just a tad. We skip the fishing. This night is a gift from Craig and Daniel. They have forwarded an excellent cut and wrapped elk to me as a present for Eliese's efforts on their behalf, so we have a lesson on cooking elk steaks. Of course, I use Alpine Touch as my primary seasoning. I now have a good supply of it for my time in the D2s. I listen as she talks about some of the most objectionable and opinionated interviewers. Eliese refuses to call them journalists.

Eliese waves her hand in an airheaded fashion and puts on a syrupy voice. "'What's it like being a powerful woman in an industry that objectifies you constantly,' blah blah blah. It's always a female journalist that has the gall to ask me that."

Eliese's eyes roll so hard, so fast, I almost think she's having a seizure.

"I respond, 'What was it like for you?' My experience is mine, yours is yours. Comparing the two achieves nothing," Eliese says. "It gets worse when the male interviewer thinks he's hot stuff because he's on the FEED with 300 million followers."

She smiles, and a female parody of a classic anchorman voice plays out. "'What kind of date would you like?'" Eliese rolls her eyes again, mockery in every word. "I mean, I'm here opening a new research center into the functional care of autism for working families. This self-centered prick is hitting on me, and his hormonal ass can't even wait until the interview is over to ask me out."

"So what should I look out for tomorrow? How I got the job?" I ask with a wink. "I can say I am dating the boss." That gets me a bit of potato thrown at me. "I'm thinking of explaining how my military experience is paying off in organizing the logistics behind the new data trunk SkipJack piloting."

"That's a fine start, Raylan, honestly. Most of it will be vapid questions. You can simply tout the completion of the last two Gate surveys. I have most of the questions they asked in the past set aside. My team will go over them with you tomorrow as prep. You only have three interviews. Whatever you do, don't answer eligibility questions. If you're taken, they'll want to know by whom, if you're free, we'll recieve proposals up the wazoo for you," Eliese says, waggling a carrot stick at me, one eyebrow raised in warning.

I nod my head. "I can see that. Will you be upset if I say you?" I slyly slide my question in, and I watch.

El smiles and says, "No, I will not." There is not any hesitation in that answer. "Yet we'll get the wedding bells question, as I'm the successor and would be the first to be married and most likely to have kids." Eliese sucks in a breath; a flash and a twinkle in her coffee eyes hits me. El asks this next part nice and slow. "Are *you* ready to answer that?"

"Hell no," I laugh. "Okay, no answering the relationship status questions. So who are my three interviewers? I am not a watch the FEED programs type of person." I smile to let her know I am willing to play along.

El is giggling so much she has to cover her mouth with her hands.

"Your face as you heard kids. It was priceless," she says. She waits until she

241

can get her fit of giggles under control, then points her carrot stub at me like a weapon and says, "Kids, kids, kids, KKKKKIIIIIDDDDS," each word eliciting more and more peals of laughter from her.

I am well into it at this point, also. It takes a few minutes for her giggle fit to recede. Finally, she says, gasping, "'FEED in' talk is one-on-one: the show host and you. Usually, you're providing commentary on the markets and new business ventures. The second is 'The Evening Round the Table' show. The topic is Gates and advancements with other Gate providers, moderated by a..." she pauses, then continues slowly, "...disgruntled man. Finally, there's a show taped in our green room. It'll air that evening on the show 'House of Talk.' It's a group of book club ladies who cover industry, fashion, investments, and very rarely, books." El's smile becomes severe. "They're harpies. Complete harpies. It's the one I'm most worried about."

"I am charming," I protest, putting on a pretentious air. "I should be good."

She counters with, "Kids." I pretend to cower, horror-stricken, as she falls into a new giggle fit.

The next morning, I receive a trim and shave, and my hair is platted by a stylist. Thap has three outfits for me, one for each meeting. Correction: four sets of clothing for today. I have a separate one for my run-through with Eliese's team. El is not able to make the study session.

The prep session goes surprisingly well. I am able to field most of the questions in the mock interviews. We then traipse over the finer points. I leave just before lunch and eat with Thap. He gives me his advice, along with the guidance of the Family's Gurkhas. Their collective opinion is to show off my "big myomere" parts. Soldiers are soldiers the world over.

For the first interview, I am seated with headphones and a mic. The "FEED in" talk show starts. The intro comes on, and the host introduces me as Lucky Number Seven. The first series of questions are general. We bandy about me only having the name Ray. Military service comes up briefly. The interviewer asks what I did as a SkipJack pilot and, like all combat SkipJack pilots, I play it off as marching on Compact Day, vehicle maintenance, tram maintenance, and unloading containers, only to load the same stuff in the same container tram again.

This is a universal skill in the Compact Military, after all: payloads must be balanced. Next, he asks how I came from out of nowhere. I mention I had a severe accident, and one of my visitors was a member of the Jankowitz Corp. That part of my recuperation was dreaming about how to shorten the build-up D2 iterations and stages. It seems like no time at all before my ninety minutes are up.

I shower again and have makeup applied. Thap stuffs me into a new suit and thrusts me into the virtual roundtable. After the introductions, it becomes clear why the moderator is disgruntled. Eliese had initially been the guest, and she tossed me in as consolation. I could be overthinking it, but I believe he is truly upset at missing his chance to make a pass at her.

The interviewer keeps coming back at me with the "what-if," exception to the rule questions. I stay out of the other pissing matches. I listen, as there are a number of corporations like GSG attempting to speed up D2 iteration growth. They are all light-years behind the innovations GSG is starting to push forward—all because I can Gate walk. All in all, I am not terrible, and I think I hold myself well.

Then it is time for my interview with the harpies. It starts badly.

Thap catches me as I leave the roundtable, and his tone is one of a sergeant giving a private an order when he says, "Change of plans, Ray. It's not a green room anymore." He pauses to open a door for us both. "It is live FEED in their North East District studio. You and Eliese are the guest stars tonight, and they are adding an extra segment just for the two of you. New duds, so get showered. Wash that makeup off and be ready quick."

I frown at Thap as I walk faster down the hall. My Segundo is moving things about on his FEED at an insane pace.

"Ray, Eliese wants you to start watching episodes, and she says to start with Trish's," Thap says as he thumbs me a message.

I bring up the episode on my FEED. Good Lord, is it bad. Bonnie Anders is the main star, and she runs the interview portion of the show. She immediately sets my teeth on edge. She interrupts, talks over, and shouts at the guests. The others do the same; they're a cackling group of gossipers. Maybe it is stage fright, but I feel as if tonight is going to be a long evening.

I finish listening to the first show as I exit the shower. I tell Thap to leave the bandage off the right wrist. I put the arm in a sling and wear the sports jacket loose. I am going to need some armor for this fight. A fresh scar and a vivid cast are always a good start.

Thap and I meet Eliese just outside of the New England District (NED), and we transfer to her tram. Eliese is vivacious in a blue and cream suit, one that happens to match my very own. The red strand of stones around her neck, not to mention her earrings, match my tie exactly.

We take her tram to NED's main studio, which is a holdover from the old New York City days. The venue is in an old theater; there are lights and a couple of hundred seats. The show will be live across the FEED network. If you believe Bonnie, our episode will receive 700 million views in the next twenty-four hours.

Eliese places her hand on my shoulder as we are about to step out of the tram. "Ease up, ," she says quietly. "You can't fight her all by yourself. We'll tag-team her." She looks into my eyes and smiles. "Raylan."

Then she blows me a kiss. Her scent, her breath so near...the battle is on.

I step out of the tram. I see a line-up of photographers with FEED cams; I turn and hold out my hand to her as Eliese exits. We walk down their faux red carpet, her arm in mine, all the way to the main entry doors. Cameramen are taking shots. I do my best to smile, but Eliese outshines me by a mile. Twists, looks, and smiles. Cut, chop, stack.

I hear in an earpiece the FEED live introducing "Eliese, future head of Jankowitz Group, the prettiest spinster alive" in a braying cackle. That is Bonnie's voice. The announcer is picking up without a hitch. "...And the newest seat at the Family table, Ray, number seven. 'Why, my garbage man is named Ray, I wonder if it is the same guy," Bonnie says, with that same raucous, braying laugh.

The green room staff are excellent. We are prepared and ready by the end of the sponsor's promo. Bonnie introduces us and shakes our hands. Her handshake is limp and oily, as if you are shaking hands with seaweed. We take seats next to each other and it starts.

"Eliese, darling, you've been away from us for so long. What's it been? Three, four years?" Bonnie asks, her nasal voice thin and reedy.

I am pretty sure it is an affectation for the show. I have heard her in interviews without that voice.

Eliese, with a smile, says, "Bonnie darling, it's been about four years. Yes, four years. How're Geoff and the kids?"

Bonnie loves her name, so much so that she has trademarked it. Her name is her image. She has Bonnie this, Bonnie that, in shops all over the world. Bonnie hates the press calling her nicknames. She is also recently divorced, number three, all twenty years older and much wealthier than her. She takes them all to the cleaners if her claims are believable. If Eliese has added the darling and the new ex-husband, well, this is going to be a slaughter. Tag team it is.

"Oh, Eliese-darling, I'm on the market, baby," Bonnie says. I watch her as she turns to me with that plastic 3D-sculpted smile. "Ray, darling! It's nice to meet you. The new number seven... And such a dashing man." The smile widens. "Rayray—can I call you Rayray?—we saw you last on the arm of Trish. How's that going? I hear she can be a handful."

It is clear she does not care one whit what I think of the nickname. Already having had my knickers tweaked, I wade into the deep end of the pool. Trish had helped me during that first Family dinner. She had guided me in and out of a minefield. There is no way in hell I am going to gossip about Trish.

"Bonnie-poo, it is a pleasure to meet you. You must have been absolutely ravishing in your day," I say, and before she can interrupt, I continue. "The GSG is new to the industry, and that requires me to be present at the job sites. I have not spoken to her for a good while now. Trish would be a phenomenal ratings smash on this FEED thing," I wave my right arm at the stage set dismissively while speaking.

I know full well Trish has been a guest on this show, and that Trish had played Bonnie like a beautiful violin. Trish's ratings were so good that the show episode mysteriously disappeared from the House of Talk library. Thap had sent me a copy to my FEED. I see in Bonnie's eyes that she now knows this is war.

Before she can insert a verbal parry into the conversation, I twist the knife a little more. "Just Ray, Bonnie-poo. No, I am not your garbage man, and I do not know him, but hats off to him. I used to do SkipJack repair for rent money.

I know how hard it can be out there. It is probably good for you that I am not your garbage man, Bonnie-poo. I doubt you could afford my garbage services."

Egos like Bonnie's build with time, becoming beasts and monsters of their own. The owner must feed them to keep in control. I wait for her to bite my proverbial hook.

Bonnie's eyes have narrowed dangerously, and there is a little trammel in her voice when she says, "Rayray, I'm pretty well off." Her tone is deceptively soft. "I don't think you want to go down that road."

I let a leonine grin start at my eyes and work its way to my mouth. My teeth flash as I say, "One-point-five million credits to the charity of my choice. I will double it from my personal account if you put in your share during this interview. That could be four-point-five million to charity. I will be there the very next morning to pick up your trash. Bonnie-poo."

Money now is next to worthless to me when I am gone half the year at a time. To her, though, money is a big part of her image. She blows through it stupidly fast. That is the reason she is now searching for husband number four.

She blanches, her face physically draining white. I have chosen my donation amount carefully, as it is her annual salary, not counting endorsements or any of her companies, which, if she does not take this, she will likely lose. There it is: I can see her prep for it in her eyes, the bite.

Bonnie straightens up, leaning back and crossing her arms, her voice shrill as she says, "My garbage day is Friday. As this is Wednesday, I'll have the funds transferred to escrow tomorrow."

I think she will back out of this as soon as we step off the stage. I should have known, however, I arrived here with a woman who brokers deals all day long means it is not just my contribution that matters. Eliese and I are a team, and together we will write our names across all the earth iterations. My siren sings a ballad, one that pulls in those lonesome sailors and brings them onto the reef, and their deaths are on the winds of her song.

Eliese looks at Bonnie and smirks while saying, "I will match Ray's contribution. I have received FEEDs from Father and Samuel that they are matching it, also." Her right wrist blinks twice. "Oh, Alverez and Trish are adding an extra half million. Darien is in for four million. That's twenty-three million credits total, minus your share if you commit today."

Eliese thumbs an embedded screen of an escrow account that Pun has sent her. The audience gasps as it hits the main screen. That is nearly enough to construct the pylons for a Gate.

Bonnie recovers admirably. She flips through her FEED and thumbs over one-point-five million in options. A forced grin weaves its way across Bonnie's 3D sculpted face, a grin that no one mistakes as real.

Bonnie snarls, "See you Friday, RayRay." Her venomous gaze turns back to El. "Now, Eliese darling, if Trish has Rayray to keep her warm at night, who have you been spending time with?"

Bonnie is a small, petty hag, and she is making a dig at Trish for upping a half-million credits. I do not know where she is going with this, but I feel as if she is now trying to slight everyone in the Family.

"I mean, Rayray is quite the catch, yet you were alone at the holiday party, if my sources have it right?" Bonnie asks.

There it is: Bonnie's attack on Eliese herself, and she is going for blood. Eliese is known for not having arm candy or having many dates at all. Bonnie has frequently called her the prettiest spinster out there, even tonight before the show started, if I remember correctly.

Never answer relationship questions. Ever. Eliese and her staff had drilled that into me from the first instant. Yet, I see that same flicker in Eliese eye's as I had Trish's when I had made my raven speech at Family dinner. Bonnie, a socialite, has challenged Eliese, and my mistress of war is going to have none of it.

I watch Eliese's body language. She does that same shake of the head—that little shake, the tell, of when she's chosen her path forward in life. That moment her mind is made up, and the whole field of battle will pay in blood. I slip my arm out from my sling, cast and all. My left sleeve is rolled up to the end of the myomere cast.

As I hear the harbinger of battle weave her song. I feel her pull on my soul; and I reach my left arm out and find her right hand reaching for mine.

"I didn't walk in here alone now, did I, Bonnie-Poo? Have you ever seen me escorted down any stairs of any tram, down any red carpet? I don't need three failed marriages to find my partner. It isn't ever about that for you, is it,

Bonnie-poo? You want fame and fortune, yes? How are those businesses doing, Bonnie? The last securities commission found your corporations at fault for 200 million in losses to investors, and you were to return 600,000 credits personally. Have you done that yet?"

A sponsor break. Her producer calls it as Bonnie's face goes eggplant purple. Oh, we have made an enemy here. As I look over, Eliese is beaming. "Well," I quip, sotto-voce, "the next segment is going to be fun." Bonnie is bringing out the whole congress of harpies. The staff is bustling about with nary a sound, placing and arranging chairs. The co-hosts introduce themselves to us.

Then it is a free-for-all. Bonnie is raving mad. The others, though, are gracious, excellent hosts. Seeing Bonnie taken down a notch endears them to us for just this night. Out comes the questions of our first date. Where was the first place we went, what did we do? They have an absolute blast with the Tree Rat Stew story, and the way Eliese plays up the whole event, meeting me at the Hill House for dinner, only to be served Tree Rat Stew.

Eliese has the whole crowd laughing. Finally, someone asks how she liked it. That is when I chime in. I talk about only having those old blue and white tin camping bowls and that I served the bowls on the Family's fine china. I comment on how she ate every last bite before moving on to the main course. I continue with how our first *date* date was a walk on the Family grounds, and we ended up talking for hours. That I messed up and brought the budding relationship out to the Family earlier, and that cost me two dinners, to be paid before leaving for a business trip. Which means I am in debt by two now, having just paid the tax of two dinners off.

I regale them with the hike, the fishing trip, the moon over the pond, and the stars. I follow by a recounting of CBN:D2 sending a gift for Eliese, which I cooked. From there, we get into the work we are doing, the advancements we have made, and little Bonnie-poo remains still, silent, and fuming.

Eliese and I leave the studio arm in arm as we make our way back out to our tram. This time the cameras and flashes almost do not stop. When we arrive back at the Hill House, Eliese seems a bit dazzled and amazed. I have a small table set up for us, covered with a red and white tablecloth. On it is a setting for two and a candle.

I proceed to butcher spaghetti. Horribly. A solid mass of noodles, a sauce that is too salty, and the bread that over-toasted, burnt. Eliese is a good sport about the disastrous meal.

"You tried, and the effort is noted," she says.

"I will take some real cooking gear on this next survey. Maybe I will improve in the nine months or so that I am away," I reply.

Eliese laughs and spends the next ten minutes sending me her favorite dishes. She recommends a couple of camp cooking sets and dozens of FEED videos by chefs that she watches religiously.

Because I now had a plan for Friday, I must move up my fourth dinner. I pick up Eliese at the Family residence after a very long day of Gate transition preparations. The tram flies us to the heart of Virginia Metro District, landing near a dock. Thap and Pun escort us on to an old, wooden two-storied vessel with lots of brass, and windows galore.

We have a three-piece orchestra, courtesy of Pun and Thap pulling together one from the Forty. The finest bon vivant French chef in the Virginia Metro District is our guide. A cruise on the Potomac leads us into the bay, the perfect setting for a chef's table dinner. We have a blast. Much of it is a good laugh over the upcoming plans for Friday. I have indeed completed number four, though being in dinner debt to Eliese is quite fun.

Eliese and I work on the timing of my garbage service over dinner. It turns out Bonnie's guy is indeed named Ray, so I set up a charity. For any refuse, garbage, and sanitation workers that have Ray in their names—Samona Ray, Bobby Ray, Franky Ray, and so on—the charity will ensure that their children would have a shorter indenture after secondary or trade schooling. Their indenture will be paid in part by this charity. I also meet with Ray over a FEED message. I purchase his shield and his first full-size garbage MLR. He purchases part of the route that includes Bonnie's residence from his current boss with his savings.

When I arrive Friday morning, Ray hands me a uniform. I put it on, and in a short time we start picking up garbage together in his new MLR. On the side of the dark blue MLR is "Ray Ray's Sanitation." I cannot help but laugh. The local film crew catches up with us as we are eating sandwiches his wife packed. We pose for pictures. I let him talk, as it is his business. It is an excellent press opportunity for him. Thap is acting as driver for the day, and we are the ones picking up the trash while walking and talking to clients. Ray asks how much to hire a guy like Thap, and I tell him the truth: a Gate in Nepal.

It turns out a lot of people had seen the show Wednesday night. Eliese is a starlet in her own right, and House of Talk had promoted the hell out of that episode all week, only to switch it to live the day of our interview. It was deliberate, to be sure.

Ray and I pose for photos, talk, and chat all the way. What would typically be a six-hour route is fourteen today. Because the news is there, everyone meets us down at the curb to chat. Ray passes out cards for haul-outs or dumpsters. As we finish, his family is waiting at the portion of the sanitation yard he is leasing for his new MLR. They have set up tables, and we have a feast, just for us Rays. Eliese joins me after about thirty minutes. We sit, eat, and joke with Ray's family, as if we have been friends for decades.

Ray asks me to give a speech, so I outline the charity. I show how to apply and access it for all the people named Ray, and what the charity can do and what it cannot. I send everyone contact info for the independent attorney's office, who is overseeing the charity as it grows with the industry. All twenty-five million credits worth, the Family's and Bonnie Anders's, are there in the charity's escrow.

It is when we are with the Ray family that I realize I need to do something for Eliese. Her help, her companionship, and her assurance that I am capable of doing the tasks before me needs reciprocation. I fire off a message to Daniel and Craig. I gave the two of them a rundown of what I am thinking about. I hope I am not presumptuous, and I do not think I am. Eliese needs a gift for the effort she has put forth in our relationship.

***

C8 S8

Saturday and Sunday are a hellacious schedule of packing, checking, testing, and repacking. I can only get one of Eliese's cooking sets into a pannier. I stow my usual stuff with it. I start early in the morning and end after dark. I am leaving Monday after the final stowage on the cargo tram. There would be a quick check, then the transit. My arm is still sore, and I am mostly through my antibiotics for the lacerations. I feel good overall, though. I will go slow the first few days and, hopefully, get things rolling.

I prepare everything by early Monday morning. I load up the cargo tram. I am wrapping up the final touches when Eliese's tram lands. Eliese sashays from her tram in blouse and skirt. I stop my work and stare in her direction, smiling widely.

Her hair weaves its dance behind her as she raises one finger to her orchid-colored lips. I cannot move my eyes from hers anymore. Those coffee-colored eyes have me spellbound. I remain quiet as she closes in on me. She is a predator in her own right as she steps up and wraps her arms around my neck. Eliese does not blow this kiss. She lets go of me a good deal later, letting her hands slide off the back of my head to my cheek.

Eliese spins and saunters back onto the tram, the skirt swaying with her movements, her black hair dancing to the motion. I almost hit the ground, and I would have had Thap not moved up to steady me. I did not know she could saunter. I like it when she saunters. I like it a lot.

Thap holds me steady, and I can tell I am more than a little punch drunk. I stand there, dumbstruck, covered in the prop wash from the engine nacelles as the tram takes off to the Family residence. I feel a hand on my shoulder. I turn to look at Thap.

"Raylan, that was the smartest thing you could have ever said," Thap says.

He directs me to my jump seat aboard our tram. It is not until I am in the air before I realize I did not say anything.

The Gate walk goes well. I make it into the D2 iteration with minimal issues. I pull to heel the SkipJacks, all fourteen of them. I am amazed at how much more comfortable I am at this now. I find this more straightforward to do than when I was in FR pulling to heel two.

For this survey, I have a complement of two construction and two demolition

SkipJacks; eight Donner V3s that I managed to sneak in one Gate early, and two demilled units. One will be at the front of the Donner daisy-chain and one at the back.

I set up camp early, open my Doc-approved food, and figure out how to cook it based on the FEED recipe videos Eliese has sent me. As the chefs on my FEED videos show, dump it all into a pot is not the answer. Tonight's meal is campfire meatloaf, freeze-dried corn chowder, and biscuits. I am planning to spend the first two days setting up base camp.

My left arm is feeling good, but I do not want to push it. The data trunk comes through on day two. I receive a FEED message that ratio slip is starting. I plan to leave base camp on the third day. My train of Donners and demilled will be ten strong. I will start my first spike and release of a balloon at the end of the eighth day.

Day two looms as I learn how to make an egg omelet in the morning. This D2 is mostly open grassland that undulates with little dotted swales and gullies of long dried creeks. I do see some game, and quite a few birds.

The demilled SkipJacks are operating in walking sentry mode. They let me know if anything more substantial than a coyote gets within a hundred meters. On the second night of the balloon journey, I am eight spikes down. I can see the whitetail deer in the distance. I have no interest in hunting big game with a broken arm. I have the food I need for now.

Tonight, it is carne asada, or, rather, jackrabbit asada dish. I shot the rabbit in the morning. After cleaning it, I have been marinating the meat all day. I put a bit too much spice in the marinade. For my cooking, it is pretty good, though. The homemade black beans with smoked pork skin are fantastic. I could get used to this kind of cooking.

I put some more beans into a container to soak and I notice I have much less water than I usually do at this point in a survey. I fly the drone, looking for a spring or a creek. I find one, and it is located two full days off my circuit. I know this radius would bring me to some eventually, so I keep at it.

I start limiting the extraneous use of my water. I have a feeling this is going to be an issue throughout the survey. Sure enough, I come across a rivulet of water on day seven. I am amazingly low on my reserves of water. It is also not the best water. Filtering it out using the portable power-supply, the water filtration pump and UV filter is a slow process. I am hoping most of the water in this D2 is not like this. It takes a day and a half to do laundry, refill the water, and charge everything back up to full. I realize now that I have been lucky with the water, solar, and wind power I was able to make use of in the previous D2 iterations.

I keep up my cooking lessons only at night. I have a limit of some things, like powdered eggs. By day twenty, I am refilling water again. This spot is cleaner, but the water here is not as plentiful as it was during any of my other surveys. I am betting that it is underground.

Day thirty starts with a thunderstorm from my nightmares. These are tremendously deep peals of thunder and lightning. My balloons let me know that it is on its way in time. I spent three days in that tent. I eat mostly MREs because I cannot cook outside. I am thankful for a cot, also, as the ground is so wet that it eventually saturates the floor, modern miracle waterproof fabric or not.

Day 35, I am slogging through mud dragging back a whitetail I have shot via a morning scout with a Donner. I put him on the portable camp table Eliese has found for me.

Within a couple of hours, I have him parted out, salted down and put into storage bags in my refrigerated food pannier. These panniers are a new Donner V3 addition. They are on the smaller side, and triple vacuum-insulated. The power draw is part of the trade-off. When I leave the mud two days later, I spend a day smoking the venison and refilling water once again.

The next morning, I drop three of my SkipJacks, one of the demilled and two Donners. I am still having issues with my metal items turning brittle. The cooking set that Eliese had found is doing quite well. My cast iron pot is looking bad. Thap sourced me a bunch of carbon nanotube knives and ceramic bladed knives. Both types of knives are too fragile for the kind of bulk work I do with them.

I have broken one by trying to use it as a pry bar between the wrist joint of the deer. I am down two rifles, my 22lr, and my hunting bolt action. I have brought spares of both. I need to rethink this issue and come at finding the solution to this metal failure from a different perspective. Double guns just take up too much space on the Donners.

I hit forty-five days when I finish my loop. I have made it through a lot of impromptu recipes and as many improvised cooking lessons. I keep at it. I certainly like this food more than my uni-pot method. I spend a couple of days at base camp. I communicate the water issue with the staff and the farming concern. I am in ratio slip, so I am not expecting an answer for at least a few days. Three days later, I have a reply: put the settlement and hothouses as feasibly close to the water as possible. We would build the SkipJack mesh all the way out to the settlement.

I use the supplied side-cutters to remove my cast. I look at the map of the area on my FEED. I pilot the drone out to the areas most likely to have creeks. Sure enough, they are there. As I had suspected, the water eventually flows over the edge of a sinkhole to disappear underground. I drop a couple of spikes and balloons, just for them to have the data FEED on the EP1 side. I place the settlement in line with their wishes as close to the water as I could. I drop the hothouse's markers as near as possible, but downstream of the settlement. I stake out the temp mesh for thirty, one-mile long hothouses, and seventy-two settlement buildings over the next four weeks.

I stake a thin temp mesh from the settlement to the demarcation area. When I receive another FEED requesting that I look into the underground water and cave as much as I can, I fly the drone into the large pit that the creeks had fallen into at some point. I kicked on its lights and explore the area of the sinkhole.

The sinkhole goes down about sixty meters deep to a massive pool of water, which then seems to flow underground from there. There are not any caves, per se, just sections of the wall rougher than the next. Here and there, little rivulets of water seep from the cave walls. I return the drone to its pannier as the ratio slip stops and the first MLR comes through.

My FEED system is already sending the FEED images of the pit as I named it. I move one of the MLRs into the area of the settlement and hothouses, then set up the second at the demarcation zone. They feed me a second dedicated trunk to put next to the settlement, starting point and power supply. That is sixteen trips of attaching the data trunks, seven kilometers to the build site.

All in all, I am here ninety-two days, thirteen of them in the temporal lock with EP1. I am lucky and have no predator problems this time. I take the three remaining SkipJacks I have left, and Gate walk back out.

I step through from late summer and into mid-fall. I meet up with Thap, and we start the process of getting things stowed away aboard our tram. It was a long, frustrating survey. The water issue bothers me. I had mentioned that to Thap in several nightly updates. He has already been looking into providing the settlement with ground-penetrating survey gear and deepwater well drilling rigs. I tell him I do not want to survey another site without something similar to our balloon spikes, but for groundwater. He nods and focuses on his work with the FEED unit.

We land at Hill House. Eliese's tram is there. I return the gear to my barn, although a new structure is completely engulfing the building now.

Thap gestures at the new shop and says, "We outgrew the barn on the last gate. This shop should suffice as a headquarters for our new GSG group. They are in the process of building the interior offices, a cage for military equipment, a cage for ammo, and then the construction crew will remove the barn." With a quirky smile, he says, "Now you need only to hire some people."

I groan and trudge up the hill. Eliese is at the bottom step of the patio with a beer.

Chapter 9
Snowball

C9 S1

I walk up the wooden lined steps to the Hill House. Eliese is breathtaking in the mid-afternoon sun. She passes me a beer as I shift the weight of my chest rig to my left arm.

I twirl in a circle for Eliese. "I am walking on my own. No visible blood or trauma, so today is a good day."

I take the first sip of beer as I get close and receive a sniff, then a scrunched-up frown.

Eliese snorts a laugh, and waggles her finger at me in mock admonishment. A moment later, that same lovely hand pinches her nose.

"What? Wood-smoked prairie woodsman is not to your liking?" I say with a grin as I head up the final steps after taking a drink. I should shower first.

"Raylan, it's a bit more than prairie-smoked woodsman," Eliese says.

I hear the lilt in her tone as I head to the shower. The shower is a long one; I scrub and wash months of prairie dust and smoke away. My hair is longer again, and it is time to schedule a haircut. I shave and step to the closet. Searching through the clothes, I find the most un-haptic suit item I can: jeans and a t-shirt. Eliese does not care about the left versus right side of me. I grab the beer and head back out to the porch and notice Thap making his way down to the barn.

"Eliese is around the back on the patio overlooking the valley," Thap says as he is walking away.

I turn to the left and walk the length of the wraparound porch. I find Eliese on a small, covered section of the deck overlooking the valley. Nearby are a small table, a couple of Adirondack chairs, and our little grill. On the table with a cover of fine mesh are some steaks and potatoes.

I sit down as the late afternoon sun passes over the house. It is a not even a question as to what is more captivating. Hands down.

"It'll be a short one tonight, Raylan. I'm leaving at oh-four-hundred tomorrow and will be spending several weeks in the old continent. I'm taking Father's place in some negotiations," Eliese says with a smile, her eyes betraying the hope that I will not take offense. "He's working on something locally here in Virginia Metro District. I think it has to do with the DGMW:EP1 Gate."

Turning to me, crossing her legs, and leaning forward, Eliese's smile fades. "Raylan, there's a major storm coming. Father's dealing with the Gate collapse. Trish sends word that one of her school buddies works for a law firm representing Bonnie." Her previous lilt changes to scorn when she mentions Bonnie. "I think Father wants us out of sight and out of mind for a while. Any chance you can stay here, or in a D2?"

Eliese's question hits me by surprise.

Thinking it over, I say, "Yes, I can be out of sight. I have a lot of organizational work to do here at Hill House," I lean over for a peck on the cheek, then say, "I need to hire people, Eliese. Thap and I cannot do it all. My biggest issue is that the Stage Three timeline has not shrunk for new settlements. I need new settlements to kick off Stage Three by the end of five years."

I pull up my feed and say, "I think if we prepare part of Stage Two dealing with water and septic systems at Stage One, we could bring Stage Two to completion a few years earlier. Getting the D2 iterations thinking of their water, power, and septic systems decouple the iteration from our EP1 teat. That is a huge morale boost to the people in a D2 iteration."

I always look forward to conversations like this with Eliese. Bouncing ideas and options between us is one of my favorite parts of being around her.

She pulls up her FEED system. The display shows the conversations her research group and Thap are having.

Eliese says, "I agree. My people are out of their depth, Raylan. I'm also holding up my side of the Family projects by dedicating them to this one. I'm not complaining. We've jump-started the surveys as a whole while trying to lift GSG off the ground. Everyone is pitching in—Darien more than probably everyone but you. All the gear, tech, and manufacturing comes through his side of the Family contacts and corporations."

Eliese gives me a look I have not seen before; it is a mixture of concern and worry.

"Talk to him, Raylan. He's proud. He...well, he's my brother, my twin," Eliese says.

By her steady gaze, I know that this last part is important to her. I am the outsider here, the newest member of the Family.

"Eliese, I have a vague inkling about all this," I say as I wave at the shop. "And who sources it all for me. I will do my best. I know he cares for you and this family."

I take a deep breath, knowing it will be a hard conversation with Darien.

I swallow my initial distaste for him and say, "He may be able to help me organize and pull some names for interviews. I have a couple I know of from the past, but I am not sure they will fit in. I am going to have Thap go over them and give me his opinion."

Breaking that statement off, I turn on the portable grill and get the potatoes ready to go on.

"I think I need mavericks: men and women who come at solutions based on what they have available to them, and not what they can procure," I say as Eliese reaches out to hold my hand after I return to my seat.

"First, there is only so much that can go through a Gate. Only so much gear I can take," I say. "Much like a guy going out to a job site in the middle of nowhere and realizing he forgot his whatchamootzit tool. Then he has to improvise with a whatchamacallit, whacked on the inverse side of the yank bearing, to get the job done."

Our talk about this Gate walk has me rethinking how GSG should go about this whole Gate survey process.

My impromptu fake shop talk elicits a raised, imperious eyebrow from El.

"What?" she says.

Oh, I am sure she understands the meaning. She just likes giving me a tweak every now and then.

I turn around and see her wry smile and raised eyebrow. "Exactly: we do not know. I need the people who do know, or at least know what questions to ask. It makes little sense to us who are not in their specialized fields. I do not need a salesman who will implore me to take or buy something for everything that could happen. I need a businessman who gets it done with what they have and knows they cannot have it all."

I gesture down at the direction of the shed.

"I think we have reached the limits that my few MLRs and the Donners can haul. Unless GSG wants to send through fifty or more MLRs at the start of the survey, there is no way for me to lower the build out time further than I already have," I say.

I am half-saying it to myself, and to carry the conversational thought process. Eliese seems to be humoring me, and I am thankful for it.

"What I would like now is to smooth out the Stage One construction and the Stage Two life while they are building out the community in preparation for Stage Three."

I have a wide smile; I love bouncing ideas back and forth with Eliese. This process always helps.

"You want to organize a group of experts in the field and pick their brains?" she asks quizzically. "A good way to do that is some sort of sponsored convention. Do it over lunch, or dinner. Make a challenge out of it with a reward or prize," Eliese muses. "How many specialties are we talking about?"

"Water related fields. Well diggers, hydrologists, and maybe a few septic or water reclamation people, for now. This last iteration showed me that we have been lucky until now," I say with a sigh. "Eventually, I will need a corresponding pick-your-brain session for any issue that comes up; especially where time spent seems like it can be reduced."

As I turned back to Eliese, I watch her play with her FEED. I notice a playful grin spread across her face, and she had sends me something. I wait only a moment before my FEED pings.

She blows me a kiss and says, "Now that you have a plan, you and Thap can have control of the special projects again. I can have my people back."

El throws me a wink just for good, playful measure. I move to the grill to season the steaks and rotate the potatoes.

I give a good laugh at that. "I knew it was coming my way sooner or later."

The final business-related item Eliese and I cover outlines Gates five through ten. It is only a simple plan for now. I have some goals I want GSG to hit concerning reducing the settlement time before I finalize too many more Gates. Achieving those goals would be a significant selling point to entice co-partners into the development of the Gate network.

After dinner, we have a comfortable evening. Eliese retires early, much earlier than I would like. I understand, though. A two-week trip is something for which one needs time to prepare, let alone not wanting to start such a journey on too little rest.

***

C9 S2

I wake the next morning and I complete my morning ritual of showering and working the kinks out. Thap heads upstairs, and we run down my conversation with Eliese. Thap agrees to set up interviews with my three candidates over the FEED system. I want his best recommendations, so I tell him nothing.

Thap will be going into the interviews cold. I have some reservations, though. None of my three fit exactly what GSG needs, other than being mavericks. Thap says he will start organizing a conference for well drillers and hydrologists based on Eliese's suggestion.

Thap also notifies me that Chen and Lily are expecting. Boss's shop is still at fifty percent, mostly because CBN has yet to hit the Stage Two mark. Chen's work is hopping, with Lily manning a desk until after their child is born.

I start working on my FEED as we take the tram to Doc's appointment. I spend the flight taking a FEED message with Human Resources, letting them know the kind of positions I have available and the staff I want.

It turns out I must have a written description of the duties and responsibilities. I guess my blank, confused face is all Thap needs to start laughing hysterically. HR pedantically pushes forward every stumbling block one can imagine until I finally say, "I will hire them myself." I close out the FEED message and walk out of the tram.

I receive another call from the Legal department. No, I cannot hire new employees myself, I must use HR's process. I want to ask the Legal department when exactly I had hired a Legal department for GSG, but relent on that idea. Then my single active braincell thinks of a stellar idea. I tell Legal what I want, then then coerce them into not only reviewing the written description, but then just writing it. I toss Legal and HR into a pit and let them duke it out.

I walk in with a grin so full you would have thought I took down an elk with my teeth. Franc is standing at the counter. After we move into the patient room, Franc starts taking all my data.

Franc asks, "What gives?"

Not being able to contain my mirth, I respond with my story. Franc has a chuckle that rolls like thunder.

Then Thap says, "Ray, he's not laughing with you, but at you. They'll get you back, both of them. You've succeeded at pissing off GSG's hired law firm and the HR department that oversees new Family endeavors."

Damn. I am not as good at this as I like to think. The majority of my time with Franc is the usual poke and prodding. The rest is a new bit of mobility and flexibility movement tests for my right wrist and left forearm.

I make my way over to Doc's office. "How was it this time, being alone for so long, Ray?" Dr Alvarez asks in that voice he has only when being a Doctor.

I chuckle. "Glorious," I say. "I have yet to meet HR department or a Legal department in D2." I muse it over. "The contact is there in a way I can deal with, FEED messages or FEED meetings, when I am close enough to the demarcation zone and data trunk. The biggest issue is still the metal fatigue, Doc," I say with some exasperation. "I mean, these Donners I am using should last ten to twelve years before a significant overhaul. These firearms and knives are as new as one could hope. I should be able to pass them down to my children."

Dr. Alvarez nods and pulls up his FEED and moves something to the FEED display on his desk. It is a ship hull with little metal plates on it.

"I think we see a kind of galvanic corrosion, maybe mixed in with some intergranular corrosion, given the findings I am receiving. It's like something eats the metal away."

Doc goes on to explain in detail how non-protected metals in alkaline water cause a charge. That charge sets off the corrosion. "For you, Ray, that would be the sweat from the skin, and maybe an amplified charge due to your myomere implants."

Alvarez pauses and pulls out an armband and a leg band. Both bands contain little flat strips of metal sown into them.

"There are many ways to deal with it. What I would like to do is get a baseline of how quickly you cause it, and how that corrosion progresses through various metals," Doc says as he hands me the bands and a box of extra metal strips. "Each one of those is a hundred grams of one type of metal or alloy. All have zero protection. I want to see what you will have the most effect on over the next week."

We sit and sip our whiskey over some idle chat about hiring practices. Along with warning me about a future feud with HR and Legal, Doc gives me some good advice: find the people I want, write the job description for them, then have them apply for it. Go through HR. They will pull them for the interviews with comparably qualified candidates, and sometimes they find a better candidate than you will.

***

C9 S3

Thap and I take our leave and head to the Family residence. I have a meeting with Stewart this afternoon and will take dinner with what family are in residence today. Thap and I make our way from the staff building, through the grounds, to the side entrance of the corporate areas. We head down the halls when we notice the workout room glass wall is open.

Darien is in the boxing ring again. This time he is sporting Kendo gear, facing off against a shorter opponent. I slow as I watch. Slight movements left or right, then an explosion of speed with a resounding thwack. I hear a third voice off to the side, talking in what I assume is Japanese. They reset. This time Darien sees me watching. The dance starts again, then a third time and the sparring is called for the day.

Darien takes off the helmet and calls out to me, "Ray, how about you step in?"

There is a near-feral glee in Darien's eyes when I pause midstep. I look at Thap, who is eagerly shaking his head no.

"It is some pain now or a big fight and a lot of pain later. Keep me on time for our meeting with Stewart," I tell my Segundo.

I know that Thap does not want me to do this, so I push a bit harder, holding my hand up to Darien.

"Thap, it needs to happen now. Eliese wants this put behind us. Do not step in; we are big boys. That goes for Phan, also," I say.

With a scowl, Thap nods.

"Sorry for the wait, Darien," I shout back. "Thap is going to reschedule some things for me. Tell me which end of the thingy to hold," I say in good cheer, as I strip out of my jacket and my white dress shirt.

The men outside the ring begin fitting me in a set of *Bogu* and tell me, not so jokingly, how to hold the *shinai*. The man Darien had been sparring with jumps in as judge when I make it through the ropes. Darien explains the concept and goes over the primary forms. Taisho-san will call the bouts from the side. The referee is named Eitsu-san, who again goes over the styles in more detail.

The bout starts. Let me tell you, a whack to the head rattles you. I am not picking up on Darien's movements. Even when I start the motion first, he is able to block, then thwacks me. Back and forth, we move around the ring.

If I hit him, it is long after he hits me. I do not give in. Reset after reset, I do my best to clash with Darien. My wrists and forearms start to swell, as well as my head and collarbone. I realize I am Darien's big, slow practice dummy. He is working on hitting me with the right part of the shinai and delivering his yell at the proper time, I think. As I do not speak Japanese, I am guessing. Darien is remarkably fast, much faster than I ever imagined him to be.

Darien pounds on me for a couple of hours. While it stings and bruises, it is a passing pain, and will all go away in time. I apply myself to the task. Eitsu-san pauses about every fifth or sixth bout to give me a little more instruction. I work at it. I think I do well. I know I take my share of lumps.

I do hit Darien. I have my opportunities to get my licks in, and I make the best of them that I can. Later, I learn it takes three things to be considered a good hit: the yell, the sword hit, and the movement of your body.

Thap hand-gestures at his watch to Taisho-san, who calls the end. As Phan and Thap remove the gear, Darien and I sit on a bench. Both of us drenched in sweat. I am happy to see he sports some welts on his arms, also, though not likely from me.

"Ray, I..." Darien's voice trails off.

I suspect he is working up to something.

"I apologize," Darien wheezes out between sips of water.

I look at him, sweat stinging my eyes, and say, "You were looking out for your sisters and the Family in general." I exhale. "That is enough for me, Darien. Though they said you hit like a girl, and I had to see for myself."

Darien laughs. "Thanks, Ray. Next time, don't just stand there in the ring. Move. You just can't take a beating like that. You will be in a world of pain tomorrow."

That I do not doubt, yet Darien does not yet understand that most of the parts he whacked were myomere.

We are still sitting and sipping some water as Samuel walks in with a bit of concern on his face, looking between us.

I laugh. "Samuel, I have him all warmed up for you."

"Oh, hell no. As a teenager, I was the practice dummy for him to get his first Dan, and he paid me. I went into the Compact Military to avoid the beatings. Plus, the pay was better," Samuel says jokingly.

He still eyes Darien suspiciously, maybe wondering how he convinced me to get in the ring.

"Samuel, lay off, please. We are big boys. He had questions, ones Eliese would not like if he verbalized them." I pointed with my thumb back to the ring. "We did our talking in there. Your brother is very verbose," I say.

Samuel takes a moment and stares at Darien hard, who returns the glare. It is Darien who looks away first, and Samuel nods.

"Good, glad that shit's over, Ray. She's my sister, too," Samuel says. After a pause, he continues, "You and I can do some talking on SkipJacks. Our research project has me stalled, and I'm stopping by to let you know that. I'm making my second trip to Brazil for those parts. The first trip was a bust. I didn't come up with any leads."

Samuel's frustration bleeds through his voice. Running down tips like the situation with these parts can be massive time sinks, most often with very little to no results.

I nod as I look at Darien's two trainers, or sensei. I am a bit fuzzy on what to call them. I have encountered their culture to a degree, but most of my studies were academic, not thwack sessions.

"Darien, you work in Japan a lot, right?" I muse, while thinking of how to phrase this. "I am wondering if I could impose a favor above and beyond the sourcing you are doing for my group. We have received some gear that is not really up to snuff. It is not bad, just not implemented the way one would expect."

I search through my FEED, and pull up the sub-dermal and haptic patch. I thumb them over to Darien.

"Right now, it is a long shot. Samuel and I both came to the same conclusion independently that someone is using stuff with those two parts to sabotage my survey missions," I say, watching Darien as he looks at them thoroughly, going over the model numbers and serial numbers. "One lead is to Brazil, which seems to be the most promising. I am not willing to put the other lead off. That lead is in Japan. Can you investigate that discreetly? Because of those two parts, I ended up injured in the second survey."

He looks them over again. "I'll look and see what I can find. How do you know it's in Japan? That information might give me a place to start?"

Samuel chimes in, "Those are not the newest or greatest, but they are mil-spec equipment. Only two places purchased both: Brazil and Japan. I know they could have sourced them from a thirdhand provider, or even separately. I want to knock out these two most likely options first, though."

Darien nods. "Sure thing, I'm headed out with them this Thursday." He gestures at the two masters with a toss of his head. "That should allow me to start looking, at least, but things like this will be hard to sort through in Japan. Parts like these are traded as currency among the Mega Corporations over there. Regardless, I'll see if I can get to the bottom of this. Thumb me the rest of the data and I'll add it to my list."

I see Darien categorizing and labeling things in his mind and on his FEED as he reads through what Thap has sent him. It seems Darien and Samuel are more alike than I realize.

I stand as Thap mentions my afternoon meeting. We take our leave and head to the flat to get cleaned up. After a shower and a quick change, I move on down to Stewart's office.

***

C9 S4

Stewart's Segundo, Lama, is at Eliese's usual desk. He shows me in as I walk through. Stewart looks to be in a better mood than the last time we met in his office. We shake hands and I get right down to the report. The ratio slip has gone well, as has the survey, given the outlined issues with water. We are working on the metal fatigue and finally may have a clue as to what is causing it.

"Stewart," I explain, "Stage Three is taking too long to reach. Ten years to have their power, sewers, and communication network up is too long."

I start thumbing the outlines of plans Thap and I have discussed, along with some ideas from Doc, to Stewart.

"I want to pull in some mavericks for my group. I want to have a convention for people in the industry for the problem we are trying to solve. Right now, that is hydrologist, well drillers, and septic system specialists."

I sit back, steepling my fingers as Stewart reviews the data.

"Eliese mentioned a tradeshow dinner with a prize at the end. I want to create competition at that dinner. I see maybe six people per table, maybe a dozen tables. Your dinner partners are your team. First, have them hash out what tools I absolutely must have, that a farm boy can use, and that will fit in our MLRs," I say. "Second, I need a way to set up a septic system, or at least mark it out. Third, it must operate without FEED system access," I say, as I wind down my magic trick. "Then have the tables vote on the best one, with a deciding vote going to me if there is a tie."

"I'll have Lama arrange with Legal to work up an NDA, pull the permit, rent the resort, and have HR do the talent scouting," Stewart says, nodding.

I suspect he knows I have more and need more, so he waits.

I swallow and say, "I think Thap has the talent already picked. I will have it forwarded to HR once he has that finalized."

There is no way in hell do I want HR picking their third cousin's neighbor for this shindig.

"I had a long chat with Eliese over dinner last night," I continue. "Her team is out of their depth on the basic subject matter. I have asked Legal to put a preliminary package of job descriptions and duties together for me." I watch Stewart cringe. "Yes, I know, unorthodox. I need to know the kind of wordings that must be used because of my military equipment and live-fire range," I point out.

"That said, here is what I am thinking. I need a historian, one who knows how the North American colonies built themselves up with no infrastructure. I need a specialist who can point me to the best places for water. I am wasting days looking for the best spot. I need a fabricator for SkipJacks, and I need two or three programmers for SkipJacks.

"Right now, I am working with re-purposed and lightly modified gear from the factory. If I am going to cut the time it takes for a settlement to hit Stage Three to five years, I need to be much more dedicated to that end," I say.

"Even with Stage Three kicking off around year five, I have concerns that single industry gates will still have an abnormally high default rate. I want to put complementary industries together in future contracts, at least three per Gate on Gates six through ten," I continue as I let my pitch wind down.

Stewart stops me with his hand. I wait as he mulls it over.

"The concern for single industry Gates is valid. However, we haven't found a way to get multiple industries to buy in on Gates together, not after those first Compact Gates went bust. It comes down to the Mag-lev time, Ray. They argue and bicker over who gets what shipment on which Mag-lev," Stewart says. "I've given it some thought in the past, though."

I think about that for a while, teasing an option out of thin air as I proffer, "I take it that they have ruled out a railroad-style partnership. Let us add an incentive to the deal, then. The sooner we get those in the contract up to Stage Three, the quicker they are off our teat. The lower our costs, the faster they start exporting in earnest. I think also having that Stage Three lowered to five years versus thirty will make this jump a lot more attractive for most industries."

Stewart muses out loud, "Give up a little now to gain more later. What are you thinking? A partnership of sorts?" He drums his fingers on the desk of dark wood. "I think that might do it: create an independent Mag-lev company for each gate that processes the exportation of raw and finished goods. Fifty-one percent owned by the Family, seventeen percent owned by the citizens of the D2 iteration, and sixteen percent by the businesses, or split equally by the D2 iteration's business and people. Any fraction is going to the people." Stewart, in a matter of moments, pulls together a fantastic idea. "I'll look into this on the contractual end. For now, float that. See if the reduced Mag-lev fees with profit-sharing will entice the businesses to band together on this."

He pauses, sitting forward, and asks in a worried tone, "Any news on the animal pilot?"

I say, "I ran into Samuel while working out with Darien. Samuel is headed to

Brazil to run down leads for a second time. Darien is looking into the Japanese aspect. I think he will get further in their society than Samuel or myself will."

Leaning back, Stewart says, "Likely so. Darien has a certain love and affinity for the culture. The Mega Corporations always seem to want to please him when he has a request. If that's all, Ray, I want to talk about the House of Talk fiasco. I already spoke with Eliese.

"Something's happened, Ray. That show has unbelievable ratings, or Bonnie shopped it around looking for dirt. Probably both. Our old friend from CGSU, Steve Jenkins, is kicking up a hornet's nest over DGMW. Most of what he is whispering into people's ears is false. Rumor has it he's out for your neck. Bonnie...I haven't figured out how that scavenger mixed herself up in this, but your charity stunt made her look like a complete fool."

He holds up both hands, imploring me to hear him out. "I wouldn't have donated if I hadn't agreed with that course at the time. However, we have to pay the bill for that stunt." He looks up and exhales. For the first time since I have met him, the man looks exhausted. "Eliese is out of the country for a while, taking over some of my dealings. She'll do as well or better than me. Use your time to lay low at the Hill House. Build up your team. Please keep your head down."

Eliese had kind of hinted at this, yet I am still a bit surprised.

"Bonnie challenged her. I knew as soon as I heard Bonnie make a dig at her for being 'the prettiest spinster,' her not having a 'man,'" I say, with accompanying air quotes. "It was either back her up or shoot Bonnie." I am careful in phrasing my last bit as only a jest. "I did not have a gun."

That elicits a snort and then a good laugh from Stewart, and he says, "Eliese and Trish are so much like their mother. Neither of them will take a direct challenge. They will stomp it flat. Don't worry, Ray, Eliese and Bonnie-poo have been doing this dance since the first interview. You tricking Bonnie out of over a million credits, *that's* what got under her bonnet. Bonnie loves money only the way those who constantly lose it do."

I stand and shake hands with Stewart.

***

C9 S5

Thap and I then make our way to the flat and continue to work until dinner. Darien has his guests, so dinner is in honor of them. Samuel has taken off for Brazil. Trish is at the residence, and she is a delight at the dinner. With overgrowing mirth, Trish outlines the whole FEED episode for our guests.

"Then Ray-san shows up Friday morning with Ray-san," Trish says as she points at me, "in a garbage man's uniform and spends all day picking up trash."

She thumbs a still image to the center FEED projector, of me in that uniform. In a fit of well-played giggles, she continues, "He then announces the charity while eating a sandwich on a bench to the news. Every garbage man named 'Ray' gets a partial payment to their kid's indenture."

The whole time, the guests look from me to Trish, the weaver of this fantastical story.

"Over the next two weeks, nearly every sanitation company and worker put in to legally change their family name to 'Ray.'" Trish smiles and laughs. "It gets better: the Rays started their private funding for the charity, calling it the 'Ray donation.' Everyone puts in five percent of their pay to build up the fund."

Trish then shows the feed image of Bonnie's face through the window of her house as she sees Ray-Ray's sanitation. This image, I have not seen. Now I can understand Bonnie's anger. I had taken her money and given it to the sanitation worker.

Everyone has a good laugh at the image. Then I hear Trish start her song. She is nowhere near as gifted as Eliese. I bet some of that will come with age and experience. She pulls those guests into her song as it arrives in full swing.

Trish was also challenged by Eliese, and wants to do some stomping of her own. "So, Ray, you and Eliese brought out the relationship to the whole Compact." She waits until the wine is in my mouth before asking, "Did you talk to Father about the wedding yet?" She waves and says nonchalantly, "That's normally how we do these engagements."

Her voice layers emphasis on the word "engagements."

"When is the date, Ray?" she asks sweetly.

It takes every bit of my control not to spit wine everywhere. I am in the stages of coughing as she says, "When is the date?"

My voice goes hoarse during the coughing fit as I hear, "Have you talked about kids yet?" An ever so sweet voice comes through as I am turning purple. "Oh my, don't tell me it needs to be a shotgun wedding!" My gaze turns to Trish, who is giving me an imitation eyebrow. Point to Trish.

This whole debacle elicits congratulations from the Japanese guests, who do not know Trish that well and take her at face value. Darien, well, he is an ass.

Darien says, in an as saccharine tone as he can manage, "Ray and I had a coming to minds today in the ring, Father. I have no objections as her brother to the union." He finishes the statement by looking at Trish and his guests, which sets off another round of congratulations from his guests.

Trish, not wanting to let the fun go, adds, "Oh, Ray, you did know about the propriety in this kind of thing, didn't you? Tsk tsk." She even sounds like a teacher who catches a student cheating. "Father, I like Ray," she continues, as I try to get my fit under control. Then she goes for the kill: "Imagine, you could have avoided all this if you hadn't canceled on me for New Year's."

My head whips around to look at her. That twinkle, that flash of blue eyes, oh, she has played me well. She is going to be hell in heels when she gets a few more seasons under her. I stop my coughing as Stewart chimes in, a great deal of amusement in his voice.

"The look on your face, Ray. I'm sorry, I couldn't stop it. I *am* Eliese's father. You needed a good ribbing over that. Don't worry, it is a statement of intent of courtship in the eyes of the Family," he says, as he waits for me to finally calm down before he digs in with his own hook. "You can come talk to Samuel, Darien, and myself before you intend to ask her."

Stewart's statement prompts one last round of congratulations from the Japanese guests. I laugh, and while bright red, nod to all of them graciously.

Then Trish sends the whole recorded thing to Eliese. I decide it is best to lick my wounds at the Hill House. We leave after cocktails and continue to work on

271

the way to the Hill House. The frame for the MKVI military SkipJack would be arriving tomorrow, the two fully kitted MKIV military units the day after. The third day is an overnight at the assembled Conference in the New Mexico District.

How Thap put it all together, I am not sure. It is up and running, six teams of six, with a 25,000-credit reward to the winning team. As we land, Thap lets me know he has a few candidates for the SkipJack fabricator he will be forwarding to me, three he found and six the HR department recommended. I will start my reviews of those resumes in the morning.

***

C9 S6

The morning is a long one in my little office. The FEED terminal has everything I need, but going through these resumes is a pain. I discard two, as they only have conventional military SkipJack design experience. I drop two of Thap's and two more of HR's for having no experience with military SkipJacks, another for being an anti-war/anti-gate/anti-transition/anti-reintroduction of lost ecology nut. You can guess who let that last one through the interview process. I have two candidates left. I ask Thap to invite them to the Hill House for a working interview on Friday.

The MKVI frame shows up in the early afternoon. The manufacturer's staff remove it from their tram and bring it into the new shed. It is a piece of art, a prototype Mark VI shell with a lot of features I have asked them to include.

I aim to standardize the mounts for anti-personnel and anti-SkipJack weapons. Currently, MKIII, MKIV, and MKV all use the same weapons, but different mounts. Armor has traditionally been hard mounted. I have several revisions to standardize that and make it much more serviceable for the troops.

The big difference with SkipJacks is the caliber. Think heavy machine guns for SkipJacks, whereas anti-personnel firearms and weapons are about the same as they have been for more than a thousand years. SkipJacks can make use of caseless ammo, integrated feed, and magazine ejection systems.

That night, I prep for my Conference and the arrival of the two fully functional MKIV SkipJacks. I set up a full pod, not one of the portable pod units I have been using over the last three Gates. The MKIVs arrive early in the morning.

The ammo should arrive later in the day. These are the same Mark IVs that Samuel and I piloted at the end of our term of service. These are good solid units. I take the time to move their docking stations into the shed. I tag them to my biometrics, FEED-lock them to me and show the delivery NCO, Sgt. Nardall, how the ammo cage locks down to me in the same manner.

"Rules are rules, Lt. Colonel Ray," Sgt. Nardall says formally.

He is not impressed by my set-up until he sees the MKVI frame. Then it comes down to two combat pilots talking shop. His infantry unit is piloting MKVs with much less armor, more speed, and a larger power cell, giving it a longer on-station and time in-theater.

From there, we go down the line of haptic suits, Donner V1, V2, V3, and Blitzens. I will send him back with two Donner V3s for my old sister unit in Force Recon. They can use a heavy pack hauler, and I want solid, independent evaluation of them. I need to know if the boys in the FR teams will break the Donner V3s in the same manner I do. If you want to know how something will fail, let the military test it.

I let Sgt. Nardall stick around for a while, mainly because he tells me of their new remote mesh spike. Instead of having a range of one kilometer or less, depending on the terrain, these new RMS units have a range out to nearly three and a half kilometers. The latency is as smooth as our old units at one kilometer out. The spikes, however, are pushing more than sixty kilos. Compare that to the ten kilos of my current mesh spike, so right now, the infantry is humping them on the backs of their SkipJacks. Nardall cannot say much more about that, but I see Thap look up when stowing the parts for the SkipJacks. I am sure Thap will look into the new RMS.

I tell Nardall to FEED Thap when he has paid his war college indenture.

Nardall stops abruptly and says, "I'm in nine years. I've paid my war college." He pauses. "How long were you in, sir?"

I straighten and respond, "I was on a work up. My mate and I were injured. We were both in just over twelve years with the FR teams, around four and a half years prior." I smile. "It has been over six years now. At some point, Sergeant, I will need someone here who can pilot Military SkipJacks. It will be work here on the live-fire range. Talk to Thap if you want, when you get out."

He salutes, turns, and boards the tram.

Thap walks up and says, "We can't just hire him, you know." He turns to look at Sgt. Nardall as he departs with a great deal of concern. Thap might believe that I learned nothing from yesterday.

I smile at my friend and Segundo. "When do you plan on retiring, Thap? When do you plan on stepping out of the game? You and I have both been there. Nardall will not leave the CM. He will do his term and take another war college course. He will keep doing that, knowing that he has a job here. It is that solace that keeps men like you, me, Samuel, and Nardall in the game. He will be injured out, or be buried out." I sigh as I watch the tram leave. "Just like me and Sam."

I look at Thap and pull my haptic suit from my rack in the shed as workers are sawing and nailing and getting things sorted. I grab my set of survey goggles and check. I have no ammo as of yet for the MKIV SkipJacks, so a bit of range time is out of the question.

Nevertheless, I am not passing up this chance to pilot a MKIV again. In my goggles HUD, I see the power levels for the MKIV are at sixty percent and my haptic suit is at ninety percent. We are golden. I do my function tests, run through the optical feeds, and look at Thap, who blanches as the SkipJack's multiple optic stalks swivel at him.

"I am out for a few hours. I have not handled one of these in six years. Time to play. Let me know when the ammo pings for landing." I am entirely too gleeful as I slowly do the final twist, arm rotation, and ankle flex checks.

Thap nods as I start. It is a comfortable jog through the length of the shop, dodging fleeing workers as they see 340 kilos of military SkipJack jogging forward and right of a pilot. For those who had never seen it, these weapons of war are pants-wetting scary.

The MKIV pounds out a steady *thoom-thoom* beat as its rubber-treaded feet hit the reinforced concrete floor. We are out of the new shed. I feel limber, like I did in my prime. I am loose, and I am stronger. I angle myself to the left of the tram and keep the SkipJack heading straight for it. I feel the weight build in my legs on one hundred percent feedback from every footfall.

The weight of piloting is mental; it is hard to learn that, let alone remember it. I have seen pilots with years of piloting experience stumble when their mind tells their body they are carrying the full weight of a SkipJack.

With an inner smile, I feel the pressure on my legs as I tag a preset command. The SkipJack leaps, clearing a large section of our tram landing area before sticking its landing. A huge grin stretches across my face. I have timed it correctly. The MKIV sinks four inches into the edge of the landing pad, and I halt long enough to absorb the landing and direct it forward with a lunge and a steadied right hand of the SkipJack.

I pilot the MKIV in front of me, building steam as we head down the pond trail. I have the MKIV jump the creek in various spots as we move along. The soil is soft, and it sticks like a tent stake in the dirt when I land. I work the MKIV free as I get back to running. I run for nearly an hour before I feel the buzz of the incoming ammo. My range time is next.

I return at a run. I walk in front of a second delivery sergeant, who blanches at seeing a full military combat SkipJack walking so easily on a remote pilot.

People who can remote pilot are a minority in our industry. Those of us who can remote pilot and dump into a SkipJack are rarer still. When Sam and I were in Force Recon, there might be one percent of the pilots in the CM who can do both. General Diomedes tests and fights for every last one of us.

I dock the SkipJack as I raise my HUD lens. I shake hands as I officially take delivery of my ammo. I look over the numbers. Not much. Enough for about six loadouts. I look at the renewal and wave Thap over. I show him and the delivery sergeant, who can do nothing other than confirm that the major who sent over this ammo would be the quartermaster with whom I should talk.

I ask Thap to get them on FEED message and to get that straightened out. I have a shit ton of practice to do. Six loadouts are not even an afternoon's worth of training. When I realize Thap is getting nowhere, he thumbs it over to me as the three of us walk back to the MKVI. I show the quartermaster on FEED the MKVI. I ask if he wants that contract filled. He laughs: the company is well on the way to fulfilling the contract for testing within its timeframe.

I turn so that my FEED pick-up has Thap and myself in the image. "Thap, buy the company. I have concerns about the quality of the 3D printed forgings."

Major Cheap Ammo says, "Wait, what? You can't."

I look into the FEED as I say, "Me? Probably not. GSG most assuredly can and will." I build a bit of heat in my tone as I continue, "That would waste my time and the Compact's credits." I smooth out into an even keel of disdain. "I would like to come to an understanding about the ammo. First, tell me why the ammo cannot be delivered to me, quartermaster."

Quartermaster Cheap Ammo, as I am now mentally referring to him, pops out a squeak of an answer. "We reserve that ammo for the Compact Military. We sent you all the CM deemed you needed."

By the time Quartermaster Cheap Ammo (QMCA) finishes, Thap has added in Quartermaster General (QMG) Cheap Ammo, a Franklin Bostich. I finish with the QMCA and within a short time, I am on live FEED message with Bostich.

"Mr. Ray, I am Quartermaster General for the Compact Military's armament group," Bostich says. He has a slight tone of arrogance as he comes on. He has been expecting this from his underling QMCA.

I have an ace up my sleeve. That MKVI did not appear out of thin air.

"QMG Bostich, thank you for taking the time just now," I say in a placating tone. "We seem to have hit a snag with the procurement order your quartermaster sent over." I am in my affable state, as this is the voice I use to get along with anyone. "I am working with the manufacturer of one of the entries to the new MKVI SkipJack program. They have sub-contracted the manufacture testing of all models to us here at GSG. That procurement order arrived with a tenth of what we need for this month's work up."

QMG Bostich is a little taken aback. "The Quartermaster General Armament Group has no interest in MKVI Infiltrator/Interceptor models, Mr. Ray."

I surmise by his look that he is working up to an articulated arrogance that the self-important have. It dawns on me that he probably has a vested interest in another MKVI test mule.

QMG Bostich lets a smug half-smile spread to his eyes and says, "I reviewed your requisition for ammo and lowered your ammo totals to levels sufficient to your needs."

I suspect that Bostich is about to cancel the FEED message.

I do my best to communicate clearly to the QMG so that there would be no ambiguity. "I see, I see. Do you know General Jermaine Diomedes? The very same general who helped set up this company as a munition's manufacturer for testing and evaluation?" I ask.

Before Bostich can respond, I continue, "I am having my Segundo bring in General Diomedes as a party to this FEED Message. You can explain to him why his Interceptor and Infiltrator MKVI units will not be tested and evaluated on schedule."

With that, Thap connects us to General Diomedes. My old Force Recon commander pops into a split view on the FEED display. General Diomedes is an old hand at the politics of the CM, and from what I hear, politics outside the CM, as well.

"Ray! My stars and bars, you look good, what I wouldn't give to have you and Sam Janks back in field command of a Force Recon units again!" Jermaine is playing it up by letting the QMG know how highly he thinks of the two of us. "Retirement as a brevet promoted lieutenant colonel seems to be treating you well. I know you had a few years to go before pulling a pension."

As always, Jermaine Diomedes is a man of good cheer. That is but a single facet of his makeup. Another side to General Diomedes is the cold, ruthless head of the Compact's Force Recon, which is the unit of men sent when something needs to be nuked without the nuke.

Samuel and I had each worked with General Diomedes for over twelve plus years. When we left, Sam was in command of our Force Recon Company. General Diomedes was very much in favor of his commanders leading from the front, doing the same crap work as the first-year FR grunts, and for twelve years, Sam and I did just that.

I light up my face with a smile so wide, it would scare a tiger. I take Jermaine's cue and speak to the general on a first-name basis. "Jermaine, I am doing well.

GSG is growing and doing well. Sam and I work it together, as you probably know. I am messaging about the MKVI models you would like GSG to work up: specifically the Interceptor and the Infiltrator.

"GSG just received our first MKVI shell," I say. Sure, I am laying it on a bit thick as I play the backstory for QMG Cheap Ammo. "Today, however, we received a tenth of this month's ammo procurement from the QMG Armament Group. QMG Bostich was just explaining why that is."

That is all it takes: nly a few in the NAC have the stones to throw down with General Jermaine Diomedes. He has been the head of the Compact's Force Recon SkipJack units for over fifty years. Well into his nineties, he still runs morning parade with his Force Recon recruit troops, piloting his MKII Skip-Jack. Every *fucking* morning. After that, he plays golf with the Prime Minister or someone from the House of Lords. The man is his own institution.

That is the start of the Diomedes power base. Like the Jankowitz Family, the Diomedes name is known far and wide. In the NAC, private ownership is nearly non-existent. The only way to "own" things is to have them under a corporate umbrella. If you have twenty-five years or more in the CM, you can submit for a corporate charter. The two largest corporate families in the CM are the Woody Family corporation in a distant second, and the Diomedes Family Corporation. There is a reason why Jermaine is called the Lion of the Compact.

Immediately, QMG Bostich states my ammo would be on the way shortly, along with an agreement for future monthly resupplies. QMG disconnects from the call, and Jermaine grins as he also departs the meeting.

Thap grins from ear to ear as he walks away, merrily looking at his FEED while whistling. The delivery sergeant stands off to the side, still as glass. The young man cannot be more than twenty-four, and he gulps as I turn my gaze on him. I privately name him Sgt. Gulp.

I say, "Oh, Sergeant, good to see you are still here! Please give me an ETA on when that ammo will be here before you leave."

I long for the day back in history when you could just buy guns and ammo off a shelf but that was a time long before the NAC.

I whistle merrily as I pull one of the four types of ammo each from the pallet. I slide them to the feet of the SkipJack MKIV. I push the Mag-lev pallet loader over to the magazine cage while whistling the same tune Thap started. The high explosive rounds go in the HE container, armor-piercing in the AP container, anti-personnel ammo in the small lock box, and anti-personnel pre-loaded frag launch tubes find their way into a specialized blast box.

I lock the cage via biometrics and FEED. Making my way back, I see Sgt. Gulp as he jogs up and says, "Sir, 2100 hours is the earliest I can be back with the remaining ammo allotment."

I thank Sgt. Gulp and bid him a safe trip.

***

C9 S7

I start popping ammo boxes for the SkipJack. Each MKIV, depending on its configuration, carries a fair bit of ammo. The ammo is fed by magazines the same way the pilot's personal carbines are. The pilot uses a preset to direct the SkipJack to pull a magazine from a storage container built into the legs, arms, or chest. The MKIV then pushes the mag into the now-empty magazine well. Upon discharging the last round of ammo, the magazine ejects up and down upon the bolt lock back. These poly-mags are somewhat of an archaic item, but no one has figured out how to shove a hundred rounds into a mag that does not jam.

Thap walks over and wolf-whistles intently and asks, "What's it have under the bonnet? I've never seen one this close."

I grin as I put on my best confident voice. "Thap, this MKIV variant is the standard grunt soldier, no command comms, no FEED up-link for the squad, and no anti-drone or air denial systems. Just plain ol' grunt. It has the best all-around speed, armor, optics, and weapons load-out. It can dish out one hell of a pain cycle with its caseless ammo. The right arm has your anti-SkipJack weapons. The left-arm contains your anti-personnel weapons," I say as I point to each of the guns and their respective mag-wells.

I start pulling out the mags and stuffing them in the magazine hard points and say, "Right arm load-out: top gun on the wrist is a twenty-five millimeter HE holding five rounds per mag, with a total load-out of forty rounds in eight mags. It is a rather stubby caseless round pushing 914 meters per second. Its damage area is about two meters, with an effective range of 1,500 meters. Pilots often choose it as an anti-personnel round at a long distance. No need to let them drop rockets on us."

I finish loading the mag pouches, but charging a round into the chamber will only happen when you go weapons hot on the range.

"The bottom gun is a twenty mm caseless AP. It has a one, two, three, four or five round burst setting. Ten-round mags are the standard, for a total of eighty rounds in eight magazines. It is pushing each round at about 975 mps with an effective range just shy of 2,000 meters. While it takes a bit, the five rounds will tear through a SkipJack's armor. That is when you drop in a HE round right behind. Many pilots run a program to drop both five-round bursts, followed by the single HE round. Reload the AP, rinse and repeat," I instruct as the mag is inserted into the mag well.

"The left arm holds the anti-personnel rifle and your pre-loaded frag tube launcher. It is a caseless 6.5 mm round in a twenty-five-round magazine, hence part of my love for the old venerable 6.5x55 swede from the old continent. You generally carry 200 rounds per load-out. It is pushing a 140-grain projectile at 883 mps, with an effective range of 1,500 meters," I say.

"The pre-loaded frag tube is a single-shot round that is something between a grenade and a mortar. It is slung under the SkipJack's left hand. It is accurate out to 800 meters with a kill radius of fifteen meters, incapacitation of about thirty-five. You carry three loaded tubes on your left thigh. Send up a drone, figure out where the enemy is. Then the squad lobs a platoon's worth of these like mortars. Head in after and make a mess of things," I say as I single-load tubes into the thigh holster and the chamber of the launcher.

"There, that should do it. I am going to run this tonight. I will get it sighted in via pod and these HUD goggles," I say, as I smile at Thap.

"Raylan, you and Samuel piloted these? For twelve years in-theater? Like pod in-theater?" Thap asks, looking at it with a bit of awe.

I explain as I get everything ready. "Thap, you know what sets pilots like Sam and myself apart from Nardall? He is a good or even great pod-based combat infantry pilot, I am sure, but he is not Force Recon material. Most pilots cannot dump into a SkipJack, as it is a violent experience.

"Others can go on reserve power, but it is something your mind has to constantly have control over. Imagine having to think about breathing to breathe. It takes mental fortitude to do it time and time again. The regular CM infantry troops are always pod-bound. If what General Diomedes says is true, only about seven percent of pilots can dump into their SkipJack more than three times during basic training. Even then, most end up in the med ward for a day or three," I explain.

"Additionally, only about two percent can remote pilot a SkipJack on a haptic suit's reserve power. With only about half a percent of either of those two groups being able to do both. Sam and I are very unique," I say as I lock things down on the MKIV. "Out of some 75 million members in the CM, Jermaine has only about a thousand FR troopers at any given time."

I look at Thap hard. He needs to understand this if he is going to keep my life contract. "We do not use pods. Just like earlier today, when I ran and jumped." I point at our tram. "By going reserve battery and at one hundred percent feedback, we double our capabilities and people on the ground. The enemy thinks they are facing twenty-three armed SkipJacks, only to find out it is twenty-three SkipJacks and twenty-three pissed-off pilots." I smile. "That is why those of us in the FR teams generally only retire one way."

I feel a bit of remorse for those brothers who fought at my side and are long gone now. In my book of names, there are ninety-three brothers-in-arms listed.

After my evening dinner, I head out to the shed. I boot into the SkipJack and pilot it down to the range via the pod. Pods do a fair bit of the target computing for you. They have a lot more dedicated processes to match up the HUD crosshairs in the pod. It is a great way to sight in the systems before swapping over to a helmet HUD or, in my case, goggles. Sighting it in is pretty dull. The Compact Military way is to use the 6.5 mm AP at fifty meters, then 200, 500, and 1000. Five-shot groupings for each. The pod will make adjustments in the

HUD for all weapons and ammo types.

The range at Hill House is basically in a long, narrow manmade valley, as it keeps the wind out. When in battle, you usually have drones out, telling you the wind conditions, then HUD does the best it can to compensate. That is the Compact Military way. It is how I start in the pod.

Once the 6.5 mm is dialed in via the pod, I check the APHE at 200 and 500 meters, respectively. I then swap over to SkipJack-capable weapons, checking the twenty-five mm at 500 and 1,000 meters. I check the twenty mm at distances between fifty and 1,000 meters; due to the twenty's rate of fire, since its inertial dampeners do wear out. I run through about a third of my ammo by the time I finish. I put it in standby, weapons cold, and prep for my hike down to the range with a Mag-lev sled of more ammo.

Thap is quite keen on seeing this part. I have to pull on my chest rig, now with armor, a personal carbine, and start my trek down to the range. We walk together, looking out into the night. When we reach our destination, Thap watches from the security bunker while I use the SkipJack to put targets and barriers in place via reserve piloting.

When I am ready, I have Thap order the targets in my HUD and send me random strings to initiate the next round of shooting, with two fifty-meter targets, and one of each of the other distance ranges. He will FEED me the string five, one, three, two and four, and I will hit them in that order using the personal carbine while moving between barriers to facilitate a better angle. Once I have warmed up after four of those, I start layering the other weapons on target.

Finally, feeling warmed up, the last two are with the SkipJack and myself engaging together as a team. The MKIV is on my right flank, and I am on the left. We have a dual layer of three, one, five, two and four for me, and five, two, three, one and four for the MKIV. Our paths cross behind barriers. During this run, my mass forces me to overshoot the distance to the barrier. I reach out with my left arm, catch the hauling clevis of the MKIV, and swing back around. Just before my momentum is arrested, I let go.

As my feet hit the ground, my body becomes rigid and I place three shots downrange. Three hits ping off my steel target. The instant after I launch that third round, I engage my weapons safety and run to the next barrier.

Then it is over. I feel invigorated. My personal carbine goes dry; as are most of the SkipJack's weapons. I have three frag tubes remaining. I go weapons cold, flagging the chamber in my personal carbine. I step over to meet Thap. We check the chambers on the SkipJack and start back up the drive. I am sure the neighbors are going to give me no end of crap over the late-night noise. Even though I am in the middle of my 200 hectare live-fire area, which is surrounded by 1,214 hectares, I know the complaints are coming.

Sure enough, we are halfway packed up when a constable tram shows up and orders us on the ground. That order is just to be ornery. The two numbskulls then land their tram in the middle of the live-fire range. When they run our IDs the military clearance for the two of us comes back. The pair lights up the SkipJack, and I watch their faces immediately pale. Constables of the NAC are rarely armed. Only one of these two carries a shock stick, and the other only has a hefty rubber baton.

I explain that I would notify them of future live-fire exercises. In retrospect, that is probably a wise thing to do. I also add Thap to their contacts for any questions outside of the live-fire sessions. I note that dropping into a designated live-fire range via tram likely is not the best way to survive. Yeah, I am a dick, but they are a significant buzzkill in an otherwise enjoyable evening. I do, however, allow them to schedule range sessions for their rapid response team a few times a year. Even for them, there are not many places to shoot at a thousand meters anymore.

They trundle up to the shed with us, just as Sgt. Gulp lands. He pops out with three more service members, and starts unloading the first of eight pallets of ammo, two of each kind. The rest of the ammo will be delivered monthly.

The two local constables see eight pallets of military ordnance and realize how close they came to screwing up by landing their tram on the live-fire range. I put them to work unloading the pallets and handing the ammo off while the three servicemen stow it in the cage in the correct locked containers. I stow the personal carbine and the SkipJack. I then return the remaining frag tubes to their locker. When it is all done, I set the locks. We all walk out of the shed, and I lock up up for the night. Tomorrow is a new day. Sgt. Gulp leaves first, and the constables after.

Thap and I look at each other and grin. That is a metric crap-ton of ammo. We head to bed. Tomorrow is a tram to Utah district for my Conference on how to find water.

***

C9 S8

We pull in a motivational speaker that is an actual clown show. He is a pretty good comedian. The speaker dials it into his audience with some old-fashioned, self-deprecating humor. The folks attending seem to enjoy the fun. We organize working groups, vendors for tools, and a mini-tradeshow in the afternoon. Following that, we have unscheduled time and then dinner.

Dinner is what brought all these people here. Meat is a rarity in the NAC. It is expensive as a product and heavily taxed. I once watched a FEED vid on how the average citizen may have meat only twice a year. Tonight's fare is beef prime rib. Thap did not skimp on the catering service. He brought in the Family livery staff to take over the venue's kitchens for the event. As everyone is seated for the evening meal, I step up to the little podium and start my pitch.

"Hello, everyone. My name is Ray, from 'Ray-Ray Sanitation.'" By now, most have seen that little exchange. I receive a nice round of applause. "I appreciate you all coming here and want to take this time to thank my Segundo for pulling this all together, especially the food. Thap, please stand."

Thap takes a generous bow, sweeping his hand out like a circus ringmaster. Once again, the man shows me up as the crowd gives him the rightfully due applause.

I smile, gesturing at Thap. "Now, why are we here? Well, I have a problem. I am in charge of surveying the Family's private Gates. My goal is to get the Gates to start Stage Three within five years, not thirty-five years that we currently see for the end of Stage Two, or even fifty years for NAC-run Gate iterations." I pause for effect. "I have a system set up that finishes putting a D2 iteration to the end of Stage One in just under nine months," I say.

I stop to let that sink in. Everyone here is a business owner or contractor. They are heavily involved in public and private works for creating the type of infrastructure I am speaking about building. The men and women here know more about what I am trying to do than I will learn in a dozen lifetimes.

With an ever so slight smile, I continue, "You are all mavericks in your fields, completing jobs that other people would not be able to do. You find solutions as a hydrologists, septic system designers, or freshwater well drillers," I say, warming up as I vocalize my vision for the Gates.

I wait as the first slide pops up in the central FEED display; it shows bullet points of the types of things that must happen for a Stage One D2 colony.

"I have run into an issue. Water wells and sewers are my primary reason for gathering us all here tonight. One D2 iteration," the central FEED display shows the big sinkhole swallowing up the water, "has the unfortunate issue of finding water, stretching the limits of our current systems."

I smile as a current view shows SkipJacks and 3D printers working solidly in what is clearly the same D2 Iteration.

"I am looking for help, and I am willing to bet the people who do it for a living can give me the most reasonably efficient set-up within the parameters I am going to lay out."

A new slide pops up in the central FEED image, laying out the interior dimensions of the MLR V3.

"First, everything, including tools, the power source, materials and supplies, have to fit in no more than two of these MLRs," I explain as the second slide pops on the central FEED.

"Second: there is no FEED system, but we do have a data trunk. Any FEED network item will not work there until near the end of Stage Three. The data trunk will not support any loads of consequence," I say when the third slide comes up on the central terminal.

I look around at everyone. I take a moment to assess how the room of men and women are looking at the challenge.

"Third: I need it to be able to test multiple areas at once. It needs to help me outline the best drain fields and where to find potable water. In some cases, like the D2 iteration you see, this includes wells for farming."

A miniature FEED video pops up with an animation of a SkipJack putting in a mesh spike in the ground. "For example, put twenty in, and then it compiles data over the initial time of the survey, around thirty to fifty days."

I am beginning to see some consternation among the group attendants. This is a doozy of a problem.

"Fourth: the power system must reside within one of the MLR V3s. Preference will go to any system that is in one MLR."

As the final image comes up, I continue. I can now see some tables are looking at this as a real challenge, and some think I am nuts.

"Fifth: it must be operable by people not in the industry. We have very few people living in the D2 during these initial build outs of any Stage One colony. Colonies simply cannot support a specialist for each role," I explain, as I step from the podium while the center terminal display lowers.

In a more cheerful tone, I continue, "Those are the parameters and here are the rules: There are six tables of six. The winning idea will be voted on by the table groups as a whole. I will cast the tie-breaking vote if it is needed. Twenty-five thousand credits to the winning table, paid tonight. I am available for specific questions, as is Thap."

I smile at the attendees in the room, all of whom are now ignoring me. The discussions are kicking off in earnest. I have one more idea.

"On top of that, should we see any innovations that will make the winning plan more efficient, it would only be fair to add another prize," I say, and plaster my best smile on as I watch everyone dive into the problem-solving. With the mention of 25,000 credits split between six people and possibly a runner-up prize, now all the tables are doubly interested.

Over the next three hours, I walk the room, answering technical questions as the staff serves dinner. After the crew removes the feast, dessert and cocktails make the rounds. The people here are an inventive sort of group. These folks are the kind of people who have a wide variety of interests.

The solutions they bandy about are often outlandish and cost-prohibitive. They are men and women of business, and they know what is fiscally feasible and what would not be. When cost is an issue, they move on.

Finally, the last table finishes their plan. We start with the first finished and listen to the ideas. One after the other, one thing becomes clear. One of my specialists needs to be a hydrologist, another a community planner, and finally someone with more historical knowledge of building a community from nothing.

I had surmised as much, and the groups outline the need in excellent detail for me. The systems they describe to me provide such detailed data that only a hydrologist can interpret it. Finally, an innovative solution rises to the top as a clear winner.

Ground-penetrating radar (GPR) spikes, with twenty-five or more units spaced about three kilometers apart. All our searches have not come up with this as a tool for finding water. It turns out these GPR spikes are not used here on EP1 to find water. GPR spikes are usually used for finding gas deposits, old mines, and other types of adverse environments. Water is overlooked as something GPR can find. They are silly expensive, but they collect data over time. The innovation award goes to table three: 12,000 credits.

The plan involves integrating the construction of the water and septic systems when building out the community's blockhouses. It will slow down each structure's build. To do this, we will be swapping the larger static, programmed 3D blockhouse printer for a smaller, piloted 3D printer, as these can more easily handle excavation, laying power, and sewer lines. Some are even designed to do that while laying MLR-based roadways.

Finally, a dedicated well driller that can be operated by SkipJack using a team on the EP1 side. It is not the fastest solution, but overall, it is efficient. It is sufficient to drill wells for homes, as well as industrial and eventually municipal interests. In the end, we can offset the speed of the Stage Two build with a second or third piloted 3D printer. I like it. It only adds about ten days overall to my timeline in a D2 iteration. At the same time, it will drop three to five years off a D2's Stage Two timeline. There is room for improvement still, but they have sorted out my water supply issue rather nicely.

That leaves me with the task of a hiring a team. I also need to arrange for enough space from which to work. We hold the vote for which table's plan wins.

I ask if anyone knows of a hydrologist that will have the experience to make this kind of judgment call. Nearly all thirty-six attendees point to a balding man in the back who goes by Ol' Jack. As Thap pays the winners the 25,000 credits and the remainder file out, I sit down next to Ol' Jack. The simple resort chair starts creaking under my weight.

Jack, the sly old fox, notices. "Yer, a stout one, ain'cha?" Jack is thin and almost 200 centimeters tall. He has wrinkles upon wrinkles, tanned leather skin, and his handshake is as solid as my myomere hand. You rarely see a man of this type anymore.

"That I am. Ray, head of the GSG. I hear you are the man to talk to about filling a position I have open," I say respectfully.

"Do I look like I need a job?" he says in a voice that tells me he likes playing the cranky old fart.

I smile, look at him, and say, "You do not need the credits." I feign thinking about it. "You are bored. You have, what, almost seventy-five years in this line of work? Your kids are grown, and you cannot teach half of what you know if you had another sixty years."

I smile as I watch Ol' Jack tune in.

"I need a man who can break new ground, one that can record how he comes about his decisions. Someone who can take this science and apply it to new D2 iteration earths. Worlds that man has never stepped on before. New theories, new hypothesis, new testing protocols." I pause, thinking of my way of going about this.

"Have you ever seen those thirty-five men and women agree on anything? Hell, they did not even vote the same for the best plan. Yet when I asked who was the best person for the job, they pointed to you."

He sips his whiskey and exhales. "Maybe I'll come take a look. I ain't promising much."

I do not know why, but I like this man of tanned, wind-beaten leather.

"I grew up in the old Arctic Wildlife Refuge," I say as I pour me a whiskey and top his off. "For four years, I lived alone in the wilderness. My parents had passed in the spring thaw one year. I joined the Compact Military at eighteen and have not been back. What I am doing, Ol' Jack, is keeping people from those long, cold merciless nights I lived through," I say in a solemn tone.

Ol' Jack does not look at me as he replies. "I grew up about ninety miles from what used to be Yellowstone park before the caldera ruptured. My extended family ran one of the last independent ranching operations, and our water rights predated the old Americas Civil War. We owned the last of the native prairie grasslands and I punched cattle on that land 'till I did my service.

"It was just five years, enough to get my war college degree. Water was always tight where we were, five thousand feet up in the Elk Horn mountains. As a kid, I was a hell of a dowser. I completed my war college as a hydrologist. I've knocked about the west for the rest of my life. One love, many kids, and two scores of grandkids. All moved on or passed."

Jack stops as he raises his glass to those now passed. I return the gesture as he slams his drink back.

"D2 worlds, you say? New iterations, new ideas? Who do you have?" he asks, and I know he is interested.

I snort. "The Family, capital F. In reality, just Thap and me. Oh, I have plans."

I explain, pointing at the still-playing scene of the big sinkhole from the farming Gate.

"I was there, Jack. I found that sinkhole. The Family's scientists tell me there is a vast salt pan underneath the soil. I walked right up to that edge, right up, and flew my drone over and took that very shot. I spent ninety days in that D2 iteration," I say. Maybe I am letting more out of the bag than I should, but Jack does not strike me as the talkative type. "Come see what I am doing, what I plan to do, how I plan to change the EP1 world for the better. Soil, fauna, and flora reintroduction," I say.

Ol' Jack is staring at me, perhaps looking to see if I am nuts or a good liar.

"Ninety days, and you saw it? You walked those plains, where no human has been?" Jack asks. A rhetorical question lingers underneath. "I can't walk no Gate. I still have a family. I...I... A new world," he mumbles, trailing off. "You want me to find water on new worlds."

There is a joy on Jack's face, the kind of wonder a consummate professional has when they realize they have not seen it all, that life has a task for them, something new, something wondrous. Work of this type makes the mind grow.

"Mr. Ray, I will come to look. I will see what you are doing and tell you what I think," Jack says, and his voice is firm, reliable, and determined.

I stick out my hand and smile. "I will have HR get in touch with you and tram you out to the site. Ol' Jack, I would like you to meet Thap. He will get you sorted. I will be on a business trip like that one in a few days," I say as I point to the center FEED video. "I would like you on-site to advise Thap and our people."

"All right," Jack says. "Beats watching you on the FEED."

A twinkle is in his eye. It seems Jack has seen our "House of Talk" episode.

***

C9 S9

We tram back out that night, taking what rest we can during the flight, and return to the Hill House. Tomorrow, I have a meeting with Doc about the metals strapped around my arm. Then I have an interview with the two SkipJack fabricators.

As dawn rises, I complete a run using my HUD goggles and the second MKIV. It is working out splendidly. Both have their quirks, but hopefully, I can get them in tip-top shape soon. Each seems to have a few standard problems. They have arrived with their maintenance schedule books. Neither had any maintenance filled out for the last four years.

The maintenance probably stopped when the CM moved to the much-maligned MKV. A couple of days each, and I can have them as new functionality-wise. I finish my jog, make notes in their rundown logs, and head into the shower.

We arrive at Doc's magically about thirty minutes before whisky time. I sit down after my tests with Franc. Doc is looking at the collected strips of metals and noticing how much they have deteriorated.

"I'll look into these, Ray, but right now I have these for you: a hundred-gram bars with cathodic protective coatings," Dr. Alvarez says. He smiles as he hands over another set of bandoleers, this time one for each arm and upper thigh. "There are four types of cathodic protective coating on each of the main types of metal. Wear these until after the Gate walk and let's see how each of these stacks up," he says as he pours the dram, and we drink.

I tell him of my first potential hire in Ol' Jack. Jack is an older man, so I ask if Doc would look at him for suitability for this job, health-wise. We get to talking about the needed NDAs for GSG. Alvarez mentions that he knows of an attorney that would do for an NDA. I mull it over and decide I want an attorney for my corporation, outside of the Family. I take down his name and Thap, of course, will set up the appointment.

We return to the shed, and the construction teams are still in full swing. We have the back section with the military gear all sealed off in a locked cage. The front-left space of the shed is full of soon-to-be offices and conference rooms. The front-right will be the main doors and is where the current barn sits. The barn will be removed while I am out on my Gate walk.

The center of the building is a workspace holding a MLR V3, one of each of the Donner variants, one demilled, and a few other SkipJacks. The far-right wall is the docking area for my usual complement of survey mission SkipJacks. I pull the Donner V1 and V2 from the center workspace and move them into the smaller barn. I have two 3D image testers and two FEED terminals.

Thap and I discuss what we want in our test. The applicants need to roughly fabricate a SkipJack as useful as the Donners, given my survey missions—for example, something that can haul, act as a shelter, be useful in a security situation, weigh less than two tons, and is easily rechargeable.

It is an hour or so later when they both arrive.

Thap shows them into the barn and introduces us in his parade formal regimental English. "Ray, this is Tom Renyolds and Tina McGrath. Tina and Tom, this is Ray, the owner of the Gate Surveyor Group." I shake hands with both of them.

"This will be a working interview," I say. "I need people who go about things from a unique perspective. I need folks who can work as a team with the other members that we are hiring to solve problems."

Tom seems mildly distracted, his eyes glued to the SkipJacks about the space. Tina is attentive and listening. The two are dissimilar in many ways. Tina is dressed in a very stylish suit. Tom is in a stained jumpsuit that has seen more than its fair share of burns from welding.

"We are dealing with problems in areas so remote there is no having the solution delivered via FEED." I look at them both as I speak. "Behind me are the two single most important tools of my Surveyor Group: Donner V1, and Donner V2. Their load-carrying capacity is the same 275 kilograms, give or take. Their run at capacity time for both versions is the same, as is the recharge. V2 differs in its panniers," I say as I point to the cargo packs. "And it is eight percent lighter." I smile as I pop panniers off and open them for the applicants to inspect. "The V3 version is a V2 with a powered vacuum refrigeration unit for each pannier.

"I am not asking you to redesign the Donner. I want something wholly new. GSG does not need a derivative of the Donner. Wholly *new*," I emphasize again. "I cannot promise I will use the design. I want to see what an outside-the-box thinker will do." I straighten, as if I am back in the CM. "Questions?" My tone is also formal, and I do not have the luxury of watching these two all night to gauge their worth.

Tina jumps in. "How long do we have, why not take a tram, and why no powered MLRs?"

The excitement of it all is lacing through her voice. This will be real a challenge for her, I suspect. I smile.

"First, you have three days, excluding today. Thap will be available to answer questions." I point to Thap, who has plastered on an impassive expression. "Lodging is set up in the community for you. A tram will drop you off for the 7:30 p.m. dinner and have you back here at 7:00 a.m.

"We work long days here, all of us. If you need more time, you can sleep in the bunkroom off to the left," I say as I point to the bunkroom and shower area. "Thap will have food brought here. This facility will be growing. Whomever I pick will be the second hire of the Gate Surveyors Group," I say in the tone I have used in so many formal unit briefings.

292

I take a step towards the 3D imaging tester on my right as I point out the basic facts. "Plain and simple: the places we operate have no way to recharge a tram or an MLR, or get them unstuck. The locations are often so remote that even the Donners have a problem busting through the brush and undergrowth. Follow that with the number of parts needed for any possible breakdowns negates their general use at this time," I say.

Tom then asks, "Wholly new? What kind of terrain must it traverse?"

Tom is looking at the unique feet of the Donners. He is a scruffy guy: unkempt hair, a face that had not seen a razor in a week or three. He is shy and will not look me in the eyes. He replies in short sentences, but he seems to listen and observe.

"I have been through snow up to two meters of deep powder and one and a half meters of hardpack. Ice is a possibility, rock shale is a given, steep mountain scree is regular, grasslands, high desert, mountains, and marsh." I think a bit more. "Also fording sandy bottom streams, muddy embankments, and fast-flowing rocky rivers, some of which are chest-high." After letting out a breath, I say, "No ocean bottoms, lake bottoms, or glaciers as of yet."

Tom and Tina look at each other. Tina asks, "Can we collaborate?" Now the excitement has hit them both.

"It is to be expected. We want the best solution, not just individual options," says Thap. "Ray, I'll take over from here. You have an appointment, one that has a strict time window. I've found a suitable stand-in for myself. He is waiting at the tram," Thap says in his regimental English.

I bow deferentially to Thap. I know he hates that crap, but these two candidates would see it as the respect it is. Hopefully, I can come back to a winning candidate, not two dead ones.

"Thank you, Thap. I will head out now," I say.

I turn and walk out of the old barn. I pull up my FEED and find that Doc's recommended attorney is only available this afternoon, so off I go. I spend some time reading up on Michael Knaggs: contract lawyer, with a decent practice under the Bale corporate umbrella. He and his wife live very comfortably in the Southern District. Busy as all get out. Finally, I hit on why Dr. Alvarez has sent me his way: Michael is an amateur historian. He specializes in the colonial period from 1500 to 1910.

I sit back as I notice a visibly worried member of the Forty sitting across from me.

"Pull the short straw this morning?" I ask as I look him over.

He looks up and gulps. What is it with gulpers?

"Dice, sir," the (very) young man says. He swallows, licks his lips, and says, "What I mean to say is, well, I won the dice toss. It is an honor."

I wave my hand. "Horseshit. Today is shit duty. Flying in a tram for hours, standing in an office while I bullshit with an attorney," I say as I look at his eyes. "Name's Ray." I hold out my hand.

The young guy shakes it as he says, "Pak, sir. I've been here for about two months." His English, his *British* English is solid.

I chuckle. "Pak, you have been in the military as long as any of your compatriots. The Gurkhas in the Forty take their job seriously. Do you honestly think they would gamble a detail away like this?" I muse while watching him.

Pak's smiling face shifts, and he looks stricken as he whispers, "I volunteered, didn't I? I never saw anyone else roll the dice. They told me I had the lowest number."

Pak bangs his head back against the bulkhead.

I smile. "That trick got me a time or three in my day. Do not worry, Pak, you would not be here if you had not proven yourself. Thap would have never let you within a ten-mile radius of the Hill House or me if he did not think you could do this as well as he can," I say.

I keep up the good-natured chatter the rest of the flight.

We land a while later. I spent a large portion of my time on the FEED system going over the work timetables for the shed, the upcoming appointments for SkipJack programmers. I review, edit, and send off Ol' Jack's new job description that I penned specifically for him. If I did not have Thap filtering this crap, I would likely not walk back over a Gate. As that thought comes to me, I consider eloping with Eliese.

I step out into the bright sweltering sun. The humidity spikes so high that I think my lungs are in the process of drowning. In front of me is a 3D-printed block building designed to resemble a wrap-around porch, like I have at Hill

House. This one is sun-bright yellow with white trim.

I walk inside to see a plush green carpet, a polite lady at a desk, and fake wood paneling everywhere. The office is nicely done up, even if the wood is manufactured and screen-printed.

I introduce myself. Her name is Carmen Knaggs. She asks us to wait. Pak and I take a seat. Out comes a fiftyish guy with a clean-shaven face, and he must have been balding badly, enough to the point that he shaves his head. The attorney has a big round belly, red suspenders, a yellow shirt with white collar, and cuffs to match. The shirt is the same bright yellow as the outside of the building. He introduces himself as Michael Knaggs. We step back into his office.

I start with, "Mr. Knaggs. Thanks for seeing me. I am looking for a third-party NDA."

With an excited and energetic voice that clips the ends of his words sharply, Michael says, "I can do that, surely. NDAs are easy to write up. What, specifically, are you looking to cover?"

I smile. "I am hiring a new set of employees. Our business line is unique, as in it has not been done before in this manner. I have to assemble a number of experts in their fields and have them organize into a group that can help my team complete tasks," I say.

Michael writes these details down. Sounding slightly distracted, he says, "What, specifically, are the kinds of things you want to be in the NDA?"

Now I need to let the hook dangle for a bit and see if my fish bites.

"I am looking at several items. One is the technology we use, how we use it, who uses it, who is on the team, and the overall plan and method of what we do," I say.

"Not many specifics in that, Mr. Ray. I'll need more than this to make an NDA effective across the whole of the NAC," Michael says, not really with frustration, but with a tad bit of annoyance.

I look around for a lure, an item to open the conversation. I see it: a pressed leaf from the big leaf maple tree.

"Interesting leaf there," I say by pointing to the enormous leaf just over Michael's shoulder. He turns and leans back in his chair, looking up at it.

"My family took a vacation a few years back, recreating the Lewis and Clark trail. We retraced their famed voyage of exploration west, and south to the great sea of Baja. That is one of my favorite souvenirs. It is from an Oregon Big Leaf Maple. My wife pressed it for me, just like Lewis and Clark did in their journals." Michael smiles and continues, "It was a four-year thing for them. We took four months, visiting and hiking most of their famous spots." He leans forward as he turns back to me. "Are you a lover of history, Mr. Ray?"

"That I am, Mr. Knaggs. I studied history exclusively in war college," I respond.

"Oh, what part of history?" Michael queries. I can see that his love for history outpaces his willingness to be an attorney.

"My particular interest is in peace, what it takes for one side to achieve and keep it. Not any one thing, mind you, but all accounts I could find in any written form from the first writings of man." I twitch that dangling hook, just a little, to see if he will bite. "There were dozens of times where I almost became sidetracked. In the end, I kept my course over the fourteen years of war college."

Mr. Knaggs is beaming. He has found another astute historian, one that could stay the course and remain focused on his interest. "I myself am partial to colonial times: what it took for new colonies to grow and flourish." He smiles. "And of course, how and why they failed. Everything from the manifests to the type of laborers brought across to the new colony, and the contracts with indentured servants."

Now I set the hook.

"It is funny that you should say that, Mr. Knaggs. I am also making history. I have started the Gate Surveyor Group for D2 iterations. I am cutting down the time it takes to go from zero settlement to the start of Stage Three while under private management. Under NAC management, it currently takes thirty-five to fifty years for them to meet the start of Stage Three. The best current private management can achieve is twenty-five to thirty-five years." I pause and let him nibble a bit more.

"Oh, now, that's a fascinating topic. I could tell you all about the bungling these NAC plans are doing. Just a terrible waste of time and resources," Michael says as he shakes his head.

I look at Pak, who hands me a plain vanilla folder.

"Mr. Knaggs, my team aims to have D2 iterations starting Stage Three in five years. Here is your job application and test. You will need that NDA signed by yourself, of course."

I tap the unopened folder. It is an unassuming three centimeters thick. Michael's eyes follow my finger.

"These are the parameters of one of the next Gate surveys I am doing: the equipment our teams currently have access to, the timeline we have. Included is the schedule we wish to beat and the people we have at our disposal. Bring me to the start of Stage Three, as close to the five-year point as you can, Mr. Knaggs," I say. "Organize it, design it, and we will change the history of man together. I will have you come on as D2 iteration project lead and set up each iteration plan to meet that five-year goal," I explain as I set the folder on his desk and smile.

Michael leans forward, staring at the folder, then pulls his FEED up and writes furiously for almost forty-five minutes. His wife, acting as the secretary, comes in, signs her copy of the FEED message just after he does. They thumb their NDAs to me. I am sure this is not the typical way of acquiring an NDA, but an attorney is the lesser of the reasons why Doc recommended Michael Knaggs to me. Then, with shaking hands, he opens the folder with enough room for his wife to read over his shoulder.

I thumb him Thap's feed and say, "I will be away for the next thirty-five to forty days. Send the bill to Thap to cover your time on this. Any questions will reach me through him."

He stands up, shakes my hand, and his wife, Carmen says, "I'll start canceling appointments, Michael. I can shove clients off here and there." I realize she is as much part of this passion as he is.

I look at Carmen Knaggs. "This is a partnership, then, this love of history?" I ask.

Michael looks up and holds out a hand to his wife, who takes it. With a brightness in his eyes, he says, "All marriages are a partnership. Who else would travel four months in a rental tram with two toddlers to visit places no one has heard about for almost six hundred years?"

I smile and bid them a good day.

Pak and I make the long tram ride back. I return late in the evening and head to the shower, and after that, bed. Tomorrow is more interviews, and then prep work for the Gate walk.

***

C9 S10

I wake up the next morning and need to work on SkipJack repairs in the shed's workspace. Like when I worked with Chen on Boss's SkipJacks, I need to bring them back to parity. I spend hours working on the MKIVs. My jumpsuit is smeared with myomere lube and various other oils, soils, and greases.

At 7:00 a.m. I walk through the shed and to where the two fabricators are working. I have enough time to nod to Tom and Tina before Thap walks in with the programming applicants. If I think Tom is scruffy, I need to readjust my base level of "scruff." Not everyone joins the CM and learns personal hygiene standards.

Thap, being the kickass Segundo he is, has rounded up five more 3D Image testers. The first two fabricators are hard at work coming up with their designs.

"Welcome, I am Ray." I proceed to go around shaking hands with every one of them. I do not bother to wipe myomere lube off my hand. While it is clear and has no odor, it does not wipe off easily. It gets everywhere. The lube transfers to any item you touch. Every person who then works with that item now has it on them. That is, until you wash your hands with a specific soap. The only bottle I have is in my bathroom of the Hill House. I want to see who can work while being frustrated.

I receive looks of confusion and disgust from some and others fail to notice. I continue over to my well-used Donners. I repeat the same speech from the previous day about what the Donners are and how they function.

"What I want is the five of you to review their code, increase the efficiency of their obstacle and obstruction tracking, their daisy-chain length, and their stability on the rocky ground like scree or slippery ground like ice."

I move about the two Donners and poke at a clump of prairie mud with my finger. The dry red soil falls to the floor with a thunk. I turn my attention back to the applicants.

"You may use these two for test mules. I expect them to be flashed back to stock when you have finished so that they can be used by the next person. Finally, and most importantly, I would like a ten percent improvement in the life of their power cells through software optimization," I say.

This last request elicits a gasp from the collected applicants, as a ten percent improvement is a big ask, usually unthinkable. However, I know that some portion of that optimization is possible, as Eliese has her team looking into it.

Susan Mickleson asks about the length of time for this project. Susan, I know from her resume, is just about to finish her secondary education. She is looking for an indenture to pay off her university costs. She is a little taller than average. She has thin, straight brown hair and slightly bulging brown eyes on a round face.

"Three days after today. You can be trammed to a hotel when you wish to shower or sleep, and dinner is available at 7:30 p.m. They offer breakfasts and box lunches to go, also, but the tram to come back leaves there at 6:00 a.m. Other than that, the limitations are yours. If you wish to stay here all three days, feel free to sleep in the bunkroom and shower in the bathroom," I say, pointing to the left corner of the barn where the bunkroom is.

Daivi Khatari steps forward and asks, "Sir, will it always be like this? Crazy tests, weird work?"

Daivi is from a different university, and she is also seeking an indenture to pay off her secondary education. She is darker-skinned, from the Indian subcontinent, I think, with black wavy hair and an oval, brown-eyed face. She stands about one-point-six meters and in general is not as thin as Susan. I know from both their applications that they missed out on some of the most sought-after indentures in the industry.

I eye her and tap my toe. "Not quite. There are intermittent periods of general work, followed by intense periods of WTF. When a programming problem comes up during a WTF moment, it will be all hands on deck," I say.

"These openings will be NDA-sealed, for life. You will never be allowed to use this work as part of your portfolio. Should you leave here on good terms, you will have the most singular complete letter of confidence from the Family to use," I say, and let that sink in.

I even hear the SkipJack fabricators in the back stop work and start muttering to each other.

"Finally, the payoff of your indenture is two and a half years, EP1 time."

That will get the applicants stewing. The single most sought-after jobs have a five-year indenture. The places that offer a five-year payoff are few and heavily fought over. Eliese knocked her five-year indenture in three and a half years through long hours, and managing twice the workload of most. Trish is on track to beat that by a smidge.

In that one statement, I have put these positions on a pedestal twice as high as the indentures these five top programmers had been vying for over the last six months. I turn to Thap, and he gives the speech about how he can answer questions. I bow to him again and head back out into the shop.

I receive an update from Daniel and Craig about Eliese's gift. They give me a timeframe of when they can start on it. Wow, it will be a good long wait. I let them know I am heading out on an inspection and I will finalize the designs with Trish's help.

I complete the first SkipJacks work up to parity that afternoon. Now it is time to prep for the shale Gate walk up north. It will be bitterly cold there. I start outfitting snow pads to the Donner's specialized feet. The pads are one of Thap's ideas after he asked me if I used sled dogs as a kid. With a couple of days of gear checking to complete, I step to it and start with the cold weather gear.

Preparing for a Gate is about triple-checking everything as I pull it from stores. While packing, I check the gear a final time as it is stowed. I will pull all the foodstuffs before departure. Looking at my list, I need to check and organize the camping gear, the mesh spikes, and double-check that the crates of spikes and mapping balloons are here. It will take me a couple of days to wrap up all my preparations, just in time to judge the SkipJack competition.

Thap keeps me up to date, and neither Tom nor Tina have quite branched too far outside the box. Both have designed a four- or six-legged pack hauler.

Tom, though, did it in style. He calls it the Llama. It is thinner than the Donner by half. It is lighter by one quarter. Its payload is 181 kilos and has interchangeable feet for the type of terrain.

"I designed it to take the place of the Donners in ice, mountain, and densely forested areas," Tom begins to explain. "I couldn't find a better option than the Donners for much of the high desert, arboreal woods, plains, or even deep snow. I worked on making something that succeeds where the Donners don't. Yes, you have less overall capacity per SkipJack, but you have something much more capable in its respective environs once the programmers," he waves his hands at the five slaving away, "get done with it. I'm not positive on the charge, as there are some savings with six-limbed SkipJacks. I'm using the same power and charging set-up. I did mount one nighttime infrared thermal optic, allowing you to circle a group of them and have them keep a security mode watch."

That is quite a bit of rearranging and packing into one midsize SkipJack. While it may not be a complete departure, it has a lot of promise.

I step back and look at Tina. I think she lost her confidence at some point during the interview process. She has a cat, tiger-sized. It is topping just about 400 kilograms. Six limbs. The payload is a paltry 147 kilos.

It features full webbed paws, with a good deal of space for snow, ice, and shale. It fits all the parameters, but spec-wise, does not have the interchangeable feet, the sentry mode, the same deep-cycle power cell, same dual-powered charging system. It only has a single solar charger.

Yes, it can manage to swim with flotation. It can jump most creeks. Yet, overall, it weighs half again more than the Donner V1, carries less and only has marginal improvements.

I sign off on the design with the statement, "Tina, I include a name in this recommendation. Forward this design to him. If he can use it, he will bring you on."

Then I thumb the design to her, and her work is hers. It is good work, better than most catlike SkipJacks out there. I put the sign off on the Famiy's virtual stationary. She will be able to sell this design and land a job to pay off her indenture.

I walk over to Tom and shake his hand, saying, "Welcome aboard. Thap will get you sorted over the next few days."

With that, I walk around the programmers, looking at their work. I can only grasp the basics of the things I see. So far, Susan and Daivi have not left, taking showers and wearing bibs from the shop as new clothes. Thap has food brought in for them. The rest are back at the hotel at 7:00 p.m. and here when the tram lands in the morning. I retire to Hill House for the evening.

I end up offering the position to Susan and Daivi. They have completed something. It seems the other three gave up mid-morning on day two and decide to turn their paltry partial attempts. Susan and Daivi have complete programs written. There are kinks, but they are functional, for the most part.

Most importantly, they have focused on and prioritized that ten percent energy savings, which will save me a two-and-a-half-day charging cycle on the Donner V3s every thirty days. With a ninety-day trip, that is seven and a half days cut. I put the three new hires together and I am looking forward to their results with the Llama V1. Their first project is to get the Llama tooled up and into fabrication for tests.

Tomorrow is the day I head out for the MWD. It is time to survey the Alberta-Shale Gate.

***

C9 S11

I step through the Gate into the marshiest zone of suck I have been in yet. It turns out this Gate entrance is basically on a floating marsh island in a bog. The train of Donners and I make it to the driest point I could find with the drone. I do some more flying and find out that it is just a crap Gate opening. Eventually, that demarcation point will need to be fully 3D printed and made safe from the marsh.

As the trunk comes through and the ratio slip starts, I get to work. I have some new ideas, new toys, and unique recipes for dinner to try. I also draw in more predators in this D2 iteration than I had the previous two. There are a bear and wolf again, although thankfully neither of them are piloted.

My growing team on the EP1 side is consulting with Ol' Jack about the marsh. Weeks in the D2 pass by as I wind up the balloon spiking and make it back to base camp. I now have perfected bear tacos and am doing well on learning how to make sourdough bread. Once I get back in range of the trunk, Ol' Jack has a plan set out for me.

I will sink some temp mesh spikes and a power source left in an MLR. Once I return to EP1, they would slip ratio it to winter. I have brought all that cold-weather gear for naught. That will allow crews to start work on the marsh area when it is frozen. It seems all the drones had come through during a freak spring storm and we thought it was midwinter.

The plan is to sink Mag-lev tracks into it as it thaws and then ignore the marsh until the D2 can drain it. Ol' Jack outlines the best settlement, comes up with suitable septic systems and well placements per plot.

I get to work surveying. It is not hard work; it is just work. Cut, chop, stack. The HUD overlay tells you where to place the mesh spike, and you put it there. The cavitating piton system drives it in. From there, I release its smaller solar charger, the wind charging balloon, and it is up and running. I exit after pulling the MLRs through. There are six, the first four carrying the necessities for the Mag-lev tracks, the data trunk extension, and the well-drilling rigs. I am out of there in eighty-three days D2 Time, twenty-four days EP1 time.

Like always, I return home to Hill House. Thap thumbs my FEED messages to me when he says with disinterest, "Eliese would be here at 5:00 p.m. to pick you up for a date night. She has sent some suitable attire to the Hill House for you. She requests that you be well-rested and have eaten before the date."

Thap does not have any kind of poker face. The disinterested voice always lets me know he thinks it is funny or will be funny, usually at my expense. I tram back to Hill House, exit, stow everything in the shed, and make my way to my bed by 11:00 a.m. Thap has me up after four hours to get showered and has food delivered for me another hour later. I then dress and walk out the door to meet Eliese's tram. Tonight is another penguin suit occasion.

My siren sings her song as I walk down the stairs. "Raylan, it is so good to see you."

Eliese waits on the bottom step of the tram in a dark, shimmering purple gown. She steps back up and into the tram just before Thap and I enter. I prowl up to her as her perfume hits me. She gives me a slight hug and air-kisses my cheeks.

"Don't you dare mess up the makeup," she says with a smile and a wink.

We sit as I turn to her and say, "Date night, huh? You look breathtaking." I point at Thap and quip, "He thinks this is funny and has been mum. What are we up to tonight?"

Ah, this is going to be good. Eliese flutters those brown eyes at me.

"Since we did a charity drive for the 'Ray Affiliated Sanitation Nation (RASN)'... Did you know that is what they call themselves now? From the sorters of recyclables to the haulers, to the guys who design the dumps: they've taken Ray as a hyphenated last name. Compact-wide. They put five percent of their earnings into the charity's early indenture pay-off program," Eliese says.

El is using her voice to serenade me as we lift off. I know she is stalling, and eventually she will get around to the point. I try to be patient, as this nervousness is a side of Eliese that I have never witnessed before.

After a while, however, I cannot bear it. "Eliese, you are stalling," I say, and she squirms a bit more.

"Raylan, I'm on the board of a charity. Their main keynote speaker bowed out with a cold yesterday," El says, a bit uncomfortably. "I was nominated to be the speaker for tonight's gala...this morning."

I nod along, waiting for the punchline. I have an idea, but I want to be sure.

"See, this gala is about creating inter-gate restoration trade for EP1 species and plants that are lost to us," Eliese says.

I look at her and smile. Then I wink.

"Okay, fine, they want us both as speakers, together. Onstage. We pulled so much for the RASN group, and they want in on it. The whole board badgered me into this while I was distracted," Eliese admits.

I laugh. "It took a whole team of devious socialites to outsmart you. That is pretty impressive." I tone it down to a smile. "We will tag-team it again, and talk

304

about the CBN:D2 and NEFC:D2 Gates. I can talk about how we are bringing the Stage Three start-up time closer to seven years than thirty-five."

"Raylan. Is that going to be enough?" Eliese asks, looking aghast. "This isn't like me. I plan everything out. I don't like stuff dumped on me last minute. It took me from the holiday party to the day of our first dinner of planning to get that right."

Eliese is now working herself into a good head of steam. I imagine that she is more than a little perturbed at being put into a corner by a gaggle of wiley socialites.

I reply with a warm smile, "We will tell our stories, I will share a bit of the dinner I attended while you were in Europe. We will talk about what the Family is doing on a macro scale to help, and then we will ask people to help on a micro-scale," I say in a soft, soothing tone.

"Thap, sort out the financial reports for the last four Gates, and what the cost of the secondary fauna and flora transplantation is per Gate. Give me a pie graph, and some financial statements from the Family to back it up," I say.

That stops Thap's smile. *Gotcha, you bastard,* I think. I am betting that Eliese would have already had her team pull that together. Thap furiously manipulates his FEED, scrambling to bring data together.

"Or you could ask Eliese," I say.

Thap's eyes shoot up to my face as he realizes I was kidding about pulling the data together. Eliese has already thumbed it to him and me. We come up with a plan. We are doing our best to work out a rhythm for tonight.

We enter on the red carpet. We stop for the cameras and the interviews. I give Eliese a twirl for the cameras, of which she takes with a grace that only she can. The staff escorts us to the backstage area. Before they attach mics, we face each other as the onstage makeup artist has at me. Pun and Thap are going to be on either side of the stage.

El says to me, "Raylan, sometimes you just have to get shit done. Tonight's a 'get shit done' night."

I am not sure if that comment is meant for me or herself. I laugh, and we part. Eliese goes to the right, and I am off to the left. It is a massive wood-flooring stage with rich, luxurious red velvet curtains. I watch and listen as her name is called, and she is introduced. Then I am summoned forth.

"I would like to introduce Ray, leader of the Family's Gate Surveyor Group," says the introduction hostess.

I walk out into the lights, looking only at Eliese's face. We reach out hands and clasp. El is planning to go for that air kiss again.

No, love. Pull me up on stage, stick me in a penguin suit, then ask me to raise money. Well, this will raise money. I deftly turn her into a twirl again. Hours and hours of mock dancing with a demilled SkipJack in the plains of old Alberta have paid off. Eliese flows with it, more so than on the red carpet. The plum-colored fabric flies as she spins into a dip.

Then a kiss, longer than the one that she had surprised me with before I left a while back. I hold it long enough to get a cheer from the crowd in attendance. I bring her back up, and her neck and face flush a beautiful pink. She is laughing the whole way back up.

As she rests her head on my shoulder, I hear her whisper, "Very nice, Raylan," and that starts me chuckling.

She defers to me, so I open with a recent story. I lead up to the day I flew to the Family home after the last public appearance, only to be asked to help spar with her twin brother. Eliese gasps at my tale of being whacked on the head, then our amiable male "bonding" as we had figured out each other, only to be upstaged by Eliese's little sister Trish. The lovely thing that she is waited for me to be drinking before dropping the bombshell that I am now on a path to betrothal. Eliese has seen the FEED from Trish, but laughs quite a bit at my retelling.

When Eliese stops laughing, she says, "You want to see the funniest face in the world?" She points at me, her song weaving through every bone and fiber of my body. "Watch close. Ray, my love..." I know what Eliese is going to do, and she just loves this too much.

"*Kids,*" she says with a broad smile.

I try, I really do, as my face morphs in slow motion while I contemplate being a future father. Then like a shotgun at the flight of a bird, "KIDS" rings out across the stage. That is it. The whole crowd is roaring in approval and laughter, and they take up the chant. "KIDS! KIDS! KIDS!"

That is why we do not hear Thap and Pun tackle someone behind us. When we turn around at the crowd's collective gasp, the man is under two very furious Segundos.

The man dressed in a cheap monkey suit. His tupee is askew, and his efforts to keep his hands free are futile as Pun and Thap pin him to the floor.

"Eliese Jankowitz, number two of the Family. Ray, number seven of the Family. You have been served," the man says.

Pun yanks free a crumpled paper from the man's right hand. Eliese's Segundo tries to slip her the envelope, but it slips from his hands onto Eliese's left shoe. Thap and Pun forcefully strap the man's arms behind him. With the help of onsite security, he is half-dragged out by the strap cuffs. I pick up the envelope and tuck it into my jacket. Everyone has heard him. I grab Eliese's hand, spin her around, and turn back to folks in the audience.

"Nope, in case you all are wondering, he's not mine," I say, raising my hands. The crowd breaks out into more laughter, drowning out my half-hearted chuckle. I decide to quickly move on.

I talk of my time working on the planning of the CBT's new venture in CBN:D2, how the CBN is preparing its second batch of propagated flora to Montana West District. I note that CBN has shipped over three million tree seedlings to the major rehabilitation zones on the east side of the Pacific Crest District.

I step back from Eliese; I start pacing the stage and engaging the attendees, meeting their eyes as I walk. I talk about how CBN is on track to meet a ten-year start of Stage Three. The GSG team is working with them to bring that down to seven and half years.

Eliese talks up the NEFC:D2. She shows the initial projections by the NAC on becoming Stage Three. Then she explains that after only one year of private ownership, it has hit Stage Two and we are projecting an eight-and-a-half year timeline to reach Stage Three.

NEFC has delivered the first of the natural transplant fish. Those fish are now propagating in their habitat in EP1: the Atlantic Ocean. She talks about how we have put together a team to find longterm water solutions and sanitation solutions for D2 iterations. GSG has found ways to speed up the 3D printing of settlements, along with the rapid 3D printing of industrial zones in places like NEFC:D2. Eliese thumbs video footage of three in-progress harbor docks to the central FEED display.

I move us back to the innovation the Family is putting together as leaders in this effort, showing that almost twenty percent of the first ten years' profit of a Gate is put back into that same Gate settlement in an effort to get them up to a stable Stage Three, at which point, reintroduction of flora and fauna will hopefully be a self-sustaining industry. I show the names of businesses we have partnered with on the EP1 side to provide discounted flora and fauna for reintroduction.

Eliese wraps it up with a bow: while the Family can help with this on a macro scale, it takes an organization like this charity to help guide these new business ventures, loan them capital, give them training, and help them and clients meet. Eliese describes our joy at being here tonight and helping fund this charity, as it will help see these seedlings and fisheries restored to their rightful place.

We bow once. I put in one and a half million credits from my personal account, as does Eliese, and we bow once more. I add a second donation from the GSG group. We exit the stage to applause as the hostess returns and starts to introduce the next MC for the second part of the evening: one Bonnie Anders.

Eliese and I look at each other. Her hand slips into my jacket and retrieves the envelope. She slips it open with a well-manicured, amethyst-colored nail and reads as we walk to the tram. We leave and head to the Family residence. While we are in the air, she reads, her legs crossed, flipping through the three pages multiple times.

Eliese looks up at me. "Well, love, we are being sued for slander of one Bonnie-poo." I almost laugh.

I hold out a finger for her to wait, and reach over and pluck the mic off the hem of her dress, then mine. I hand them to Thap, and he proceeds to put them in a round red canister. Pun pulls out a small box from under the seat and begins scanning us, then themselves. Finally, the canister in Thap's hand opens, and he scans the mics. They are still transmitting. Thap closes it again and hands it back to me.

"Go ahead. The mics will not transmit from here," I explain while tapping the box. I tilt my head. "I like the sound of that, by the way." I smile.

"My comment about her only being out for money pissed her off. She's made some allegations that we blackmailed her into that one and a half million-dollar donation. I have a deposition in a few weeks on the matter, and you..." She pauses. "...Are not scheduled.' Looking over the three pages again, my love says, "That's strange. They don't have you sitting for the deposition, for this, at least. Yet you are a part of the lawsuit."

As El talks, I am doing a bit of digging. It turns out that since our appearance on the show, Bonnie has made friends and been seen with four out of the nine ladies on the charity board. I show Eliese the list of the ladies on the charity board, then start looking one by one at the public pictures released two days after our show. It seems three of them have even had their own interviews on House of Talk.

Eliese fumes. She goes full FEED, almost a thirty-inch view, and starts sending messages to personal attorneys and staff. You must have some severe and significant upgrades in your FEED system to manifest a view screen like that. We land and make our way to meet Stewart.

Thap thumbs a FEED to me: a pre-taped interview with Community Council member Steve Jenkins. The former CGSU member is blaming the Family in a conspiracy to pull the plug on the DGMW:D2 settlement. We walk into the room and see Stewart watching the same FEED.

Steve Jenkins leans forward in the screen, almost frantic with energy as he says in his burbling and spluttering voice, "What I am positive of, Bonnie, is that the Family was losing money on DGMW: D2. They then used a bumbling guard by the name of Ray."

Jenkins shakes his head emphatically. "You met RayRay, right? To cause a terrible 'accident,' one that killed an old lady and left another guard braindead. Ray convinced his former girlfriend to sign the transfer order for a terminally ill patient out of the local hospital out of spite, all because his manager wouldn't put Ray on day shift," he says. The accusation hangs in the air, and while that sinks in, he whispers, "All so Ray could complete his mission."

They continue with complete tinfoil hat crap. Bonnie then comes back after a sponsor break and asks, "What's next for Community Council member Steve Jenkins?"

Steve slathers on the smile of a lizard and says, "Well, Bonnie, I'm announcing my bid to run for a seat in the House of Commons as a representative of the Montana West District. I just had a donor put one million into a PAC to help my campaign." He licks his lips, and the burble and lisp fade a bit as he says with a voice that is now a shrill cry, "When elected to office, I plan to get to the bottom of this DGMW:D2 failure. I plan to see Ray jailed. Justice for DGMW:D2!"

I laugh. I can't stop. "I still have Jacki's 'Dear John' letter," I say. "Is there an attorney assigned to me?" I ask as I quickly type a half-dozen names into my FEED. The names and contacts of the attorneys for this new debacle arrive from Thap and Pun. I start a message and move the list of people to depose about Jacki and how she left.

"I have spoken to several staff members who worked with Jacki. She was not well-liked, even more so after bailing on her indenture after convincing the local eligible batchelor, a doctor, to vouch for her indenture payoff. They scampered within a day or two." I think for a minute. "I don't know where Mark is, and he would also be worth deposing." I write, deep in thought. I hope Mark was not watching this load of garbage.

Stewart slaps his desk and growls, "Damn it. Consolidated Gate Securities United went and filed for bankruptcy. Somehow, they ended up misplacing a great deal of money, equipment, hard assets, and if you can believe it, personnel. How do you misplace your people? On top of that, we've issued a Compact-wide probe into their failure to staff Gates properly. Steve Jenkins was the number three guy, and at the time he was the acting Chief Legal Officer and Chief Financial Officer.

"It looks very suspicious to me. We've been waiting for depositions and financial statements for months now. I am going to make this priority number one. We might have even been overbilled. At the very least, we were underprovided by our contract," Stewart says.

The head of the Family turns to all of us in his office, his face livid with anger. You can see his distaste for dealing with lying scum. Stewart paces behind his boat-sized desk. Eliese holds my eyes, letting me know this is not the time to speak.

"New plan," Stewart says. "Now you two go everywhere together. Every function where you're not working with your teams directly, the two of you are one. We can't have this...this..." Stewart waves at us. "...Thing. Whatever you're calling it. We can't have it be called a sham."

There might be heat behind Stewart's words, but I do not think they are directed at Eliese or myself. No, this anger is solely meant for those who are trying to take their pound of flesh from the Family. Sure, Eliese and I are catching some of the blowback, but I do not take it personally.

Eliese visibly stiffens and says, "This isn't a sham. I don't care what that bitch says. I am *not* some whore for money the way she is."

I gently reach out to find her balled fist with my hand. Her voice trails off, although her rage is still evident.

"We need to, and we will be seen. I can do that. It would be the pleasure of my life, Eliese, my love. However..." I turn to Stewart. "When we are here, or at Hill House, we will be left alone. Period. No interviews at our home," I say, ending with my own myomere reinforced growl.

Stewart does not like that. Whether he is planning something or does not want me dictating terms to him, I do not know. The irritation leaves his face quickly after a tense stare-down between us.

He softens as he turns to Eliese and says in a mollifying tone, "Yes, I see now. Personal space. I understand, Eliese and Ray. You'll be left alone here and at Hill House."

I bring Stewart's attention back to me and say more calmly, "Stewart, thank you. 'This thing,' as you put it, is love. We will do it at our pace. Not Bonnie's, not your pace or anyone 'elese's.'" I let out a deep breath as Stewart slowly nods his agreement.

I muse about something Jenkins had said while Eliese and Stewart are talking schedule re-arrangement.

I mutter just a smidge louder than I should have. "I have two MKIV Skip-Jacks. I can always drop a frag tube on her while she is hosting." Then it hits me. "Stewart, subpoena Jenkins's office for a donor list, including this PAC he mentioned. Then subpoena Bonnie's account. She put a lot of effort into tonight. I bet, I know, but cannot prove it is her funding."

Eliese is back to calculations. "I'll handle the financial statements. Trish owes me for her stunt with you at dinner. She can help me wade through them with our forensic accountants."

Eliese points her finger at her father. It is not accusatory or aggressive, but a way of laying out her clear battle plan for all. I understand now; Stewart did not choose Eliese as his successor because of the Darien stunt. He wants Eliese as number Two because she plans, organizes, and executes actions with efficiency like none I have ever seen.

"You handle Jenkins and this whole Consolidated Gate Securities United," Eliese says. She turns to me. "You'll be issued a deposition. You and your group of attorneys find any and all hospital staff, Mark, anyone who works there and knew you before or after the accident."

She takes a breath and straightens, as if for another battle. "Father, I'll be at Hill House with Ray. For a long while." The song Eliese sings is that of a commander shuffling pieces around on a table like an old-world war game, and her voice is the final word in this matter. I see Stewart's reasoning for succession in this one conversation, and she will one day lead the Family. Samuel has that trait on a smaller scale. Eliese, like Stewart and his father, have that singular trait of being visionaries.

Eliese waits as her father stares back at her, neither saying a word. I have the impression this is the first time she has challenged him openly.

El raises that eyebrow when Stewart is about to say something; when he demurs, she lowers it. Eliese laces her voice with warm conviction for Stewart and myself as she says, "He sleeps on the futon in the living room, Daddy, and I'll take the bedroom. We're serious, but not serious like that. I haven't seen Raylan or spent time with him in two months. He and I need to work on things...work on *us*. He's gone a month at a time almost four times a year. We're not jumping into this without a long conversation and a clear understanding of us and how it will work."

Stewart nodded as he says, "Ray."

I also nod and reply, "Stewart," as he points to the door.

We exit. Next to Thap and Pun are two more Gurkhas, Pak and another young guy. After the door closes, I point at Eliese and say, "Private," then at Thap, "not private," using the knifehand with each. Thap will make it clear to the rest.

"They're the staff we'll be using at the shed and range. The barn will move down to the range. Soon it'll be converted into a small barracks living space. Those two will oversee the range and the barracks. Once we get the organization situated, we'll receive one more, plus one every third weekend for relief," Thap says.

I bet Thap and Pun have been cooking this pot for a while. With as much time as El spends at Hill House, it is a natural progression.

Thap continues, "Pun will share my apartment for now. In a week, the rest of the workout room downstairs will be renovated into a second apartment."

I nod as we stop at Eliese's door. She invites me in, then proceeds to show me the main living area: hardwood floors, ornate, beautiful furniture with wood on the arms and stripes in the cloth. Not a stitch of fur or leather anywhere.

It has a lot more light than my apartment here at the residence, and a lot more space. She pulls me over to her room while Pun and Thap remain in the sitting area. She stuffs me in the pink chair with white stars.

"Sit, help me with my wardrobe," Eliese says.

My education as to why you need more than five outfits begins—specifically, five outfits that do not include three haptic suits and two chest rigs. Eliese heads into the bathroom with armfuls of clothes. A moment later, she returns with a twirl. She uses the look on my face to gauge her own little model runway. I fear I am not that helpful, as it does not matter if it is a dress, skirt or pantsuit. They are all fantastic. Then I remember the jeans, the walks, the plaid.

"Love, Eliese, I live at the top of a mountainous valley in the woods. Leave that stuff here. Jeans, sweats, and comfortable clothes," I say.

Eliese frowns at me and continues bringing me things to look at. I relax and enjoy the time in her presence. It has been a mesmerizing evening. In two hours, we have narrowed it down to five suitcases, and only one of the suitcases will fit in the Hill House closet. She is happy, and I am so glad to have her there with me at Hill House.

We then leave for the Hill House, all six of us. For now, I help settle the new guys in with Thap. Then I make my way back upstairs to hear music.

"Raylan, you didn't only practice cooking," Eliese says with a smile as she wraps her arms around me, and we start dancing. She leans her head on my shoulder as we sway to the music. "Were you serious, Raylan?" she asks softly. "That this is love?"

I keep moving us to the music, dancing all around the main living space. Her perfume and the dress are amazing. It nearly short-circuits my brain. The song changes, but I keep swaying.

"I think about you constantly," I whisper as we sway. "My days are darker when I am not around you. When I am near you, I feel fearless. There is no way I would have gone on stage and said half of all that before I met you," I explain. It forces me to take a deep draft of her perfume, and I shudder under the spell of her scent and touch. "I am happy you are here. I am glad I can tell you how I feel."

We sway a bit more, and her head lifts. "You haven't yet." She lowers her head back down. "You have said 'my love,' 'love,' and 'this is love.'"

We keep dancing to the soft music. I work in a twirl, and El graces me with a flowing spin. It is her smile as we return arm in arm that seals the deal for me.

"I love you, Eliese," I whisper into her ear. I can feel her shudder and relax even further into my arms.

I hear her repeat those words, a little louder, with more precision. "I love you, Raylan."

We dance to a couple more songs, and as we both have work in the morning, we call it a night.

Eliese turns and pulls her hair up and says, "Would you, please?" She gives me the side-eye as I reach to undo the clasp at her neck upon her request. "In your dreams, Raylan."

My face flushes beet-red. "Most definitely in my dreams tonight," I say, as Eliese glides to the bedroom.

I strip out of the penguin suit and lay the clothing neatly on the breakfast bar. I check my FEED: it's nearly two in the morning. Not much time left to sleep. I walk over to the futon and sit down. I exhale with exasperation at the day I have just finished. As I drop onto my back, the futon breaks, one side now tilting askew. I roll my eyes, fluff my pillow, and unlike a normal night, I am not out in under a minute. I lay awake, pondering, even after I hear a soft "Good night."

***

C9 S12

I am an early riser by nature. Sleeping in happens but only rarely. After my morning ablutions, I make French press coffee well before Eliese stirs. I knock on my bedroom door, and on the second knock, I hear a muffled and groggy, "Come in."

I step in and proffer the cup of God's greatest beverage as a gift.

"Here, this will help." She sniffs, and I see those chocolate-brown eyes surrounded by black hair widen as the first hint of coffee hits her nose.

"I hate our bed," El says, laying with the covers up to her chin.

I chuckle. "Why do you think I sleep on the futon? Which I broke last night, by the way."

"We need a new bed. This mess won't do," Eliese says for a second time as she moves the hair from her face. Taking the cup, she says, "We need a new bed. I mean, *I* need a new bed," she corrects a little sheepishly as her face turns a shade of pink.

I laugh. "Nope, you are caught fair and square in your Freudian slip," I say, waiting for her to take umbrage. Eliese does not take the bait. "I need a new frame for the futon at least. Truth be told, Eliese, anything said pre-coffee is inadmissible." I head to the other room, saying, "Would you like me to bring the food in here, or are you going to come out of the room?"

I close the door, leaving Eliese with her coffee. I start some groats with a generous helping of Doc's mineral powder on my eggs. I am dishing out the food onto plates when she comes out in a white and pink silk Dragon-print robe. She has on blue fuzzy slippers. The light of the pre-dawn sun is just poking over the top of the patio. The windows lighten as the daylight hits them and the room lights up.

Eliese lets out a groan and says, "Turn it off."

El She shuffles past the breakfast bar and sits on the broken futon. She wraps my blanket around her legs and then looks out at the day, sipping at her coffee.

I ask with a great deal of apprehension, "When this is over; when it is just you and me, will you still be here?"

"Raylan, you know," Eliese says as she keeps looking out over the patio. "It's only been a few months for us, a few dozen evenings here and there." She turns and looks at me, a cup wrapped in both of her hands. "Not including the several hundred FEED messages a week," she says in a tone that is soft and carries a warm vibe.

"I will wait, Eliese. I have time. I love you and would love even more to wake up next to you every day." I sigh. "You said we needed to talk. I laid there all night on the broken futon thinking that I am happy with you. I have not been happy for a very long time," I say softly, slowly.

I pray silently, that the feeling is mutual between us. Maybe I have had more time to think it through when alone those long months surveying a D2 iteration.

Eliese sips her coffee. "That isn't how this works, Raylan. You can't just wake up and say I'm going to marry you." I sit next to her.

I hold a plate of eggs and a bowl of groats and honey. Two forks and two spoons are in my other hand. I keep the plate so we both could nibble for a few minutes. She is fully reclining into my side now, watching the sun come up.

"Yes," Eliese says, her song bright and strong.

"Thank you, Eliese," I say quietly.

We finish things off sooner than I expect. Unbeknownst to me, Eliese's blood is coffee-based. I come back with more and sit.

"You know you are going to have to talk to Father. I also will need a ring," she says in the softest of happy voices.

I kiss the top of her head and say, "I messaged your father at 4:00 a.m. Wait here."

I move to my hospital duffel bag from Dillon. I pull out my charred and cut-up haptic suit. Dr. Alvarez had saved this for me, and maybe he had studied it or just kept it for sentimental reasons. Whatever the reason, I am thankful he did. I return to the lopsided futon and sit down.

In almost a squeak of fear, Eliese asks, "You messaged daddy at 4:00 a.m. to ask permission to marry me?"

I slowly open the suit. On the inside, in a pocket where you would store military ID, is a tiny plastic pouch. The suit is burned, charred, and melted at every haptic patch. The power cell had exploded and eaten at the fabric covering of the back.

With a bit of levity in my voice, I say, "Heh, no. I told him I had thought about asking you to marry me for the last three months in D2. I had planned to wait for the Family Holiday party. Instead, I would ask you this morning. Then I closed the FEED."

I have kept the suit for one reason. It has my parents' wedding rings in the ID pocket in a pouch. I carried them on a leather thong while alone in the north. I wore them with my ID tags while in the CM. They are all that is left of the name I do not know, of my parents, of a history I was never taught.

"In the north, Eliese, you never wear jewelry in the winter. It can conduct the cold to the flesh." I say in a quiet voice, "My parents would take these rings off in the fall, then complain how fat they had become in spring when they try to put them back on."

I smile and look at her. Eliese is so still, you would think her frozen. The only tell that she is alive is that her hands display a small tremor while gripping a cup.

I continue with my story. "It was late winter and early spring. It had been too warm during the day, but violently cold at night. My parents had not put these rings back on yet, as sometimes, in extreme cold snaps, metal can flash-freeze to the skin."

I open the little pocket and I pull out a pouch that was once clear. I pull out a charred necklace with two rings clanking, although the rings seem okay. They are titanium, something with enough heat resistance to withstand the lightning. I separate the rings from the crumbling necklace, along with the little bit of plastic pouch fused to them.

I pull them out, buff them off as Eliese puts her left hand out, shaking slightly. "Your mother's?" she asks quietly.

The band is plain grayish steel. "There is not a stone, just a bit of whatever alloy they both had. I have always thought they are awesome. The perfection of the symbol of marriage." I am whispering, and my hand shakes as much as hers.

I smile as I slip the ring on her finger. "Yes, and my father's," I say as I hold it up. "Because of the cold weather, no one wore jewelry for almost two-thirds of the year. My parents did not have these on. They were hanging on the chain by the door when they died. These are one of the few things I left the cabin with."

With the ring on her finger, I put on my father's ring, and seal the melted pouch. The pair is a good fit.

"I love you. We will fight this together. Steven Jenkins and Bonnie Anders will not get away with this crap." I take a deep swallow of coffee and say, "I have a meeting with Dr. Alvarez this morning. Are you busy?" I ask, then I joke, "Your father ordered us to 'be seen' together, my bride-to-be."

That receives a snort. "Oh, that would grind Daddy into a fit if we had a twenty-four-hour drive-through marriage." She sips a bit more coffee and then brings up her FEED. "I'll be on FEED except for the actual meeting."

She looks at her ring. Then Eliese sits up and does her little head toss, stretches out her hand and proceeds to take a FEED video of it, then swaps it back to her face. Out of her pursed lips comes the loudest raspberry I have ever heard.

I ask, "What gives?"

"Trish," she says with a smile in her voice.

"Can I do one? I owe her, also," I say as I set her coffee aside and pick her up as she wrapped her legs around me. "Ready?"

She nods as we spin slowly, looking into each other's eyes. I am holding my right hand out to capture our spin. I kiss her slowly and thoroughly. I end my video and set her down.

"That will get her," I say as I send it to Trish.

Eliese giggles. "Okay, we have to get ready, shower dibs," she says as she darts to the bedroom door in her blue slippers. As I hear the door slide shut, she adds. "The bathroom gets a remodel." She pauses. "The bedroom, also."

I hear faint mutterings as she continues to talk. I am not sure if Eliese is speaking to me, or herself, or to her fellow deities of battle. I go over to the counter and finish my groats and coffee. I am happy, on cloud nine content.

After I shower and shave, I get dressed for the third time. Eliese and I make our way to the tram and head to Doctor Alvarez's office. Eliese is on her FEED taking care of her work. Her Segundo and team are making adjustments for her to be working out of Hill House. Much of that, according to Thap, is meshing our two schedules together. Thap has a second appointment with Michael Knaggs scheduled for today, so she adds that to her day.

We sit down, her in a chair, myself on the patient table. Franc enters the room and starts his tests. I set the bands with the metal bits to the side. He stops when he sees my ring. He then turns to Eliese, who is fully involved in her FEED. He twists his head around and sees hers.

"Congrats," Franc says with a big grin, pounding my shoulder into the table as he pats it. I am now pushing 164 kilos, and his congratulatory pat is not so little.

We head into Doc's office and sit down. I hand him the bands with the cathodic protected metal bits. He takes them out and is looking them over.

"I'll see what we can come up with here. Some seem less damaged than others," Doctor Alvarez says. He smiles as he sees Eliese. "Well, this is a pleasant surprise. How are you this morning?"

I bet that the Doc is engaging Eliese in conversation as to pull her off her FEED. Eliese finishes a message quickly and dismisses her FEED system. She looks up to her family friend and graces him with a lovely smile.

"Well, Peter, I was served papers on Compact-wide FEED last night and made a fool of by a woman whose sole claim to fame is marrying older men with more money than her," Eliese says. She sighs and rolls her eyes. "Then I got into to it with Father and was told I have to travel around with Raylan and him with me till this is all over." She feigns an overly dramatic and drastic flair of her left hand, and she continues, "So I decided to get back at them all and marry him."

Doc sits still, bewilderment on his face. "Congratulations?" he says, somewhat skeptical, moving his gaze from her hand to me.

I laugh. "This is for us, Doc. The Family. We will deal with the wedding when we have squashed pants-peeing Steve Jenkins and Bonnie-poo." In a polite and more serious tone, I ask, "Speaking of those two, would you and Franc please sit for a deposition on the accident and your interactions with Steve Jenkins?"

"Sure, I think we can manage that. And call me Peter, if you would," Peter says, extending his hand to me. "You are to be family in the very real sense."

We shake and return to our seats. Peter steeples his fingers for a moment.

"So, Raylan, you are gaining weight. Your broken arm tests came back very well. Everything seems to be coming along nicely. Have you started piloting heavily again via battery reserve?" he asks as he hands out his little dram of whisky.

I respond, "I am as fast or faster than I remember. It feels more natural. I have less shift in perspective when running on battery reserve at a hundred percent feedback. I pilot a pair of older MKIVs on our range. There is a Mark VI chassis I am going to be building up to meet my needs better in D2." I pause, then say, "GSG also has a custom order for an Interceptor and Infiltrator MKVI SkipJack build. Those two projects are going to move forward here in a few months."

I know that I am rambling a bit and need to pull my mind back on task.

"We are headed down to speak to Michael Knaggs after this. He will, if all goes well, be coming on as my team lead. I plan on having him organize and decide priorities and timelines for the GSG. The goal is to get it down to five years for Stage Three."

Doc is well into his notes as he types. Just like last time, he pulls out another set of bands for me.

"More of the same, though this time fifty-fifty coated and uncoated on each one. Would you do me a favor and see how they hold up over the next twelve to fifteen weeks?" he asks in his Doctor's voice.

I finish my drink and stand.

"Will do, Doc. The last ones held on at just about the twelve-week mark," I say as I hold my hand out for Eliese. She rises, and we make our way out to the tram and head south. I end up being the one on the FEED this time, reviewing the updates on Ol' Jack, Tom, Susan, and Daivi. We have a lot of work to cover.

The Llama prototyping and programming are coming around. They are hoping for a first-run trial in about five months. Jack, it seems, has hit it off well with Michael Knaggs via FEED. Tom is itching to get to work on the MKVI—so much so, he has completely overhauled the MKIVs past the parity point.

Our tram lands, but the sign for "Knaggs, Attorney at Law" is missing. Now it sports a sign saying that it will be returning to the Community Block commercial leasing structure pool. Carmen meets us at the door and ushers us into Michael's office.

I introduce Michael and his wife, Carmen, to Eliese. This time, Eliese is FEED-off. We sit in the seats left in a nearly empty office. He holds the folder to me.

"We worked on it nonstop. I think...*we* think I can get it to five years and five months with what you're currently using," Michael says excitedly.

I stop him. "Carmen, we ran short last time. I take it this is a partnership? You are part of this project, and this is the type of work you want to do?" I ask. They look at each other a bit worried.

"Yes, he's the historical understanding and the planning, but I am the organization," Carmen says with resolve. Her shoulders straighten. "We are a package deal."

I nod and take some time to bring things up. "What I have available is," I pause, "too big to be done remotely. I can see you are already making changes, but you will need to relocate at GSG's expense." I watch as relief hits them. I now need to rein in that excitement just a tad. "It may not be full-time for the two of you together on each project. What Thap has told me I need for the group is an admin, a master of the organization, if you will. What I have open, Carmen, is a position for operations officer that will communicate through Thap to me. Someone to sort out all the relocation arrangements for our people. Part of that will also be as a project manager to build out the Hill House complex."

I smile as I go on, thumbing over Carmen's duties and responsibilities statement. She will be the organization of our crew.

"After the buildings are completed and the crews are moving forward in a more normal capacity, you will be coordinating the MKVI I/I project for me. You will also cover procurement, supplies, and all the related needs of our GSG group. We will be growing in the years ahead. Are you both up for that?"

Carmen stands beside her husband Michael, nearly bouncing out of her shoes. "I take it from your excitement you are interested?" She nods emphatically. "Okay, walk me through the plan." I am happy they are both joining on. It would be good to have another partnership within the team.

In short, their revised plan comes down to staking everything, then use the new, smaller piloted 3D printers. This plan can add months to my time in D2, but maybe I can make use of the new temporary mesh stakes that the military is using. Those will offset the increased staking this plan calls for me to do. From there, it comes down to pre-loading a lot of the design into the piloted 3D printers.

The most significant downside is the load on the data trunk. We can only have two 3D printers in operation, piloted or otherwise. We will take the two we use for structure and sanitation construction and change them over to power and water first: one for buried power line construction and one for water and sanitation line construction. Complete the water and power before the actual structure building even begins. Once the structure and their sanitation are in place, then piloted SkipJack workers can finish the detail work.

The colonists will hook up the power cells and wells during Stage One. The infrastructure will only need to be hooked up to a Community-wide water system, sanitation system, and finally a new power station some time in Stage Three.

As for industrial work, their plan will extend another data trunk to the D2 iteration. From there, we can move two more piloted 3D printers to the D2 iteration and repeat. The industrial area seems to be significantly less in size than the citizens' living accommodations in most D2 iterations. There would be phases of higher activity, but much less working on top of each other than we currently have. I still have some issues with this plan, but I think GSG can work with it with a few minor tweaks. Once the colony moves from Stage Two at 2,500 colonists to Stage Three with up to 25,000 residents, they can begin to manage their own building projects.

I nod as Carmen and Michael finish their presentation. I look at Eliese, who seems to have questions.

I let Eliese take the lead, and she says, "It might be cheaper than how you are doing it, Ray." She gives me a wink. "How are we planning to staff these extra SkipJacks, let alone supply the raw material needs of the 3D printers?" Eliese is into her FEED as she continues, "We are staffed at ninety-five percent capacity via data trunk on EP1 piloted SkipJacks. Supplying the raw materials for added piloted 3D printers already occupies seventy percent. We do not like going over that seventy percent for raw material shipments to D2 iterations, as any interruptions in the supply chain could set us back months. That also doesn't take into account how dangerous it is sending that many Mag-lev containers through the Gate during this phase of their build out."

Carmen tilts her head and confidently says, "The Mag-levs will have a slight change in priority for now, a shift in which materials go through first. Because we are putting in power, water, septic and sewer systems before building homes and structures, there is an adjustment, but not an increase. This adds time to Stage One, but drastically decreases the time for the iteration to move into Stage Two."

Carmen continues at the raw edge of being without enough breath to speak. "Meaning, once a piloted 3D printer is up and running on industrial projects, the remaining printers can be working on new housing, Mag-lev roads, wells, and so on. A Stage Two iteration could go from a hundred new colonists a month to about 500 a month." She smiles as she explains, "Once they open Stage Three, they should start looking at producing their ferro-concrete and doing their surveys for mining. That will be in addition to building their power systems, sewer systems, and low-orbit FEED network."

I hope this is the right way to pull this off. I have been throwing money, power, and my brute strength at this project to bend it to my will. I have made progress, but that singular effort by me is showing diminishing returns. I need to get the time to Stage Three down if I am going to make this viable without the NAC stepping in and taking over.

"Michael, Carmen, what am I missing in my team, or who am I missing?" I ask carefully.

"A construction lead. You need someone onsite organizing these SkipJack pilots as they work," Michael says. "A community planner who isn't stuck-up. Someone who can help design these places and lay out everything well. We think we have that down, but it would be good to double-check. I don't have a recommendation for the job slot, though. Sorry."

Well, crap. Looking at Carmen, I say, "Thap, send Carmen a message about finding a construction lead for the SkipJack pilots that will work out of the Gate facilities." That earns me a thwap from Eliese. I chuckle. "Thap, send Carmen."

Another thwap, this time from both Carmen *and* Eliese. With a good-natured laugh at my own poor humor, I say, "Welcome aboard. We will be working together a great deal." I forward them the NDAs Michael has written up.

They once again read and sign them. "Working together a great deal," I say again, this time letting the bomb drop. "Each time I Gate walk."

It takes a few seconds for that statement to percolate through their minds.

Finally, Carmen says, "You...you're the Gate Surveyor Group! Not just the CEO."

Eliese rolls her eyes. "Oh, you just think you're something special." She smiles as she starts to walk about, looking at the photos of the kids. In under a minute, she has coaxed their names, ages, and the year they first had braces out of Carmen.

I take the time to introduce Michael to Thap, who forwards information on three temporary living spaces. The tiny town near Hill House has limited options, currently. These will have to do until a permanent house can be found within commuting distance. We say our goodbyes and start to tram back to Hill House.

Eliese comes over and leans her head on my shoulder. A moment later, her heels are off and she turns the row of seats we are sitting on into a couch for her.

"You know, Raylan, if you weren't as lumpy as your bed, this would be the perfect spot for a nap," Eliese says with a smile, and that smile goes all the way to her eyes. "They're good people, Raylan. I think you've found good people for your group so far."

I am just happy to have Eliese next to me.

She is asleep within a few minutes of the tram taking off. That night we stay in for dinner. We cook non-butchered spaghetti. She puts on her robe again after dinner, and we sit listening to the music playing from the FEED system. I hand her the blanket I use at night. El looks at her ring, turning it about her finger.

"Regrets?" I ask.

"Never," she says emphatically. "I'm wondering if you've carried this every-day up until the accident."

"Usually on that lanyard you saw. I put it in that little plastic case when wearing my haptic suits."

We sit and listen to music. I use my FEED to bring the lights down, and we drift off. When Eliese rolls over on the lopsided futon, I wake and carefully pick her up and carry her to bed. I cover her with the bedding, gently.

***

C9 S13

I rise from the futon in the main room before 5:00 a.m. It is time for me to run. I go down the porch steps and pick up some steam. I run the loop from the little pond at the ridge down the backside to the live-fire range. From there, I move up to the shed and back to Hill House.

I make my way back into the house and start the coffee and groats. I knock on the door to our room and bring in the morning's go-juice on the five-count. Eliese is awake this time. She accepts the cup with a smile.

These first few weeks at the Hill House together are terrific. We have a chance to get to know each other and our quirks. She sings into a hairbrush when showering. I prove to be clinically unable to find a clothes hamper to put any dirty laundry in.

Every morning Eliese inhales the scent of her coffee before sipping it; it is a waking-up ritual that she likes to do.

"Why do you bring me coffee every morning Raylan?" El asks. I sit in the pink and white wingback chair that mysteriously appeared in the small bedroom one day.

Taking a long drink of my coffee, I tease, "Well, love, it gives me an excuse to come in and use the bathroom." I receive a snort for that joke, and it almost causes Eliese to spit coffee. "You like waking up slow. We get a chance to talk, figure out the plans for the day. It is...peaceful," I say in complete sincerity.

Eliese almost purrs as she sips. "This room has to go, Raylan. The bathroom, also. The kitchen needs to be redone, and we need offices. The guys down below also need their own spaces..." She stops speaking mid-sentence.

Whatever thought she has been working through flitters away with the view as the auto-dimming glass shifts to let the sunrise in. El looks out over the mountain valley, and then she turns to me.

"I love the view in the morning, and I want to work things out so I have this view in the living room, bathroom, my office, and most of all, here in the master bedroom," Eliese says.

The joy in her smile brightens her voice as she keeps going. "I have a plan, Raylan. Give me a few more weeks, and I will show you what a magical place our home will be!"

Eliese's excitement is palpable. Her FEED pings, and with an eyeroll, she brings it up.

"Ugh, major buzzkill," she says.

Eliese now sports a severe frown. Then that look shifts and solidifies into something just shy of "slay them all."

Eliese says, "We have a meeting this morning. We're being deposed today at our Family offices." Eliese takes her final sip and finishes in a less disgruntled tone. "Before dinner, we have a meeting with Darien, Samuel, and Father. In between, though, you have a meeting with an estate attorney at the office."

Someone dared interrupt Eliese's morning coffee routine, and though she has only started this routine when she moved to Hill House, there will be bloodshed today.

I stand up and kiss her the top of her head. "I have to fight your brothers and your father?" I ask.

She snorts. "They would be paste on the floor, but no. It's likely due to some information Darien and Samuel have turned up. Trish has unraveled some interesting financial things."

Elise is not looking at me, but working on her FEED. It is almost scary how easily she manipulates a FEED system. I have never seen someone take to it as well as my love.

"It seems Mr. CFO Jenkins was padding the billable hours on the Gate contracts. On top of that, he was vastly overstating the number of people working each gate. DGMW reportedly had five guards, plus Mark. We paid for six employees, so we have that corruption and fraud to work with. There are also rumors he was able to reduce employee costs by almost thirty percent, which locked everyone into their current positions," she says, stretching. "We have leverage there with the NAC's employment regulations."

I look down, and she looks up. She puts her finger on my lips and shakes her head. "You still have to ask Daddy. A FEED message is not sufficient," Eliese says with a laugh.

I pound down my coffee and dash to the bathroom, yelling, "Dibs," finally winning the race to the shower in these last few weeks. I make it out of the shower, toweling off, then step out of the bathroom. I head to the closet for clothes, and I need not have, as Eliese has a set laid out for me. I dress and have my breakfast groats without my love, as she is skipping them today. We board our tram and head to the deposition. Eliese goes into one conference room, and I step into another.

My deposition is almost laughable. Did I intend to pressure Bonnie into selling off 1.5 million credits in options to give to a charity for garbage workers? I answer questions as directed by my attorneys. It comes down to Bonnie's claims that I am her garbageman and my fiancée the prettiest spinster, so I met her challenge by saying she could not afford me. I met her money with mine. She agreed on the Compact-wide FEED show. I delivered on picking up her garbage, and I also provided the money to a charity of my choice, which I discover is currently valued at thirty-one million credits.

Then Bonnie's attorneys leave, and in comes Steven Jenkin's new attorneys for CGSU, which is suing me in civil court for ruining their good reputation. They sit down and start in on the questions. Again, I answer the questions at my attorney's discretion.

The first question my attorneys object to is: "What was my role in the conspiracy to remove the dimensional lock on DGMW?" I do not answer, as it is akin to the infamous query of, "When did you stop beating your wife?"

There are a few minutes of intense discussions between my two attorneys and the three representing CGSU. With agreement from the arbiter, the deposition resumes.

"Mr. Ray," says the thin man on the left of the stack of CGSU attorneys.

"Can you run through the events that led up to the gate collapse? Those memories, as far as you remember. Start with your discussion with District Gate Manager Mark MacCalister."

It is not that I dislike this thin man, and I do mean thin, narrow, bone skinny. This attorney, Mr. George, is the personification of "thin and delicate" everything: eyes, lips, long fingers, limp, patchy angel hair, an elongated face, and a neck that needs stacked rings to hold it up. I listen to the whisper and the almost gasping wheeze of his voice. I nod, after being given the go-ahead from my attorneys.

"Mr. George, I spoke to Mark on a Thursday evening just before my shift. We covered a variety of issues, part of which was the lack of staffing available for our Gate. We were supposed to have a staff of three guards. We had two. Mark asked if I knew any military retirees who might want to be hired on. Mark suggested we would split the referral bonus. I pressed him on moving to the day shift."

I can tell the three knew all this. I keep my story straight and true. "Mark lets me know that the whole company is short-staffed, and the entire industry is short-staffed by forty percent," I say.

I continue as I kept an eye on all three. I am looking for something, but what that is? I do not know.

"Mark went on to tell me that our yearly inspection had happened the day before. That inspection was moved forward by almost four months. The inspector had spent all the previous day at the site. Dillon Gate Montana West passed with all top marks, better than we had the two previous inspections."

The CGSU attorneys have me break down the list on Mark's big FEED display. I explain Mark's concern that CGSU would not forward us a third, fourth, or fifth man because we achieved all the top ratings.

The third man, a CGSU attorney is scratching things down on a piece of paper. He holds it up for the other two. Maybe that is the thing I am looking to expose.

"Mark and I discussed how his wife was at the hospital, how he had tried to retire and could not. That CGSU was supposedly holding him there under pain of prosecution. How CGSU had pulled him out of his week of vacation to return to work," I explain. More intense scratching. Interesting. "That morning when I returned home, I had to tell my then-girlfriend that I would not be moving to day shift. I explained CGSU's lack of personnel to her."

I watch the "three amigos." No writing or sharing this time.

"Jacki, my girlfriend, stormed out of our blockhouse. She had her bags packed and had taken Friday through Monday off to visit her sister in the old West Virginia. I was supposed to leave that night for a Saturday and Sunday visit with her family. I was told not to bother until I got the move to day shift worked out."

I engage in eye contact with each as I prepare for the next stage of the story.

"I went to work. I was a little behind, so I FEED-messaged a single-ride share in order to arrive before work. I waved at Abuelita as she was exiting her apartment. Mark had left his office for the day due to a family emergency, or so David said. David was undressing from his haptic suit when I arrived. He could not hear me over his earbuds."

I pause, testing the reaction before continuing, "David let Abuelita in, and the two of them set food on the table. Abuelita passed me a letter to send through the Gate to her missing grandson Jesus. While I was booting up my demilled, I saw through its ocular feed that Abuelita had left and was heading for the Gate. David was not in a haptic suit, so I dumped into my SkipJack at forty percent boot and ran after her in person and with the SkipJack."

There is a loud snort from the previously motionless middle attorney at the table.

"Mr. Ray, no one dumps into a SkipJack. Not even the CM encourages dumping into them, let alone at forty-percent boot cycle." He snorts again. "Stop playing the hero, Mr. Ray."

I look at my attorneys, and they are stone-faced. I am on my own on this one. "That is medically *retired* Lieutenant Colonel Ray, over sixteen years in active service, twelve of that in Force Recon under the command of the Lion of the Compact, General Jermaine Diomedes," I let my voice hit a growl as I continue, "Six individuals in this house have seen me dump into a SkipJack at as little as twenty-five percent boot cycle. Would you like to depose them?"

The third amigo scribbles on the pad and holds it up. First amigo, thin man, frowns and asks, "Did you eat at that time, Mr. Ray?"

No use of the rank, so either they want to verify my rank, are extremely rude, or did not understand. Lieutenant Colonel is not as unique as it used to be in the old pre-NAC militaries. The CM has a plethora of highly ranked individuals. Promotions are passed out with medals, and twice on Sundays. I dislike being critical of the CM, but their penchant for promotions due to time in service is one of the things I take issue with. Force Recon, however, is a different bird. In the FR, you *earn* your promotions. That achievement is only watered down by the rest of the CM's bad habits.

I am waiting to see if they will give a bit when the second attorney speaks up. "Answer the question, Mr. Ray."

"I arrived almost twenty minutes early. I ate and was booting my SkipJack up a full ten minutes early for my shift," I say. "It is at that point, as I have stated, that I saw the lady we called Abuelita moving towards the Gate. I dumped into my SkipJack, yelled at David to help, and ran out the door."

The man in the middle is not happy, the third amigo is still, and thin amigo is patient.

I continue, "I ran for Abuelita, and my SkipJack caught her cardigan just before the Gate. Abuelita slipped out of the overshirt, and my SkipJack was able to grasp on to her wrist. That is when David's SkipJack ran into mine and sent us all forward a few more feet. I tried to pull physically backward as everything went white." I pause before moving forward. "I woke up in the hospital."

The three amigos look at each other. The middle amigo then pulls out a FEED fob. Middle amigo says, "It is a recording from the opposite of the SkipJack shed. The camera is a recording from the corner window of Mark McCalister's office."

The image pops up in the center of the table's FEED display. I watch as Abuelita leaves, and about thirty seconds later, I see my SkipJack initiation start. About two minutes into the initiation, she passes my SkipJack, continuing to the Gate. At some point, you can see my SkipJack lurch forward as it comes under reserve battery and a hundred percent feedback.

We watch my demilled run the distance to get a better intercept on Abuelita. She reaches the Gate area, and it shows that my SkipJack is holding her, I am nearing my SkipJack just as David's grabs mine and starts to pull on the clevis.

It slips and falls. That is when I grab David's clevis and the lightning hits. The FEED image cuts out.

We go over that FEED video a dozen times. Each time, they ask silly questions in a minutely different way. Middle amigo even wants to know if I had used the SkipJacks to control the lightning bolt.

Thin amigo goes on to ask me about all these dates I am supposed to have had responded to Steve Jenkins via FEED messages.

I am calm and carry a matter-of-fact tone when I explain to each of them, "I did not have a FEED system. You can check with my Doctor, the hospital staff, and my physical therapist. My FEED unit had melted into my bones."

Undoing my cuff links, I begin to roll up my right sleeve. their inane questions. I show them the scarring, tiger striping, and the vertical cuts to relieve the pressure.

All three blanch at the ruined mass of melted, oddly mixed skin.

I explain in detail. "The majority of my skeletal system was surgically removed, as it was severely damaged. Doctor Alverez printed a new skeletal frame and musculature after taking samples from my left side. After being released from the hospital, I had to go to my bank to receive a banking fob so that I could get a new Compact ID card. The ID arrived in fourteen days. I was unable to use any FEED system for six months after leaving the hospital. I had to operate the FEED terminal at the Community Center building using my valid ID."

I watch as the three amigos become very squirrelly. Paper scratcher amigo furiously writes and waves the pad at the faces of the other two. I wait till it nears a crescendo of paper flapping before I say, "Those recordings of what I searched, listed, and communicated with are now part of the public record. I am sure you can subpoena them from the Community Center. I know my attorneys have copies."

I watch as the fluttering paper stills, and the three amigos look at me, then at my attorneys. Our attorneys have copies of all my usage times, and the affidavits from Doc and Franc that I had no FEED access from the day I woke till the day Franc installed it.

The three move out of the room for a quick conference in the hallway. When the three amigos re-enter the room, it is the thin amigo who asks, "Why did you steal the haptic suits?"

"The suits were sent to me after Steven Jenkins terminated my employment," I counter. "Jenkins said CGSU would ship my effects to my residence. On the outside of the box was a manifest of my private property. The manifest lists those haptic suits as my property."

That is when my attorneys hand them a copy of the manifest. I had kept the manifest, courtesy of Boss, who wanted a duplicate with every haptic suit he bought. It is not that I think these three attorneys are yahoos. I think they took Steve Jenkins at face value, or at least part of his statements, and now they look like yahoos.

My FEED beeps; I open it, and nod. I stand. "That is all the time I have for this session," I say. I excuse myself from the room.

I have another meeting. Thap guides me down the Family's Corporate Center hallways. I enter another smaller conference room, one with only a small table and chairs. A little FEED display tab rests on the table. There sits an older woman, and a younger secretary stands by her side. I introduce myself and relax into a chair.

I ask, "I am unsure how I can help you. I have no family left alive."

The old lady looks over her glasses at me. "Are you Ray? Just Ray, no last name? Formerly employed by CGSU in Dillon Montana West District?" Her accent is familiar, if more pronounced.

I look at her. She is in her late sixties, an attorney, her curly hair just frosting with grey, swan-rimmed glasses, with a chain to hold them around her neck. A white shawl graces her shoulders. You could have easily assumed her to be a grandmotherly family attorney, but she is not fooling me. She could have hammered those three amigos into the ground. "I am," I say confidently.

"I have no biometric or FEED data from which to test that. Can you verify the last thing you talked to your boss about in his office before he left for the day?" Her tone is harsh, almost accusatory.

That is an interesting question. My boss is Stewart of the Family, but she cannot be referring to him. Prior to my time with CGSU, it was General Jermaine Diomedes, so she must be speaking of Mark.

"In the office, we talked about his wife being ill and how my former girlfriend wanted me to move to the day shift to start a family." I pause. "I told him to give his wife my love."

I am thoroughly perplexed now. Then it hits me: she is a close resemblance to Mark's deceased wife, Morgan.

The no-introduction grandma attorney looks at her aide, who in turn nods. "We verify you to be Ray. I am giving you this FEED fob provided to me by my former client, Mark McCalister. It remains unviewed, as you can see from the security stripe. You are to view it alone, per the instructions in his will." She stands and motions to the door. "Good day, Mr. Ray." She passes by her aide.

The aide whispers, "Good kiss at the charity," then scurries out behind her boss.

Staring down at the FEED fob, I decide now is as good as time as any. Thap sends for a small scanning kit and checks the fob and room for monitoring devices. He steps back out after a thirty-minute search. I tap the fob, and it starts up on my FEED.

Mark looks like hell. To call the short chubby man thin is an understatement. He looks like a medical skeleton of bones with a thin skin wrap. His cheeks have sunken deep, and his eye sockets are deep purple, possibly bruised. His hands are wrinkled, with loose skin almost dripping off his fingertips. The man looks horrible.

"I'm dying, Ray. I'm not going to last long. I spent the last two years investigating who ordered Morgan moved. I have depositions from everyone at the hospital. They show that Jacki started an affair with the doctor. She needed you to be on day shift so she could claim this family you were to start together was yours. She got pregnant. That would have cost her the indenture and the doctor his career, as there is a no-fraternization clause," Marks says.

His words come out in whispers and gasps. He has a breathing mask that he puts on for a few heartbeats. He removes it and speaks maybe four words, then returns the mask to his face.

There is a slight shuffle, and an external FEED mic slides forward on the table, closer to his mouth.

"The Doc and Jacki colluded to get her indenture paid out when she learned you could not move to day shift. He verbally promised, as did she, to stay at the hospital for one more year. They left, vanished two days before you woke up. The indenture was paid off in part because the hospital thought she would hang around due to your injuries. The two of them vanishing left the hospital one doctor and nurse short."

I watch Mark suck in deep breaths, but not gathering any air. Mark lifts that little clear mask from the table to cover his mouth. His face is starting to flush as he pulls in more oxygen.

He gasps frantically as he starts up again "All because I did not move you to day shift and it ruined her first plan. She struck out at me, moved my wife. Jacki convinced the doctor to sign the move orders. Maybe she thought you would get my job, I don't know."

He pulls out a handkerchief that is covered in reddish-brown blotches and starts coughing violently. I see new, fresh blood spread on the little bit of fabric. Mark even has blood on his hands as he takes deep breaths with the oxygen mask.

"Ray, they Gate walked. They got cleared in record time somehow. The pair found a position for a Doctor and a Nurse in a Compact-controlled dimensional iteration down in New Mexico District," Mark says.

He pauses here, breathing through his mask. I think over the implication of the many details Mark has relayed so far.

In a raspy voice, Mark says, "Ray, I was the one who gave that FEED to Steve Jenkins's attorneys. I viewed the whole FEED video, not just that short version they possess. I know you can Gate walk through and return to EP1. It's dying here, Ray. It dies with me. I edited that feed video. I need your help."

I watch Mark's eyes fill with moisture as the sobs start, and his frail body shudders even as the coughing fit spews more blood about the table and mask.

"I need you to Gate walk and bring justice to my wife and myself. In exchange," Mark growls.

There are a ton more coughs and more blood, and a lot more breathing from that mask.

After a time, he says, "When Jenkins fired me, I was fired in his office. It was the very next morning. I knew you would't destroy a Gate. Ray, Jenkins didn't care two people died. He immediately accused you of destroying the dimensional lock."

I see the strain in Mark's body as he tries to breathe enough to speak.

"Ray, you were just taken to the hospital that previous night. I had just left the long-term care facility after staying with my wife in her room. No one knew what had destroyed the dimensional lock on the Gate. No one from the Family had arrived yet to inspect the Gate. How could Steven Jenkins know that lock was lost and that it had fixed on a new iteration?"

He pulls the handkerchief up to his mouth and starts coughing again. This time, there is so much blood that it drips from his chin and his teeth are stained red. He is gulping air and coughing bloody phlegm.

"Ray, he left the room, presumably to report the accident and to call the authorities on me. I knew, I *knew* you wouldn't do that. I stepped over to his desk FEED terminal and thumbed everything to myself. His terminal wasn't locked to his FEED or biometrics, Ray!"

He laughs and coughs yet more blood.

"He was so blatant about his crimes, he didn't even lock his terminal. I thumbed the whole network to my FEED system. I was then escorted off the premises when he returned with a security team, and Steve Jenkins fired me outside the corporate office. I had made it to the steps of the building when two constables arrested me for the Gate accident."

Now Mark grew in size, sitting up, staring fiercely at the FEED recorder, bloody bubbles boiling out of his mouth and the corners of his nose.

Mark's voice is nearly gone, and what was once probably meant as a growl of anger only comes out as a wet, hoarse whisper. "I spent that week in jail, and my wife died during that time. Once I got out, I did my best to get all the evidence I could. Everyone was saying it was you who destroyed the Gate, and when I realized it was Jacki who transferred Morgan, I snapped.

"I attacked you, Ray, that day at the hospital. I am sorry. Weeks later, I started to read the stuff on my FEED from Steve Jenkins's terminal," Mark says.

A wheezing fit attacks Mark again, and his chin is rust red from the blood he hasn't completely wiped away. Mark starts aspirating into the mask. An aide comes into view and helps to clean the mask and calm Mark down.

"You'll see. I'd already returned to the security office, and I retrieved the video

I had of you from the security office cam. I edited it then and there. I am about to be deposed by Steve's attorneys next week. My attorney is going to give them that shorter video as part of my last will and testament. She is my wife's first cousin. She knows Jacki killed her. Please don't hold it against her, Ray. Do what you must bring down Steve for keeping me from my wife in her last days. Then someday, somehow, go find Jacki."

Mark devolves into a horrific fit of coughing. This episode goes on and on until the aide returns and places a new air mask over his nose.

Damn, Mark. I am sorry. I cannot promise I will succeed, but I will try.

I pick up the FEED fob and thumb everything to my own feed, then exit the room. I stop and look at Thap.

"I need some time before this afternoon's meeting with the rest of the Family," I say. "Is the FEED terminal in our quarters as secure as it can be?"

"Raylan, each of the FEED terminals in the residences is top-of-the-line secure. If you have data to review, research, or transmit to another Family member, it is safest to do so from there," Thap says in his formal British regimental military tone.

He is already guiding me down the hallways.

"Thap, thank you. Thank your team. If I end up distracted and don't thank you enough, know it now," I say as we come through the door to our flat.

I sit down and spend a couple of hours organizing the data Mark has forwarded to me. Most of it goes to Stewart, as he is dealing with the Gate inquiry. There is not a whole bunch I understand. Mark had a lot of contextual data we are missing in these reports. Hopefully, Stewart and his team will be able to make more sense of it. I send everyone a copy of Mark's video.

I stand, enter my master suite, and take a shower. I scrub hard. I feel like I did those first days out of the hospital. Reliving those memories through Mark's testimonial has stripped my emotions raw. Seeing Mark in such pain, knowing he spent the last two years running things down, and that he was forced by a failing body to ask me to finish his quest for justice has laid me out for the first time in over a year.

***

C9 S14

I exit the bathroom to find a suit laid out for me. Thap is in the living area working on his FEED, communicating some instructions to Carmen. When I round the corner, he turns and looks at me. With a nod, we head for the meeting. On the way, he fills me in.

Carmen has viewed the temporary living block homes and chosen one. She went to the Community Council and put her family on the list for one of the blockhouses nearest us. She also was able to use Michael's attorney status to do the same for the rest of the newly hired staff. Because of the increased demand for living arrangements in an area closest to us, the Community Council is looking at building to suit. GSG will foot part of that bill, of course, so our people will have housing close by.

Thap and I meet up with Trish and Eliese in Eliese's office. We are the last to arrive. Eliese ushers us through Stewart's office's massive wooden doors to find a new table occupying the space with chairs for the seven of us. Our seating arrangements mirror the dinner table, and it is a wonderfully crafted table.

The chairs are charming inlaid wood and have fantastic cushions, except for mine, which is steel. I chuckle inwardly at the snarky humor. This chair is Pun's work, without any doubt. He has an offbeat sense of humor, and he has a practical-joker streak a mile wide.

As we sit, Stewart speaks. "Family, we will be speaking of these events, evidence, and repercussions in here only. Given what Ray passed on to me today and Trish's findings, we best keep it here. Let's start with Trish, cover Bonnie, then move on to Steve Jenkins, and finally, Darien and Samuel's info. From there, we can move on to questions."

Stewart looks to his daughter Trish.

Trish's face is a wintry leer of contempt. It was Trish's appearance on the House of Talk that had turned things from an amicable Q&A interview to a nasty harpy festival. Bonnie had tried her darnedest to embarrass Trish about something the then-teenage girl had done.

Trish handled her with grace and composure. Bonnie, in turn, ended up looking a petty middle-aged shrew, so much so, she removed Trish's interview from her show's library, the only episode to be removed, up until our evening interview. The Family accounts for the only two episodes removed in over fifteen years of airtime. Even though the Family has done two dozen interviews prior to Trish's interview with House of Talk, Bonnie still took it personally.

Trish's tone is harsh, and I think she is out for blood when she explains, "We subpoenaed Bonnie's personal and corporate financial statements. I spent the full week of leave going over her various financial statements with the independent auditors our attorneys hired. Bonnie was and remains broke.

"The money she put forward for your little bet was her advance for her latest book deal. She was running about six hundred thousand credits in debt at the time, and this does not count Bonnie's responsibilities for the number of properties she leases."

Trish nods graciously to Eliese as she continues, "You were right, Eliese: her divorce claim of cleaning him out is false. She was offered very little, and she had lied about her financial situation to him at the time of her marriage. That deception was his basis for the divorce, which netted her 1,700,000 credits, which she promptly used to bring a 2,000,000 credit debt down to 500,000. Since the divorce, it has increased up to 600,000."

I receive a little nod. Trish puts a chipper tone to her storytelling. "That book deal, Raylan, was to pay off that six hundred thousand credit debt and give her enough to live off during the writing. Her pay from the FEED network is barely enough to cover the metro blockhouse lease and the monthly transportation to the studio. Last year, the studio yanked her wardrobe budget after it found out she was taking kickback payments for mentioning the designers on the show."

Trish pauses and takes some time to peruse her list of findings. "Bonnie is currently embroiled in a lawsuit over that kickback scheme. The studio is suing her to pay back a full nine years' worth of wardrobe budget. It's not an insignificant sum; they're asking for 367,000 credits."

After a moment, Trish's voice tightens as she continues, "I investigated the

PAC that put forth the money to help Steve Jenkins. The donations of three other charities forms the PAC. Those three charities have received their donations from a larger charity that dispenses the funds out to smaller District-wide causes.

"Bonnie has ties to all but one. By ties, I mean she is on the board of the larger charity that sends the cash down to regional charity groups. In this case, it split off the cash to three smaller but less known charities. Bonnie is on the board of two, and friends with several board members of the third. The one thing she has no direct tie to is the PAC." Trish frowns and says, "It's that old 'you know it, but can't prove it' adage."

Trish sits down and nods to her older sister, Eliese, who straightens and says, "All of the Family subsidiaries pulled future advertising from her FEED show and anything her production company produces. In this area, we only have one month remaining in that contract. She mocked the Family for that during the deposition.

Just a little while ago, I pulled all advertising from the studio that airs her FEED show or any show her production company produces." With a cheshire grin, Eliese continues, "The Family has four months remaining on that contract. I let the studio attorneys know we then allocated that advertising budget with a twenty percent increase to 'The Doctor Sean Tallomer show,' which runs an hour before hers from a different studio. That got her attorneys buzzing. It seems that while they're representing her and her production company, they're expecting the studio to pay the fees."

Eliese smiles as she moves the conversation on. "We'll see if that pans out. Both parties taped the deposition, and you all have the FEED copy of it. She tried to drag my love life out in the deposition, but the arbiter shut that down."

My love is beaming now. She nods to each of us at the table, and her hands move as she thumbs a file to the group seated at the table.

That smile reaches her coffee-brown eyes as she says in a grim avenging refrain, "After speaking with our attorneys, I am fairly sure the judge's panel will throw this out. While she did mock us, we did the same to her. Bonnie uses this as her basis for the claim of slander. However, we had no say in the publication of that slander, as she owns the company that produces the show. That slander was produced by her and ultimately distributed by the studio. The term blackmail she has been throwing out on the FEED is not part of the lawsuit or trial."

With an even more severe tone, Eliese continues, "The interview with Steve Jenkins that Bonnie aired does provide the Family an opportunity to sue for slander. It's a back-and-forth session, produced by her, and distributed by the studio. The studio is covered, as her show is considered an opinion piece. However, that gives us the ability to go after Steven Jenkins and Bonnie. I haven't fully reviewed the data that Raylan just sent out today. For me, that's as good a summary as I can give."

Eliese takes a seat and looks toward Dr. Alvarez. I turn to Peter, and I am almost startled by the hulking, silent form seated against the back wall. I had walked past Franc, and I had not noticed his presence at all. Franc lets out a small rumbling chuckle at my reaction to his presence.

Peter rests his head in his hands, his glasses on the table, his creased dark skin in contrast to his neatly curled white beard. He sits up and speaks in that Doctor's voice he loves so much. "Last week, I was deposed by CGSU's attorneys over Ray's injuries, David's brain death, and one 'Abuelita's' death. We covered Ray's care, pre-injury and post. As he is a former patient of mine, I covered that care, also.

"I used generic terms: lower leg, ankle, and foot reconstruction. I kept to the same for this particular accident. They asked a lot of questions I could not answer. Mostly, the questions were about David and what happened to this Jesus that went missing through a Gate," Peter explains.

"Finally, they addressed Ray's meetings with Steven Jenkins. I mentioned how Steven Jenkins barged in there the second Ray was awake, against my specific orders. I told them how Mr. Jenkins threatened you, lied to you, Ray...he was never your hired attorney. Jenkins was acting in CGSU's best interests.

"It was reprehensible how he soothed you by saying you weren't responsible when he thought you culpable. That's what the new attorneys are looking to find: who is culpable. As best as I can figure, they're not CGSU's attorneys. They're CGSU's *creditor's* attorneys," Peter says as his anger climbs.

Dr. Peter Avarez is a very amiable and gentle man. His patients are his friends, and he protects them fiercely. I shift my eyes back to Franc, and it hits me why the two are loyal to each other. They carry a mutual respect for each other. It is the kind of respect one earns over decades of friendship.

Peter's pause hangs a little in the air, and he says, "Ah, yes, your 'meetings' with Steve Jenkins. When they found out there was just the one meeting where he fired you, they were a bit surprised. They tried to contest this, but I provided the visitor's logs, which you had only the one other: Mark McCalister. They became concerned, then."

The doctor sits back up, smiles, and looks to me, his dark hands uncharacteristically fidgeting on the table top.

Peter says, "They then tried to dispute that with FEED messages over the full term of your recovery in DGMW. I simply showed them your original FEED unit, as fried and crispy as it was from my medical files. I went in to specific, if not graphic, detail how the thin bio-electric trunk of your FEED system melted into your bones during the lightning strikes.

"I showed them the invoice CGSU refused to pay for your replacement just before you moved here to Hill House. I then showed the bill for the surgery to put the new one in at Community Dillon Hospital," Peter explains with a vulpine grin. "They argued that CGSU did pay your bill, and even tried to verify that with CGSU's bank. When pressed, they admitted there seemed to be a discrepancy in the accounting data the bank had and what CGSU provided them."

Peter sits back, pulls a small flask from his pocket and proffers it to Stewart, who declines with a shake of his head. Peter dispenses a dram into an empty glass, watering it with his pinky from a glass of water. He turns to me and raises it in salute.

I lean forward and gave a synopsis of my deposition with the CGSU attorneys. I then go on to explain the FEED video supplied by Mark that I forwarded to everyone. I go over the files as Mark had asked, but I simply did not have the context to understand them. That is why I forwarded them to Stewart in the hopes he can give them to a group that will parse out the issues Mark described. I am simply the least informative in this group, so I turn to Samuel.

Samuel sits ramrod straight. He has always been this way when his mind is working hard to pull bits and pieces together. I think this is a large part of why he was so effective as our FR team leader. From the FEED messages General Diomedes sent to both of us recently, Sam's brevet promotion at his medical discharge was to a full bird colonel. If ever there was a man who earned that rank, it is Sam Janks.

For the last month or more, Samuel has been in the Brazilian Union. To say that Samuel looks frustrated is an understatement. His face is gaunt, drawn, and his eyes have a certain haunted look to them. I get the impression that somehow sending him to research the beast that nearly killed us both was not a kind thing to ask of him.

"I've checked every lead twice. There just isn't any connection in Brazil to the attack six years ago or Ray's second Gate attack. I have nothing on that front, simply nothing. I did get an interesting FEED message, but that we can cover later," Samuel says.

Sam turns to his brother and chucks him lightly on his shoulder.

Darien grimaces. "It wasn't easy. I traced those parts using my contacts at the Mega-Corps. They searched all over South East Asia. The places that had both types of products simply did not have any missing and used them in very different applications. There was no way for them to end up together at the same factory. I had run the leads down to the end like Samuel. That is when Phan and I were invited to play golf. We saw a sign when visiting a southern Japanese Island."

Darien smiles and raises a hand to calm everyone down, his showmanship nature bleeding through. It is easy to see why Darien gets along in the corporate world. His body language, his way with words, and even his gestures pull you into his orbit.

Darien explains, "The real business in Japan is done during leisure activities. You make a request formally at the office and receive a formal answer. The negotiation happens informally on the golf course, baseball game, or dinner outing."

He let out a sigh as he senses the table's collective eyeroll. Even I doubt Darien would turn down an excuse for a round of golf.

"All around us as we played our round of golf were old static signs for a company. This company serves as an automated electronic parts recovery and recycling center. It is where you go to find old parts in good condition to be able to get older models up and running. It's the only industry in an otherwise farming and recreational island," Darien says.

Darien shifts and brings up the FEED of the company for us all to see. It is a dilapidated building near the edge of a small port. The facility has a few of the smaller MLRs that Japan favors parked at the doors of its main facility.

"They have twelve workers controlling about thirty automated systems," Darien says. "These systems pull about 100,000 to 150,000 dedicated parts a day out of broken tech only a few cycles out of date. The tech is then categorized, labeled, and sold in bundles."

A new series of images pops up in the table's central display: Darien and his Segundo, Phan, on a guided tour through the facility.

"One place stands out as a purchaser of these two items. Med-i-Care was a bio-tech firm leasing the Senkaku Islands from the Chinese Confederacy. Once a month, a ferry from Japan used to head there to drop off supplies, and to take staff for leave. However, Med-i-Care failed almost twenty years ago. The buildings should be empty."

Darien is enjoying telling the story. "It gets weird from here. These serialized parts bundles were sold to Med-i-Care three years ago. Someone picked them up in person. The lady labeled the container and shipped it to the Med-i-Care biotech firm on the Senkaku Islands via the Chinese Confederacy port of Wenzhou."

With a gleam in his eye, Darien says, "That's where the current monthly ferry originates. I made a few inquiries into firms I have dealings with in the Chinese Confederacy. Due to my notoriety with the Family and the sensitive nature of the CC, I kept inquiries vague and about the nature of the old facilities only as a possible future site for a Pacific-based joint Fishing Conglomerate D2 iteration. Phan and I have yet to hear anything back."

Darien sits back. I am genuinely interested. I now have a spooky place to investigate and, hopefully, something to shoot. "Do we know if anyone is on the island currently?" I ask, hopefully.

Darien says, "Due to its proximity to Reunited China and the Chinese Confederacy, no. We could petition the Compact to launch a drone and call it research for that joint D2 iteration fishing site. I could, I suppose, try to travel there from Japan with the Chinese Confederacy's blessing for inspection of the property for a D2 gate."

"No, Darien, that is my job as the head of the GSG. You get me that ferry, I will bring my gear, and take a look around." I pause. "This is a lead to a deserted place, and someone laid out this clue years ago."

"It's a trap," Samuel says.

"I agree, Sam, it is a trap. Someone put it together years ago, expecting either Samuel or myself to go," I say in a flat voice. It is a voice I have not used in years.

"Ray, I'll go with you," Samuel, my brother of the mud and the blood, says.

I had known it was coming. I had known he would want to. Samuel is as good as he likely ever was. What he does not know, comprehend, is that he is not at the top anymore. That wolf would have killed him, and that cat nearly had. I will probably be facing many piloted beasts and likely more than one type of piloted beast. *No, Samuel,* I think. *You should not go.*

I look at Samuel. He has as much right to go as I do, as much reason to go, and he has the skills. I am not his keeper, and I do not have the right to tell him no. I do have an obligation, one to my brother in war, to my soon-to-be wife, and the Family. I must put terms on him coming.

"Samuel, you have not touched a SkipJack in over six years. I have concerns. I have one SkipJack MKIV not sighted in. Come sight it in. Then, if you match my time on a course called by Thap, I will be glad to have you at my side once again, brother," I say.

I see the rest of the Family stiffen as they realize finally, in all its completeness, that we were never postal clerks. Samuel nods and looks at his father, Stewart, who, to his credit, is sitting at the head of the table and taking it all in.

"You can do this, Samuel?" Stewart asks, and raises his hands to pause Sam's response. "You can do this again?"

Samuel gives one nod, and Stewart continues, "The files from Mr. McCalister are in only the most basic sense of order. I have my team looking at each file, comparing it to the data we received from our subpoena. That will take time. There are large amounts of data to organize and sift through. Samuel, do you have something else to ask?"

Samuel coughs. His face works into a few different masks as he is trying to figure this part out. I know in an instant what it is. Samuel has this tell when he is trying to be snarky.

In his best bad-joke voice, Sam says, "Trish forwarded me a FEED video and put her order in for another 'Ray,' one model newer." He coughs as the FEED video I had sent to Trish begins to play. "So, Raylan, Eliese...anything you two want to talk about?"

I see Eliese inspecting at her left hand. "I asked Eliese to marry me when this ends." I gesture at this discussion table. Turning to Stewart, I say offhandedly, "Stewart told me to be in her presence in public until further notice."

Stewart looks at Eliese, and me. "I received a FEED message at four this morning." He plays the FEED message for everyone at the table.

He chuckles and plays it up as he says, "For decades, I've thought about a young man sitting in front of me, begging for permission to marry one of my daughters, or even a lady seeking to snag one of you two roust-about boys." He looks at Eliese. "I never expected to be told via a FEED message at 4:00 a.m." Stewart's rumbling laughter echoes in the room. "She's happier than I have any memory of her ever being. The two of you should make an announcement, maybe after Bonnie's case is done."

Eliese and I return to Hill House. We have a light dinner of grilled chicken; although I have five helpings. Eliese is working on her FEED on a new futon. After slipping into a haptic suit, I head down to look at the shed to see how the construction is going.

I say hello to Jack, Tom, Susan, and Daivi. They are working late on an update of the panniers on the Llama V1 to fit the new mesh system that Sergeant Nardall had mentioned. I go to the weapons cage gate and slip on my goggles as I bring the two MKIVs out, one at a time. I spend some time looking over the MKVI units that Tom is itching to work on.

Compact Military SkipJacks, specifically the Mark IV series, are a humanoid shell with myomere muscles and myomere steel bones. From behind, I hear Tom walk up. I can tell he has stopped by the MKVI.

"Boss, when can I have at it?" Tom asks, barely holding in his excitement.

"I have not decided what I want to do first. Infiltrator platform with speed, battery capacity, sound deadening, long-range priority, and short-range defense. Or Interceptor platform speed, short-range SkipJack weapons, extended remote battery capacity. Maybe just a soldier unit like the MKIVs with their better armor and good battery life," I say, musing out loud.

"I can dream up a couple of variants: something on each end of the extremes and something in the middle. What kind of armament do you want on it?" Tom asks.

"For the Infiltrator, standard 6.5mm PC rounds, 300 hundred rounds in mags for the left arm, 20mm caseless for the upper right arm with 120 rounds, and an APHE tube with two extra rounds. Use that as a starting point and you can adjust up and down from there. It needs light and solid SkipJack-level armor. See if you can put the noise-canceling system from a Prowler drone on it. The key is sound suppression at speed," I say.

I remember the wolf attack. "For the Interceptor, though, give me some sort of hatchet, hammer, or blade I can use in hand. I want a close-up shotgun with 120 rounds and a 20mm with 150 rounds. Speed is king here. I am thinking of a denser version of a pilot's poly armor. See if we can get a sustainable thirty KPH out of it."

I look at Tom and say, "There are some things I would like you to work on. I want hard points. I do not wish to have static-attached weapons like the MK II, III, IV, and V. I want it all to be detachable and replaceable. I want the power system to be hard point mounted. When it is dry, pop in a new one.

"I want the weapons to be swappable in the field. If the pilots have the need to go from standard MKIV soldier load out to four 25mm guns, I want that to be an option. Our carbines have an accessory locking system. How come we do not do that with our SkipJacks?

"Finally, I want replaceable hard point armor panels. Give me two open hard point mounts for mission-defined accessories on the shoulders, say a pannier, noise-canceling system, or an air denial drone. Move the commander's network from the MKIV into the accessory mount, as well," I say, gesturing here and there about the MKVI's frame.

I continue, "I want one base SkipJack so versatile that it can fit ten different roles. We will build up to five or six standardized variants as a standard SkipJack trooper unit. The pilots and commanders can modify those to fit the mission profile, if needed," I explain.

Turning around, I walk us back to the MKIV and say, "Walk me through, Tom. When I last left, we were at parity on one."

"The load out is the same," he replies. "I dropped some armor on the second unit, just to lighten it up a bit. We are down from 340 kilos to about 313 kilos, before ammo. It has some gains in speed. I kept all the optics the same. I had to make some choices. It came down to more replacement of myomere bundles and skeletal members than anything else.

"Yea, I have them at parity, but they wouldn't have stayed there for long. They gave us old, worn-out scraps. Now I have them near as new as I can make them," Tom says distractedly.

I turn to the young man, who is facing away from me and staring hard at the MKVI. It is plain for anyone to see that Tom's mind is ninety percent on the new MKVI build-ups and ten percent on explaining this pitiful MKIV to an old warhorse.

I spend some time inspecting the SkipJacks. All the ammo feed systems and bores are clean and bright. I take a moment to drop the lenses on the goggles and start up the two sets of diagnostics. Now, as the two go through their system checks, I start looking over each joint flexible area.

There are a lot of new parts on both. Tom does solid-looking work. The units are in very good condition, as near original shape as one could make a thirty-five-year-old MKIV. I bring the lenses up and push the goggles up, as well.

"Tom, we are going to field these tomorrow on the range. We are going to be running and gunning on reserve and via pod. They will be banged up and beat to hell. I need them in as good a shape they can be," I say.

I am not sure my warning is heeded, though. Sam and I are going to put these two through some very heavy workouts. Turning to Tom, I smile, letting him know it is not personal. We simply have not worked together long enough to joke in this way yet without an explanation.

"Samuel and I will be swapping off units tomorrow. I will need the ammo taken down to the range in the morning, at least a full pallet of each," I explain. I look at the HUD lenses again as I drop the view goggles down. "Then I will likely want to make some changes to one or both." I begin booting them up and take each of them through the movement drills again and put them back in their docking station. With a handshake, I head back up for dinner. Tom is a solid guy, and I know that the MKIVs will be ready for me tomorrow.

***

C9 S15

Samuel arrives early the next morning. He is wearing his old haptic suit. Like my old one, it is a bit tight in a number of areas. I meet him at the end of the log steps. He chuckles when I pull the Eliese eyebrow at the haptic suit.

"Lay off, Raylan. I'm sure your old one was tight on you," Samuel says.

I chuckle and start the run: two laps of the pond, range, shed. To my surprise, Samuel is not gasping, but I can tell *he* is surprised at the pace I keep. We turn into the shed and get a start loading the SkipJacks with ammo from the cage. Tom and two of the range guards are there to move the ammo down to the range. I forgot the cage is biometric locked to me and my FEED.

A number of guests arrive just as the SkipJacks leave the docking stations.

Thap says, "Samuel has the range first, then he will have a couple of runs of a called course to set the time. Then Ray will run the course on reserve."

Samuel grins in his pod. The SkipJack starts moving out of the shop and down the hill to the range. He spends several minutes doing his run-down tests. When the live-fire range goes hot, Sam starts the same sight-in procedure I did a few weeks ago.

When he finishes, he has the range called cold and leaves the pod and jogs down to the range in full battle rattle, including plate carrier, ammo, and personal carbine. I notice that the weight of the gear is something Sam is not used to anymore.

The plate carrier hangs on him nicely, just not as smoothly as it would for a guy who lives in it as we had once upon a time. It may seem a small thing, but a man gets used to his gear sitting a certain way upon his frame. That frame, like mine, had changed in the intervening eight years. The carbine bounces more than it should because the sling is not set quite right. A few quick fixes, to be sure. It is these small things that come back the more you work with your gear.

When Samuel stops at the bottom, I spend a good ten minutes helping him get all those little things sorted out. Thap tells Sam the first three runs are for practice, which is good, and it will help Samuel to loosen up. He reloads the MKIV's own ammo pouches and tops off his PC's ammo load out.

The one benefit Sam has is an old military helmet, with its full display HUD, as opposed to my helmet and civilian HUD goggles. It is not a MKIV helmet like we used, but one of the earlier versions. I have no idea where he found it.

Sam's first two runs are hesitant and a little bit jerky, though no one here but me would know. To everyone else, Sam is a rain of hellfire unleashed upon our range. I consider his third run a good deal smoother.

Sam starts his timed runs at fifty-two seconds for the pair, which is not bad for a thousand-meter range with barriers spaced on a fifty-meter wide area. He steadily improves. Samuel's fifth run is for a good forty-nine seconds.

For his sixth and final run, Samuel is excited, driven, focused, but loose. He is oblivious to his father, two sisters, and his brother watching. They have never seen the way we Force Recon pilots bring hell from the ground and spread it around. There is sheer, shell-shocked amazement as Sam hits forty-three seconds on his final run.

That time is maybe two or three seconds behind when Sam and I were at the top of our game ten years ago. The issue is, unbeknownst to Sam, the top of the game is now at a different level. I feel terrible about this. I have advantages that Sam does not.

Thap announces the final time to the watching group. Silent amazement mixed with horror is on every face. Samuel lets out a war cry of triumph. I can see the fear dawn on the faces of his family members. They now know that Sam will be going into battle. They have not previously known with such visual and auditory conviction.

The members of the family have no idea that Sam has done this a few thousand times. I catch the look Stewart gives me; he is pleading with his eyes for me to deny his son, my brother in arms, the right to fight by my side.

I walk past and give Stewart a nod as Samuel discos from his MKIV. Sam starts reloading the MKIV, saying he is going to do better. I nod, waiting. I cannot let my brother go; I cannot bear Sam Janks's name written large in my book of those I have lost.

When I walked back through the Gate, the world had changed. Not just knowing that men, even if that knowledge is only of one man, have a way to go back and forth between iterations. I know that a man can do more, can pilot more. When my brother of the mud and the blood finishes loading the MKIV fully, I FEED message Thap. I will be ready shortly. I know now, finally, how I walked back through piloting two SkipJacks.

Samuel stands next to his family as I pull his SkipJack to heel. I force-dump into it as my second piloted SkipJack. It is pressure, a lot of weight, but registers not as physical but mental mass. It is your mind that lifts such weights.

I take that mindspace I use for piloting and force another mindspace to manifest. That simple action of creating a third split in my mind is pain, it is fear of the unknown. I layer and marry the MKIV directly to it. With a blinding white light behind my eyes, I split a third mindspace for myself.

The mass of piloting is mental, and at a hundred percent feedback from both SkipJacks, my mind believes it is holding up 680 kilos of weight. My knees sag under the mental strain. I have not really thought how haptic feedback works when piloting more than one SkipJack before.

The haptic suit does not do an actual one-to-one ratio. The haptic suit buffers your muscles at a rate of one-to-one hundred. The feedback is the percentage of one-to-one hundred that you carry and move in. Right now, I am hefting about sixty-eight kilos of imagined weight on top of my thirty kilos of battle rattle.

The haptic feedback is not just the weight or the pressure of the mass above your center of gravity. It is the density of resistance your own body feels during movement. That density, that resistance, compresses around every portion of your body beneath the haptic suit.

With each step, it is like walking neck-deep in non-Newtonian fluid. Slow is smooth and fast is hard. Very hard. It takes a tremendous amount of concentration and mental effort to navigate or move through that barrier your body puts in front of your mind. I am not a fan of forcing your way through that mental safety barrier. I have seen pilots rip muscles clean off their bones trying to do it by brute strength alone.

Maybe this is why I am different. I see now how my mind is different. I will a fourth, fifth and sixth mindspace. I allocate two extra mindspaces to each MKIV. The perceived mass my mind is holding is cut in half, then down to one third. I do not know if others have envisioned bending their piloting mindspace before. Today, though, I know it will work, as I have done this before.

I do some bouncing and flexing of both units. I complete their rundown tests as Sam is describing what it is like to pilot the deadliest munitions system in modern warfare. I order my preset commands for both SkipJacks.

Samuel stops talking as a look of horror washes over his face. Pulling to heel is one thing, but I am doing the impossible. No one operates two SkipJacks doing two separate flexing protocols at different stages. Imagine drawing a square with your left arm counterclockwise while drawing a circle with your right arm clockwise. It is a standard test for pilots, and few can complete it effectively. Now add in bobbing your head up and down to a rhythm in your mind. Got it? Now start skipping.

I have one mental space open for my human eyes, one mental space open for my human body. A pair of mental spaces open for my left SkipJack, and a final pair of mental open spaces for my borrowed SkipJack.

It is the same basic principle the CM teaches you in boot camp. The first mental space a pilot opens generally puts you down for up to thirty-six hours. That head-partitioning agony of opening the second mental space has kept pilots from trying to open a third. Here, I am bulldozing through to a sixth space.

I was more than hesitant about trying to open more than the two mental spaces you use as a remote pilot. I had, after all, woken up in the hospital the last time I piloted two SkipJacks. I can feel the brain-splitting pain, the pressure, as I look to Thap. With a nod to my Segundo, I pray that I can hold this long enough to prove my point: to drive home to Samuel this game has changed, and his time has passed.

Soon, I have one SkipJack at each side of the range. I am about thirty-five meters behind them, giving me some room to run and pilot. Thap calls ready, and on the count of three, I am off. As Thap calls the targets, I pilot both SkipJacks using both of my dropdown HUD lenses.

Where the HUD fails, I have years in D2 worlds and a vast number of very useful presets built up, several hundred more than I ever made in the FR teams. Today, I need the fifty most common presets to jink and jive the two MKIVs from one target destination to the next. They slide past each other when crossing during their own firing phases.

I am a tad behind, picking shots with my personal carbine, shooting much less than I had the other night weeks ago. Yet, I was only piloting one MKIV the other time. Now, though, the MKIVs are firing nearly dead even with each other. I am not a fan of splitting my mind six ways like this, with live ammo.

I feel the world's worst migraine building, and I feel the stretch and pull of my mind. The mindspaces are pushed to their limits. I cannot call it doubling down, but that is essentially what I am doing. I bring two more mindspaces into being and marry them to the MKIVs.

The mass on my mind lifts, and I know there is a good chance I might be out for a day or two. The last target Thap calls is the 500-meter number three target. I let it have two salvos of the 20mm AP ammo from each MKIV. The ringing of four five-round bursts echoes through the Blue Ridge mountains as I stand my SkipJacks down.

I feel horrible, not just from the growing, brain-dividing migraine. Samuel and I had been in almost every battle together since we joined Force Recon. He is as good a pilot as anyone, ever, in Force Recon. I have seen him match the Lion of the Compact himself on the range.

The world has changed, just like it had the first time SkipJacks hit the southern border battlefield all those years ago. The three of us turn and see Samuel is in complete shock. I pull both MKIVs to heel. A separate mindspace is reloading each of the weapon systems as I walk. I walk up to the Family, as that is what this is: a capital F meeting.

I do not need to hear the time. I do not need the time called out to further shame Samuel. Thap walks up, and he must have felt the change in my run or maybe he simply understands an old warrior's pride. Thap shakes his head no to Samuel. I feel a relief, one I have never felt before. I cannot take my brother back into war. Sam's time is past, and Samuel needs to move past our former life.

There is but one way out of FR, and by the grace of luck, God, or gods, Sam Janks found a second way. I cannot take him back into hell; to do so would spit in the eyes of whatever fates granted him leave from such punishment.

I hear his voice, quiet and respectful. Samuel phrases his question just barely above a whisper: "Thap, what is the time?"

Samuel's face is a mixture of awe and fear, and I hope that I conveyed the message that needed to be said. I pray that Sam knows I have done this to show him, that he knows this is the only way he would understand.

Thap clears his throat, then announces quietly, "Twenty-four point fifty-seven seconds." My Segundo looks at Samuel, softness and sorrow in his eyes.

I walk over to Samuel and hug him, touching helmet to goggles, our faces inches from each other. I whisper, "Brother, I need you to plan. Plan this op for me, for all of us. Figure out this attack for me. I have never been as skilled at that as you. Leave the door-kicking to me. Please."

I see the tears in his eyes as my friend of so many bloody days and nights realizes he will not be with me this time. I hold him, even after I feel the nod.

I feel the whole GSG and Family are here. All the Segundos and all the supplementary guards are here at Hill House. Everyone is a bit curious as to what is going on. I am betting most have no real contextual basis for understanding what has just happened.

I hear them asking why did Samuel not use two MKIVs? Why does it matter that Samuel used one? That I used two? How? Why does the time difference matter? I think they see the shudders of a man's pride cut low and do not understand. They voice that desire to answer the unknown in a thousand questions that one can never explain unless you have lived it. It is Darien who shushes them, and he does so politely and with a bit of deference.

"What you saw is a professional realizing that their time at the top of their game has passed, there's a new team on the field playing a new game. One for which he is ill-equipped to play," Darien says. He sighs and speaks up a bit more forcefully as the murmuring starts up again. "You saw Samuel beat a quarter of those targets every ten seconds. Ray defeated half in just over twelve. That difference would mean death on the battlefield. It had to be shown, not spoken. There is no way to tell a person the truth of it, and Samuel had to live it."

Darien's voice is the final discussion on the topic. He walks over and slaps me on the back and whispers, "Thank you."

I let go of Samuel. The range goes cold, and I clear the guns in Samuel's MKIV.

Samuel pulls or pushes that loss aside, stands still for long second, and then he turns to me, a slow smile on his face. "Let's have some fun," he says, meeting my eyes. "Brother."

I grin as he force-dumps himself into his MKIV. After this last run, I am quite a bit slower. My mind is still shuddering under that eight-way split. His rundown tests finish, and we decide to be showy as Thap calls targets for us.

Piloting a single MKIV is excellent and refreshing, damn near restorative to my mind. We are not running our personal carbines. The two of us are just piloting the SkipJacks. The best we could do together is a very rusty twenty-eight seconds. It would take months of us working together daily to trim those final three seconds, even if we could.

We have ammo, we have frustration, anger, fear, and so we expend that ammo, frustration, anger, and fear into that range. Calling it cathartic is an understatement. There are not many things like feeling the recoil of a gun, or the haptic feedback from the arm-mounted weaponry. We will be tired when done.

Both of us are sweating by the second reload. Most have somehow found some lunch and picnic tables around the corner of the range and are sitting and talking over the volume of noise. We finish by using our frag tubes at the 800-meter targets.

We disco and pull the MKIVs to heel. We walk up to the shed and put the two SkipJacks in the maintenance docking stations. Tom is already there. "Back to parity, Tom. I will need to know more about where I am going before I make any decisions about what loadout I want," I say, as I strip off my HUD goggles and stow them on my chest rig.

"I need a proper helmet before this kicks off, Samuel," I say, pointing at his old one. I have no idea where he had picked up that ancient thing. Helmets are not like tuned haptic suits. They can be reused and are often full of top-level CM encryption. "I'll need to talk to you during..." I stop when I see his face. I smile, as he is grinning like an idiot.

"Ray, I'd forgotten how much fun that is," Sam says and then laughs. "I'll see what I can get a hold of. I've had this since before Basic. I bought it as a teen and hid it in my rooms at the Family residence."

We store all but the cleared MKIVs in the cage and walk out of the shed.

Chapter 10
Work up and duck

C10 S1

It is later in the evening. Eliese and I are lounging on the futon, enjoying a cup of her favorite tea. Our view is the vermilion sunset out the windows on the porch.

"Raylan, could he do it? Can Samuel make it through the fight that is coming?" Eliese asks in her anxious and soft voice.

I take a sniff of the tea in my hand and sip. I have a heat pad over my head, and my eyes are closed, as the migraine is fighting to rip my brain out of an eyesocket. Nevertheless, I know what Eliese is asking.

I have said many times that Samuel and I were as good as any of our fellow unit members. Her concern is that without him, she might lose me. With him, she might lose him or both of us.

"I am not the same, Eliese...not any longer. This fight will be brutal, it will be swift, and violent, as all fights are. It will also be twice as fast as he remembers. You can train for that to a degree. It will not be enough, not today. eight years ago, maybe," I say, turning to look at my beloved. "Trying to keep him alive would likely get both of us killed."

I push up the heat pad and lift one sore eyelid. I put as much love and care into my voice as my heart would allow, when I say, "It will be a while out. I need more information, and I need a layout, a plan. Samuel is great at planning. With him devoting time to that planning, I can do the work up and training. As much as I am different from him in this fight today, he has always been from me in planning. My typical plan was to lob APHE till the place was ash and then shoot anything that twitched with the 25mm. As we go through the workup, we will do our best to button down any loose flaps."

She smiles weakly. I can tell my explanation only mollifies her anxiety minimally. I feel the trust given to me then as she moves that concern to the side and brings up her next topic. Eliese's Queen of industry persona is in full swing now. Maybe this is her way of doing what she can to aid us in this fight.

"Raylan, you have a good deal of work, also. I'm thinking we put a hold on any new Gate walks until we can bring the lawsuit and this Steve Jenkins thing under control," Eliese muses. "It'll give you a good chance to get your team settled and work on a few projects together."

"I have pretty much come to the same conclusion," I tell her. "I want to set Knaggs and his team to review each of the settlement build-ups. Suppose he can get them close to five years; we will then be well ahead of government sponsored gate, including those here in the Compact. I would like him to focus on them in order and tie in the new plans with any new tools, equipment, and supplies."

I tilt my head back, copying the family's affectation of thinking. "Out of what we have done, time and data have been our biggest issue. We have tried to keep the data trunk expense down. I cannot see it paying out, Eliese. We must have that time down to at least five years. I think we need to bite the expense bullet and drop another data trunk in, maybe two," I say, doing my best to articulate my thoughts.

"That would support a third, fourth, and maybe fifth building crew via SkipJacks. Once they get to Stage Two, their colonies end up with a skilled labor problem. Being able to supply a twenty-four-hour shift in the D2 will help," I explain. I remain unsure if I am providing solid reasoning or solid justification in my little speech.

I feel her long-fingered, soft hand on my shoulder. I turn and see the dark violet of her nail polish and kiss her fingers. In her business voice, fear and anxiety are pushed aside in favor of what she can direct and control.

Eliese says, "What does that do to our costs? I know when we looked at it before your first Gate, we would go from footing about fifty percent cost factor to nearly eighty percent with a second data trunk and crew."

I know I can get the answer, but with this pain in my head, I let El do the heavy lifting, so to speak. The way she pulls and flips through her FEED, it is not necessary. Her mind is racing and far outstrips mine in raw business acumen. Even if I do beat her to the exact data she is looking for, she will pull it up on her FEED to view it there. She despises sharing someone's FEED.

"This last shale Gate is almost a thirty-three percent cost factor for us. Raylan, you knocked fifteen percent off. That's very impressive," Elise says. Her fingers slide through the data on her FEED display. I bet she is figuring what my new team would add to that. I think even if we hit forty percent for Gate number five, number six will be lower, and seven lower than that. This idea of going back to the first four and hammering them out, ultimately, will make the next few Gate builds that much less expensive to open.

"With your team, you'll push to a sixty percent cost factor with what we have now," Eliese muses. "That's a second data trunk, plus three more around-the-clock SkipJack shifts and equipment, roughly."

Eliese is now about to start what I call idea-juggling. It is a combination of putting ideas in the air while she moves about Hill House's living area. It is one of my favorite things to watch her do.

"We can use that time to refine better tools for the settlers that are there. As for the population, build some partnerships for complementary industries to buy in, as you've intended. Bring our remote SkipJack tech up to date, update the temp pods, and reduce the lag in D2 for their pilots. We're spoiled here in EP1 with our satellites. I'll see if Darien can partner with any of the Mega-Corps for an extended survey range spike that can handle overlays for piloted 3D printing of buildings, docks, piers, pipes, power stations, and septic systems," Eliese says. She is up, walking and turning and doing a pace down the most open section of Hill House and back.

"I will have Knaggs look into complementary industries to introduce the first four to. CBN will be a challenge, as it is more a homeland than a business enterprise," I muse out loud as I sort things on my FEED. "Farming...I think we can sell that, provided they are amicable." I am currently looking back through old FEED messages for one. "That brings me back to something Knaggs has been saying: 'Success of colonies is often due to their access to shelter, clean water, and the ability to create their food.' I will need more info from him on that," I mumble.

Our night goes on like this, the two of us talking to ourselves and commenting on each other's mutterings for the next few hours. Together, we hammer out a list, a schedule, of sorts, for Knaggs's first team meeting. Tomorrow is going to be a busy day for them. It is way past dark. I have since moved the futon to face the window. I am reclining and watching the stars. Eliese is leaning on my shoulder under the blanket. She seems to be perpetually cold. I drift off to sleep, wondering what will come in the next few months.

I arise the next morning and find that neither of us have moved from the futon. I lay Eliese down and cover her while I get ready for a run. I find Tom has finished bringing one of the MKIVs back into parity.

I slip into a haptic suit and start it booting. After it finishes booting, I start my run slowly, as I have that lingering migraine combined with somewhat cramped muscles. I avoid my previous loop. I am beginning to tear up that trail with the combined weight of the SkipJacks and myself. I move past the trailhead to the gazebo and jog down to the range. I find Thap and the Gurkhas doing laps. I join them.

After about five laps, we wind it down. It is a good run. While running, I find out the old barn is scheduled for dismantling today and will be rebuilt at the range as a small barracks. Then there will be about four weeks of remodeling for the interior to turn it into three separate block flats, one main living area, and a training room. I am guessing Thap is eager for that.

I head back to the shed near Hill House. I park a mud-caked MKIV in the repair bay and hit the sonic washer. I pull a lens down after MKIV is clean and send it into the cage docking station. Locking everything back up, I return to the house and start coffee and breakfast.

Eliese will head off to the Family residence today while I nail down the plan with the group. First, though, I need to make a design decision regarding my gift for my beloved. I have heard back from Craig. CBN is ready and waiting on a final choice. With Trish's help, I have an idea of what she likes, so I make my choices and move on to my coffee.

Knaggs is running the team meeting today. I am going to be around just in case there is an issue, and if necessary, they can get my final take on it. I will also hit Knaggs up for finding a secondary industry partnership for those first five Gates. Samuel is planning to stop by with a preliminary plan for training.

Later tonight, we are off to a small gala for something Deloite is putting on. Trish is attending, as well, as part of her indenture. The partners cornered her to pass on an invitation to us. Name recognition, I suppose. Thap informs me it is "about the training of the under-skilled in an age where trade indenture-ships or indentured higher education reigns supreme."

I am in the bathroom shaving when I get a peck on the cheek good-bye for the day.

"Raylan, I know you can become dedicated to a passion," Eliese says with a wink, her face and torso just inside the door. "We must leave at 5:00 p.m."

That is a pleasant reminder not to be late. Eliese has me dead to rights, though. I am as likely to get sucked in today as I am any other day.

Knaggs leads the meeting well. He brings them all together and discusses their backgrounds, how each of them will help change the way new D2 iterations are settled. There is a lengthy and healthy review of where each Gate stands on its path to Stage Three, and what they need to be able to provide their own power, food, shelter, water, sanitation, and finally, he adds the FEED system network. I am hesitant about that last one, but Knaggs has made a convincing argument for why we cannot keep adding data trunks. A localized mesh system will only go so far and still requires EP1-based data trunks. Those data trunks operate off our EP1 FEED network, increasing our costs on the EP1 side. The longer the D2 data trunk, the higher the latency, and the more likely there will be data artifacts. Putting up their own network is critical.

Ol' Jack and Knaggs will be lining out the settlement's future power, water, and sewer networks with a civil engineer they are bringing on to act as a city planner. His name is Mordecai Rothman. His whole family will be making a move to our area from the Great Lakes District. Mordecai's wife is taking a job with the local primary school. Their kids are about to head off to their secondary education. They are both looking forward to a quieter life.

Daivi is hard at work finishing the follow and stability programming for the Llama. She is figuring she has about four days until it is ready for first-round trials. After that, her job is to reprogram the two new piloted 3D printers to lay out sewer, power, and water systems while printing a paved road system for MLRs to make it off the demarcation zone. One of the printers will be doing the digging and the printing of the water and sewer pipes, and the other 3D printer will be laying the power and printing of the MLR roadway.

Susan is doing her best to increase the efficiency in which the five-axis 3D printers can work. Calling them a printer is an excellent way to get a lecture from her, as they complete the ground leveling, digging, and waste removal. When fed components for reinforced concrete, they print out structures. When fed materials, they print things like piping, conduit, and cable when combined with the proper tool head.

Our D2 iterations will be able to print out power, water, and septic systems in the future. Once the printing is complete, people piloting SkipJacks can go in, install all the fittings, furnishings, wall panels, fixtures and finally connect the power, water, and sewer.

Carmen is behind the scenes sorting out individual projects with everyone. Suppose they need an appointment with an outside vendor, SkipJack pilot group, 3D printer manufacturer, or simply need input on a what-if. Carmen is available, and capable, the staff officer with her hands in every pie, keeping everyone on time, under budget, and guiding them in their moments of floundering. I am beginning to understand why Michael Knaggs's attorney practice was so busy.

Finally, there is Tom, the odd man out. Tom is helping organize all the requests from SkipJack pilots into more accessible, dedicated tools and machines, from a treaded, trenching SkipJack to one that has a self-sharpening saw blade for logging. We even have smaller SkipJacks for laying power, water, and sewer in areas that do not need the larger 3D printers. He is also looking at minimizing the huge agricultural SkipJacks for small, family-based garden and food production for Stage Two colonists. These new SkipJacks allow for that much-needed food portion of Knaggs's plan.

***

C10 S2

Samuel arrives close to noon, and we have a chat as we sit down on the floor, eating a tray of sandwiches that one of the Forty brought to us.

Samuel is excited. "The problem as I see it, Raylan, is that this fight isn't against men piloting a SkipJack. It's against animals: faster ones that have natural weapons, and no sense of mercy."

He outlines as he points his sandwich at the unused animal SkipJacks.

"So far, you've faced two sets of animal SkipJacks. Up till now, they haven't had integrated modern weapons. That doesn't mean these animal 'Jacks will not have weapons in the future. Given the kind of torture that the wolf went through—steel teeth or steel claws—it's only a matter of time until it happens. Raylan, what if it has a shotgun for a tail?" Sam asks, snorting as he sees my face trying to picture such a monstrosity.

"Raylan, I want you practicing with the heavier shotguns out there. Spread that damage a tad. If you can get one pellet into the brain or spine, you can put them out of the fight," Sam says, tapping the last quarter of the sandwich into his hair. "Finally, you've always sucked at hand-to-hand. You never gave it the work it needs. That's got to change. You seem to favor knives. As close as the catfight was, I think swords and similar weapons are out for now." Sam grabs half of another sandwich from my seven-sandwich pile.

"I talked to Lama, Father's Segundo. He's sending up two more Gurkhas. One is the best small-arms guy he's ever seen. You'll work with him on handguns and shotguns. He's going to make you move, fire, and reload. The plan is to have you shooting three days a week," Sam explains as he chews.

It is as if we were huddled in a thicket waiting for our orders to pounce. Propriety is gone. We eat and we talk in the same low whispers as we had during so many missions, but most of all, I listen to Sam's plans.

"The second guy is simply scary. He's the best hand-to-hand man in the Forty, and he specializes in short-range weapons like batons, sticks, knives, and the Kukri. He's willing to add a hammer or hatchet to the regimen. He'll work with you every other day, three days a week." Samuel is still eyeing the pile of sandwiches. "It's going to be a ton of work, Raylan,"

I remember this Sam, the military Sam, stripped of the capital family name, scarfing food, doing a rundown, explaining his plans, or a doing a simple post-operation review while chewing enough food to make his cheeks puffy. I message Thap to let him know we have two more Gurkhas coming, that possibly we should scrap the barn and build a proper barracks for the guys, only to find out Carmen has it in hand. She has notified Thap and taken charge while telling me, "Bless your heart." I can almost hear her amusement in those words.

I sit through Samuel's telling of my new schedule, and I have one thing I need to get off my chest. "Samuel, yesterday was for show. I do not know if I can pilot two with any effectiveness. I still have a migraine today. I doubt I can do it well enough to stay alive in a real fight. Well, not without some serious training. I can probably do it in a pod. Out in the open, though, I will end up being easy cheesy pickings," I say, as I imagine a few animals running past my SkipJacks, then pouncing on me.

"I know, Raylan, and I realized it last night. The world has changed. You are but the first step. That said, I agree: I am out. I feel much more relieved than I rightfully should. I'm sore today, sore like the third day of boot camp. I can help best by taking charge of planning that you want. I also know you need to focus on one SkipJack, and you. One SkipJack, one Raylan, or Eliese will have my head," Sam says, and he chuckles.

I know he likes his sister. Yet, as anxious as she seemed last night, maybe Eliese is more worried and anxious than I initially thought. I nod and slide the plate of sandwiches over to me as he reaches for another half. I grin and set it between us.

"I will be ready," I say.

I have more to say when a pair of boots and legs stops in front of me. The boots are perfectly shiny, and the pants bloused into the top of the boots have their own creases ironed into place. I follow those creases up and find myself looking at a man of wired muscle and tendons.

"Mr. Ray, we train now," the man says.

I hear the knifehand in his voice. The regimental English is not as precise as Thap's or even Pak's. He has likely learned it in his home country of the Nepalese Concordant.

"Food later. Run now," the man barks. I start moving involuntairly. My body responds as it had all those years ago in boot camp. I know the six miles I ran this morning are not going to matter to this man. We set out on a short jog down to the range.

Thap is there with Carmen, who is overlaying a FEED image of hers with the new proposed barracks. He waves at me as I jog down from the shed. Then I see him grimace as my instructor walks around the corner to the range. It seems I have pulled the hard ass for hand-to-hand combat. I have a sense that this will go the same way my time with Darien in the ring went. This is going to be a lesson in pain management.

"My name is Rana," my new instructor says as he jogs past me. "You are slow. Big and slow."

We start on form with an Applegate Fairbairn knife. When I am wrong, it is corrected one time by Rana manually. Every time after that, Rana fixes it by a judicious application of a wooden baton. I laugh when the first baton breaks over the back of my right elbow. It is Rana's way to have me keep my elbows tucked in.

I know our future time together will be very instructive. I am poked, stabbed, cut, hammered on, and thwacked on the head so many times by a man who looks as if I could break him in half with one hand. We work on speed, parrying, disabling blows, and blows to end it in one go.

I go to work on my close fighting skills under his tutelage. I will learn to punch, kick, and take a beating like I never have before. It is not a codified martial art, per se, but a foundation from which to win. It is dirty, mean, and nasty. It suits me just fine.

I finish my first day of how to be slapped with a stick by Rana, training. I head to the shower; I have layers of bruises. I cover the bruises on my neck as best I can. I dress, and head to the tram. Thap stares at me and shakes his head.

Thap, I think, feels sorry for me. "Rana's the best, Raylan. Just...he...well, duck. Duck more, duck faster," Thap says, and I laugh.

I wince a moment later as the laughter puts pressure on the bruising around my left ribs. Thap and I talk about this gala, and what I am to do. I am Eliese's fiancé, number seven of the Family, so I am, of course, arm candy, but arm candy that is moving Gate D2 iterations to Stage Three fast, which is likely why they want me there. Much of the complaining about the marginalized untrained peoples of the Compact comes from them making up a disproportionate amount of Gate walkers. I do not mean people given leave by the NAC to walk a gate; I mean people who, in the dark, in the rain or snow, sneak through because they believe it is their only chance at a new life. I will have to think about that. Setting up trade schools for the D2s might help those workers and colonists before they apply to Gate walk.

Eliese is stunning in a black dress. I am happy to see her after a mild day of being hit by a rolling pin. Her hair is pulled up, leaving her neck visible, tasteful earrings, and a stunning amethyst necklace. As always, her perfume is alluring to my mind, and it is very distracting.

Eliese reaches out with one finger and touches my head, tilting it gently to the left. Her perfume lifts from her wrist to my nose, short-circuiting my brain. She then inspects the bruise peeking from the collar of my shirt.

Her eyes go flat. She turns to look at Thap, and my Segundo flinches.

"Training today," I murmur to my beloved. "Rana..."

El's eyebrow raises, and her gaze whips back to Thap, both of her eyes settling on him entirely. This time Thap does step back.

"El, Rana is my hand-to-hand instructor," I say, intervening. "Knives, batons, and hammer. I was a bit slow today. I will get better," I do my best to mollify her, and to pull pressure off Thap. He has zero to do with Samuel's schemes.

"Raylan, I'll do my best to hide this. You will *not* mess with the collar tonight.

No playing with the monkey suit," Eliese says with a warm smile that makes the bumps and bruises I am now sporting well worth it.

I return the smile and inquire about the general premise of this gala. We chat for a moment, and I tell her of my idea for trade schools. Eliese informs me that setting up the trade schools should be done in the D2 iteration. The Compact does not like letting any trained labor go so easily.

Apparently. there is a lottery for trained personnel and their families. The lottery encompasses each of the needs a Gate has. Generally, any leftover slots go to unskilled labor. First to arrive, first through the Gate. They can go to any Gate that will take them. Usually, only new Stage Ones or Stage Twos will take on unskilled. Eliese talks as she is layering cosmetics onto my neck, while shushing me everytime I try to ask a question. Speaking makes my neck move.

"Would there be repercussions from doing that? I mean encouraging the Gate walk and having training available in D2?" I ask as I sit in the exact way she wants.

"Maybe, but with our Gates, likely not. Some other private Gates may not see this kind of arrangement as a problem," Eliese says.

She is thinking it over, I can tell. It is a way of looking at the issue that we have not covered. Ever the brilliant one, she is considering it from many objective points of view.

"The Compact won't stand for it, I think. They'll want us to train them and have their indentures paid here and put them into their queue. If it's to be, it should be done discreetly by the D2 iteration. Accept Gate walking colonists and offer them what trade school training they can, but have them pay their indenture in D2. Most of all, don't tell the NAC about it," she says with a double wink.

Our tram flight to the venue is smooth. Eliese spends the flight prepping me on the partners we are meeting this evening. We meet Trish inside the golf course's main ballroom. She is sporting her own arm candy for the evening.

Trish and her arm candy are there together this evening, but will not be together after this evening. He is too numb to be a vulture or mongrel. His name is Jason Miles, and he works with Trish at Deloitte. They met on one of the audits, and she asked him to attend with her tonight. She is deftly keeping him in line, much the way she had done with me. That gives me a chuckle.

"Raylan, what's so funny?" Eliese asks as we are circling through the room.

"Trish is doing the same thing with Jason that she did with me at the holiday party. I wonder if he will turn out as I did," I say, as I follow her lead between conversations with one of the partners for Deloitte's North East office whom Eliese has met before.

"Raylan, you don't have a clue how miffed Trish is at me for poaching you. On top of that, she's very put out with you for canceling on her," Eliese says, her voice a whisper of song that reaches only my ears. She sighs as we finish another meet-and-greet. "And no, Jason won't be like you. I'm sure he's a fine man, just not a Family man. Trish knows that. She'll let Jason down easily if she hasn't already made it clear."

I realize Trish already had. "He said 'to attend.' Not be arm candy, date, or go with, but 'attend,'" I muse, as I snag an hors d'oeuvre from a passing attendant.

Eliese gives me the side-eye as I am looking to snag more. I steel myself to resist.

"She's not in the market, as she says. With her work and her indenture, she doesn't want the distraction," Eliese explains in response to my statement.

"How often do you talk?" I ask, wondering.

"We message daily. That's what caused the issue when you blurted out about our relationship. I hadn't mentioned it in any of my messages. I must have tipped Trish off, though. She clued in even a bit too fast for her at dinner," Eliese says.

We are sitting at the dinner table, just as three other couples find their way over to our table: executive partners of the firm and their spouses. I begin to see what Darien had meant about Japan doing business on the golf course. For these three partners, two women and one man, business is done at the galas.

It seems there is a superficial interest in keeping Trish on after her indenture. Eliese's response is Family-typical. That is Trish's domain, not hers. I know well that Trish has no love for outside the Family work. She has been working towards her own division her whole life. It will have to be one hell of a deal to keep her there.

We talk and commiserate with the plight of non-indentured workers. Much of it is complete pap, but I can understand their point of view, even though I do not agree with many of them. The speaker is engaging; she is a young day worker who has just received notice of her acceptance into the hospice trade school. She is happy at having the chance to improve her life and those of her family. Hospice, I learn as she continues, is not quite a full hospital nurse. They are the primary caregivers for the elderly and infirm who have moved out of hospitals to facilities.

I pay more attention as I think of Mark and his wife, Morgan. The speaker outlines that with the increase of median living age above 140 years, people are, for the first time, coming to grips with extended periods of living at an age where hospice is a part of daily life. The view of hospice care has changed in the last few decades. No longer is it relegated to being a place to die.

I flit through the data packet provided by those putting on the Gala. The speakers make no mention of the other side of the hospice industry. There is a stark rise in genetic dementia, the resurgence of drug resistant cancers, and that hospices serve as a recuperation place for those who have rejuvenation procedures. These facilities do well as care facilities for folks recovering from their own printed organ transplants.

The evening is a beautiful and I am happy to spend it with Eliese. I meet some interesting people, but ate way too little food. We retire soon after the dinner and return to Hill House. I spend the rest of the night having Eliese rub pain relief cream on my upper torso and arms. I am damn near in seventh heaven at her touch. It relaxes me so much that I wake up the next morning late for my training.

***

C10 S3

The firearms training instructor's name is Ghale. I learn that he is one of three members of the Ghale family serving in the Forty. To say Ghale is an odd duck is an understatement. A shorter man, with a prominent forehead, he loves guns, has a sly wit, and a healthy sense of humor.

Ghale starts me on shotguns. Through Ghale's instruction, I learn how to load, shoot, and then speed reload pumps, autos, rotary mag, and box mag shotguns.

When it comes to handguns, my preference for big bore revolvers is not appreciated until he sees that my grip mitigates the heavy recoil. Ghale relents, and I have my 454 Casull back. We focus on using cover, getting to cover, and setting up shots. This part is not new to me. What is new are the weapons themselves. I end up carrying two 454Cs, each with five rounds and several speed loaders. The shotgun holds eight rounds and I carry some strip loaders to reload it on my chest rig. While it is not as physically punishing as yesterday, it is still exhausting.

Ghale does not allow me to walk, stroll or even jog. I must sprint from place to place. It is the worst kind of torture for a man in full battle rattle.

I make my appointment with Peter Alvarez. We talk about the metal deterioration of items at Hill House. He has come up with another set of bands for me to wear. All the bands are thin flat bars that will touch my skin. Doc wants to see if having a sacrificial metal would help stop the corrosion of the other metal items I interact with over time. We start a long series of experiments. The bands never bother me. They are more unseen jewelry than anything else. I do notice over the next few months that I am getting much longer use out of the firearms, SkipJack parts, and other tools I am using daily than I have in the past.

In the evenings, Eliese and I plan the full remodel of Hill House, including the master bedroom, two closets, two vanity sinks, one soaking tub, one massaging tub, and a double shower. The central change is the wide wraparound windows that would encompass the living area, master bath, master bedroom and Eliese's office. They will cover from just above the floor to just below the ceiling, all the way around two-thirds of the house.

The kitchen will be changed to include a dining nook for the two of us, with a larger, more formal area for dining with guests. We are also building out the wraparound porch just off a new doorway on the left side of the living area. The porch will include a brick oven, a smoker, grill, and space to clean up.

Where the stairs are to the apartments below will become an office, and nearby a hallway will lead to the laundry area on the right. On the opposite wall of the laundry will be new stairs heading down to Thap's and Pun's private flats.

Behind the master bedroom, down the hallway will be two separate offices with full Family integrated terminals for Eliese and myself. Going straight by those offices, a hallway leads to a second full bath and two bedrooms. Bedrooms, Eliese says, are for kids. Eliese enjoys telling me about the dozens, or hundreds of kids we are going to have.

For my part, I am allowed free rein on the gazebo at the pond. The pond is to be dredged, widened, and deepened back to its original size. A small fishing dock will be installed about fifteen feet out over the water. The downside is now that the remodel is about to start, I will be commuting daily from my flat at the Family residence. Eliese will come to Hill House as needed. I am forced make the best of it that I can.

My team is up and running at full speed. The civil engineer, Mordecai Rothman, and his family have settled into their new blockhouse. They are observant of their Jewish faith, so his schedule, for the first time in his working life, includes time for that faith. He is a tall, medium-build guy who, over the last couple of decades, has designed the municipal planning for the Great Lakes District's new Communities. The three of them, Knaggs, Jack, and Rothman, seem to get along as well as three grumpy old men can. Jack and Rothman are betting who can grow a beard the fastest. Carmen tells me it came out of a weekly poker night. I leave them to it, as I need them to work together. I suppose if that requires a poker night and a beard, then Grizzly Adams they can be.

Carmen asks to set up a commissary with staff for the employees here at Hill House. She has noticed many of them are working later and skipping meals. I discuss the matter with Eliese. When I get back to Carmen, I make sure there will be concessions made for Rothman's and Daivi's individual faiths.

There will be a Kosher station, an Indian sub-continent station for the Gurkhas and Daivi, then a general Compact station. Carmen adds in a halal station just to round out the package. I am sure it will be a hit as soon as it is up and running. Other than that, they are making significant progress in revising the plans for the first four D2 iterations.

The next three months pass rapidly. It has been nonstop working for everyone at GSG. I am that much further into my training when the Hill House's remodel is finished. The printing of the barracks finished a few weeks back. The construction crews finished up the interior work a week or so ago. For now, we have the range crew settled into the building. Pak and his range management men are enjoying their new space in the barracks. We have a dozen small apartments in the barracks building available for future residents. Thap and Pun now have separate flats below us at Hill House.

Our first night back in the Hill House is going to be terrific. Thap and Pun help me with my gift to Eliese. Daniel and Craig have hit it out of the park. Pun orchestrates her schedule to keep Eliese at the Family residence on the day it arrives. Thap and I spend the afternoon taking delivery, putting it together, and installing the various pieces throughout our new home.

Eliese will return home tonight to do a walkthrough and create her punch list. The furniture selection will happen after that, or so she thinks. Trish has been feeding me FEED messages from Eliese. With the help of Trish, Pun, Daniel, and Craig, we have taken care of the big stuff.

I have a custom bed with nightstands made from old-growth Douglas Fir. The legs of the bed are ten inches wide, and the back is a rearward curved arch. The nightstands are matching Douglas Fir. I do not have the bed built on a log theme, but a finished Douglas Fir plank and beam construction similar to her beloved coffee table.

The CBN craftsmen build a massive formal dining table out of red oak with thirteen separate leaves, stretching a total of six meters long. Finally, we have six sturdy chairs that can withstand my weight. Trish assures me that Eliese will love it.

Hill House has turned from a cozy cabin to a lovely home, a significantly larger home with recycled IPE wood floors. Ironwood, or IPE trees, are about the only wood that can handle my weight while I am tromping about it repeatedly. They make excellent furnishings that I have pulled together. I still have my futon, even though it is now relegated to my office. I prepare elk steaks for our dinner tonight. I am enjoying the music from the FEED as I prep everything at the counter. I can hardly wait for Eliese to arrive.

Eliese lands, and I meet the tram down at the new landing area. My beloved gives me a peck on the cheek before we make our way up to the completed Hill House. Eliese was last at Hill House a week ago. There has been a slew of things completed since.

We walk up stone steps to our new front entry. A wanigan, as I call it, although Eliese informs me "mudroom" is the proper term. I put on slippers, and it is in an effort to deaden the sound of my weight as I stomp about.

I turn to show Eliese the new basic kitchen. My effort to slowly unveil the gifts stage by stage does not work. I hear a squeak of joy and a rustle of fabric as she dashes to the table. I can see her inspecting the joinery of the table. No screws or glue, just like the coffee table she had purchased for her office. Eliese's hand glides across the exposed joints as she admires the artisanship. Then she flows over to the chairs, and her hands again caress the joinery.

"I commissioned it from CBN, and they have been working on it for most of a year," I explain. "Trish and Pun helped pick the types of wood and styles you would like best." I pause for the next bit, to better see her reaction. "For all the items they made, it is a big commission for the people of CBN:D2. Every man, woman, and child has put their hand on the underside of the table and bed in blessing."

Eliese's head slowly rises from under the table, and her long black hair frames her face as her lips start to move without sound. I have seen the hundreds of handprints on the underside of the pieces as I put them together. To say it is moving is an understatement.

I walk over to Eliese, and she melts into my arms. I see that her emotions have overtaken her. I sit down on a chair, and she slides onto my lap. I hold her for a very long while as her tears fall onto my shirt.

"I remember the coffee table, the pride you have in your first purchase. That first night, you described the details of the master craftsman who built it. I wanted to give you that same craftsmanship for our home," I whisper.

"You still have not seen the master bed and matching nightstands. The leading craftsmen are a pair of brothers who studied Sashimono-shi in Japan. They joined CBN when they learned there were openings. I think you will like what they came up with for us." I keep talking as I rock her on my lap. "They built you a bed out of old-growth Douglas Fir, and it is a masterpiece, Eliese. The same kind of craftsmanship as the table here."

Slowly, the tears stop. "I can't believe you remembered, that you..." I wait as Eliese snuggles closer. "Thank you, Raylan. I love you," El says in the softest of whispers, and her final sniffles fade.

She then wipes her nose on my shirt and slides off slowly, and goes to the guest bath down the hallway. In a few minutes, she returns. Her eyes are only showing a hint of puffiness.

"I'm ready to see my other gifts." Eliese puts a playful spin on it, tears forgotten.

I lead Eliese to the pair of pocket doors leading into the master bedroom. She takes a deep breath and opens them to a wall of windows shining into the room. The bed sits in the center, facing the windows that overlook the valley below. The nightstands sit to either side.

A small pair of his and her vanities sit on either wall, with small Douglas Fir stools to sit upon and remove clothing. Eliese says nothing, merely wanders the room, touching and feeling the wood and fabrics. Trish is a godsend. She has dialed in the linens, the materials for the stools, and purchased a matching settee. Under Trish's tutelage, I have learned that olive drab haptic suit material is not a suitable choice for linens.

Eliese has made her loop around the master bedroom. My vision of beauty stands before me on the opposite side of the bed. I see that she is holding back tears again.

"Thank you, Raylan. I love it. All of it: the colors, the fabric, the sheets, the bed, especially *MY BED*!" Eliese squeals in joy.

With a hop into the air, she flops onto the bed and looks up at the ceiling.

"My bed," Eliese says again with that same joy. Her eyes roam about the room, coming to rest on the crown molding, all of it intricately carved. It is the work of another tribal nation, depicting a Raven carrying fresh water to the world. It tells of how the Raven sometimes tricked, borrowed, stole, or just gifted the world with the sun, moon, tides, and most importantly, water. Eliese turns her head to see me. "I love it, Raylan!"

"I am glad you love our bed, Eliese..." I am unable to finish the sentence.

"My bed, Raylan," Eliese corrects impishly. "My bed, my table. You still have the futon in your office. You gave them to me. Mine."

My beloved is trying to hold back giggles as she is mimicking making snow angels on the bedcovers.

"If you say, 'I do' at the right time, I might be persuaded to let you join me in my bed." Eliese raises an eyebrow, then winks at me over the top of the fluffy duvet cover.

"Then I had better prepare my lady's dinner before the Morrigan unleashes her displeasure upon me," I say, giving her an equally playful bow.

I exit and slide the doors closed behind me. I still have a good deal of prep time. El can run through the rest of the master bedroom area and make her punch list while I finish dinner.

We are leaning on the counter, having a beer while the outside grill heats up. Eliese has been uncommonly quiet.

"Raylan, I've been thinking over Senkaku Island. I know you and Samuel haven't come up with a way to get there undetected. I think I like Darien's idea," she says.

I hear that song of hers in her voice. She only becomes that way when angry or vengeful, and this is probably a bit of both.

"If we partner Darien's Japanese Mega-Corps and NEFC on a gate on this little island here..." Eliese says as she brings up a FEED image to the central entertainment terminal. The map shows its close nature to the Senkaku Isles. "From there, we can use the NEFC to get you close to the Med-i-Care complex on the main island."

I turn from oiling the grill and walk back through the sliding doorway. I make a circuit of the kitchen counter.

"I have kind of put this on the backburner, love, what with training, and the new outlined plans for the first four D2 iterations," I say.

I move the FEED image to get a better look at the topographic maps of both sets of islands. With a zoom here, and a long considering look, I agree with my wife-to-be.

"Senkaku is tiny. I like this, though. It gets me in the general area and gives me a plausible reason to inspect the fishing grounds stocked with depleted species," I say with a clack of the tongs.

Walking out onto the patio, I put the steaks on as Eliese finishes setting the table. The elk steaks only require a few minutes on each side. It is time I use to parse out this new opportunity Eliese has presented me with.

As I bring the steaks and potatoes over to our patio sitting area, I say, "I have a meeting with Stewart and Samuel tomorrow. I will get their take on this. Thanks, love." I give Eliese a peck on the cheek as we sit at her new table.

As the evening progresses, we chat about the way the update on the house has turned out. The new windows overlooking the wraparound porch are a tad taller and allow more light through. Eliese is in love with the whole place. Hill House is her place of refuge and quiet as she organizes and leads her division in the Family enterprises.

"I like my office," I say, thinking of one of the pelts that Eliese had the contractor hang for me. The three squirrel tails above the door are a humorous reminder of our first evening together. I do not have a desk, per se, but a Family FEED terminal set to the side of a heritage wooden workbench. It is as big as a table stationed in the center of the room. In the middle is a 3D image tester for SkipJacks. I can review, comment, and if I want to, change things forwarded to me from the team.

My office has a cave-gray wall, as Eliese puts it, with light, fake wood flooring and a light-colored hardwood bench. I can see myself spending a great deal of time there. It seems like most of my recent Family-related work right now was in a chair, and not in a haptic suit.

We retire for the evening. I have an early meeting with Stewart, Samuel, and now that Eliese has mentioned it, Darien, since he returned from Japan.

***

C10 S4

I walk into Stewart's office the next morning and play the secretary role and pour the coffee. I end up discussing the changes at Hill House as a form of small talk. I sit with Stewart and Darien as the three of us are waiting on Samuel. I am on my fourth cup of coffee for the morning. I do not know why Stewart's coffee is so much better than mine. Samuel enters Stewart's office as we are wrapping up our morning FEED messages.

"Sorry, gentlemen," Samuel says. "I am running a bit behind this morning. Thanks for taking the time to join us, Darien," he adds. "I've been working on part of the plan for Raylan, the one that he forwarded to us last night." He keeps talking as he is pouring what looks like his fiftieth cup of coffee. "Darien, is this even a possibility?"

With a pause, Darien leans forward and says, "This is the type of historical thing the Japanese like to do, and the type of project the Mega-Corps get behind, initially. They won't sustain it, but they will help get it off the ground and use that as excellent public relations within Japan. Protect and honor their previous fishing grounds, protect and honor the history of Japan, that type of thing."

"They could possibly pull this off themselves, but their Stage Three timeline is about the same, if not a bit slower, than the NAC's." Darien looks around. "I will try. I'm going to need a couple of detailed plans, the minimal, the big ask, and then the one you want to actually do." He catches all of our eyes. "I owe them a favor, to begin with, for the effort they put into helping me find the sub-dermal and haptic patches," Darien explains with a great deal of emphasis. "This will come at a cost."

I say, "I can work with NEFC and see if they would be interested in another partnership. So far, the Compact fishermen are giddy about being back out and making a decent living. Even if it is just farm-raising and releasing, initially, it is all subsidized based on the price of the fish coming through the NEFC:D2."

I think we are all wondering it, but Darien clears the air.

"It took me a while to understand why I flew from Tokyo to Ishigaki Island to play golf. They wouldn't come out and tell me that the place I was looking for wasn't an end purchaser, but a recycling facility of parts," Darien says. "Even after the time I've spent there, the subtlety of what is and what isn't acceptable gets me. For this request, it wouldn't surprise me if they want an additional two or maybe five Gates surveyed by the GSG."

I pause at that. If we do this one Gate, I will have to complete five more. To do five more outside the Compact will be a challenge at this stage of GSG's growth. The opportunity is now, though, and despite our former animosity, with Darien, the Family comes first.

"I am amenable to that offer, provided it is in exchange for me doing at least one, preferably two Gates here, and we use our teams at our rates. I want our pilots and construction crews through Stage One," I say, giving a so-so twist of my hand.

"I'll see what I can arrange, Ray," Darien says as he nods. "That will sweeten the deal, for sure."

Stewart brings it around to his part of the meeting and says, "My end of this fiasco is figuring out what Steve Jenkins has done or is doing. I've forwarded tons of questionable over-billing to the NAC authorities.

"There's now a three-judge panel assigned to the matter. They're looking into multiple counts of fraud by CGSU. The issue is, Steve doesn't have the money. CGSU doesn't have the money. That makes me believe Jenkins is a pawn, a low-run charlatan in a group that is significantly larger.

"My staff and I have yet to discover who is pulling strings. The good news is, with the Compact looking at him heavily for fraud, his political aspirations have tanked. I'm hearing through the backchannels that your deposition, coupled with Peter's, and that video deposition from Mark McCalister, have raised several red flags with his story for the creditors of CGSU," Stewart says.

I am always amazed by Stewart's manner during these meetings. He has this way of laying things out smoothly and concisely.

"Moving on to more distasteful news: the presiding judge has granted Bonnie-poo and her lawsuit a postponement. At the earliest, it's six months out," Stewart says with a grimace. Stewart rates talk show FEED stars lower than scummy politicians. His lips twist into a Cheshire grin of his own as he teases, "Given the delay in the trial, I would like to see an announcement on the engagement soon, Ray."

I grin, so vastly that Samuel makes gagging sounds.

"I bring it up with Eliese regularly," I say, and a frown appears on Stewart's face. Evidently, Stewart is not going to cross that rubicon with his daughter. "I will let her know the change in the lawsuit. The woman is prescient for gossip like that," I say offhandedly.

Samuel, now about two and a half a cups in and no longer twitching from the caffeine overdose, says, "Got bad news, Ray, Ghale says it's time to play footsie with SkipJacks. He's going to start you out with marker rounds."

It is my turn to grimace. "Let us get to it. I have a workout with Rana today."

The meeting breaks up, and I head back to Hill House, where Rana waits for me. Things do not quite go as planned. I am not fast enough, and I do not see Rana's tells soon enough. At some point during our session, I use my head to block his baton. Twice.

Please do not get me wrong, Rana is not a sadist. He does not delight in the pain I endure during our training sessions. He just makes that day as if it is a fight to live, to survive, that death is the only other outcome. Rana has no way of dialing it down a notch or three.

Eliese has had it out with Thap on more than one occasion. In these past months, I have come to love soaking in ice baths. Eliese flies down to the barracks after she sees the blows I have taken to the forehead and temple, which leaves a goose egg three inches wide and an inch thick. My scalp is also seeping from a small laceration behind the ear that Thap platelet-glued shut.

I watched Eliese leave to confront Rana. She orders dinner at the barracks commissary. I do not know what Rana has told her. Eliese stays there for most of the evening.

When Eliese returns to Hill House, she says, "Raylan, get faster. Don't use your head to block his baton."

Then she retires to the master bedroom. That is it. Rana's reign over my training continues, uncontested. I seek out ways to increase speed and reaction times. My weight, even with my moderate build, is my Achilles' heel. I am heavy. Not big and bulky, but solidly heavy. I can run with ease and at length, as my endurance is fantastic. My speed is okay, but Rana is much faster. I keep at it, and with time, I know I will improve.

Over the next month, I secure the NEFC buy into the Ishigaki Gate. Darien acquires the Gate contract from the Mega-Corps. Japan does the Ishigaki:D2 iteration fishing, and the fishing product pays for NEFC fishermen to run the floating farms near Senkaku Island. It takes me a couple more months of prep work to get my group to do their part of this job. They are itching, as it is the team's first build from the ground up. It will be the first test of the Llamas and the first time I take the MKIVs with me. I am also taking fishing gear with me this time, along with a double-hulled inflatable dinghy and motor.

Ghale is also not happy with my speed. In comparison, my speed is excellent for a SkipJack pilot in full kit, but I am woefully behind most competitive athletes. My weight is the primary issue. Ghale has worked me months and months of sprints, since our very first session. My sprints are from one sideline of the range to the other, with the odd interval of a random distance shouted in. Months of running back and forth to my barriers, then doing it all with guns and gear. I have improved. I will not be a world-class competitor, but I am much faster. I am improving each month significantly. I am thrilled with my achievements. Ghale and Rana think I can be faster still.

Along with all my Family duties, training, and other responsibilities, I also spend the time honing the MKVI with Tom. I settle on the Interceptor as the model I plan to take to Senkaku. It mirrors my capabilities as a pilot nicely.

I have taken the MKVI chassis out on a dozen runs. I am going with a semi-auto SkipJack shotgun on the left arm. The SkipJacks require much more to put down, and their shotguns are four-gauge, use hulled ammo, and sport a four-and-a-half-inch long polymer carbon case. Each hull holds four poly-coated, twenty-eight-gram tungsten cored lead balls, with a total payload of 113 grams per cartridge.

The MKVI's shotgun is pushing each of those balls at 655 MPS. Even in heavy chicken-walking assault SkipJacks, you feel that round go off. The MKVI will be carrying seven rounds in each of its magazines, with twelve mags on the thigh and chest, for a total of eighty-four rounds.

In the right arm, I have the venerable 20mm and its ten-round mag, with a total of fifteen mags stuffed in the remaining pouches. The final weapon is a type of hatchet, stowed for emergency use. It has a seven-inch blade on one side and a hammerhead on the other. I am not sure how trials will go with this as a backup weapon. As a rule, SkipJacks are meant to carry firing weapons, not those for thrusting or chopping.

For the MKVI's armor, I go lighter. Rana's baton has made a lasting impression on me. Speed is king, where I am going. I need to adjust, be faster, and I tell myself that, repeatedly. So I have chosen thin, durable poly-composite armor, suitable for human-held weapons. I have yet to face a SkipJack, and I am pretty sure if I see them first, I can win. I am not as confident with animals. Speed is the rule. Shoot, move, repeat, keep moving.

The most significant change is the modularity that Tom works into the design. We designed this Interceptor model for running down SkipJacks. This model can change into a Commander's SkipJack in under two hours. For that matter, so can any of the seven variants that Tom and I have designated.

The seven designs are: Soldier, Communications, Squad Heavy Machine Gun (HMG), Command, Air Denial, Infiltrator, and Interceptor. Tom's solution is not a groundbreaking, new technology. They are scaled-up versions of what has worked in the past for people. Latches that lock the weapons down onto railed tab systems. Modular slots to hold sections of rails. The armor is a buckle-type system that allows you to apply all-new pieces of armor in thirty minutes.

The MKVI is one chassis with one power plant, seven different weights, three top cruising speeds, seven weapon load outs, each with its own pannier pack, reserve battery, ammo mags, and armor plates. Tom and I now have seven MKVIs to work on. Five are always in the standard configurations. The last two of my seven initial MKVI chassis are workhorses and test mules for weapons load outs, armor types, and so on.

I showed Samuel the new MKVI, and he was in awe at the speed and ease of its use. He must have quietly informed General Diomedes to come and inspect the work. I am quite happy to see General Jermaine Diomedes walking through my shed, past all of my GSG staff. Diomedes's three aides walk alongside him. I hold up my hand to Tom, as I realize who is here. Off to the side, Thap calls an early lunch for the GSG group and sends them down to the commissary.

I step forward and meet Jermaine. "General." A flash of white graces his face as he puts his hand out to shake mine. He then wraps me in a trademark hug and pats me on the back.

"Ray, you've put on some serious muscle," General Diomedes says. "It's good to see you. I decided to stop by and see if you've made any progress on our project. I have a little time before heading to a hearing in front of a House of Lords committee."

Jermaine's assertion does not fool me, as Samuel had been here two days ago. Samuel, you little sneak.

I have a genuinely bright smile on as I say, "That we do. Let me introduce you to my primary SkipJack designer, Tom. His compatriots, who do the programming, just left for an early lunch."

I watch Jermaine eyeing the seven MKVIs behind me. I turn out of his way and walk over to them. I repeat the names out loud for him: "Soldier MKVI Variant A; Communications MKVI Variant B; Squad HMG MKVI Variant C; Command MKVI Variant D; Air Denial MKVI Variant E; and the last two are our two test mules. They will be the Infiltrator MKVI Variant F and the Interceptor MKVI Variant G."

I go over to our armor test mule. "Tom, please bring ultra-light poly, light, and heavy SkipJack armors over."

We have them all on one cart. I grab the chest piece while Tom pulls the shoulder pieces off the sled.

"The CM needs modularity, so we are giving it to them. The MKVI is one chassis with seven roles. Any chassis can fill any role in under two hours," I explain as Tom and I start buckling the Ultra-Light poly armor of the Interceptor model onto the test mule. Then we take that off and replace it with the light and heavy plates.

Jermaine stares. He walks over and picks up all the armor plates one by one. Traditionally, they are welded on, and it takes hours to replace just one piece. He turns one over to see a snap-hinge that clamps to a corresponding snap-hinge on the chassis. He walks up to our mule, pops the clamps, removes the old one, and with a little fiddling, snaps on the new one. Jermaine then redoes the six clamps to hold it firmly in place.

"We have always wanted something like this. How did you pull it off?" Germaine asks Tom.

"Well, I, uh..." Tom stammers. "They're not people. That's the short of it.

381

The SkipJacks are not people," Tom says.

Tom can quickly become flustered. I find it best to slow-roll Tom. When I go slow and deliberate with my explanations, Tom does well. Seeing the top special forces general here inspecting his work has Tom just shy of fanboy glee.

Even Tom understands the General's patient stare. "Every other attempt has treated the SkipJacks like humans, with human organs. They waste space, and weight, protecting parts where humans have organs, limiting how armor is attached to the same way humans have armor attached," Tom splutters out quickly.

Tom is not a person to ask to give a speech. He is, however, a good man who works hard and enjoys his work. I will go further and say that Tom is a savant when it comes to SkipJacks.

"I, uh...well, I decided to protect the central processing spine, power supply, ocular systems, and finally, joints. I found ways of making and building clamps onto the main chassis. From there...well, it is a layering effect of armor," Tom says.

I gesture to the weapons test mule, and with a smile, I pull Tom back from a lecture on his many attempts. "Please show General Diomedes the weapons mule."

Jermaine whips his head around, pausing in attaching a shoulder pauldron. "You have a *weapons* mule, also? The armor is revolutionary, Ray, you..."

He stops midsentence as Tom hoists a cleared 25mm to the arm of the mule. Jermaine goes silent as it clicks, latches, then locks down with buckles.

"Modular mounts?" The general almost gasps in surprise.

He moves so quickly to the MKVI weapons mule that Tom starts, as if scared. Even at his age, Diomedes is a formidable warrior and an even more deadly remote pilot. Tom hands him another gun mount, this time a 20mm, and Jermaine promptly mounts it to the underside of the same arm.

With a hoot and a whistle, the Lion of the Compact slaps Tom on the back. "Boy, are you married? I have a great-granddaughter about your age."

Tom's round puffy face goes deep purple.

Jermaine turns to me. "Do they work?" he asks.

"Programing is being done. The Interceptor is the only one we can function-test." I bring up my FEED, make some changes and say, "Tom, pull an ammo load-out for the Interceptor for General Diomedes and meet us down at the range."

Turning back to Jermaine, I hand him my goggles and say, "There is a pod over there, or you can go reserve and follow me down to the range."

My goggles are snatched out of my hand before I finish my sentence. Tom and I have the weapons mule configured to the Interceptor in a matter of minutes. I can see Jermaine starting the boot-up, and I start walking down to the range, gesturing for Jermaine's aides to follow me to the shed.

Thap meets me outside the barracks with an impromptu lunch under a pavilion. He had put the commissary staff to work as soon as the general's tram landed. Diomedes is fast—not as fast as Samuel or myself, but quicker than any of his green recruits. When he finishes giving the MKVI a rundown, Jermaine pilots the MKVI into the range docking station and hands me back the goggles. His haptic suit uniform is showing sweat and dirt from his piloting. With a handover, I stow my goggles.

"Susan and Daivi are the primary programmers," I say, introducing the rest of the team.

Jermaine sits at the table, grabs a free plate, and starts to load up his tray as any soldier will do. If food is in front of him, he will eat, because he does not know when he will eat next. His aides take his lead and sit quietly at another table, munching on their plates of food.

"Ray, this...this is a game-changer. These will likely be improved, but it solidifies everything we have asked for in an MKVI. I have seen the other trial MKVIs and none has anything like this. No other nations can be onsite for double the reserve time of our MKVs. GSG has incorporated a pack, battery, ammo... Ray, no one else does this." He keeps at his sandwich until finished, and then he continues, "When will you be ready to test the other four?"

I turn to Susan and Daivi, who have moved to our table. "Ladies, what is your realistic ETA on programming?"

Susan and Daivi look at each other. Daivi pipes up, "We started with the Interceptor first because it is the fastest. Programming the point its balance shifts is much more difficult on fast SkipJacks than it is on slow. We have maybe three more months of programming for the MKVI Interceptor, and that's not including final weapons HUD programming adjustments. All the variants will have the same HUD and weapons programming. It just needs to be tuned for the variant."

Susan steps in, informing General Diomedes, "I've started preliminary work on the Infiltrator. The issue there is working with its noise-canceling pack (NCP) during movement. The MKVI is a very fast SkipJack, and we're trying to slow it down enough that the NCP functions smoothly. Slowing it down will allow it to be operational in the field much longer than it's currently capable of being." She smiles and finishes, "I figure about four months for preliminary, nine total for the final iteration. Then the other five SkipJack variants are just a function change of the first two. So maybe a year for full trials of the programming."

Daivi and Tom nod in agreement. Jermaine looks at all three of them. "I can hardly believe it, Ray, a small team like this pulling it off. I'm eager to see what comes of it all." Jermaine rises from his seat at the table, his aides again following his lead. He shakes everyone's hands and works his way back up to his staff tram. I return the MKVI to the shed bay, and Tom and I finalize our changes to our problem with the shielding the ankle joints from dirt, mud, and everything in between.

***

C10 S5

I reach the point where Rana is using his baton on the SkipJack as part of the training. This is one hell of a workout. My job as a pilot during these sessions is to keep Rana from being able to hit my MKIV with a baton, so my MKIV is dodging, weaving, bobbing, and rolling all around the range.

This leads up to Rana showing me how to implement and integrate the hatchet into fighting hand-to-hand with the SkipJack. With the mass of a MKVI, the hatchet will be a devastating weapon. Other than pummeling, there has been no advancement to SkipJack hand-to-hand combat.

You usually just knock something down and stomp on it; that is normally the extent of training. We use one of the demilled units. He shows me how I can lock up joints with a hammer swing, cut myomere muscle between armor seams with the hatchet, and how I can destroy ocular sensors.

Finally, Rana shows me how to put it entirely out of commission by sticking the hatchet in the haptic input connections to the power cell at the back, above the hips. Tom is not thrilled to receive the demilled SkipJacks back in pieces.

Ghale is now just as bad as Rana. Everyday, I am running his courses with my SkipJacks while doing his courses of fire. I have a SkipJack component and a Ray component. When my revised pilot armor comes in, I groan. It is lighter, but it is also thicker by half. It is not the same level of armor I am used to donning in my kit. I am bumping into things and my body has not quite become used to its girth.

It rubs my skin in a hundred different spots, so if I am not tripping over myself, I am rubbed raw in very uncomfortable places. The basic idea is to get me out of things that contain metal as much as possible. This new armor lightens my load and speeds me up, but the individual pieces are thicker. Because of that, the gaps at the joints are more significant to accommodate movement.

Michael Knaggs takes to calling me the "Polymer Knight." I work at it, day in and day out. Three weeks later, a second revised set of armor arrives. This armor is a bit thinner. I worry about the even less protection, less weight. I will live with it, though. I can move much more comfortably and much faster than I can even with my old traditional military chest rigs and their heavy plates.

The prep for the Gate at Ishigaki Island is starting. We have our agreement. As the weeks and months tick down, I make an appointment with Doc for another round of metal bars to take with me. Right now, I am going through the bars at about forty-five days.

"Ray, things are going well, and all your tests on blood, liver, and stool functions seem fine. No excess heavy metal content. You seem to be stabilizing in the normal from being slightly low in many minerals," Peter says as he pours me a drink. "We'll get your boosters up to date. I'm sending you several antibiotics. Cuts and abrasions can easily become infected in the southeast seas."

"Thanks, Doc. Do we know what is going on? I have my guesses, but find them hard to believe." I have been avoiding this topic for a while.

"My guess is your body is pulling the minerals from the alloys to use in your myomere bones and myomere muscle groups. Since wearing these, your intake of human food has dropped down to only Olympic athlete levels," Peter says with a wave of his hand. He does not mention it in his Doctor's voice, though, and I am a bit taken aback. "This is pretty much theory, at this point. After you return, I will know for sure."

I roll that over in my mind. "I have had my suspicions, and this is pretty much what I had come up with," I sigh. Tilting back in my chair and with a wry smile, I mutter, "Raylan, the living cyborg."

"Nah, you are as much human as anyone else," Dr. Alvarez smiles. "When do you leave?"

I bring my chair back to the floor. "This coming week. The estimate is about two weeks of ratio slip, and 120 days, give or take, on the Island. This trip, I am taking an inflatable boat for the ocean spiking and fishing gear. I need a break and plan about four or five days of fishing. Six months under Rana and Ghale, and I am ready for a respite and some solitude."

I sit down the next day with the team to go over the approved plan for the Ishigaki:D2 Gate. Knaggs and his team take the time to outline the program for me. Michael looks up from staring at the stack of papers on the table.

"We think the best place for the dock is the same place it currently is in EP1. We agree with Japan: build a mirrored Ishigaki city in D2. Ishigaki Gate is the first Gate we're going into with a solid plan to get to Stage Three from the get-go, once the survey is done, and you've had your island 'vacay,'" he says, with an eyeroll and air quotes on the word "vacay." The whole team has been ribbing me for going fishing. "We'll roll in five sets of the new Mini Mag-Lev Rollers (MMLR), and two more data trunk lines. We'll be running five sets of crews," Michael says, as he turns over the soapbox to Mr. Rothman.

"The biggest issue will be building the breakwater, harbor, and docks," Mordecai explains. "That will be the job of crew team one. Crew team two will be building the facilities to assemble the boats. The Japanese fishermen have a slightly different boat design than the NEFC uses. This crew will be their own SkipJack pilots. The third team crew will build the infrastructure, power, water, sewer, and MMLR roads."

Today is my first time listening to Mr. Rothman. We have chatted a couple of times briefly via FEED message.

"There's a spot they want to build a desalinization plant from the start, so that will be their priority. The fourth crew group will be building the structures for the fish hatcheries. The hatcheries will spawn the fish there, raise them to smolt size and then transport them through to EP1, from there to the nets near the Senkaku Islands. Finally, the fifth crew will be working on the actual structures," Mr. Rothman explains. He is a verbose man who does not like being interrupted, so we all let him speak.

Susan takes over for the rest. "Jack's been working with the Japanese on the desalinization plant. Daivi, Tom, and I have worked hard on getting the new MMLR 4/5 out. They will contain forty SkipJacks for construction, one per construction group. The second MMLR 4/5 will carry the other needed equipment, like the parts for the 3D printers.

"The main group of 3D printer machines will roll in after you clear out, boss. Japan's making this Gate a full fifty meters wide and twenty-five meters high. They're going all out. We can shove almost complete boats through. They'll need minimal assembly once inside D2.

"Daivi has updated the software on all the MMLRs and Llamas. I recoded the military spikes. Tom and I redesigned them for anchored use in water. You only need to worry about the bay. For the first couple of months in the area, Japan will be putting these buoys in," Susan says.

She takes a breath and then adds, "Our construction equipment is our own. However, the Japanese have contracted with us for the design of their equipment to be used there. We're sending you in with the first trials of this equipment. You're using our Llamas and MMLRs, to start. The best one of those is an MMLR temporary base camp, with built-in accommodations like stove, refrigerator, shower, bathroom, and sonic washer for laundry."

There is a little clap from the side, and I turn to see Tom grinning wildly. He is super excited about this new MMLR. He has never really cottoned to the idea of me living in the wild. We go back and forth over the plan that afternoon. It is an exciting conversation and well thought-out plan.

The first part of my trip will likely take a bit longer. The second part will be far shorter. Pull the MMLRs through. The bulk of the mesh spikes will follow me through the Gate. Hopefully, there will be enough of them once the ratio slip starts. The build teams can take it from there. They will be starting the day after I exit the D2 iteration back into EP1.

Over the next few days, I finish up our tests on the Llama and do some final outfitting on the two MKIV SkipJacks. I pack my gear and load my SkipJacks into an HLT. I pack all the panniers, double-check my gear, then triple-check. One thing left before Eliese and I head to Ishigaki Island to meet the Japanese contingent is the Family's Holiday Party. I missed the one last year while in D2. I have made arrangements not to miss this one.

***

C10 S6

I am out of the shower, trying once again to fix this silly tie. I am standing there, yanking the tie around my neck for the 300th time, when Eliese's perfume hits me. Her hand covers mine and she effortlessly glides to stand in front of me.

"Here, let me," she says, and her tiny admonishment holds me in place. As she ties, she smiles. "I think tonight is a good night to make a public announcement about our wedding. Don't you?" she asks. That last bit is said just as she tugs the tie tight. I cough a bit as she laughs.

"Anything special? Do I need to give a speech?" I ask, somewhat bemusedly. "I mean, it is a first for me."

"Dinner, barring any unpleasantness, and we can have a toast then. Yes, a speech will do nice. Short, though. You can ramble, Raylan," Eliese says, as her lips brush mine. "I am telling you now because I know you would have obsessed over it if I had mentioned it earlier." She smiles sweetly at me.

The kiss, though, sends me up onto my toes. I could not have chosen a better Morrigan. She has styled her black hair up beautifully to frame those lovely dark brown eyes. An elegant new silver dress. A beautiful necklace of thumbnail-sized opals and matching earrings. As we finish getting ready, she applies the lipstick I notice is missing from my face.

"When are you thinking? Winter, spring, summer? Or maybe tonight I can have Thap become a minister before dinner is over." I receive a snort and a peal of laughter I have not heard in quite awhile. "Tonight, then," I say and start pulling up my FEED and messaging Thap. The look that teases onto her face is fantastic, almost an equal mix of sheer horror and absolute delight.

As my beloved turns to talk to me about this, I kiss her and assume my fair share of the lipstick. I then dance her out of the bathroom. She is in a fit of giggles. After a moderate amount of protest, I put her down. I step back and wait while she fixes her mascara from laughing so hard.

We board the tram and make our way to the Family residence. We exit ours just as Trish exits hers, sans Jason. We meet before the steps to the entrance and she slips her arm through my left one. The three of us start to walk in. As we reach the top of the entry steps, Trish lets go of my arm and air-kisses me on the cheeks. She then does the same to Eliese, saying in a whisper only we can hear, "Congratulations, Eliese, on the engagement."

As Trish goes in first, I give Eliese a look of bewilderment. Sotto voce, Eliese says, "We talk, Raylan. Since I poached you, it's only right she be the official first person I tell." She smiles at the door attendants as we walk through. "That's why there's no arm candy, as you like to put it. She's running interference, so to speak. Soaking up the attention of the vultures until the announcement."

I smile and shake hands with guests as we enter the main ballroom. We speak with members of Darien's pair of teams, or Stewart's, or Samuel's. I am even able to meet Eliese's primary team, finally. They are an odd lot, all spread out over eight or nine nations. I learn that is so Eliese can have her hands in the Family's local affairs directly. Her team works together as one, but has teams of their own for local and regional issues. To say that Eliese is a far thinker is an understatement. The only one close to that is Darien, who has an NAC and Japan team, usually working on two different sets of goals.

Eliese introduces me to several Community Council members from the Districts where I have completed surveys. My team's efforts have made considerable strides to bringing those Gates to Stage Three. The exports from those D2 iterations are starting to pick up significantly, and the local economies are enjoying the benefits. I run into my friend, Craig Standing Elk, among the Montana West group.

"Craig, how is the family?" I say as we shake hands and spin to continue to people watch. "I want to thank you for the help with the furniture. Eliese was moved to tears."

"The family is well, and my daughter is getting married next summer—to a man from the Crow nation. It will be a big event," Craig says. I look at him and grin.

"Congratulations, I wish them the best," I say. "Are they planning on heading to CBN:D2?" I ask carefully. I am unsure how I would feel if a daughter Gate walks with a new husband.

"No, not with CBN:D2," Craig says. He pauses, mouth agape while staring at me "Ray, you got a second? Is there someplace we can talk?" he asks quietly.

I turn back to him, nod, and we head to my flat with Thap in tow. When we enter, Craig quietly stands, surveying the flat.

I say, "This is my flat here at the Family residence. It is a far cry from the cabin I grew up in, way up near Cold Foot." I gesture to the table, and we sit.

I can tell Craig is working up to something. I ramble, explaining to him the first time I had walked into this room. Thap enters shortly after that with a pot of coffee, cream, and sugar. The act of me making us each a cup seems to give Craig time. He looks askance at Thap when he sits at the table for a brief second, then goes off my lead of not caring.

Thap opens his FEED to take notes and says, in that perfect regimental English, "Ready when you are."

I know it is complete bullocks, as Thap would say. He only does it when he wants to play up the butler or Segundo role. Craig looks up, grabs the bone china cup emblazoned with the Family Crest and clutches it for warmth. That tiny thin cup sinks into the palms of his two hands.

After a sip, Craig begins, "We are the first nation, the *first* First Nation, to make a D2. It took all we had, about thirty years of collective funding. We had to pull in colonists from many other Tribal nations, and we had to accept people into the tribe who were not part of the blackfoot nation."

Craig looks at me, not with any harshness. He is letting me know the cost of diluting their nation.

"We were made fun of for those thirty years. We were the butt of all the Indian jokes," Craig says, and takes another sip. "When we had the money..." His eyes go wide at the second sip. "Boy howdy, this is good coffee." He and I both smile at the non sequitur. "When we had the money the Compact wanted when we first made our contract, we went to the NAC and asked them to build us the agreed-upon Gate. They said the price had changed, that it was thrice the price given to us back when we started."

I know this part, and it is a big reason why I chose this Gate as GSG's first survey. We have a Gate in the area that is traditionally their lands. Not only is it located in their traditional lands here in EP1, but the D2 iteration opens inside those same historic lands, so it worked.

Craig continues, "When we contracted with the NAC, they stated that our price was firm and inviolate till we had built the gate." I can see the pain in his eyes, as once more, the government had lied to the tribe. "We knew the Family had a Gate nearby, and we knew the Family's Gate costs were higher than our agreement with the Compact." He finishes the first cup as he starts again, "You know the bargain you struck with us. The help the Family has given. You are the First Nation man in the Family."

I fill his cup again as Craig says, "What you may not know is the stories of the First Nation man who walked our Gate and surveyed it for his people, only to leave to live his own life. The gift he gave to a belittled people." He sips. "We count a couple of hundred people from three dozen tribal nations as part of the CBN. They've been telling this story since you walked back out of the Gate, Ray."

Craig pauses, looking at me, and maybe he is waiting for me to deny it. I do not.

"My brother Daniel was in Newfoundland until he walked the Gate. He rarely dealt with our people after his indenture, as he was a voice for our people back east. He caught a tram to the DMZ and walked the Gate the same day. The only way someone would mistake him for me is if they saw him on the other side," Craig says with a smile.

"He would not answer questions about the man who had surveyed the CBN:D2, even though he was the man's main contact, from what I understand. It's for that reason that I knew you walked that Gate. He is protecting his word and would only do so for a gift like the one you gave," Craig says, and his head bows for a moment.

After a few moments, Craig leans back, holding his cup, stretching out his large frame. He is more at ease now, as he knows he is on the right track.

"That tale of the lone Gate surveyor has gone throughout the aboriginal peoples of the world, Ray. Around the whole world," Craig says. He breathes deeply. "It has played well in the many North American Compact Tribal Nations. The Crow Tribal Nation...they want their Gate and Nation. They have more than we did at the start, but are starting much later. They're looking for a Gate, any Gate that can get them to their own CCN: D2. I'm worried they will make a bad deal." Craig pauses, frowning.

"That isn't why I'm here, Ray, why we're talking. This boy my daughter is marrying is planning on being that surveyor. They have it in their heads to do it together. To be the start of the CCN:D2," Craig explains. He has a tremor in his voice as he sits forward. "She's my only child. Ray. They need guidance. They aren't like you and me, kids born in the trees and woods. They both grew up in the cities. Nevertheless, the tribe has given them leave once they find a Gate to contract into."

I sit up. I look to Thap, and he says, "I will go to the next room and speak to Carmen. The barracks will house them. Not comfortably for newlyweds, but it will do." Thap goes into the office space and begins FEED messaging Carmen in the ballroom. Within minutes, an attendant has brought her to the room.

I introduce Carmen to Craig. We get down to sending out applications for becoming part of the GSG. "We are going to send these to Leticia and Jackson, Craig. I will give them guidance and training as much as I can. They will both need to be SkipJack pilots. There is going to be an indenture for that. I will not let them leave untrained or unskilled. It will be a minimum of five years." I pause as I think. I am definitely freewheeling with this idea.

"I will talk, and that is all I can promise, to the Family about opening a Gate near the Crow tribal lands. Right now, we have 240ish Gates made. Of those, only about fifty are up and running with a lock on a habitable D2 iteration, and of that fifty, only four have been surveyed," I say with caution.

"I cannot put the Family's financial needs behind the desire to help people to an extreme. It may help if Crow Tribal Nation will partner up with a few other entities. It can even lessen the cost for each group. Yes, they would share a Gate. They would also get into a Gate faster."

I do my best to lay out the realities for him, bleak as they currently are. I watch the relief hit Craig like a ton of bricks. He visibly slumps as his tension releases.

I say, "You know, if this works out...maybe, maybe," I mumble, tapping my fingers on the gaming table.

Carmen takes a swing at my thought process and hits it out of the park. "A school for surveyors? Fit them with sub-dermals, a five-year indenture, a five-year training program? Have the indenture pay off by completing a survey of a Gate."

I can tell Carmen is not comfortable letting slip I can walk Gates with impunity. Neither knows that the other knows, and that is fine with me. Carmen and Craig wrap up a few details as we walk back to the ballroom. I have received a FEED ping from Eliese, but I am not worried. She likely saw me head out with Craig.

I meet back up with Eliese in the ballroom just as she is finishing up a conversation with a couple of gentlemen. One is a vulture. Ah, non-believers in the rumors we are engaged. I give Eliese a peck on the cheek as she leans over for one. I then beg forgiveness from the vultures, and we head over to Darien's Japanese delegation. I see Trish off to the side, pulling in her vultures. She uses humor, laughter, and just enough flirtation to keep almost all of them interested.

Eliese and I introduce ourselves to the Mega-Corp men and bow. She talks about the upcoming Gate survey and how GSG has built it to their specifications, using our tech. They seemed to be happy with the results. From the smiles, they are enjoying themselves.

One young man cannot take his eyes off Trish. He looks at her sidelong, occasionally staring, sometimes with peeks through the crowd. It is time for a little payback. Trish has helped me and has worked with me on Eliese's present.

As Eliese entertains the corporate types, I step over and secure an arm candy for Trish. I have no clue who he is, but next to Trish is the right place for him to be. Trish will take care of everything else. The pair stand next to each other, and they chatter back and forth. It really throws Darien's mongrels and vultures into a tizzy, now that both eligible daughters are occupied for tonight's festivities. I almost feel sorry for the poor young lads, since they spurned a number of eligible ladies here, all in the hopes to have a chance at Trish or her elder sister Eliese.

Dinner is about to be served. Our seating has changed slightly. Stewart, of course, is at the head of the table, Eliese to the right, and Darien across from her. I, however, sit at her right hand. Samuel is across from me, then Trish and her arm candy, then Peter, Franc and the beginnings of Darien's guests. We sit, and Stewart makes the toast for the evening. I am sure it is a fine toast about something. I am a bit preoccupied, realizing I have not worked on my speech yet. Stewart sits and looks at Eliese and me.

I swallow hard, a lump of ice building in my stomach. I half-rise before I copy his glass-tapping as I stand up the rest of the way. I clear my throat twice. Only before a lopsided fight have I ever felt this much trepidation.

"Friends, family, guests. If I can have a moment," I say with a small pause. I look around to see that I have the room's attention. "I would like to announce that Eliese and I intend to wed this coming summer. I cannot have imagined a more able and capable partner for my life. Eliese constantly challenges me to be the best I can be. I have a confidant, a friend, and soon a lover in my future bride. We are excited to start this new chapter in our lives together. We are happy to share this moment with all of you. Thank you." My pronouncement of our intentions is not the best, but in my defense, I only had about an hour and a half of warning. I lean over and give Eliese a small kiss.

I was about to sit when I realize my siren has yet to sing her song. Eliese's brown eyes sparkle as she stands next to me.

"I met Ray at this very dinner two years ago. It took a great deal of work to poach him from Trish, but I have won," Eliese says with a light laugh. Her voice is a triumphant ballad as she continues, "In this battlefield, I am victorious. He brings me the most effortless joy. Together we talk and dance the nights away. I am looking forward to our life together as husband and wife. Thank you all for being here to share this evening with us."

El is not satisfied with a small kiss. I see her mocha-brown eyes gleam in satisfaction. Her territory has been surveyed and staked.

We sit, the rounds of toasts go on, and I start the perfunctory tip of the glass after the third. The staff serves dinner eventually, as the follow-up toasts to our nuptials are that many. The meal, as expected, is exquisite. Soups, roasts, and fish dishes combined with sides of potatoes and cabbages. It is a fantastic dinner.

I do notice that Trish seems to be enjoying herself. Also, her arm candy seems to have relaxed after the toasts. As the dinner wanes, I am amazingly thankful for what I have, and who I am about to share my life with.

After dinner, cocktails, and deserts, we dance. I have practiced over these last six months, dancing with Eliese at Hill House. We hit the floor and have a ball, pun intended. Surprisingly, Trish and her arm candy are right there with us. There are going to be some severe rumors tomorrow. Darien and Samuel are out and about on the floor somewhere, entertaining the ladies of the ball. When we finally end the evening and return home, it is very early in the morning. We sit on the futon, looking at our stars in the quiet and darkness.

"I love you, Eliese. We will change this world together." I have no idea why I am thinking that, other than the concept of a school for surveyors has been bouncing around in my mind all evening. I tell her of the conversations with Craig and Carmen. The school could allow GSG to open a significant number of Gates, without having to spend years behind a D2 iteration away from Eliese.

"I like the idea and the opportunity it unfolds for GSG as a team. It's the chance to bring many more of these Gates into functioning operations for us as a Family business. We have a couple close to the Crow tribal lands, but they're as close to other tribes, also," Eliese says while leaning her head on my shoulder, a blanket covering her.

"I'm scared for this Gate walk, Raylan. I'm worried like I've never been before. I don't want to lose you, Raylan. Please come back." I hear the fear and apprehension pick up in her voice as I look out over the deck and the light of a new day starts to peek over the valley below. I am drowsy, and I know she is tired.

I hear her voice trail off as my eyes close. Two more days and we tram to Ishigaki.

We make the trip to Ishigaki via multiple heavy lift trams (HLT). It takes us a few hops across the Pacific. When we land, it is the dark of night. We move to our lodgings and take a much-needed day of rest. Tram flights are uncomfortable, even more so over long distances. Tram flights, while also carrying tons of gear, hopscotching up and down across the Pacific, is exhausting.

We need to force our biological clocks to the current timezone. That means a decent meal and an early night. I do have a Gate walk in the morning. We spend dinner together before retiring. Eliese is worried, and I chalk up her unease to our recent public engagement statement. Eliese closes the door to her suite after saying goodnight. I make my way down a dozen steps to my door. Thap opens it from the inside.

I am doing my best to focus on my job and last-minute meetings with my staff and the Japanese clients. My time in D2 will be ninety to 120-plus days with a slip ratio. For the GSG team here in EP1, it will be about eight to sixteen days.

I have fewer overall mesh spikes to install. Thankfully, it is no longer necessary for me to spike every property outline. That process is dealt with by the pilots of the 3D printers, using the preloaded map overlay that each spike has.

Spiking the balloons is going to be essential, as the possibility of a tropical storm or a tsunami necessitates having them up as soon as feasible. Finally, my inflatable and I would be dropping spike mesh buoys around what will be Ishigaki:D2 harbor and some of the surrounding seas. We have dredges and 3D printers coming in to make the breakwall for the harbor. All in all, less work for each project part. I just have a half-dozen additional projects, so in total, just as much time.

The possibilities of tomorrow weigh on me. This is the first real test of GSG, the culmination of months' worth of work for my teams. It is the largest Stage One to Stage Three buildup plan GSG has devised, to date. On top of all that, we are doing it with another country, where there are language barriers, social barriers, and even barriers between our gear and tooling.

I worry and wonder if we got it all worked out in the planning phase. Do we have a plan in place for those things we did not? I am still a little stiff and sore from tramming in yesterday when I finally wake. I shower, shave, and pack my toiletries. I find Eliese waiting for me on the veranda of my bungalow. She is wearing a light linen dress, something to hold off the humidity as she rises to greet me.

Eliese's voice sings a lament for the first time since we met as she says, her voice almost a whisper, "Return to me. Come back whole. You'll beat this, Raylan. Don't give up."

I look at her, and I am puzzled as to why she is nearly at the point of tears while leaning on my shoulder. I can smell her perfume, and feel her shudders as she holds back the sobs.

I am still confused as I do my best to be jovial and joke, "With you here, Eliese, I will rip the Gate open to come back."

As she sniffles, it dawns on me why she worries. Today is the first stage in a plan to take on the depraved pilot of the animal SkipJacks. Only a fool would not see it as such, and I am one such fool. I have been so busy planning this Gate that I have not thought of it that way at all. To me, it is another Gate, another survey. There are too many new wheels and parts my team have put together in their first Gate. My concerns have revolved around the many more steps I am scheduled to do, those numerous new projects. I have not effectively connected the dots of this Gate: opening the eventual travel to Senkaku Island and the lab.

"I will come back. I have no doubts, none. I will be back here soon," I say, the conviction in my voice as hard as my muscle and bones.

I wait while she finishes dealing with her now-puffy and reddened eyes in her room. She comes back outside in a short while, sporting large, opaque sunglasses and a smile. A bright blue straw hat with a cream satin band and bow covers her head. She has a matching loose linen summer dress fitted with a full cream band with satin bow at the waist. For this alone would I tear a Gate open to come home. Eliese is my vision of perfection.

I am now in my complete surveying kit. While the armor plates are new, the rest of it has been through six months of Ghale and Rana. It is faded, worn, and in some places, torn. It fits, and as uncomfortable as the new poly armor is, I need it. I have the latest battle rattle layered poly armor, all free from scuffs and marring. I plan to use this armor daily for over ninety days, to live in it. The armor and myself need a real shakedown together. I pray that it will help me unlearn the old military armor sets.

Unfortunately, the guns stay at home. Japan's strict laws will not allow me much here. I have one small 22-caliber pre-charged pneumatic (PCP) air rifle for birds and small game. I am looking forward to fishing to supplement my diet. I take with me a good number of fishing rods, reels, lines, hard and soft baits. Because of the lack of large animals on the island, Doc has beefed up my fresh food portion. There will be a large amount of fresh and frozen foods in one of the sections of the MMLR that will go through with me.

Eliese steps up to me, tilting her forehead to mine. With a whisper and an aria, she says, "I love you, Raylan. Don't forget that. Ever."

Her lips nibble mine as her arms wrap around me over my shoulders. It is a slow, deliberate kiss, the kind of kiss that keeps your soul burning for decades. With a final sigh, she lets go of the embrace and pats my cheek.

"I've got work to do, Raylan. Be safe, love," she says, turning and making her way over to the control terminal for Japan's Mag-lev rail system.

I gather all my SkipJacks to heel: two MKIVs, ten Llamas, and a couple of the new MMLRs for the Llamas to tow. One contains an intricate base camp set up for me. The other includes my staples, clothing, food, inflatable, medical, and small power supply.

A drone launches to confirm, for the twentieth time, that I will not be Gating into the middle of the Pacific ocean. The first two iterations we linked to via this Gate were about five meters above the open sea. Not all D2 iterations have the exact same landmass. I am sure that is something to boggle the minds of Gate folks on EP1. I Gate walk. As soon as we get a go-ahead, multiple data trunks are pushed through the Gate.

Chapter 11 Rage in Senkaku

C11 S1

I step from early morning sunshine and sweltering humidity into cloudy skies and buckets of rain falling right down on top of me. It takes me a second to orient myself. The growth here in this D2 iteration is far too thick for me to keep plodding through with my MMLR's. The Llamas can tow them, but not through thick vegetation like this. I pop out a drone and start sending it up and around in this rain. In an area 200 meters away, there is dense vegetation but fewer trees. Past that, I will be into thick and heavily wooded areas.

This is not something I had expected. Sure, I had an idea from the drone flights. You always seem to forget how much traipsing around in the jungle sucks until you are back in the jungle. I put my drone up for now. I start up the SkipJacks in a daisy-chain.

I begin to walk in circles, hours of trudging on, around in ever widening circles, with my troupe of SkipJacks and MMLRs. I am slowly able to flatten an area out to set up camp. As near as I can tell, I am where I expect to be: somewhere east of Miyara Bay EP1 and north of the town of Ishigaki EP1.

After a couple of hours, I have ample enough space to pull everything into a wagon circle. I string a couple of tarps up behind the MMLRs over to a couple of Llamas as a rain fly lean-to. It does little to stop the seepage of wetness. Within minutes, the water is drifting through the rain fly down to the ground.

The torrential rain does not let up that day. I eat a smaller soggy, warmed MRE for dinner. Thankfully, the wind never really picks up that night. A couple of hours after sun-up, the rain lets off, and I can put the drone up again and look for a place to put my base camp. The sheer amount of ground I need to cover is something the GSG team considered.

The demarcation zone is five kilometers from where the 3D printers for the breakwater will need to be built. If I turn the opposite direction, it is over three kilometers from where Japan wants its power plant to go and even further for where I am supposed to stake the water desalinization plant.

The central demarcation zone is here. I do not want my base camp here, or really, in any line of either of those three spots. Even though it will mean a walk for me every morning for the first few weeks, I feel that I need a better place for my base camp.

I find a beautiful area south of Banna Park EP1. It is four kilometers due east, not a long trudge for me and the SkipJacks, but puts me out of the way of the first two primary construction pathways. Before I leave, I put a FEED message through the data trunk, letting folks know where I will have my base camp.

While it is not a long hike, it is a full day trudging. I pull up a HUD on my goggles and stake out the first zone for the demarcation point. Later in the day, I also drop two mesh spikes on the direct line from the power plant to what will become the port. My bivouac area is still a mess. It takes hours of trampling the vegetation down.

Finally, I am able to kick open my MMLR and start putting the camp together. I do not finish until well after dark. Though this type of base camp does allow me to move it, I am reticent to see the functionality over a tent. Maybe if you were on a much longer trek having the Llamas or Donners pull, this would make sense. Right now, I am just glad to have a place to set it up and get out of mosquitoes for a few minutes to get dry.

The MMLR's mini shelter is much like my hard-sided shelter from the last few Gates, except it is far more extensive than that four point four square meter tent. The MMLR shelter is more along the lines of a thirteen square meter trailer that pops out to make a thirty square meter shelter. There are hard sides to put on once it is extended, for insulation and wind resistance. The hard sides allow you to use the roof as a solar panel, along with a pair of staked, long-range balloon chargers. There is a spot to fill up a reasonably large bladder tank for water, and that is currently empty. The interior has a place for a folded futon mattress, a full shower, a small kitchen area, a sonic washer for clothing, and a composting bathroom.

Now that I see it set up in a D2, I realize that I am going to be living in style while I am here. After I connect the power unit, siding, and the balloon chargers are in the air, it is well into the night. I go in and strip out of my sopping wet clothes and hang them to dry in the shower. I make some food as the shelter cools down and the interior humidity decreases to something approaching livable. I understand the reasons why this was well worth towing into a D2 iteration.

I am up with the daylight. I dress in new clothes and empty two of the Llamas. I put some water bladders in their panniers, and I head off to find potable water. I have a good idea where the Isobe river should be, just west past the demarcation point. After two trips, the water tank in the base camp is full. The second MMLR contains all my pack gear and food. I start unloading a small portion of it from its storage spaces to fill the base camp refrigerator and freezer. There is a lot of refrigerated and frozen food in the second MMLR.

What is neat about this new second MMLR is the refrigeration and freezer system. They are vacuum systems. Every time I remove something from them, it pumps out the oxygen and pumps in an inert gas at a very slight vacuum. Yeah, it should not have any gas in it when in vacuum. There is always some, and pumping in inert gas keeps the food fresh much longer.

I refill the Llamas with their payload of spikes and put on my full kit of poly armor. I will do anything to keep those mosquitoes away. With a grunt, I head to the demarcation point to drop the first of the mesh spikes. This facility and build is about triple the size of any of our other previous D2 build outs. While these three-point-five-kilometer mesh spikes make for less overall spiking, the size of this DMZ makes it nearly as many.

It takes me a week of staking them into the ground to become concerned. I do not receive an update message from EP1. I check several times. The Gate has a dimensional lock; I am sure of that, as it displays that on the controls. I check the ratio slip next. "Damn, that went sideways," I say out loud to myself.

I stand back as I do the ratio slip math. I should be on a one-day EP1 time to about twelve days D2 time. If my math is correct, I am on a one-day EP1 time to a little over fifty-two days D2 time. That would put me here for anywhere between 427 and 835 days, around two years.

I drop a message confirming I have seen the ratio slip error. I will be expecting a reply to trickle in starting in the next day or so. I realize that it depends on when the ratio slip went askew. For now, though, I have a job to do. Before I can get to work, I need to mull over how to survive nearly two years in this D2.

What I cannot do is panic. I have a lot of supplies and tools at my disposal, much more than most colonists in history have ever started with. Thankfully, securing mesh spikes with a SkipJack is not difficult. It allows me a great deal of time to figure out how to stretch my food, find food, grow food, and what to do to keep me and my mind occupied.

One of the things in the forefront of my mind is, what happens after two years? What state will I be in physically? I am not worried about my mental state, although maybe I should be, but I have done the live-alone thing before. I do not want to lose the recent skills I have worked so hard to gain.

I decide to work on the skills Rana and Ghale have taught me every morning with a pair of wooden sticks. I want to keep my knives for as long as I can, and I hope using the sticks will lessen the corrosion throughout the knife steel. Thap has been working on a new knife design for me. Unfortunately, they did not make our departure date. I do not even bother pulling out the Air Rifle from its case in the MMLR.

A message from EP1 comes through the data trunk. It does so slowly; one letter every three days or so. It is a very simple note, 'Wrknnt.' GSG and Eliese understand that data transmissions are also affected. That is all I need to know. There is not anything I can do about it here in the D2, and I have my survey work to finish. I make some adjustments to my work process. I am working slower, steadier, with more deliberation. I will be here a considerably long time, so my mornings are workouts, my early afternoon focuses on Gate work, and evenings become an endeavor of figuring out how to survive.

After finishing the demarcation zone, I move down to Ishigaki Harbor. This area will become the breakwater for the colony. I pack up my Llamas with my inflatable, my tent for camping, and the camping gear. I start down to the coast. I make it about twenty-five feet before I hear the lock on the door of the base camp. I go back and unlock it.

Old habits die hard. The last thing I need is to return to a locked base camp, as my FEED system is unable to open it. The trip to what will become the port and breakwater slowly becomes less congested with vegetation. Even with piloting the lead Llama and the rest daisy-chained, it is rough going. The plants are stout, bushy, and flex back into position easily. It is a long, hot slog.

When I hit the beach, I find a series of old stumpy shrubs and pitch camp there. I line up the Llamas as a windbreak and begin to work on unpacking gear. The inflatable, its power cell, the motor, the fishing gear, ropes, stays, and anchors all require some assembly. This ridged inflatable is reasonably good-sized. Just a tad over twenty-two feet, it has a standing central console that I have to put together with connectors and tools.

I can carry only two buoys at a time, plus my fishing gear. Thankfully, to prep I went nuts on that, tons of lines, reels, and five poles. Lures, well, let us say it takes up a whole pannier between line, lures, and baits. It takes two days to bring the boat up to full charge. While the charging system is working on the power cell, I travel up and down the coastline installing the mesh spikes.

The buoys have ninety-five meters of engineered cable and a cavitating piton that fires into the sea floor at three different directions. Once that is fired, I drop a ninety-kilo concrete weight around the line to secure it, then toss over the buoy. Once the 3D printers arrive, they will either retrieve the buoys or fully secure them in place. Other than the initial rainstorm upon entering the D2, the weather seems to be cooperating.

I spend a month spiking the mesh system for the port and breakwater. I have been in this D2 iteration for forty-six days. My daily reports are still hitting the data trunk. I am still getting the abbreviated 'working on it' messages. I think something or someone is playing havoc with the systems. I have every confidence that Eliese and GSG will get to the bottom of it.

Fishing has become an early morning and late evening pastime. I have salted and smoked a fair amount of fish in the evenings. I pack up the camp and stake the inflatable above high tide. It is time to replace Doc's metal bands and take an actual shower instead of taking a dip in the sea. I look forward to eating a real hot meal and taking an extended look at supplies and ration them as best I can.

I had three sets of bands from Doc. Each of them will cover forty-five days. As I see it, I need them now to finish the work, not later. Once I complete the work, the metal bands do not matter.

It takes a couple of days to figure out a ration plan to stretch 120 days of food for over two years. One thing I keep an eye out for is fruit of any kind, or vitamin C might become an issue. I do my best to propagate the seeds of the oranges, lemons, and limes I have as fresh fruit. I have the most success with the lemons.

I create a small area for them to grow and make sure the little seedlings are out of the wind and mud over the next few weeks. To do this, I made my big circle spiking the balloons in three-day hikes. Then it's back to base camp, filling the camper's water tank, then out for another few days of balloon spiking.

What should have taken me forty-five days is now pushing sixty, and I figure I have about twenty-five more days. The terrain of the forest and brush are slowing me down. The big thing, though, is charging up the boat between runs out to the individual Jima Islands. Almost all of them are in my fifty-kilometer radius. Thankfully, I do not have to link them with buoys, also. They are close enough to each other to make a connection with the data trunk via the mesh spikes. I am a full 130 days into this D2 iteration when I march back into base camp and spend a day to get clean.

***

C11 S2

I am now just over one-third of a year into this mission. I have not received FEED messages or anything else resembling human contact through the data trunk. I keep sending mine through, since my reports do not get kicked back. I get back to work the day after my return from submitting my Day 131 report. Yeah, I do not have to walk to the Gate to submit my reports, or to receive them. It has become a mental thing for me, a necessary reassurance that I have a connection to home. I must make that trek, submit, check, then make the trek back to base camp. Routines, projects, things to do are what will keep me sane. Cut, chop, stack.

Before heading out to spike more areas, I clear a bit larger space and start to plant a garden with all the vegetable seeds I saved from my initial food supply. Potatoes just do not grow; it is too hot. The tomatoes do, and I continue to keep their seeds as I eat them. The melon seeds I have previously saved also grow. My little lemon tree flourishes. Most everything else is not meant to grow in such a warm, humid climate.

Thankfully, by the time I finish the power plant and settlement spiking, I have a full twenty plants of tomatoes, and a dozen melon plants. I can never remember the difference between cantaloupe and honeydew. Whichever it is, I am growing the green one. I add most of these to my daily meals.

Everywhere I place a spike, I clear ground and plant a few seeds. In places I have put spikes in the soil in the past, I return, clear land, and plant more seeds. I even make return trips to Iriomote-Jima and plant stuff at a few different areas there. I fish on the way there and back. Fishing here is straightforward: simply put something in the water with hooks on it. Drag it behind the boat as I cross the sea. I will be pretty sick of fish, tomatoes, lemons, and green melons when I finish with this D2. Once I finish planting my gardens, I get back to work on staking in the docks.

I do not have to do this work; I have long since completed my portion of the survey. It comes down to having the supplies, the time, and needing something to do. Keeping oneself occupied with a task and setting small goals is key to being able to survive alone. Spike these three points on the shipyard, then fish for an hour. Spike these two sections of dock for the build crew, then return and check on the gardens. It is all about keeping your mind and body busy.

It is during this time that my first MKIV fails. I have been trading on and off between the pair of MKIVs. A short week later, my second MKIV fails. My first

Llama goes shortly after that. By day 255, I have completed all the spiking and placed all the buoys that crossed the Gate with me. It is two or three times the work GSG had planned on me doing for this D2 iteration.

It is time I get serious about survival. I start living out of the base camp. I keep the seeds of the plants I grow. I keep only fifty percent of my garden in the base camp in case of crop failure. The rest, I simply go on walkabouts with a single Llama and plant. I fish every other day. I harvest crabs and eat a lot of crab legs and claws. I have no way to test for red tide, so I avoid clams and mussels.

I keep my eyes open and cook everything thoroughly. On the anniversary of the first year, I return to the demarcation zone. I write an extended update; send FEED images of my camp, and start day 366 of my trek to two years.

I rotate planting plants for the better part of a year. I start at least ten every fourteenth day. I probably do some severe ecological damage by planting things all over the islands. I do not care. To me, this means getting home. I will do whatever I must to return to El, even if I have to rip that Gate open.

I keep fishing and smoking fish. I do well and I am pretty creative with how I cook fish. Even with my experimentation, there is a lot of roasted melon-juiced fish. Honestly, I am far better off here than I had been as a young teen at my cabin in Alaska.

I start doubling down on my time training with surrogate knife-shaped sticks. I keep working on my running and my speed. I go down to the beach at low tide and sprint, day in, day out. I survive. I continue to use my stores and stocked food rationing system. It is helpful to have that little bit of flavor everyday. It is not much, but it lifts my spirits as I continue until I can walk the Gate back to EP1.

It is day 450 when the first letter of a new message comes through. It is only a partial message. It is only two words, and they light up my life. I do not know how, but Eliese sings her song from a world away, and I hear it as clearly as if she were next to me.

'Hvepln.'

That is all I need. I triple my training and double down on being prepared. I work in my gardens, I train, I run, and I fish. I receive a similar message every fifty-three days after that. The third time, the message simply reads, "Have a plan." I keep sending my FEED reports. I lose my last Llama on day 609. I am down to only myself now.

I have to carry water from the river. I keep the pump and filter at the river. I pull a power supply from the demarcation point and leave it next to the pump and filter. The first sentence is on day 662: "Stay strong, Ray. We have a plan."

Day 710, I run out of my rationed food stores. Despite my best planning, I lose some stores to spoilage along the way. That kind of loss shows on a long-time scale like this. On day 715, I receive a FEED message coded to my biometrics, and it is from Eliese.

"The Family all on-site. Someone sabotaged the ratio slip. In hindsight, we should have expected that. I am sending this coded to only you, Raylan. We have not heard from you since the first message confirming a safe Gate walk. I know you, though. You said you would 'rip that Gate open to get back to me.'"

"Not many know you have lived longer and in harder places than this. I will see you soon. We are going to try and bring the time ratio slip back to parity on day 725. Should that fail, we have a plan for day 750. If necessary, we have back-up plans if those first two fail. We will be sending supplies through first. Expect an MMLRs. We know you need them. Don't Gate walk until we know there is a solid lock on the ratio slip parity between the two iterations. Eliese. P.S. I love you."

I have rarely spoken since arriving in this D2. My ill-used voice erupts in joy. "Eliese is one smart woman."

El sent the message coded to my biometrics. When it returns opened, Eliese will know that I am alive and have read it. I hope she is well. Hell, I hope she did not lay waste to the island sorting out this problem.

My last knife crumbles on day 719. It started as a full-length, ten-inch kitchen knife when I arrived. It dies as a three-inch chipped piece of steel that has been flaking apart for the last week.

I move to retrieve the small PCP air rifle, only to find it severely corroded. All that remains is a puddle of near-liquid powder in the bottom of the case, almost as if it had started falling apart the first time I touched it. I am thrilled with my armor, my haptic suit, my boots, everything that is not made of metal. Other than those items, I am a walking rust monster of insatiable destruction.

My next few days are okay. I have enough dried fish for about twenty days. I supplement that with what I can forage in tide pools. I have some fun using long thin sticks to fish out little creatures from nooks and crevices. I treasure the octopi when I can find them, and squid is a much-welcomed treat.

Most of my reels and fishing poles have died at some point. Even with as little metal as they have, eye loops or reels in general just do not hold up. I now use the poles without loops and only a length of line and bait attached. I swing the line out over the water and tug a bait in overhand. This process takes longer, but I am able to relax on the beach and fish.

I am doing well. I shower on the night of day 724. I wash my gear that cannot be sonic-cleaned in the sink. In a mirror of my first day in the shelter, I hang it all to dry in the shower. I do my best to clean up my little home for two years, and give the whole base camp a similar treatment.

As I wipe down my mirror in the bathroom, I realize that my facial hair needs a trim. I do not grow a beard. It has never been a beard, only a representation of a bear with mange. My razors and scissors are long since gone. I am stuck with it, I suppose.

In a moment of inspiration, I remember the safety shears in the first aid kit. After retrieving the equipment, I open it up slowly. I peel the layers of the package apart till I find the white and clear pouch with a pair of hermetically-sealed safety scissors. I cut that mange off my face as close as I can. I follow up with a bad, bad haircut. I chop it off as close as I can to the nape of the neck.

I have carried this same medical bag across two other gates. I have only opened it to check its contents. I have never opened the sealed pouches. The needles are excellent; the thread for sutures, the staples, and staple gun are fine. All things metal in this kit are pristine. I will remember this for my next talk with Dr. Alvarez when I return home.

***

C11 S3

I stride to the demarcation point on the 725th day. The front end of an MMLR pushes through the Gate around midmorning D2 iteration time. I must keep the momentum going, and I have no SkipJacks.

I have had days to give this some thought. I have lots of rope, even a snatch block that has yet to see use. I secure the snatch block to the old MLR that sits on the ground at the far side of the demarcation zone. I loop my rope through and pull both ends to the MMLR as it pops out of the Gate.

I tie a bit of boat rope to it and started yanking as hard as I can. On a Mag-lev road, an MLR will move under power; forward, turning, or even reversing its momentum. There are not any real rollers or wheels, just a rolling change of the magnetic currents in opposition to the ones below it. Without the roadway, the Mag-lev Roller will hover as long as it has power. If it stops moving, then it is a pain in the ass to get moving again.

An MMLR fully loaded requires four Llamas each to pull from a dead stop. The larger MLR MK4/5's take six Donner V3s to move. The older MLR MK2s and MK3s take four Donner V2s each. There is no chance I can get it moving again without some serious mechanical leverage advantage.

I can, however, keep it moving. With the most significant effort I can manage, I pull it through the Gate and into the demarcation zone yard. Even using the snatch block and pulley, it is very difficult to keep moving. I hold a steady pace across the demarcation zone until it hits a small embankment near an old MLR and stops, resting a bit canted and off-center.

I pull up my FEED. Sure enough, there is a message via the data trunk.

"Ray, there are supplies in the first container. The second is full of Donners so you can clear the demarcation zone."

First container? There is only one. "Container" is an odd term. It is an MMLR. Maybe it will come through soon. I make my way to the first container/MMLR and pop its seals. It is a smaller base camp trailer of a type that GSG does not use. Maybe GSG sourced it locally? It is not as large of a fold-out shelter, more storage than base camp.

After I set it up, I find it has metal bands from Doc, though I am not sure I need them. Food. I pop a couple of CM rations and some pouches of what the CM calls peach fruit and start eating. I go through and find a pannier. I open it and smile.

Inside the lid is a note. "Be careful, Raylan. Someone sabotaged the Gate. We are working on it. Don't Gate walk just yet. Thap sends you a gift: two diamond-like carbyne linear acetylenic carbon (DLCLAC) knives. Eliese."

I continue to eat, to think. Eliese is still expressing concern. I strip, put on my bands from Doc, put on my haptic suit, and layer poly armor again. Then I pull out the knives. One is an Applegate-Fairbairn-style knife, weighted at the pommel. It has a double-edge blade just a tad shorter than the length of my hand. I try to flex it, but it is like steel, and it seems stable. It is solid black in color, except for a tiny glint at the edge. It smoothly shaves the hair on the back of my hand. Superb edge.

The second blade takes me by surprise. It is made of the same material, and I know it is a gift from Thap and Rana: a Nepali soldier's Kukri. Just over one and a half lengths of my hand, and it is as dark as night. The handle is made from a solid composite with a lot of aggressive texture. The forward sloping blade also shaves the hair on the back of my hand. This is what Thap has been working on to get around the metal limitations. I like these knives: just enough mass, not too heavy for extended use.

I strap the knife to my chest rig, and the Applegate tucks in sideways under my empty mag carriers, which puts it on top of my belly pouch. It is a little bit cramped, but doable. This makes it easy for my left hand to grab. I sling the Kukri on the left side just behind the hip. I find it is easier to pull free this way with two hands, as opposed to one hand on my right side. It is a forward and out motion, versus an upward, out, and shift grip motion.

I have a place to stay, I have food, and I have enough water for now. I sit and wait. It is near sunset when the second MLR comes through. It moves into the DMZ a tad too fast. The MLR is a full-sized one, with the Family's logo.

Something ticks in the back of my head as I start towards it. I think it odd Eliese would send an MLR when the MMLR is what is contracted to fit Japanese transport specs. I do not need forty Donners to move these. The hair across the good side of my body stands on edge as all the pieces of the puzzle click into place, just as the cargo door opens.

I received two messages, the first via the FEED system, and the second hand-written by El. Someone else sent that FEED message. Eliese never calls me Ray in a message, and on top of that, Eliese always signs her messages. Whoever put this charade together does not know that. Our mystery assailant who sent the first FEED message does not know we refer to them as MLRs or MMLRs, and not containers. Someone is still playing games. I pat my knives, and I give a quick prayer of thanks that Eliese sent through the MMLR before our opposition got his plan into place.

Under scrutiny the MLR is not one of ours, and it is not a V1, V2/3, or V4/5. It is a Compact-surplus MLR made to look like GSG's color schemes. My team would never have sent it through the Gate at that speed, either. There is no way you can put forty Donners in that MLR. Our older MLRs hold eighteen humanoid SkipJacks, max.

I hear noises, grunts, growls, and howls. I know what is here, and a sense of dread hits my stomach. I watch the roll-up hatch on the MLR. My right and left arms automatically work to draw the Kukri, then the left arm grabs the Applegate.

A black ursine head pokes out, rotates and locks onto me before it drops from the MLR to the ground. It is not but a second before it charges. I notice a white sun patch on its chest as it runs towards me.

Most people do not know a North American black bear can run fifty-six kilometers an hour for an impressive few hundred yards. I hope the Asiatic black bear is slower, but as it gains speed, I realize it is not. Some humans can run as fast as forty-three kilometers an hour in a sprint. To put it another way, most horse breeds gallop between forty and fifty kilometers per hour. Bears are powerhouses of nature.

Damn, it is a fast bear. I lunge forward to meet it. I am no lightweight anymore. I am much heavier and more substantial now than when I came here two years ago. I suppose that is what two years of absorbing the metal from SkipJacks will do to you.

As we close the distance on each other, it tries to bullrush me. I drop low and shoulder-check with my right shoulder. We spin wildly off each other. I take the worse of the confrontation as its four paws give it more stability than my two feet.

I feel its right paw scrape against my armor. My Applegate flashes out, scoring a deep puncture to its left abdomen. After we pass each other, I roll back up to my feet. I reach up with the left hand, feeling the gouges on the armor. The bastard has steel augmented claws. Score one for Samuel's paranoia. I feel blood on the far-left side of my torso. I watch the bear when it shakes its head. I dive to the ground, rolling forward.

I come up with the Kukri, sweeping from lower left to upper right and missing the cougar that has stalked me from behind. Had I not noticed the bear shake its head naturally, I would be under ninety kilos of furious cat.

The Applegate scores enough of a hit to push the paw off to the side. The descending righthand Kukri follow-up blow takes off the cat's second paw swipe at the wrist. I am back on my feet spinning out of its way, trying to bring the bear and the cougar into view when I see the second of two wolves hop out of the MLR.

This just got a lot worse.

That is all the distraction the cougar needs to latch on to my trailing left leg at the calf. I stab down as my weight starts to fall. The Applegate slices deeply along the left side of its neck. The blood starts to flow freely. This cat twists and yanks its head, like it is playing tug of war. I know it is trying to keep me off balance. I can feel steel-capped teeth start to curve behind the armored shin guard and puncture the leg. My next two swings with the Kukri bring nothing for my efforts.

The bear is facing me. I notice a shadow flanking me on my left, and one wolf in front of me. I do not think my assailant can pilot more than one of these beasts. The bear and wolves are currently being natural opportunists. With a swift boot to the ribs with my right leg, I bring the cat up short.

The piloted cat shudders, and it releases its hold on my leg slightly. Its head shakes, only to find the Kukri in its skull. I twist violently. I race back towards the inside of the MMLR sent by Eliese.

The bear does not turn as fast as the closest wolf. I kick out a foot just as patchy-haired wolf lunges, and apply my heel to its nose full force. Its forward momentum stops, and it yelps as it crumples backward.

I check on the bear to see him almost upon me at full speed. The Kukri leads in a downward chop on its right shoulder, and the Applegate stabs into its neck as I let it bowl me over. I hammer that Applegate home like a power hammer forging steel. I pierce its neck a second time, its shoulder, then ribs.

The bear tries to reorient to my new position, but the pilot must have expected me to stand and face the charge as I had done previously. He overshoots me and his momentum rolls me up to my elbows and knees as the bear passes over. Being rolled like a burrito by a bear in a forced yoga pose is its own new kind of painful.

I can feel blood on my chest from the first swipe, blood leaking from my left leg, and blood on my shoulder and arm from this last pass. I cannot keep taking damage like this. I need be smarter, I need to be faster, I need to move. I startle in surprise when my right leg goes out from under me. The second wolf has grabbed my foot from behind and is in the process of yanking me down as the first wolf comes for my neck. I manage to snap-kick the wolf down on its nose.

I vowed to Eliese that I would return home. I have always been willing to fight. I have always been open to fighting. I have always carried this seed of darkness that revels in blood and gore my whole life. I grew up as a young man hunting for survival, all alone in the cruel cold of the Nunavut north. As a kid in boot camp, the drill instructors teach you how to wall away that primal desire to make you into an effective team member.

In my mind's eye, I enter that mental space where I constructed the megalithic wall to keep things about myself hidden. There is no hesitation as I start pulling those megalithic blocks down, yanking those mental barriers out of the way.

When the wolf hits me again, I tuck my chin and catch it in two thrusts. The first thrust is a sideways jab with the right hand into the ribcage, using the Kukri. The second is a forward angle cut from the base of the lower jaw towards the eyes.

As we clash together, I roll with it, dislodging the grip of the wolf on my right foot. I keep rolling with the snarling, biting, growling wolf pinned between my knives. We stop when I have put the MMLR between the bear and myself. I hammer the wolf's skull to paste with the butt of the Kukri.

I keep bringing those walls down in my mind. When I spin up and off that canine mass of mush, I can tell the pilot did not have the time to disco from that forced mutation. The wolf is twitching violently, thrashing in a final set of seizures.

I feel blood on the inside of my thigh and do a quick check. No arteries. I see the moment the pilot dumps into the second wolf, the one that prowled about the edges of the fight. This wolf has a better coat, with less patches of missing fur. I feel that it is now wary of the two-clawed beast it faces.

The pilot seems hesitant, lost, almost, in its control of the wolf. I use the time to check my surroundings until the pilot finally elicits a virile sense of control. He, as the wolf, comes at me in a rage, a pure rush, teeth barred, eyes open only a slit. While being piloted, the wolf cannot understand the law of self-preservation that every wild animal has.

I meet it with my reinforced combat boot out of instinct. The field goal kick to its head sends it ass over teakettle. I put my full-181 kilo mass into that kick. I can feel the reinforced toe of my combat boot buckle briefly as I connect. I hear the bear chuffing, and dash to my left a few steps and then spin slowly to face him.

The bear shakes its patchy furred head as the pilot leverages another dump to gain control of the beast. I watch that these animals fight the mental whammy as the pilot forces his will upon them. The more my adversary dumps into them, the harder it is for him to gain control the next time. It walks forward, not charging this time. I notice the glint of steel on its teeth and claws.

When the bear closes the distance, it stands and roars. The pilot tries to fight me on two legs. This pilot does not play to the animal's strengths. If he had stuck with the bear from the get-go, the two wolves could have finished me off. If not just them, the cougar would have. He is no real predator. He is a man playing at being a beast.

I dart in, swiping down with the Kukri on the backside of its right-paw swipe. Three more hits with the Applegate to the lower ribs, then I spin off the bear's right side. The Kukri catches in its forearm and rips from my hand. That yanks me off balance for when the bear backhand tosses me to the ground. I roll with it. I come up and see it turning towards me. Its first few steps finish breaking the right forearm where the Kukri is lodged. The Kukri falls free as the right paw goes limp.

I turned to the wolf I had kicked. It is trying to rise, but is not capable yet. I back up towards the Gate now, and I shift the Applegate to my right hand. I am moving smoothly, and I feel no significant breaks, only those few bleeding wounds. The bear gallops at me in a three-legged hop. With each meter forward, it gains speed.

I step forward, to the bear. I challenge it with a bellowing yowl when we close. There is that moment of disconnect when the primal challenge for dominance brings the bear back in control of itself.

The pilot cannot reassert his control of the bear faster than I can assert my will using the Applegate. I hammer that DLCLAC blade into the base of the skull.

"Mice to elephants, the good Lord has made us all the same. Skin one animal, you have skinned them all," my mother had once explained.

That adage has proven true a thousand times over. I aim to hit right where I know the spine connects to the head. The Boker starts to skip along the bone, until the rest of my mass and strength drive it through cleanly. I twist and let the bear fall. I continue walking past, and I hear the bear thrashing as the pilot tries to disconnect too late.

I make my way over to where the Kukri lies. I turn to see the bear still twitching. That pilot has still not disco'd. He is going to learn the hard way one day. Too many of those late disconnects, and he will be a braindead meat bag.

I review the field, looking for movement, taking a quick step back to the wolf, which is having problems trying to stand. I pick up my pace. I slice down with all the force I can. The Kukri hits flesh and bone. The DLCLAC blade impacts at the left eye of the wolf. The wolf is out of its misery. Then the twitching begins. The pilot had dumped into the final wolf.

I retrieve the Applegate and move to the fake Family MLR. The inside has cages, but only four. I return to the temp shelter MMLR. Once inside, I start applying compression bandages on my wounds. It is not bad, nowhere near arteries. I will be stiff, likely for weeks, and I know I do not have the time to recuperate. The pilot knows where I am, why I am here. I grab one of the spare haptic suits and stride over to the Gate.

As I advance to the Gate back to Eliese, back to EP1, I am still tearing that megalithic wall down.

***

C11 S4

I surprise the hell out of everyone as I step through and out of the Gate. There is not even a single machine-like sound, no voices, nothing but light wind. I do a quick check, center on Eliese, standing near Doc and Franc. I walk over and kiss her, blood-covered armor, bandages, and all.

"Tell me that Samuel is coming with the MKVI. I must go to Senkaku now. This was all done to keep me from heading there," I say to Eliese, who looks back in confusion.

Franc does not look confused as he pushes me back over to a series of packing crates and sits me down. As he unbuckles gear, Doc jogs over as fast as an aged man can. Franc's voice rumbles like granite. "Sit, Raylan. We've got time."

Thap yells from the side, "ETA on Samuel is ninety minutes out."

"Patch me up, Franc. Enough to get me through the coming fight. Staple, glue, whatever you must do," I growl.

With that, I stop resisting the tender mercy of Franc and Doc. Eliese starts walking my way. I see Stewart, Darien, and what must be thirty people of the Japanese contingent. My team, including who I presume are Leticia and Jackson from the Crow Tribe, are near the control center.

Well, that secret is out. Turning toward the Gate, I see a work area set up, a small stage with dozens of FEED monitors. All are showing the battle area at the demarcation zone from the perspective of the MMLR. Yep, that is going to be all over the news FEEDS.

"The Family's Number Seven beats up rare defenseless animals." Bonnie is going to have a field day.

Eliese looks at me. I watch fear, love, and rage bloom on her face.

"I love you," Eliese says, with a hand over her mouth as tears start to well. "I-I..." She stammers as she looks down at herself, her hands, her dress.

I notice the color begin to drain from her face. I have transferred blood all over her dress, and it covers her arms and chest, where I had briefly held her.

"Carmen! Trish!" I shout. Trish is there first, Carmen right after. "I love you, Eliese, and this fight is not over. They are going to get you cleaned up and changed."

Both ladies nod as they head for a separate MMLR that must be Eliese's quarters. Doc and Franc are yanking a boot off now, trying to pull it. Franc finally just cuts the laces. I looked down at my swollen right ankle, not so much the myomere groups, but the skin. It will be stiff for a while.

Off comes the chest rig armor plate carrier. Thap is beside me now. He starts pulling parts off, salvaging what he can. Pak is beside him, pushing a Mag-lev crate full of a new set of armor and gear, a whole load out of kit. A new haptic suit, new boots, and poly armor plates complete with pouches of full magazines, and speed loaders for the shotgun and a revolver.

I hear Thap in a distant voice. "Raylan, calm down, slow down. Samuel is coming. A pair of men pushed that MLR through early this afternoon after setting the ratio slip back to parity. No one expected that. When we approached them, they took poison. We could see you waiting in the D2 for the all-clear."

Franc gently pushes me back down as I try to peek in the crate again. Franc and Doc are platelet-gluing and stapling me closed where needed. Pak is now wrapping dressing on areas they have finished with. I bet this will be a hell of a bruise when I finish.

I have enough deep cuts that they are adamant that I sit still. I watch as Thap goes through my old gear, transfers what he can over to the new kit, and lets me see everything as he double-checks, then triple checks the load out.

I am dressing when I notice a strange tram land. This one is an old NAC CM drop tram. It left service well before Sam and I entered the FR teams. It must be Samuel. Besides the side loading door, I see the stubby chute for dropping

SkipJack spikes.

A SkipJack spike is a pointy tube, like a nail that the SkipJack rides inside of during freefall. It has a mesh system on it. A team needs twenty of these mesh systems to lower the latency enough to use a SkipJack in a fight with other SkipJacks. I hope Sam has thought of that; although I am sure he did.

Samuel is always about preparation. That is why our team did so well. Sam prepared us as a team, himself as leader, and finally us as individuals. If the opposition force caught us off guard, the fight would be fifty-fifty on good days. When Samuel preps for a battle, he is hell on wheels. I see him step out and jog over as Thap and Pak are putting the last pieces of armor on me. The final things they attach are the Kukri and the Applegate. Pak has cleaned both knives.

I flex, bounce, and adjust things how I like as Sam makes it over. I say as soon as he is in earshot, "Am I a go?"

All I need is his nod. All around us, the Mega-Corp men flinch as I holster the revolver, sling the shotgun, and load its ammo into the mag carriers. I finish by putting the speed loaders in their pouches. I turn to Sam as I notice Trish and Carmen leave.

"Five minutes, Sam," I say, and start for Eliese's trailer.

She exits a few seconds behind the two other women. A pair of dark sunglasses hide the red-rimmed eyes again. Her long, black hair is tied back in a ponytail. She walks to me with purpose, vengeance written in her face.

The kiss Eliese places on my lips is a tremendous perspicacious gift. Her strength of will and passion flow from her mouth to mine. My heartbeat rises in time with the kiss. I feel more robust, more aware, and part of my nature starts to click together in perfect synchronicity. To have her here, to stand with me before battle as I ready...that means the world to me.

I read somewhere once that men would do unspeakable things in the name of love. It has always been confusing to me.

Now I understand it. I am about to bring hell from the ground and spread it around.

I am sure for everyone else the kiss is uncomfortably long. When we break the kiss, her teeth catch my lower lip and hold it just long and hard enough for me to feel her fear and love. Afterwards, I see Trish standing next to "not Jason."

That is interesting, and it is a very bold statement by Trish at this time.

***

C11 S5

Sam is about six feet from me, holding a sleeker-looking helmet, an MKVI one, I am guessing. It does not look like the MKIV I have used in the CM and has the wrong antennas for an MKV. I put it on and start organizing it as best I can. Usually, this process takes weeks of training and fiddling. Everytime they make a Mark revision, all the systems reorganize. It forces old pilots to relearn. Stupid practice, but that is what they do.

Sam and I walk to the drop tram. Sam updates me on the flight time. Estimated ETA is just after dark. He does have a dozen of the three and half kilometer mesh spikes for the drop, all the new mesh spikes that GSG uses, so a considerable radius compared to the previous ones we used in our days with the CM. The SkipJack will drop first, hammering through the main building. I will land on the roof.

I smile. "It's that simple," I say with no question in my voice.

"Make them pay." Sam meets my eyes. He is all commander, all business. "I'll drop you. When you've cleared the Med-i-Care buildings on Senkaku, I have an eight-man Gurkha team on standby to do a bag-and-tag on intel for each of the islands. They'll prep the structures with a sprayable thermite paste coating. When we're all clear, the Forty will torch it off, melting it all to the ground," Sam says with a vicious and vindictive grin.

I nod and say, "Thanks for getting it all planned, Sam." I almost stop walking when I realize in this setting, my brother of the blood and mud has become Sam Janks again; when in a Family setting, he is Samuel. I wonder if I have such a dichotomy in my nature.

Sam nods, turning back to monitoring the flight plan. These drop trams are not armored or armed. He makes sure no one will inconvenience us. I sit in a jump seat, adjusting the HUD and helmet feed. I pull up the camera and FEED them to the HUD display, get the display color, lighting, and width set for me, check the built-in comms system, and boot uplink with the MKVI. Then I start setting the fire-control links, the static command links, and my many hundreds of preset commands.

Sam has done a bang-up job setting most things how I liked them back in the military days. However, I have been operating sans helmet system for nearly seven years EP1 time, add in another three if you include the D2 time. In all that time, I have used the nonmilitary HUD goggles. There are things that I prefer differently now. I am mixing and blending the two on the fly. Not my favorite thing to do, but there will not be a better time to hit this bastard.

Customizing the helmet settings is more work than I anticipate. I am finishing when I hear Sam call, "Fifteen out."

I start packing and loading up the MKVI with ammo. I charge the weapons, close its drop spike, then step into my back-up chute and buckle everything into place. I squeeze into my own spike. I call ready as I lower the lid on the man-capable spike shut.

A minute or three later, the drop tram starts to shudder as the dozen mesh spikes fall free. They will impact at terminal velocity, and the MKVI will hit the ground at about a third of that velocity. My drop spike will arrest my fall just before hitting the roof. It will open a vast round parachute about a hundred meters up, slow the descent, then the petals of the spike would open at the bottom, making landing pads for the spike.

In the final instant before landing, all four-door petals will fully extend with a rip-away chute and nearly bring it to a dead stop in the air as it hits the roof. That happens in theory. It works that way about thirty percent of the time, or so says my anecdotal evidence of over a hundred drops. We will see. So long as it gets me down fast, without the unpleasant sudden stop at the end.

I feel the schump of the SkipJack going just as my pod releases. Sam will be painting the landing zones for the spikes to hit. It will put the SkipJack down in fifty seconds, with my spike landing on the roof in approximately a hundred seconds. I wait, it is always a less than thrilling ride. There is no part of hurtling to earth without seeing the ground that is enjoyable. The winds knock the spikes about until they obtain enough velocity to stabilize their flight.

When I feel the first chute slow, then release as it pulls the second chute free, and the moment it releases as it pulls the last chute free, I prep for impact. The nose blows full as its petals spread wide to land on the roof. Then the sides of the spike blast outwards and up into a mini-chute of their own. My drop spike hits with a thunk and steadies. I bring the shotgun to my shoulder, safety off, and exit, clear my area, then focus on getting the MKVI moving in a new mindspace.

Through the one pulled-down HUD display, I run my system checks. I dump in as my other eye searches the roof. There is movement up here. The first cat comes at a run, with leaps over the building's rusty ductwork.

I step around and left of the spike. The shotgun barks twice, and two rounds hammer into the cat. It takes a shot to the head and front chest to deplete it of its nine lives. I push in two rounds in a quick reload.

I move to the right to find a wolf scrambling across the damp roof. Because of the shotgun reload, my right hand is already near the revolver, which I draw and let roar. The first hits the shoulder, the second misses, the third shot slams its head. Re-holster.

Back on the shotgun, I sweep left and right to be sure I am clear. Good, I send the command. A *FFFFWUMP* rattles the roof, and moisture and loose pebbles dance up. I have just blown the SkipJack spike panels off.

I pilot the MKVI and exit the spike. I see a bear in the near-empty room coming at me, and put one round from the MKVI's shotgun into its head as it charges. There is a pause, and then a second round of SkipJack buck hits it. A human shotgun is one type of horrific weapon. A SkipJack shotgun can single-shot most animals alive on EP1. There was no need for the second shot to the bear, because it is disco twitching after the first. I shift its views to thermal for a minute. There are too many thermal blooms of where others have been. The building is dark. I swap back to low-light vision and start the MKVI forward.

Above, I hear the bellow of the two SkipJack blasts as I thumb in a couple of replacement rounds into the 454 Casull. I re-holster again and get back on the shotgun. Moving to the left, I snake my way up to a tremendous air handler. After doing my corner peek-check, I keep shuffle-stepping around the side. I hear a raspy feline hiss: another cat. I swiftly bring the shotgun around the corner and let the cat have it as I see the pilot dump into it. The cat had gone from a hiss to the shake of its head when the pilot tried to take command.

What I am not expecting is the ursine charge from directly behind me. I can feel the animal moving as the roof shakes, and hear it bellowing as it drives at me. A quick pivot and a four-step shift are all I need as I let four rounds of buckshot loose into its head and chest. It drops into a heap. The bruin's lungs are heaving, and its soon-to-be lifeless head slaps against the roof in pain.

I keep my head on a swivel as I feed the shotgun with four rounds from the feed tube on my plate rig and one from the single-shell holder. I react as I see a trio of wolves coming at my SkipJack in the drop-down HUD.

The SkipJack has shouldered its way straight through the short drywall partitions. As it clears, I see the three wolves pile in. The lead is the pilot, and the back two seem to be pulling to heel as I do with my SkipJacks.

The 20mm speaks its wisdom, and the right rear wolf's chest becomes mist. The MKVI's shotgun roars, and the left rear slams to the ground. As the MKVI walks forward, the 20mm denotes its superiority again, dropping the piloted wolf.

I focus, taking the time to reload both MKVI guns. The MKVI ejects the 20mm mag while I stow the partial shotgun mag. Pushing through or throwing aside more office and lab debris, I keep the MKVI moving forward.

There is another trio of bears coming forward, being led by an enormous black bear on the left. An additional two more come in from the right. I open up on the lead bear on the left with the 20mm. I shift aim to the second on the right and release the second five-round burst. The shotgun roars as it puts one into the leading left bear.

Turning the MKVI slightly, I take the last two, now trying to hide their flanking movements behind desks. Silly pilot: cheap office furniture does not stop rounds from a SkipJack Shotgun. There is a lesson there for new pilots. You need to consider your cover and concealment differently when facing SkipJacks.

Based on the muffled sounds of the rapid firing of the MKVI, I know it is slightly ahead of me and below me. Doing a quick peek over the small maze of meter-high ductwork that I am concealed behind, I see another bear. Looking behind it, I noticed the shoulders of more wolves and cats. I shift to the corner of the duct, waiting until the bear rounds the corner to me and I hit the head with lead. I drop two rounds in it, just to be sure.

I then vault up onto the duct, twist my torso and drop the single cat. I skip back two interconnecting sections of ductwork and put one round in the trailing wolf. The other is safely behind a bit of an air handler. The shotgun seems insufficient to hit him through the machinery.

I have one round left in the shotgun tube after that exchange. Dropping it to the sling, I pull the Casull out. I hop two more layers of duct work to the right. I see his rear flank and put one round in his rear hips. The bullet exits out the other side, shattering both legs at the hip bones.

Sure enough, as I close in with the shotgun, the wolf is twitching from the forced disco. I reload as I close. One final shot puts it out of its misery. Topping the shotgun and the revolver off, I kneel on the duct, swapping between standard cam and night vision. I have about twenty-five meters to the edge of the building. The roof looks clear. I start my way over.

Reloading the SkipJack, I send it forward. I skip the door in the wall by making my own. The shoulder rush puts me in a room with two sets of chest-high drywall partitions, and there are rows of cubicles on either side. There is an aisle down the center, breaking up the room into a partial tic-tac-toe board. Swapping between night and infrared does not help. There have been a lot of things in here recently. I see the main entrance area and the reception area through glass walls on the other side of the room.

Back in night vision, I walk around to the left. Humans, almost exclusively, gravitate to the right. I peek my MKVI around corners as stealthily as I can, and it is not till the end when I see them: about nine to fifteen beasts huddled in a mass. My adversary is holding the animals back by piloting a bear, with some wrapped around a little corner. I drop back. I know he is piloting that bear, and he is waiting for something. I recheck ammo and turn my attention up top.

With a quick helmet camera shift, I check the remaining portions of the roof. I dash over to the edge and look down. I see nothing directly below me. It is about a six-meter drop to the ground, not my favorite. I do not know how I would fare if I make that drop to the concrete below.

The main door leads to a small patio, with a staircase going down like an extra-wide fire escape. Switching to night mode, I use the shotgun's IR illuminator to light things up. The stairs are not straight up and down the cliff like I had thought, more like a snake crawling up the side of a steep hill. They weave back and forth, with a thick railing on the outer edge. The railing is much thicker than needed.

It dawns on me: this is how the Med-i-Care employees brought equipment up from the boat or tram dock. The railing is probably strong enough to keep the Mag-lev sleds from falling over the edge. I catch movement at the bottom towards the edge of my shotgun's illuminator.

There is a simian shape. Is it walking or galloping? It hits the bottom rail and launches itself over the second rail. By the time I bring my mind around to what I see, it is climbing past the third rail. Damn, I turn and run for the hole the SkipJack spike made in the roof.

With the sight of the freaking gorilla, I bring the SkipJack around the little cubical and take a knee. The 20mm hits the bear and exits. I had assumed that knee in case any rounds hit and exited the bear, in hopes they might deal some small damage to those behind it. I let the second burst loose on the right side.

It is too late, and the game is up, the lot of them darting into the maze of cubicles. Only three animals are down. I can hear cats coming from the right. With a twist and two booms from the shotgun, those two cats go down.

I pull the hatchet free with my right hand. Dancing back around the corner where I had knelt, I put three rounds in three wolves. I hit another cougar with the hatchet, slicing through the cougar's spine as it latches onto my right leg.

I see four wolves come from the left, with the pilot leading. I put a round into the lead wolf, only to realize the pilot has disco'd and is piloting a cat to my right. I put the last shotgun round into a trailing wolf before I turn my attention to the cats.

A number of cats are in the air as they try to tackle my MKVI to the ground. I smack the piloted one away with my right arm; it slaps down hard onto the office floor. The second one receives a punch to the chest, caving it. I finish it off with the hatchet as the first of the last two wolves latches onto my left leg.

Spinning the hatchet around, I whack the wolf on the back of the head with the hammer end. It drops to the ground, and I stomp its head flat with my left leg. The piloted cat is up. I take that same wolf-smashing foot, and donkey-kick backward. That kick propels the piloted cat into the hard concrete wall.

I turn to the remaining lone wolf; which is running now. I hear a deafening roar as I start the reloading process while moving to the center of the room. I put a 20mm mag in, then insert a shotgun ammo mag.

I drop down to the top of the SkipJack spike. I hang there and listen and finally let go, falling to the ground. My legs absorb the impact. I orient to the destruction doorway my SkipJack has made. I start running. It is only about sixty meters, but I do not have much time as I hear the first bellow from the simian beast.

I know there is one wolf somewhere. I make good time and do my best to be alert for movement and noise. I enter the lab space and hear the wolf moving around nearby. I hook left again, peeking and peering around corners. We dance around this room, almost completing two circuits looking for each other.

I do not see him, though I do hear his augmented claws on the tile as he tries to gain speed. Again, the beast comes at me from behind. I put him down with three rounds. The wolf twitches because the pilot is late forcing the disco. Interestingly, this pilot's disconnects are becoming slower and slower. I reload the magazine tube for the shotgun and check the 454 revolver. I step lightly as I head to the other side of the lab.

The first roar shakes the glass panes separating the cubicles from the entry area. How none of the glass shattered during my fight with the other animals, I do not know. There is a second roar, then shortly after that, an explosive rumble as the front door comes sailing in. It hits the glass partitions in front of the SkipJack and sails through.

I dive the MKVI aside to the right. Scrambling up, I realize I am too late. Following right behind that third roar is a piece of railing that the simian uses as a club. The heavily augmented and armored gorilla hammers the club into the left arm and shoulder of the MKVI. The left arm of the MKVI is firing at it as the club slams home and sends my 300-kilogram MKVI staggering.

I do not know if the gorilla is wearing SkipJack level armor or what. There are only two little spurts of blood before the MKVI staggers a few steps. The simian's arm reaches out and grabs the left arm of the MKVI. The beast spins in a circle, tossing the MKVI like a discus.

I take the fall, rolling into the landing, and come up. The HUD flashes that the shotgun is inoperable, and the left shoulder has little mobility. It is on me before I can do anything but dive to the left. Somehow the beast has reclaimed its club, which sails above my MKVI in a tremendous swing. The railing pierces the back wall when it connects.

The gorilla has me on reach, and in hand-to-hand battle, the MKVI will lose. The monstrosity sports a near eight-foot arm span, almost double that with the club. I dive again behind it as it pulls on its club, now stuck in the wall. If I can get outside, I can open the range on it and use the 20mm.

When that club comes free, the simian uses the momentum to spin around and face me. Hundreds maybe thousands of gallons of water shoot into the room. I know that I will be in a world of hurt if I let that beast get a hold of my MKVI. I configured my MKVI for speed, for movement, not for slugfests. It might be able to go toe-to-toe in strength, but the damn simian has some serious reach on me.

I watch from the hole that my SkipJack had knocked into the cubicle area. The golf swing it took at my SkipJack sends it staggering. I step through nice and low as the gorilla uses my MKVI for track and field. I notice that the simian does have some kind of armor.

It seems the perverted scientist who did the work has placed hard armor plates under the skin above the haptic suit mesh the pilot is using. I can see only two welts of blood on the lower abdomen and two concave areas bleeding slightly where the armor is. I sling the shotgun. I cannot let this simian beast get close to my SkipJack. If it has SkipJack-level armor, then the 20mm is the only thing I have that can punch through the damn beast.

Once again, I stand in my mental space facing a mostly dismantled wall. I must go all-in. I pull the last few megalithic stones out of the way in my mind. The man that steps forth from that dark place is me as a thirteen-year-old, understanding that I was on my own. It is me as a young man fighting the tribal elders to allow me to become a soldier. It is me the first weeks of boot camp, and it is me as a career soldier. It is me in every battle during my term of service. It is me as a soldier seeing that first attack on Sam. It is the living ferocity I had that night in the fight to beat the first piloted cougar. It is me in every sweaty, sour, hard, bloody day in my life. It is me in that hospital bed after the lightning bolts hit me. It is me and my determination during those days, weeks and months of physical therapy.

I see my stubbornness, my determination, my rage, my cunning as I step forward and become whole. All my many traits weave together in a solid core of lethal grace. I pop up from behind the cubicle, the front sight of the 454 Casull already falling into line.

I put the first round in its throat, the second near its far collarbone and the third round into its right elbow as it tosses the club at me. I dive to the right, so it can see me. I spring back up, holstering the 454, moving the shotgun into place as I roar my challenge. Either the simian is immune to that tactic, or I am just too puny. My gut leans towards both. It charges me, right arm trailing behind it. I put three rounds of buck towards its head as I move for that hole in the wall my MKVI had made previously.

I juke and jive out of its grasping hand. The simian's limbs pound the ground as they propel it forward, but the gorilla turns like I had before my lessons with Rana and Ghale. Gone is any sense of simian grace. As I stop at the hole in the wall, I hammer twice more at its head with the shotgun. Out of those five rounds I fired at its head, I might have hit it twice.

The way the simian runs with three limbs, the head bobbing and weaving, there is not a great shot. I dive through the hole as best I can. The floor is slippery and wet, and my lunge is off. I hit the ground hard. As the air sucks back in, and I try to rise, a grip grabs the left heel of my boot. It feels like a vice is squeezing my foot. I twist as much as I can. Its left arm is poking through the hole. I pull the revolver from under me.

Distraction, Raylan, remember you are the distraction. I put two rounds into its armpit. There is no armor there. I can tell those rounds hurt the beast, as little shuddering spasms ripple through its body. Nevertheless, it pulls me through the hole on my back now. My feet are near the edge of the gaping hole in the wall. I fumble with the revolver reload. Ghale will kick my ass in training for this. I chuckle at the mental idea that training over the next few weeks is going to be revolver reloads while being dragged by the feet over very bumpy terrain.

My SkipJack regains its feet and starts to sprint, but slips on the wet floor. I pilot it back up and realize how slimy this water on the tile is. I Pilot the MKVI up carefully second time, as I have seen my body dive through the hole. I am moving those fifteen meters closer, when I hear the two shots. I can see my feet through the MKVI-made doorway now. I need only move a tad further.

Reload done, I put a Casull round into the left knee of the gorilla, then one into the left elbow. The roar that follows shakes the room and is like thunder inside your head. The eruption of noise deafens me as much as the gunfire. The knee shot has shorted the pilot's control. I see the simian try and straighten as it shakes its head. I know I have won as the grip on my left foot falls away.

The pilot has lost control as my SkipJack steps parallel to the simian. The gorilla turns its head as some primal instinct understands the real threat is those dozen meters to its side. The first five-round burst tears through the upper left arm and creates a massive chest cavity. The hole is nearly a foot wide and is above the jerry-rigged side plate armor on the simian. The second five-round burst vaporizes everything from the neck up. Red mist hangs in the air, then drifts down to coat my helmet's visor.

I see the body slump to the ground, like a marionette with its strings cut. I reload the revolver. I unpack myself from the hole, pull out my shotgun, and start reloading it. Kneeling, I finish my reload and start back through the hole. The MKVI is making its way out the door.

I must help reload the 20mm. The left arm is unable to get the angle right. Its function is down to about eight percent left-right movement and about fifteen percent up-down motion. There is no function at the elbow or from the forearm shotgun.

I clear the shotgun ammo from the weapon. However, the fingers can still grasp. As I stand at the top of the stairs looking down, I see a thermal bloom from a tram's engine nacelle through the MKVI's thermal eyestalk. I put an end to that. I reload the 20mm again and start down with the SkipJack leading. I am using it as cover until I hit bottom. Once there, we cover the 500 meters to the now-damaged tram.

I have the SkipJack pry open the side door via the emergency hatch release.

When that is open, the MKVI enters. In my HUD, I see a pod with my animal SkipkJack pilot. There is also a cage that looks like it had once housed the simian. I enter the tram behind the MKVI.

The stench from the cage is unreal. I see the pilot is in a pod, not one I have seen before. His goggles are down, and his chin is the color of paste blue. His lips are cherry red. He gasps as if choking, and I see he has no teeth.

The pilot has a tracheostomy in his throat, a small breathing tube sticking out that exits to medical equipment in the pod. The area around the tube is red and very inflamed. He has his haptic suit on. My adversary is covered in bile, stains, and suddenly, I am not sure the stench in the tram is from the simian's cage. Attached to his stomach is a feeding tube, along with a colostomy bag. The tube is feeding him some sort of creamy white slime. I can see tremors in his body as he goes into shock. It seems that all those forced disconnects screwed him up.

I try to figure out how to remove him from the pod. I move to the back and see a full set of vitals. I start a force disconnect from the pod but he goes into cardiac arrest. He starts foaming blood from the mouth and is dead in a few minutes. Brain function ceases while I watch the medical equipment on the pod.

I pull up my comms via the helmet and let Sam know where to land, and that this site is mostly clear. In just a few minutes, a team from the Forty lands on Senkaku's main island with Sam. They have staged on the Q-ship that I originally had planned to launch this mission from. They bag biometric samples from everything, pull any FEED data from any local device they can get their hands on.

Each man pulls a small Mag-lev cart full of sprayable thermite paste. One even sprays the entire interior of the tram. Several hours later, everyone is spraying their way back to Sam's drop tram.

I step from the dock into the tram and look at Sam. He has seen the FEED from my helmet cameras.

Sam nods to me and says, "Per Thap, all islands are clear, all forces accounted for and in the air. Ray, we're ready to take off."

***

C11 S6

The tram climbs to cruising speed. Only three of the islands have structures. We see the thermite fires light up the night sky. The bright white flames are hundreds of feet high; even the 3D-printed buildings are burning to ash and cinders. Sam turns around as we head back to Ishigaki.

"Stow the weapons and ammo in a pod, boys. Ray's stunt when we took off is going to have Japan's Mega-Corps in a tizzy," Sam says with a roll of his eyes. As an afterthought, he adds, "Even the knives, Raylan."

"Damn," I say with more than a little bit of remorse.

I am just getting to like these knives. I take all the ammo from the MKVI and place them in the designated pod with everything from my plate carrier. When that spike drops, we pull the guns off the MKVI and place them in another. Sam sends that spike to the bottom of the ocean, also. The men with us had set the thermite containers in that tram on the dock. There would be little left. We land on Ishigaki at a couple of hours before sun-up. Our other teams would be returning directly home.

When we land, a military cordon surrounds the tram. The military searches each of us individually, one by one, as we exit. They do it professionally, with dispassion and courtesy. It is comprehensive, including metal scans, diamond-like carbon scans, and we are stripped to our skivvies. They find not one bit of our weaponry.

I watch Trish and the young not-Jason talking. He walks over to an older man at the back of the military cordon and speaks in a clear, concise measured tone for a heated few seconds. We keep our hands where they can be seen, and we keep quiet. The older man and the young man walk over.

"You are Ray-san, yes?" states the older man. It is not a question.

"I am Raylan, number seven of the Family, leader of the Gate Surveyor Group," I say in military precision and enunciation.

The older man nods. "Your contract is to secure this facility, survey it, and to find out who was propagating the crime of sabotage, yes?" the officer asks, looking at me intently. Clearly, this military man does not buy his younger counterpart's bullshit story.

"Yes, that is part of the contract. I am also responsible for bringing this settlement to Stage Three within five years. If I fail at that, there are hefty fines due," I explain. I gesture slowly, with an open palm, to the young buck Trish seems to have taken a liking to.

"Why you?" the visibly frustrated man asks. This is his final stab at unraveling this complete farce of a story.

"Because I am not Japanese," I say with a straight face, in complete sincerity. The sentiment being if I failed it is because I am not Japanese, and if I succeeded, it is because the Mega-Corps knew I am the best man for their job.

The old man nods, and nods again slightly. His eyes narrowed and appraising. He knows full well that the young man fed him a line of bullcrap, but he can find nothing to call the young man on.

He turns to the young man. A rapid-fire stream of ass-chewing happens. The young man does not even twitch. It ends with what I think is a question.

He receives a simple *"hai."* Yes, to something then. The older military man and his subordinates march off to their own tram.

The young man looks at me, at the blood and bruises, as I pull my SkipJack to heel out of the drop tram.

"I owed you for the introduction to Ms. Trish Mr. Ray-san. I hope this makes us..." The young man pauses. "Not even, but square."

I stick out my hand, bloody gore and all.

"Call me Raylan. Thank you for your help. I do not know when the hostile party there would have targeted someone else in the Family." I say as I wave at the Gate. "It has tried for Samuel and me." I hope I have articulated the issue well with out saying that Trish might be next on the list.

"It?" the young man says, clearly catching the implications of my chosen words.

I look at him. He catches on fast; moreover, he has been with Trish. If he is not Family material, she would have let him down before now. I nod once and pull the helmet cam footages from my FEED and send them to him. I code the whole thing to his biometrics.

I explain, "After you view these FEED vids scrub them. Be wary of passing them around."

The young man peers at me, nods once. Turns and leaves to talk to Trish. He and Trish climb in a tram and lift off shortly after that. I head with Samuel and our team to our Family tram. There is a dismantling group of locals already fast at work on the old CM drop tram. Soon it will be sent into the nearby D2 Iteration for scrap.

We make our way to the other side of the Ishigaki island demarcation zone. I find Eliese there, waiting. Samuel drops me and Thap off and takes off with his Segundo. It is turning dawn now as I walk across the DMZ for the Gate. Eliese opens the door and smiles. Thap and Pun stand guard outside as I shower and dress. Eliese bandages me as best she can.

Eliese and I walk out into the morning sun, cross the lined walking path in the demarcation zone as dozens of MMLRs are transiting through the Gate. Work is in full swing, she explains. The teams had left for Hill House last night. We board our tram and start hopping back across the world. We do not land at Hill House; instead, we return to the Family residence. Franc meets me once I enter the Family wing of spaces. He pulls me along to the infirmary as he calls it.

"Damn good fight," Franc says as he cleans and gives me dressings for my injuries and double-checks all my bumps and bruises.

I do not know why, but praise from Franc is almost frightening. When Franc clears me from his care, I find Eliese waiting, showered, and changed. Once again, she waits for me in my flat as I clean up. My wounds are numerous and very sore; the platelet glue and staples hold me together in patches of white gauze and tape.

Eliese has been somewhat silent; not giving me the silent treatment, but silent. I know we have a meeting with Stewart shortly. When dressed, I walk into the sitting area, where she waits; her hands fumble with a cup of tea. Thap comes in with a pot of coffee for me. I give him a look. He nods, and with Pun, stands outside the main door.

"We should talk," I say very gently. Since we left Ishigaki, I have been returning those megalithic blocks to their wall. Surprisingly, the other me is helping me lift and place them from the other side. I understand that only one part of me can exist in a civilized world.

In my mindspace, I am up to my knees in blocks when Eliese looks to me.

"I saw you, Raylan. I saw the moment you decided to come home at all costs. When that bear ran over you, it is as if your soul changed," Eliese says while looking at her cup. She takes a few deep breaths before she starts again. "For me, Raylan, I step from the darkness of a garden as leaves start to fall, as autumn wind snakes through the trees, and the first true frost lays itself on the world. When I step, the world changes behind me. In front of me is the green wonder, and behind, barren cold of a new moons winter." Eliese says in a whisper, "What is it like for you?"

I am pouring coffee. "It is simpler. It is a wall. A megalithic wall with stones the size of trams. Once open, a more complete me is there. I take every bit of blood, tears, pain, cunning, love, hurt, joy, and loss and weave it into a man that is good at one thing. When I walk, I tow behind me the mental SkipJacks of death and destruction on leashes," I explain, taking a sip. The understanding of why we are drawn to each other so fiercely clicks into place. "Right now, we are building that wall back up. We are layering those blocks, mortaring those megalith stones in place," I say.

I am trying to show El that other nature and I are working together. I hope she does not think this nature has sway over me.

Eliese looks to me then and says, "We plant vines that grow and bear fruit. It holds her back until I trim them back. It's a...'gate' of sorts." She smiles weakly, gives that shake of her head as she looks up at the ceiling.

Her chocolate-colored eyes flash as she lets loose with a hymn or an anthem in her voice. No, it is a blending of the two, I realize.

Eliese says, "This weekend, with the Family at the Hill House. I will not wait until the end of summer; I will not wait until autumn has begun. What time we have, I want to spend together." Her will is absolute. There is no room for argument. "Your secret is out, Raylan. The world knows that the Family's seventh member is the only man that can Gate walk. A copy of your fight in the

D2 hit the FEED networks. Combine that with you walking through bloody as death itself and kissing me..." In her song is a twinkle of humor and a lot of love.

"I was merely marking my territory, love," I say with a smile. I continue to look into her eyes.

Eliese lets out a peal of laughter at the marking my territory remark. It takes her a moment to calm down. I see the laughter for the fear, worry, concern and frustration that it is. I am unsure if El has ever dealt with such things before.

"El, this weekend works for me. I will be there."

"Raylan, honey, no one will face you openly after watching that FEED stream," Eliese says with a smile and wink before she continues, "We have a meeting with Father. I'll message Trish. I need her to start planning. I assume Samuel or Chen will be your best man?"

I shake my head and put on my own Cheshire grin. "I owe a man," I say with a wink to Eliese. I see the recognition dawn on her face as her eyes flash at me again.

I ping Thap, and as he and Pun walk in, I stand.

"Thap, the wedding is this weekend at Hill House," I say and wait a good three seconds for that to sink in. Pun's face erupts into a frown so big it could span rivers. This means a lot of work for him in very little time. "Would you be my best man?" is the question I follow up with. Watching Thap's face go from horrified to horror cubed is well worth it. My friend has earned it. "Samuel, of course, and Chen from Montana West District, will be groomsmen," I say as I start pacing the flat. "That should do. Can you manage that, Thap? It means Pak and Pun will take charge of security under your oversight." I see a smile split Thap's face as Pun stomps his foot and marches out of the room, realizing he had been handed the short end of the stick.

Thap smiles, and in a lazy British accent, which I have only ever heard him use when speaking to other Gurkhas, he says, "Sure, I'll speak to Pun; he and Pak can deal with the security."

We are now heading out the door when I smile at Pun to let him know I am just teasing and that planning his indenture's wedding is not falling solely on his shoulders.

Epilogue

Epilogue

The meeting with Stewart, Darien, Doc, and Samuel starts once we arrive. I grab the bottle of whisky from Peter as I pass by, and glasses from the liquor cabinet. I set one around the table for each of us, then proceed to pour a dram as I walk around. Trish will already know. Once I sit down, I then lift the glass.

When everyone else does likewise, I say in a rather triumphant voice, "Here's to seeing you at my wedding this weekend."

That gets a couple of coughs and a little playful slap from Eliese.

Darien, being Darien, says, "Wait, you had to give Eliese a glass? Does she know? How's Trish going to feel about this?" I am not sure who kicks him, but he jumps a couple of inches in his chair. "All right, all right. I'm just joking. I will be there," he says with an extensive grin.

"I'll kick this off with a question. Ray, did you know, who you introduced Trish to?" Darien asks, peering at me quizzically. "No? That is Tenno Hei-ka's fourteenth son. He is a royal prince of Japan. You dragged him over and stuck him with Trish. The poor man." Darien grins. "They've hit it off well. Asahito-san is not in line for the throne, so no worries there. He is, however, on the board of two Mega-Corps out of the seven." With a wave of his hand after another sip of the whisky, he adds, "He's the reason the Gate went forward in the first place. He lobbied on behalf of it. He wasn't in any of my contacts or

435

communications. So it added to our totals in the final vote tally."

Darien has this natural self-assurance as he lays out his side of the deal. He is much of the reason we have been able to pull this whole thing off. Our differences aside, Darien puts Family first.

Stewart looks at Darien. "The fourteenth heir. Does Trish know?" he asks, then abruptly waves it off by saying, "Never mind, she would have charmed it out of him in the first two minutes." He looks sideways at the whisky. "This weekend? Eliese? Couldn't you give me more warning?" All he receives in reply is a raised eyebrow and a stare as cold as the frozen barren wastes of the north. "This weekend it is. Small wedding, I take it?" Stewart asks with a hard swallow.

"A couple, Father, just a couple. It will be at our Hill House. You three," she says, pointing emphatically at Darien, Samuel, and Doc. "Plus one only. The same goes for Trish. This is small, private, and our day. A Family day," Eliese says with a smile on her face.

"Peter, please extend an invitation to Franc for me," I say. There are a half-dozen looks of bewilderment at my statement. Doc assents with a tip of his glass after only a fraction of an odd look.

Samuel quips, "Where am I to find a date that fast? Come on, Eliese."

That elicits a clink of glasses from Doc, Darien, and Samuel together. I roll my eyes at the idea of Doc trying to scrounge up a date.

Sam continues, "Now that *that's* covered, I need to talk fallout. The drop tram was sent through the Gate and is scrap for the Ishigaki 3D printers. It will be turned into plumbing or something, so that part is clean. We dropped the weapons in 2,700 feet of water. Finding them, though, will be a pain." He breathes in, takes a sip and continues, "The Gurkhas...they would never talk, so that contract is complete. We have everything that we pulled from there. Doc has some specifics, and I will go over the island itself."

Sam says, "The Chinese Confederacy is pissed. They know something about the island. It is quite possible that the Confederacy was feeding, funding, or managing the man on the island. They know the place is now slag. All three isles with structures are gone. The largest structure was full of cages, hundreds of animal cages, but only a few had animals in them.

"The Gurkhas put everything out of its misery, then they burnt everything to the ground. That team expended every ounce of thermite paste and emptied their tram of all secondary explosives to get the upper buildings destroyed. The third island was possibly a private residence at one time. No one had used it in at least fifteen-plus years. Only a few bits of information remained," Sam explains.

He sighs before continuing. "It gets weird here. It was a research facility for human-animal gene splicing. Somehow the original people left, were let go, or killed off. One man remained. We know him as Rivas March. He was supposedly killed by the replacement more than fifteen years ago. I have my doubts about that." He waits for that bombshell to hit home. It certainly does. Darien and Eliese stare at each other.

I start to interrupt, but Samuel cuts me off. "Raylan, hold on" he says, knowing I have some questions. "The replacement is *not* Rivas March. We have a record of his biometrics." He sees me ease back. "The issue, Raylan, is that if Rivas is dead, who had the hit put out on me seven years ago? I think Rivas simply slipped his leash and left. Someone else comes along and says they killed him, then takes over the assassin-for-hire business." Sam turns to Doc. "Your turn. I have more for after this part."

Doc looks around. "As Samuel said, Rivas was not the pilot that died. We had no direct or ancillary match to the DNA or biometrics. There's one thing similar: that the pilot fed on a nutrient bath full of minerals, of a similar size and makeup of what one would need to have a myomere muscle and bone replacement surgery. Similar, but not exact. I only know of one other person who has ever lived through something like that," Peter says as he gestures with an open palm to me.

"Raylan here goes through metals at an alarming rate. It has been a transformative nature of his condition since the first attack with the cat. He's been able to accept and expand myomere muscle and bones. I had thought him deceased almost eight years ago. But when I go back to my original records, his myomere bone and muscle both grew during those seven years, about half of one percent."

Peter is all smiles, now fully into his Doctor's voice as he professes the basis of what I currently am. "I thought I was getting old and just misremembered it. I went back and compared it in the last couple of days. He did grow one percent. It was then that his desire for mineral-rich meats and legumes came to my memory.

He was eating primarily Indian style foods with mostly legumes, pulling in as many minerals as he could afford." He takes a small sip of his whisky. "They were not enough. Once he was able to get the bone replacement after surgery, then he was eating better at the hospital and home. Things took off when he started Gate walking. Raylan is now a tad over 180 kilograms. Much of that is his full myomere bone skeleton and his full myomere muscle."

He looks back at Samuel, who picks up the thread. "We have a real Island of Doctor Moreau. The island was used as a base from which to launch or house assassins. I, for one, think this is just where they came from, and this person Raylan ran into...I'm not convinced he was the man in charge. He might have been the one who attacked the Family three times, but I even have my doubts about that. I think the real man in charge is Rivas March." Sam turns to look at Stewart and says, "We found his files for the plan to infiltrate the boarding school Darien and Eliese attended. We found his cover name only. From the read of it, he was operating alone. Grandfather had something he wanted. After he left for the school, some twenty-eight years ago, he only returned sporadically. Fifteen years ago, this new pilot shows up and assumes the Rivas March moniker and claims to have killed the previous version."

Sam leans back, as a thoughtful silence descends upon all of us.

Stewart downs the remainder of his whiskey. After a moment, with his eyes closed, he says, "Ray's nature is now known worldwide. The interview requests haven't stopped coming in. Neither have calls for inquiry into how he can do this."

Stewart looks to me, possibly thinking about the last interview I had given, the conversation where the Family spent over twenty-three million credits and are now embroiled in a lawsuit.

"For now, we're going to stall. Eliese and Ray's wedding gives us about a month to let things simmer down. We can hide you at the Hill House for a time, although eventually, they'll head there. Is there someplace remote you two want to go to for a time during your honeymoon?" Stewart asks as much as advises in this last statement.

I answer, "Yes, we will head there the day after the wedding. I will make the preparations, and make the necessary switches with the tram flights." I have not been back there in a long while. It would give my team time to work up the next couple of Gates. Eliese...getting out on our own will do her some small amount of good, also.

The meeting ends after another hour of talks about Ishigaki's finer details.

It is two nights before my wedding, and I am on my futon, dreaming. I hear the thump at the door. I walk over, but I am not at Hill House—I am in my old cabin. My hands are small, young, not even coming into their strength as I reach for the door.

It is late February, early March in the old Nunavut wilderness. I am so worried. My parents are late, so extremely late. I pull the door in, and there lies my mother. It takes all my strength to drag her cold form inside. From her chest down, her outer clothes are a sheet of ice.

Her lips are as blue as the tattoos on her chin. I pull her over towards the fireplace, then I stoke the fire. With the dampener open, I start getting her undressed. I pile warm woolen blankets around her torso, setting the rocks we kept on top of the stove to dry out mittens and boots onto the blankets to keep them hot. I work for hours, heating her slowly from the core and head. I am leaning against a bed by the fireplace with her back pulled to me, my skin to her skin. My mother is so cold. Wrapped in these heated blankets with her, I sweat.

My mother starts mumbling. "Raylan, Raylan."

"Yes, Momma?" I say in Inuktitut.

It is her native language. Tears falling freely from my eyes.

"Stay with me, Momma. Warm up, Momma." I already know that if Dad is not here, he will not be coming back.

She seems to warm up in the next little while, her eyes fluttering open and locking onto the fireplace or the tiny kitchen across from us, and then fading back closed.

"Raylan, my son, my beloved son," my mother whispers, now using my father's language, Malimiutun. "I should never have let them make you." Her voice is so quiet now, that I can only hear it in this dream. "You are our son of war, our son born for war. Your name is War."

I am awake, soaked in sweat. I feel the heat of the blankets and fire on my skin. I have been planning our remote tram and MMLR up to my parent's old cabin in the Nunavut District all week. I believe that there are answers at the cabin, answers the other part of me needs. Now I remember why.

I get up and pad over to the kitchen as softly as my weight will allow. I pull a cup from the cup hanger and drink some water from the sink. I feel my siren's arms slide around me.

"What are we, Raylan?" Eliese whispers.

I can feel her tears as they land on my skin. I know without asking that her other part has spoken to her soul, also.

"We are husband and wife, friends, lovers, travelers. The day after tomorrow, in the afternoon, we start our journey together, El. We will find our story, and we will write it across all the worlds," I say as I grip the counter. I turn around and hold her tight. I pick her up and head back to the futon. I sit there with her leaning into me under the blanket until the sun rises, and it is time to get ready for the guests to arrive for tomorrow's wedding.

The end of book one.

Glossary

1. Anti-Personnel High Explosives (APHE): another name for most modern CM SkipJacks' preloaded frag tube. It is a cross between a grenade and a mortar.

2. Balloon Spikes: these high-altitude balloons will tether to the earth initially while they compile their logistical data. After that, they will float freely around the atmosphere for decades relaying weather, lidar mapping, and temperature data to the spikes on the ground.

3. Blockhouse/home: prefabricated building of basic living standards. Four walls and a roof. They range from studio to three bedrooms in size. Blockhouses are rented from the community pool.

4. Brazillian Union: Brazil for short; colloquially, the Union is dropped from its name.

5. Chinese Confederacy: the confederated nations of Southeast Asia. The government is a blend of oligarchal communism and despotism.

6. Commissary: a restaurant in an office, barracks, or other institution.

7. Comms: interpersonal communications networks, sometimes between people or HUDs.

8. Community Ride Share (CRS); the only flat ground transportation

inside a Community in the NAC. Private property ownership is not allowed. All ride shares are pre-purchased from the community CRS vehicles.

9. Community: the government that comprises towns, villages, and cities within the NAC.

10. Compact Military (CM): the combined branches of the NAC military. Navy, Army, and the rarer Marine Troopers.

11. Consolidate Gate Security United (CGSU): the private security corporation that Raylan worked for in Dillon, Montana.

12. Daisy-chain: the mode for incorporating multiple SkipJacks to heel or follow mode by use of a physical cable.

13. Data Trunk: a line that carries the bulk of the information into a new D2 to facilitate using SkipJacks, 3D printers, and assemblers. It also delivers data, messages, and FEED-based items to the settlers. Without a data trunk in a D2, piloting SkipJacks would be limited to the DMZ area.

14. Demarcation Zone (DMZ): the basis hub for all EP1 to D2 iterations.

15. Demilitarized (demilled) SkipJacks: MKII trainers that have had their weapons permanently removed and are often used as security patrols for civilian and community installations.

16. Diamond-Like Carbyne linear Acetylenic carbon (DLCLAC): a material dense enough and strong enough to work as a replacement for steel.

17. Dimension two (D2): the separation designation from Earth Prime. If a DMZ has one Gate, that world is designated D2. If the DMZ has more than one Gate, which is not common, they are designated D2, D3, and D4.

18. Dimensional Gate Dillon Montana West (DGMW): a gate owned by the Family corporation. Ray worked the night shift as a guard.

19. Disco, or disco'd: short for "disconnect." It refers to the action of pulling one's mind free of the connection with a SkipJack.

20. Donner: a ubiquitous survey SkipJack that is often pulled to heel by surveyors as they do their work. It is the best all-terrain workhorse available to the GSG surveyors.

21. Earth Prime 1 (EP1): designation of the earth, the origin of humanity.

22. Forward Elliptical Educational Display (FEED): a system that uses a root line under the human skin to power itself. The more extensive the FEED root system, the larger the FEED display screen. It utilizes a small, semi-opaque curved display that is useful for any number of personal amusements.

23. FEED Fob: a small tab that acts as a designator. Can be used for banking codes or as a key to a door. Most often, they are used to store and contain data.

24. FEED vid: a pre-recorded video or message displayed on a FEED systems display.

25. Force Recon (FR): FR teams are the NAC's remote pilot assault and reconnaissance forces. They usually comprise of anywhere from eight to twenty men, not including the SkipJacks they pilot.

26. Forced Disco: when your mental connection is forcibly removed from piloting a SkipJack. Forced Discos have a certain amount of feedback, as pilots are often unconscious for minutes to hours.

27. Gate Surveyors Group (GSG): a company Raylan starts under the Family's corporate umbrella.

28. Gates: doorways that lead from Earth Prime to a second dimensional Earth, usually designated as "D2." If more than one Gate originates at the DMZ, they will be designated separately as D2, D3, D4, etc. Stepping through a dimensional Gate is a one-way affair. A person can go from EP1 to a D2, but it is suicide to return from a D2 to EP1 if you were born in EP1. On rare occasions, children of a D2 immigrate to EP1.

29. Great Lakes District: one of the primary districts of the NAC.

30. Haptic Suit: a thin jumpsuit worn against the skin. Its receptors interpret a signal from the subdermal inputs in the human pilot. Those inputs translate into movement in the SkipJack.

31. Heavy Lift Tram (HLT): flying cargo ships. HLTs are designed to move mass from one point to another.

32. Heel: a piloting term used by remote pilots to tow along more than one SkipJack. It takes immense concentration to bring multiple SkipJacks to heel behind your primary piloted unit. It is not generally done over long distances, as it is easier to use a wired connection to bring the SkipJacks to heel.

33. High Output Light Emitter Diode (HOLED): a very bright output LED light.

34. Hill House: the name Thap comes up with for the cabin where Raylan lives.

35. House of Commons (HOC): the equivalent of the old Canadian parliament and old U.S. Congress. The representatives are voted into office by constituents inside their Districts.

36. Indenture Broken: a notice on your FEED account that you failed to complete your Indenture. Like a Gate walk, it is one way. You get one

chance to pay your Indenture; should you fail, you earn the Indenture broken mark. You will find borrowing money, obtaining leases for housing, and permanent work hard to obtain.

37. Indenture: the prescribed time a secondary education graduate has negotiated to work for a corporate entity to pay for their secondary education. Years of Indenture and how much residual pay you receive are common negotiation points. The highest value Indentures have the shortest time, with moderate residual pay. You cannot be employed by any governmental, community, or district office unless you have paid your Indenture.

38. Living Dining Kitchen (LDK): a 2LDK blockhouse would have two bedrooms, living, dining, and kitchen spaces.

39. Local Mesh Grid (LMG): a series of rebroadcasting antennas that allow for a very robust and quick uplink between pilots in pods and the SkipJacks. They are often used in war or applications where piloting is very hazardous. Sometimes operators of industrial sites use an LMG to avoid paying the data hash fees of a LOSS-based piloting scheme.

40. Low Orbit Satellites Systems (LOSS): the other way SkipJacks are piloted. They are still used in war or where extreme uplink speeds are unnecessary. There are transactional fees for piloting via a LOSS link.

41. Mag-lev: a transportation system that utilizes cars and a single-piloted MLR to control them. It is a cross between our freight trains and tractor trailers. Mag-levs are the primary means of moving bulk goods across the land.

42. Mag-lev roller (MLR): a simple vehicle that uses magnetic rotors to propel them forward. They hover above the ground; there are no wheels. They vary in size, from single-seater delivery vehicles to multi-ton vehicles that haul cargo and supplies.

43. Med-i-Care: a biotech research firm that leased the island of Senkaku from the Chinese Confederacy.

44. Mesh Spikes: the smaller localized repeater stations for a data trunk line. They can rebroadcast an uplink for piloting SkipJacks and transfer data over short distances.

45. Military Occupational Specialty (MOS): a coded number for every NAC CM job.

46. Mindspace: a construct a remote pilot uses to portion the duties, controls, presets, and commands given to a SkipJack when piloting remotely.

47. Mini Mag-lev roller (MMLR): a cooperative base camp system designed by GSG and the Japanese megacorps.

48. MKII SkipJack: The second-generation primary fighting machine of the NAC military.

49. Montana West District (MWD): the NAC district comprised of areas of western Montana, western Wyoming, Idaho, eastern British Columbia, and Alberta.

50. Myomere muscle: the primary building block of SkipJacks. It is denser, heavier, and stronger than any known animal muscle. Myomere contracts and extends with similar electrical impulses as animal muscle. It was once thought to be a cure for amputees, but the human nervous system does not take well to myomere integration. Although prosthetics can use myomere, there has been no direct human muscle replacement aside from Dr. Alverez's limited success with Raylan.

51. Nacelle: the primary flight engine for trams. They have multiple rotors that are enclosed inside ductwork. They allow for vertical take-off and landings.

52. Nepalese Concordant: the home country for all of the Forty who serve the small 'f' family. The Segundos, save for Franc, all originate from within the Forty.

53. New England District (NED): the NAC district comprised of the upper northeast coast of North America.

54. Noise Canceling Pack (NCP): an option on the MKVI infiltrator SkipJack.

55. North American Compact (NAC): the combined former nations of United America and the Canadian protectorate.

56. North East Fishing Conglomerate Gate:D2 (NEFCG:D2): a gate set up to take advantage of the D2 world-rich Atlantic fisheries.

57. Pacific Crest District (PCD): the district along the western coast of the NAC.

58. Pannier: a box, cooler, or a water-tight container that a SkipJack carries. It can be configured in many different ways to fit a SkipJack's needs.

59. Piloting pods: the circular housing pilots use to move, manipulate, and guide their SkipJacks. The pod interprets the movement, preset commands, or both to the SkipJack.

60. Platelet glue: an instant adhesive that a body can absorb as it heals. It aids in closing cuts and lacerations from the inside out.

61. Presets: a list of commands that form a specific function when piloting SkipJacks via a pod or remotely. The more presets, the more agile the SkipJack, and the more agile the mind behind the piloting.

62. Preventative Maintenance (PM): necessary tasks to keep all equipment running at peak efficiency.

63. Reunited China (RC): a small group of natural and manufactured islands off the coast of southeastern China. They deem themselves to be the proper Chinese government.

64. Rideshare: a community vehicle used to pick up and disperse employees at various destinations.

65. Rundown log: a pilot's way of recording issues, quirks, or general diagnostics of their SkipJack.

66. San Diego Dockyards (SDD): a construction, freight, and dockyard corporate consortium that is union-based. They operate the most prominent blue water ship manufacturing facilities on the west coast of the NAC.

67. Scandinavian Commonwealth: the combined states of Norway, Denmark, Finland, and Sweden. It is a Luddite nation that opposes every technological advancement that might lead to AI.

68. SkipJack Docking Station: systems which contain the charging apparatus for Skipjacks. Sometimes they also include a sonic shower system to clean the units.

69. SkipJack: a machine with no sentience that a human pilots in a pod. It mimics the human's movements and follows preset commands or both. In very rare cases, it is piloted outside of a pod.

70. Standalone FEED unit: a FEED system in the form of a rugged tablet. It can do most of the functionality of a FEED system, save for ID and banking information.

71. Standard Compact Currency (SCC): the official currency of the NAC. "Credits" for short.

72. Subdermal Inputs: small nodes tied to human musculature to aid in the piloting of SkipJacks.

73. Temp Mesh Networks: these run off the data trunk lines. They are used by EP1 SkipJack pilots when building out a settlement in its various stages.

74. The Family: a corporation that houses tens of thousands of businesses under its wings. Due to the NAC limitations on private ownership, all businesses must be part of one of the limited corporations. As a result, the Family is one of the world's largest.

75. The family: usually descendants of the Jankowitz lineage. They run the large F family corporation, and each has a seat at the Large F corporate table. However, not every member at the large F corporate table is a direct descendant.

76. Tram: a flying bus, car, or heavy lift vehicle for transporting goods, people, or materials. They utilize engine nacelles to lift into the air. Most routes are preprogrammed flight paths, and little piloting skill is needed to fly one. Bush pilots can and will pilot by controls without preprogrammed flight paths.

77. Virginia District (VD): the NAC district comprised of the area we know as New Jersey, Delaware, West Virginia, Kentucky, Tennessee, North Carolina, Maryland, and Virginia.

78. War College: an affiliated secondary education system for those in the NAC CM. As they serve their country, college is free, and when they complete their term of service, there is no indenture to be paid.

About the Author

Evan is a believer in the idea that the world is too small to live in one place; he has spent the last 25 years moving about with his wife. He serves as chief cook, bottle washer, skate mechanic, and storyteller. Together, they have lived on both coasts and the central/mountain time zones. His wife assures him that she will not trade him for a less attractive model. Undisputedly, the most remarkable dog breed is English Springer Spaniels.

Also By

My Name is War is the first book in a five-volume set. I've completed the rough drafts of the other four volumes. My editor and I are working through them diligently to get them published for you. In the meantime, I have numerous short stories set in the same Earth Prime Universe.

The Earth Prime series:

My Name is War

I am War

At War

War at Large

A War to End it All

You can find my short stories in Raconteur Press anthologies:

Ghosts of Malta: "Finder"

Knights of Malta: "Precursor"

Falcons of Malta: "Family Matters"

Space Cowboys: "Drover"

Space Marines: "One Way Out"

Pin-up Noir: "Last Call"

Upcoming projects in the works:

"Lion of the Compact," the story of General Jermaine Diomedes

"What it means," the descendants of Letecia and Jackson Medicine Crow

Made in United States
North Haven, CT
25 July 2024

55423498R00251